Finding Paradise

"If anyone here has a right to be angry, I do," Edward declared. "I'm not the one who divulged a secret that had been kept for a quarter of a century."

"I didn't do it to hurt you," Eden insisted. "You were miserable. Your father was forcing you into a marriage you didn't want and making you feel responsible for Worlege, all in the name of duty. I figured if you knew you weren't really his son, you wouldn't feel duty bound to do everything he wanted. I had no idea you'd disappear."

"What did you think I'd do?" Did she have no idea what she'd done, how it had affected him? "Did you think I'm the kind of man who would cling to a title that wasn't mine? Did you think I could live with myself knowing I'd cheated Patrick of his birthright?"

Eden bit her lip. "I didn't think of that at all. I was just thinking of you. I never said..." She turned her back to him. "I wouldn't have said a word if I'd thought anything like this would happen."

Edward didn't know what got into him, but the next thing he knew, he'd taken Eden in his arms and was kissing her.

Other books by Leigh Greenwood:

THE RELUCTANT BRIDE	The Cowboys series:
THE INDEPENDENT BRIDE	JAKE
	WARD
COLORADO BRIDE	BUCK
REBEL ENCHANTRESS	DREW
SCARLET SUNSET, SILVER NIGHTS	SEAN
	CHET
THE CAPTAIN'S CARESS	MATT
ARIZONA EMBRACE	PETE
SEDUCTIVE WAGER	LUKE
SWEET TEMPTATION	THE MAVERICKS
WICKED WYOMING NIGHTS	A TEXAN'S HONOR
	TEXAS TENDER
WYOMING WILDFIRE	

The Night Riders series:
TEXAS HOMECOMING
TEXAS BRIDE
BORN TO LOVE

The Seven Brides series:
ROSE
FERN
IRIS
LAUREL
DAISY
VIOLET
LILY

LEIGH GREENWOOD

Texas Loving

LEISURE BOOKS NEW YORK CITY

A LEISURE BOOK®

April 2008

Published by

Dorchester Publishing Co., Inc.
200 Madison Avenue
New York, NY 10016

If you purchased this book without a cover you should be aware that this book is stolen property. It was reported as "unsold and destroyed" to the publisher and neither the author nor the publisher has received any payment for this "stripped book."

Copyright © 2008 by Leigh Greenwood

All rights reserved. No part of this book may be reproduced or transmitted in any form or by any electronic or mechanical means, including photocopying, recording or by any information storage and retrieval system, without the written permission of the publisher, except where permitted by law.

ISBN 10: 0-8439-5686-0
ISBN 13: 978-0-8439-5686-3

The name "Leisure Books" and the stylized "L" with design are trademarks of Dorchester Publishing Co., Inc.

Printed in the United States of America.

10 9 8 7 6 5 4 3 2 1

Visit us on the web at www.dorchesterpub.com.

Texas Loving

Chapter One

It would have been difficult to ignore the rider if he had been riding through the streets of San Antonio or Galveston. That he should be riding up to the Broken Circle Ranch made his appearance even more surprising . . . and intriguing. He was ancient. Well, maybe not exactly *ancient*, but certainly too old to be riding a horse alone through the Texas Hill Country on a horse at least two hands taller than the average cow pony. But it wasn't the size of the horse or even the age of the man that drew Eden Maxwell's attention. It was his clothes. Used to men who dressed in scuffed boots, Levi's, a cotton shirt and vest, and a battered Stetson hat, she wasn't prepared to see a horseman who wore a coat with tails, a white shirt and a tie when riding a horse. He was actually wearing a top hat. She had seen such hats in pictures, but she'd never seen one on a man's head. The man's pants were skin-tight and pale tan. Even at a distance, she could see the light reflected off the high gloss of his boots. Set against a background of scantly forested hills and rocky outcroppings, he looked like a character out of a storybook.

Eden's first instinct was to rush inside and tell her mother, but Isabelle was visiting Luke's wife, Valeria, who had given birth to Valentine six weeks ago. Pete's wife, Anne, had presented him with twin boys, Kane and Kent, only last week. Now everyone was awaiting the birth of Will and Idalou's second child. Jake, Eden's father, said the county was turning into a big nursery.

"Who is that man?" Junie Mae had come out on the porch to bring Eden some lemonade. It was a warm afternoon and the cool drink was welcome.

Eden's parents had given Junie Mae refuge when she found herself pregnant without a husband. Though several men had shown an interest in courting the beautiful young woman, she had been content to stay at the ranch, cooking and taking care of the house. Isabelle was delighted because it gave her more time to visit her grandchildren.

"I don't know." Eden looked to see if Scotty had followed his mother before remembering he'd begged to accompany Isabelle. Junie Mae's son was best friends with Will and Idalou's son, Riley. The boys played together whenever they could.

"Do you think he's coming here?" Junie Mae asked. "I mean, dressed the way he is, maybe he's lost."

That thought had occurred to Eden, but the rider didn't look like a man who would get lost. It wasn't just the horse or the clothes. It was the way he rode, tall and straight in the saddle despite his age, the way his gaze seemed to miss nothing of the countryside as he passed. No, he wasn't lost, but Eden had no idea what he could want with anybody on the ranch. Or the surrounding ranches of her brothers and sister.

"Do we have any lemonade to offer him if he wants to stay to talk to Mama or Dad?" Eden couldn't imagine what this dandified old codger would possibly have to say to her cowboy father.

"Your father won't be back for hours," Junie Mae said, "and when your mother gets near a baby, she loses all sense of time."

"Then I guess we'll have to entertain him." Eden glanced back at the man, who was now less than a hundred yards from the house. "I get the feeling he might be a lively old gentleman who'd appreciate the company of two young women."

Junie Mae giggled. "He looks old enough to be your grandfather."

Eden's smile faded. Except for a brief visit to her father's mother in Santa Fe, she'd never known her grandparents. "He shouldn't be out here by himself. It could be dangerous."

"Do you think he'll want to stay overnight?"

"From the size of his saddlebags, it looks like he's planning to stay for weeks."

Eden was looking forward to meeting this man. Maybe it was that he represented something new and different. Maybe she was a trifle bored with her life now that she was out of college. For the past year she'd attempted to stuff some of her acquired knowledge into the heads of nearly two dozen children, many of them nieces and nephews, who'd rather be riding pell-mell over the countryside or swimming in a river than sitting in a schoolroom. She was proud to be a schoolteacher like her mother had once been, but something was missing. She just hadn't figured out what it was.

"I'd better get the guest room ready."

Eden put a hand out to stop Junie Mae. "There's no point in putting on fresh sheets until we know they'll be used." The man was looking at her with intense interest even though he was still fifty yards away. When he finally came to a stop at the foot of the steps, his face relaxed into a broad smile. Age had been kind to him. It was easy to see he'd once been a handsome man.

"Welcome to the Broken Circle Ranch," Eden said. "I'm Eden Maxwell. If you'll tell me who you're looking for, maybe I can help you find them."

The man's smile grew broader even though he looked tired and a little sad. "I've found who I'm looking for."

"How do you know?"

"You look just like your grandmother did the first time I saw her fifty years ago."

Eden had spent the last two hours answering so many questions about life at the ranch that she was tired and a little edgy. No detail seemed too small to be interesting. The man said his name was Alastair Davenport, that he was from England, and that he was a relative of her mother. Beyond that he wouldn't say anything, preferring to wait until Isabelle came home. He was clearly disappointed Eden didn't know much about her great-aunt Deirdre, who'd died before she was born. She breathed a sigh of relief when she heard her mother enter the kitchen.

"I apologize for being away from home when you arrived," Isabelle said when she'd been introduced to the visitor. "I was visiting my newest grandbabies."

Isabelle didn't sit down until she was certain her visitor had been well taken care of. They were in the front parlor, a retreat for the adults when the families converged on the ranch for their periodic get-togethers. The sofas were dark brown leather, the chairs covered in bright florals, the walls hung with pictures of the family, and the floors softened by hand-braided rugs that could be washed when they got muddy. Isabelle refused to have a room that wasn't made to live in.

"Your lovely daughter has been telling me about the family you've made," Mr. Davenport said. "Now I'm going to tell you something about the family you come from."

"Aunt Deirdre would never talk about them," Isabelle said. "She said there was some sort of scandal."

"There was no scandal," Mr. Davenport said. "Deirdre made certain of that."

"Oh?"

"Deirdre didn't exactly tell you the truth," Mr. Davenport said to Isabelle. "She wasn't your aunt. She was your mother."

"That can't be true," Isabelle said. "She told me—"

Mr. Davenport held up his hand to stop her. "She fell in love with the younger brother of the Earl of Southampton. About the time she became pregnant with you, the earl died. The younger brother succeeded to the title and wanted to marry her, but she said she wasn't a suitable wife for an earl. Despite the new earl's pleading, despite his wish to give up his title, she moved to America, where she gave birth to a daughter. Where she gave birth to you."

If anyone else had told such a fantastic tale, Eden wouldn't have believed it, but there was an earnestness about Mr. Davenport that didn't allow disbelief.

Isabelle sat up ramrod straight in her chair. "Are you saying I'm illegitimate?" she asked, fire in her eyes.

"I'm saying you're the daughter of the Earl of Southampton," Mr. Davenport stated, his eyes glistening with moisture. "I'm saying you're *my* daughter."

For the first time in her life, Isabelle Davenport Maxwell fainted.

"Are you sure you and Scotty wouldn't be happier staying with Will and Idalou?" Isabelle asked Junie Mae. "It'll be awfully lonely when we're gone."

"Idalou has enough on her hands with the new baby," Junie Mae said.

Isabelle Haskins, "Belle" to the family, had been born eight days ago. With no more births imminent, Isabelle had accepted the earl's invitation for her, Jake, and Eden to spend the summer in England. He said he was an old man and wanted to get to know his only child and only grandchild before he died.

Eden practically trembled from excitement. The little she knew about society and London made her curious to learn more. She loved the Broken Circle Ranch and Texas, but she wondered what it was like to live in the middle of the largest city in the world. Isabelle had almost refused because she said she and Eden didn't have anything suitable to wear. The earl said they could take care of that after they reached London. Jake had balked when he found out he would be expected to dress in a tie and tails for dinner. Only the prospect of being separated from Isabelle for four months had convinced him to change his mind, though he stated that he intended to eat in the kitchen with people who dressed sensibly. He wasn't at all happy when Alastair told him the servants were even more punctilious about their dress than the aristocrats.

Mr. Davenport was such a kind, energetic, happy old man, Eden couldn't think of him as some snobbish peer who would look down on her. He was just Mr. Davenport, an unlikely conjurer who'd appeared out of nowhere to turn their lives into make-believe. The orphans—Eden's brothers and sisters all adopted by the Maxwells—thought it was a hoot Isabelle was aristocracy. They said she'd been ordering them about all their lives as if she were a duchess. Jake didn't like it, said ragtag cowboys didn't go around hitching themselves to daughters of earls. He stopped complaining after Isabelle told him she wouldn't be too good for him if she'd been the daughter of a king.

"Just think of all the new clothes you can buy when you get to London." Junie Mae had worked in her aunt's dress shop for years and had never lost her interest in clothes.

"Clothes I won't have any use for when I return," Isabelle said.

"Maybe you'll want to stay," Junie Mae said. "Your father keeps asking me if I think you might."

"It doesn't matter who my father is," Isabelle said. "I'm a Texas rancher's wife. That's all I want to be."

But Eden wondered about herself. She looked forward to the chance to visit England, to meet her new family, to experience the world of the truly privileged. After such an experience, she wondered if she'd be content to be a rancher's wife.

Worlege Manor, England

The two horsemen leaned forward in the stirrups, driving their laboring mounts forward with strong hands and shouts of encouragement. The horses thundered up the incline, neck and neck, their nostrils distended, flecks of sweat whipped from their straining bodies by the breeze that cut across the freshly mowed meadow. The two riders laughed and whooped as they drove toward a towering oak of enormous girth. They shot past the ancient tree, the dark bay a neck in front of the chestnut. The heavily muscled man riding the bay pushed his raven hair out of his eyes and twisted in the saddle to face his slim, auburn-haired companion. "That was a damned good ride, Patrick. You're going to beat me one of these days."

Patrick patted the neck of the sweating chestnut. "I expect I will if you keep giving me the faster horse. When did you buy this one?"

Edward Davenport burst out laughing. "I won him on a bet. That fool Evelyn Montgomery thought the horse was faster than Crusader. He's such a terrible horseman, I gave him fifteen pounds and a head start, and still beat him." The laughter left his eyes. "Your father tried to make me give it back."

"He's your father, too."

"You could never tell it by the way he treats me." The half brothers dismounted and led their tired mounts toward the stable. "Sometimes I think he must have hated my mother for dying, but if she hadn't, he couldn't have married your mother and had you." Edward could remember when his father loved him, when he felt wanted, but that started to change after the two boys grew up to be so different. Now it was painfully obvious the viscount adored Patrick and would have put him in Edward's place if there had been any way to do it.

"He doesn't hate you," Patrick said. "He just doesn't understand why you don't see things the same way he does."

"Then why did he never take me to London? I was left here to be brought up by my nurse and that thieving estate manager." It was an old story, one he couldn't change, so there was no point in getting upset over it. "I wouldn't care if he'd just leave me to manage Worlege. If he'd follow the budget I gave him, I could get the estate back on its feet."

"I expect that's why he gets so irritated with you."

"No, he gets irritated because I'm not the perfect son like you. He's particularly irritated right now because I haven't asked Daphne to marry me."

"Why haven't you? She's a wonderful girl."

"Then you marry her."

"I'm not the heir," Patrick said, "the complete horseman, the smartest estate manager in England, the best brother anyone could have."

The admiration in Patrick's eyes made Edward feel uncomfortable. He was taller than his brother, bigger, almost rawboned, with the broad shoulders and powerful calves of a man who enjoyed physical sports as well as physically demanding work. He was perfectly coordinated on horseback and could shoot better than anyone in the county, but he couldn't remember the rules of etiquette, was a complete failure at clever conversation, felt uncomfortable in anything but work clothes, and had two left feet on the dance floor.

Patrick, on the other hand, was suitably tall, elegantly slim, with flawless features, and a body perfectly suited for any style of dress. He rode and shot well, but he handled social etiquette perfectly, could converse with anyone on any subject, and danced beautifully. He liked London, parties, and women who were so quiet and well behaved, Edward sometimes wondered if they were fully awake. Yet as different as they were, they'd always been each other's best friend.

Edward gave his brother an affectionate shove. "If I'd known you were going to grow up to be perfect, I'd have drowned you."

"No, you wouldn't. You'd have made sure I got to shore even if you didn't."

"At least Father would have been happy then."

Patrick's grin faded. "He just hates being on an allowance." He sighed. "He swears Great-uncle Alastair is going to live forever."

"I hope he does. I like the old buzzard. It was just like him to head off to America to find his only child. I thought Father would have a stroke when he told us."

"He's afraid Uncle Alastair might decide to give to the child everything that isn't entailed."

"That *child* would have to be forty-five by now. He or she is probably married with a large and hopeful family who would like nothing better than to batten on to an English earl gone sentimental in his old age."

"That's what Father said when he heard Uncle Alastair was bringing his daughter and part of her family to London."

Puzzled, Edward asked, "Why is he bringing them to England?"

"I don't know. Perhaps he's bringing back a beautiful heiress for me."

Edward laughed. "Then you go meet them. I'll stay here."

"You can't. You have to be in London to propose to Daphne."

Edward felt the familiar tightening in his stomach. Daphne Bidwell was a beautiful woman, intelligent, and possessed of a dowry large enough to ensure his family's financial future, but he'd always envisioned himself with someone more down-to-earth, someone who could share his life with him, living in the country instead of a suffocating society milieu governed by the rigid and stifling rules of a queen who'd been in deep mourning for nearly thirty years. Daphne knew nothing about the country and he cared nothing about the city. Their worlds didn't meet, yet they were expected to make them merge into a successful marriage. He didn't want to marry a woman whose conversation was entirely about her friends, parties, or clothes, and who disliked horses.

Daphne had lived her whole life in London, waited on by a platoon of servants and attended by her old nurse, a governess, and now a suitable lady's companion. The only child of a wealthy banker, she'd been groomed to marry a title and become a dutiful wife. As far as Edward was concerned, she'd been molded and shaped until they'd squeezed the life out of her.

Edward intended to do his duty, but he could never forget an old school chum's description of the year he'd spent in the American West working on a cattle ranch. The stories of untrammeled freedom from the strictures of society, of weeks spent camping out during roundup, of whole days in the saddle, had fired Edward's imagination. He told himself such a life wasn't possible for him, but it was real enough in his mind to make his impending future difficult to accept.

His back was against the wall. His father and his great-uncle had no concept of what it took to *earn* the money they spent so thoughtlessly. No matter how hard he worked, no matter how many times he explained the need to invest in the land rather than wringing every possible penny from it, the family fortunes had continued to dwindle until the Davenports were on the verge of bankruptcy. As the next person in line for the title after his father, it was Edward's duty to marry a woman with money.

He'd tried for Charlotte's sake. He liked his stepmother. She had mothered him with warm affection when she married his father soon after his mother's death. He'd tried for the earl. The old man was almost as bad as his father about spending money, but he encouraged Edward in his efforts to improve the estate. Edward *really* tried for Patrick, had never held it against his brother that even a casual observer could tell their father adored Patrick as much as he disliked Edward.

"I'd marry an heiress if I could," Patrick said, "but no one is interested in the second son. Besides, no female is going to notice me when you're in the room. Even Father admits you cut a noble figure."

"In broadcloth. I don't do well in satin." Edward wanted an uncomplicated life, a family that felt like a family, a home where he felt that he truly belonged instead of feeling he'd somehow been dropped into the wrong place and time—even though Patrick constantly tried to convince him he'd make a good earl.

"Stop being so critical. You look very impressive in your dress clothes. Besides, you're the most caring person I know."

Edward threw his arm over his brother's shoulder. "You've always come to my defense, but it's time you started looking out for yourself. Davenport men marry young. Can't have a hot-blooded young buck like you on the loose."

Patrick laughed heartily. "You're older, so you have to be sacrificed first. Besides, if it comes to being hot-blooded—"

Edward laughed. "Not another word. Whatever you've heard is undoubtedly an exaggeration. Do I look like the kind of man to be chasing after women?"

He didn't have to. Women chased him. Women who had no more in their heads or their hearts than his great-uncle's title and the position in society it would give them. He wanted a woman who would love him for himself, but he wasn't sure that woman existed.

London, England

For a month Eden's anticipation had been building to the point she thought she might burst. Her grandfather had told her endless stories about England, the city of London, his country estate, and the several members of his family. She'd heard all about the bad temper of the viscount, who was the son of the earl's deceased younger brother, about the wonderful qualities of the viscount's wife, Charlotte. She also knew about the difficult nature of the viscount's heir, Edward, but her interest had settled on the viscount's second son, Patrick. It wasn't hard to figure out that her grandfather would have been delighted to have Eden and Patrick fall in love. Eden had never thought of marrying an Englishman, but the earl made Patrick sound like such a wonderful man, she wasn't willing to discount the possibility. However, she was a practical woman, not given to wishful thinking or fanciful imaginings. England was a foreign country. She didn't know if she would like it . . . or any of its inhabitants.

After such a long period of waiting, it was hard to believe now that she was actually in the heart of London, the biggest city in the world. She stared out the windows of the hansom cab as it rattled over the cobblestone streets and its driver disputed the right of way with other cabs, private carriages, men on horseback, wagons of every description, and pedestrians who appeared to think all traffic should stop when they wanted to cross the street. In some ways, it wasn't very different from Galveston or San Antonio.

"I expect our ways will seem strange to you," the earl was saying to Isabelle and Jake, "but Cyril and Charlotte will be happy to take you under their wings. I don't think you'll have to worry about this young lady," he said, winking at Eden. "Patrick will make sure she's well taken care of."

Isabelle had joked that it would be a wild twist of fate if Eden were to marry into English aristocracy, something her own mother had refused to do. But Jake wasn't amused at the thought of his daughter living nearly five thousand miles from Texas or marrying a man who was puffed up with his own importance and talked funny in the bargain.

It was all a great adventure to Eden. She'd smiled to herself several times thinking of what some of her classmates at her fancy Eastern college would say if they knew her grandfather was an earl. And if she were to marry the brother of the future earl, well, there wouldn't be enough envy to go around.

She told herself to stop being foolish. She was in England to enjoy herself, and learn something about her grandfather's life, not to find a husband. Still, her grandfather's description of Patrick had piqued her interest. If the man was only half as good as the earl made him out to be, Eden was surprised he wasn't married already. Twenty-two might be considered too young to get married in England, but in Texas Patrick would have been considered a man for at least five years.

"I don't know if you'll meet Edward this evening," the earl said as the cab turned into an avenue that was amazingly quiet after the noise of the main thoroughfare, "but Patrick will make sure you're not neglected."

"I hope you won't make him spend all his time with me," Eden said. "I'm sure he has his own friends, his own plans."

"Once he gets a look at you, he'll be happy enough to forget his friends," the earl said. "You're a very lovely young woman even if you aren't quite as beautiful as your grandmother was." He patted her hand. "Patrick will be as charmed by you as I am."

Eden was certain she would never again see anything as incredible as the city of London. From the beautiful buildings to the enormous tree-filled parks to the cobbled streets choked with traffic, it was all she could do to keep from staring like a provincial. But it wasn't until she found herself in the entrance hall of her grandfather's London home that she began to understand what it meant to be an earl. The whole house appeared to be made of marble: columns of green veined with white and black; walls of white flecked with gold; floors of alternating black and white squares; stairs of pure black.

Life-sized portraits adorned the walls. She noticed the earl's immediately. His angular features and white beard made him stand out from the others. His gaunt face was pleasantly cheerful despite being lined by suffering. By contrast, the viscount's portrait depicted a tall man with soft pink skin and a satin waistcoat stretched too tightly over his stomach. Smooth-shaven with thick brown hair combed ruthlessly into submission, he appeared to be suffering from the same sour disposition as most of his ancestors.

"The drawing room is on the second floor," the earl said as he accompanied them into the entrance hall. One servant held the doors while others were already unloading their luggage from the cab. "You can rest there until the housekeeper comes to take you to your rooms."

Just then a handsome woman appeared at the head of the stairs, accompanied by a man with a pained expression. "Welcome to Southampton House," she said. "I'm Charlotte Davenport. This is my husband, Cyril, Viscount Wentworth."

Cyril's forced smile did nothing to hide the anger that puckered his brow. Acting as though she hadn't endured a long ocean crossing and an even more tiring journey from the port, Isabelle marched up the steps with the energy and decision that had characterized her whole life.

"I'm sure you're horrified to have to receive me," Isabelle said in her forthright manner, "but neither I nor my family want anything from you. After a short visit, we'll return to Texas and you can forget we exist. For now, however, I would appreciate being able to sit down in a comfortable chair without being rocked from side to side, being choked by smoke, or having my teeth rattle in my head."

Charlotte appeared to be only slightly less stupefied by this speech than her husband, but she recovered quickly and led them into a room that could only be described as sumptuous. From the velvet curtains to the painted ceiling to the elegant chairs, the room bespoke a luxury only the very rich could afford. Eden couldn't picture her brothers coming into such a room after being on horseback all day. Jake looked ready to bolt.

"I apologize for not having everyone down to meet you, but we arrived in town later than expected," Charlotte said. "Would you like something to drink? Tea, perhaps?"

Jake's face had lit up at the offer of a drink, only to fall at the mention of tea, but the earl was already offering him something more to his liking. Eden's attention was drawn to the quiet entrance of a handsome young man of slender build and thick auburn hair. His complexion was fair and without flaw, his features finely formed and assembled into an uncommonly attractive face complemented by a charming smile that drew Eden in immediately. Though dressed in a white shirt, tie, waistcoat, and form-fitting suit, his style was casual.

"Patrick, come meet your cousin." Her grandfather turned to Eden. "His half brother Edward stands between him and the title—but the two of them still manage to be great friends."

"Uncle is always teasing me about Edward," Patrick said with a quick smile, "but Edward will make a much better earl. I don't have his stature, or his command over a horse."

Eden liked him immediately.

"There's a lot more to being an earl than size and horsemanship." The viscount's displeasure—Eden wasn't sure at what—was plain to see.

"Where is Edward?" the earl asked.

Patrick turned to him. "He had some last-minute business with one of the home farms. He won't be able to come down for several days."

"It wouldn't be something earthshaking like the birth of a foal or the purchase of a new ram, would it?" Cyril grumbled.

"I never inquire into Edward's business," Patrick said with an open expression.

"Patrick is making excuses for him as usual," the viscount said with a frown.

Eden thought she saw a flicker of uneasiness, but Patrick was obviously too well trained to betray his feelings before strangers.

"He *must* be here tonight," Charlotte said to her son. "Daphne and her parents are coming for dinner."

"I'm sorry, Mother. I can only convey Edward's assurance that he will be here as soon as possible."

Charlotte Davenport's harrumph was more expressive than words.

Eden had been under the impression that sons of the aristocracy had to obey their elders. It seemed, however, that Edward was different, something Eden found as interesting as Edward's family appeared to find annoying.

"We're expecting Edward and Daphne to announce their engagement any day now," Charlotte explained.

"Edward is fortunate that Daphne is an undemanding woman," the viscount said.

"Daphne is fortunate to have found a husband who doesn't neglect his estate," Jake put in.

"It's stupid to put managing the estate above his obligations to the family," the viscount sneered. "We hire people for that."

"His work at Worlege has increased our revenues," the earl pointed out.

"He wouldn't need to worry about increasing our revenues if he would marry Daphne."

"You've done your best with the boy," Charlotte said to her husband, "but everyone knows how stubborn he is." Charlotte smiled fondly at her son. "He's nothing like Patrick."

"You ought to be glad of that," Patrick said with a self-effacing laugh. "I'd have no idea which animals should be saved for breeding and which were good only for slaughter."

Eden couldn't see anything wrong with Edward's knowing how to manage his livestock. In fact, she wouldn't think much of any man who left the conduct of his business entirely in the hands of someone else.

"Edward and Cyril seldom agree on anything," the earl explained, giving his heir an impatient glance. "Though I don't find the goings-on in the farmyard to be of any interest, I don't see why it's such a problem that Edward does."

"Because it makes him seem more like a farmer than the man who will someday inherit your title," Cyril said.

"Young people often have different ideas from those of their elders." The earl turned to Isabelle. "I wonder what Deirdre would have thought of your cowboy?" he asked.

She reached out to grasp Jake's hand. "Probably what I thought of him when I first saw him," she said with a hearty laugh. "Fortunately it didn't take me long to realize a wonderful man could come in bad wrapping paper."

Eden loved to see her parents show affection, but she could tell Charlotte and Cyril thought it was unbecoming. Even Patrick looked surprised.

Just then the housekeeper came to announce that their rooms were ready. The earl made his excuses and slipped away.

"I'm so glad to meet you," Patrick said to Eden. "It's rather exciting finding that I have a cousin I didn't know existed."

"Even if she is an American?"

"Even then. I hope you won't let Father's irritation prejudice you against Edward."

"I'm sure he doesn't need my approval. I have a feeling the earl is rather fond of him."

Patrick smiled ruefully. "*That* irritates Father even more than my defending Edward. Now don't let me keep you from your room. I'm sure you're anxious to rest before dinner."

"I'm not such a feeble female. I'm used to helping cook supper after working all day."

Patrick looked surprised.

"I grew up on a ranch," Eden explained. "I have ten brothers and one sister. We all had jobs. I also liked to work with Dad and the boys when they'd let me."

Patrick seemed at a loss for words.

Eden laughed at his perplexity. "Texans expect a man to work for his living. If he can't, or won't, we don't consider him much of a man." Eden supposed she shouldn't have been so direct, but she wasn't about to let anyone look down on her or her family. "Now before I offend you so badly you won't speak to me again, I'd better go to my room."

Eden decided that one advantage of living in a ranch house was not having a bedroom on the fourth floor. After climbing so many stairs, she might need that rest after all. Her room was small but beautifully appointed. Though she appreciated the luxury, the view from her window was of the back side of another house, not the panoramic view of the hills that surrounded their ranch. Yet it was so quiet it was hard to believe she was in a city of more than four million people. There weren't half that many in the whole state of Texas.

A knock sounded on the bedroom door and a maid entered the room. "The family is gathering in the salon," she told Eden. "Dinner will be served in half an hour."

After giving her appearance one last glance, Eden stepped out of her room and was nearly run over by a man hurrying along the hall.

"Pardon me," he said and moved aside to let her pass.

Eden's initial feeling of irritation that he should be in such a rush vanished when she got a look at him. She didn't know how to address him. He didn't look like a servant, yet he didn't look like a member of the household either. From his boots to his cap, he was a study in brown. His boots were worn and slightly muddy, his pants wrinkled and showing age. His shirt had probably been clean when he'd put it on that morning, but he hadn't bothered with a tie. His coat, though cut well and of fine cloth, appeared to have been subjected to use in all kinds of weather. Yet despite his rumpled appearance, there was an air about him that bespoke a person of consequence. He started to move past her, then apparently changed his mind.

Eden wasn't sure she appreciated the way he looked her over. It wasn't rude nor was it lewd. It was simply open and appraising. She couldn't tell whether he liked what he saw or whether he was making a list of her flaws.

"Do I meet your approval?" she asked.

She was pleased to see him flush.

"I shouldn't stare, but I hadn't expected to meet a stranger in the hall. Who are you?" he asked point-blank.

"I'm Eden Maxwell. Who are *you?*"

Chapter Two

$\mathcal{E}$dward had met many women in his life—most paraded before him in hopes of becoming the wife of a future earl—but he'd never met one who stopped him in his tracks. Even more confusing, he couldn't tell what it was about her that was so unexpected, so arresting . . . so mesmerizing. She looked like a perfectly ordinary woman, more beautiful than most and with a figure that caused a stirring in his loins, yet he knew right away he'd never met a woman like Eden Maxwell.

"I'm Edward Davenport, and I'm going to be unforgivably late for dinner."

"I'll forgive you."

Some of the tension left his body and he laughed. "Thank you, but I'm afraid that won't help."

She surveyed him from top to bottom, apparently not finding much to her approval. "From the look of things, you'll need an hour to get ready."

"At least."

"Then you'll either be really late coming to the table, or Charlotte will have to hold dinner so long, the meat will be dried out. I suggest you not tell anyone you're here. That way they'll be pleasantly surprised when you enter the salon after dinner. You can send a message to the cook to send your meal up to your room."

It occurred to Edward that this young woman might be the daughter of the illegitimate offspring the earl had gone to America to find. He'd been so busy with the estate and uninterested in the possibility of new relatives—even ones who, according to his father, were bound to arrive with their hands out—that he had put them out of his mind. For him, America was as distant as Australia.

This young woman wasn't dressed in a fashionable style, but she didn't look as if she would be asking for handouts. She certainly had an ample supply of self-confidence. From the way she'd concocted her little plot on the spur of the moment, she was obviously intelligent.

"Would your mother let your brothers get away with that?"

Eden's laugh was unexpected. There was nothing controlled or cultivated about it. It was simple and natural, the way children laugh when they play. He found it charming.

"She would never start supper until everyone was home. By the time the boys had taken care of their horses, washed, and changed their shirts, supper would be ready."

"Your mother cooks?" He'd never given any thought to how things were done in America, but he couldn't imagine a daughter of the earl cooking her own dinner.

"My mother and I both cook," she told him with a frown and a tinge of annoyance. "Food doesn't cook itself, not even in London."

He didn't understand why he was acting so dull-witted, or why it was important that this young woman like him. He just knew it was.

"You probably think I'm terribly rude. I shouldn't be talking to you without a proper introduction, but I don't have very good manners." It was just one more way he had failed to live up to his father's expectations. "No matter how hard I try, I always get it wrong."

Eden rolled her eyes. "You haven't done anything wrong. Even my brothers wouldn't find anything to complain about."

He couldn't believe she'd rolled her eyes. English women *never* did, never showed emotion or expressed disapproval of the men in their families. They might glance demurely at hands clasped in their laps or concentrate on a flower arrangement, but they never talked openly with a strange man.

"I'd better not hold you up any longer. I need to get down to the drawing room before they send someone to look for me, and you need to get to your room before anybody knows you're here."

"You really think I ought to hide in my room?"

"If you want to make the evening uncomfortable for everyone, by all means let your father know you're here. I'm sure you think you have a good reason for being late and dirty, but I doubt he'll agree."

Her expression was hard to read. There was a little bit of impatience, some lingering annoyance as well as disapproval, but there was curiosity as well. Whatever else he might say about her, the chit had spunk. And a smattering of insolence. He was certain she knew he was the heir, but that hadn't stopped her from saying he was dirty. He admired her for not being caught up in the trappings of society. Daphne would have fainted before she would have talked to him in his present condition. Nor would she have been likely to find the kitchens, much less know what to do when she got there.

It was hard to imagine a woman as poised and beautiful as Eden cooking. Kitchens were hot, noisy, crowded, and everyone in them ended up looking blowsy. He couldn't picture this young woman except as she was now: calm, collected, and slightly amused. "If I get caught, may I tell them it was your suggestion?"

Her annoyed look was replaced by a laugh and twinkling eyes. "That's probably the sort of thing your father would expect from an American. Of course, you might have difficulty explaining why you followed any course suggested by a woman. Most likely he'd consider that a failing."

Edward lost all desire to laugh. Either Eden Maxwell was a mind reader, or his father had behaved with his usual arrogance toward people he considered inferior. The weight of his situation came crashing down on him. The surprise was that, for a moment, Eden had managed to make him forget it.

"I'll take your suggestion and claim it was mine," he said with a forced grin. "As far as everyone is concerned, you haven't seen me and I haven't seen you."

"Edward," Charlotte exclaimed, coming to her feet. "How wonderful that you could join us. It's a shame you didn't arrive in time for dinner."

Edward crossed the drawing room in long, athletic strides to greet his stepmother with a kiss on the cheek. "I had the kitchen send up something while I dressed."

Eden thought Edward glanced briefly in her direction, but she couldn't be sure. He didn't look comfortable in evening clothes, but they looked marvelous on him. He wasn't as handsome as her brother Will—God simply didn't have enough material to make two men like that—but he was dazzling in the manner of Sean or Hawk. He was big . . . several inches taller than his father and brother. Patrick was handsome and sweet. The viscount and earl were imposing because of their inborn sense of consequence, but Edward stood out for the sheer force of his masculinity.

"You should have let me know you were here," Charlotte said to Edward. "I would have had the cook hold dinner."

"Certainly not," Cyril said to his wife. "If Edward doesn't have the decency to arrive on time, he can eat in the kitchen."

"You should have come to the dining room as soon as you arrived," Charlotte insisted. "It would have been no trouble to lay an extra place for you."

This time Eden was certain Edward did glance toward her. "I wouldn't think of embarrassing you or your guests," Edward said to Charlotte.

One of those guests was pretty Daphne Bidwell. "That's Edward," Daphne informed Eden in a stiff undertone. "The viscount has asked my father's permission for Edward to ask for my hand."

Eden thought that was a strange way to go about asking a woman to marry you, but she didn't know anything about the inner workings of English society.

She couldn't tell whether Daphne's annoyance stemmed from Cyril's remarks, or Edward's lateness and apparent lack of contrition. Eden looked from Edward to Daphne and back to Edward again. He looked a bit like a wild animal forced to pretend to be tame, but she found that exciting. What woman would want a husband who was completely predictable?

Edward turned and crossed the room to Daphne. She stiffened like a starched apron in a March wind. Edward looked just as uncomfortable. Edward bowed from the waist. "I must apologize for being so late. I have no suitable excuse."

"You don't need one," Daphne said, the sharp edge to her voice at variance with her words. "I'm sure you have many important things to do."

If Eden hadn't known better, she'd have supposed they were strangers meeting for the first time.

"Nevertheless, it was unforgivably rude." Edward looked like a puppet with someone else pulling the strings and putting the words in his mouth.

Daphne turned to Eden. "Let me introduce you to Eden Maxwell. Your stepmother tells me she's your second cousin."

Eden had already been informed by the earl that Isabelle's illegitimate birth and real connection to him would not be discussed outside the family.

"I'm delighted to meet you." She looked him up and down as brazenly as he had her earlier and was amused to see his eyes widen with surprise.

Daphne's gaze narrowed. "My father says Edward makes a very distinguished appearance."

"But not as distinguished as Patrick, don't you think?" Edward suggested with a grin.

Daphne looked so annoyed, Eden was relieved when the earl told Edward to come over and be introduced to Eden's mother.

"She doesn't look old enough to be the mother of a young woman," the earl said of Isabelle. "Must be something about Texas that keeps its women looking young."

"Texas loving," Jake said with his usual cheeky grin.

Isabelle laughed at her husband's remark, gave him a tender smile, and squeezed his hand, but Cyril and Charlotte cast disapproving glances at both of them. Daphne didn't appear to understand what Jake meant, but Edward made no attempt to pretend his eyes weren't dancing with amusement.

"Are you willing to give advice?" Edward asked Jake.

"If it's not inborn, it can't be taught," Jake replied.

Edward seemed to unbend, become more like the man Eden had encountered in the upper hallway. "That means I'm permanently handicapped."

"I get the feeling you've got damned few handicaps," Jake said.

Daphne puckered up like she smelled something sour.

"You're embarrassing Daphne," Isabelle said, "and I doubt Charlotte thinks this is a suitable subject for her drawing room."

"I think love is an acceptable subject any time and any place," the earl declared.

"Love is always on everybody's minds when young people are present," Charlotte said.

Eden didn't miss her pointed glance at Edward, which had the effect of rendering him wooden once again.

"There's nothing improper about courtship when it's handled in the appropriate way," the viscount declared. "There was little that passed between Charlotte and me before we were betrothed that couldn't have taken place before Queen Victoria."

"Edward's of a different cut from you," the earl stated. "Sometimes I wonder how he could be your son."

Eden could understand why the viscount wouldn't like having his uncle make such a remark before guests, but she didn't understand why he turned white and appeared to struggle to control some strong emotion.

"Not all sons are like their fathers," Cyril managed to say.

"Patrick is like you," Edward offered. "He has perfect manners, always knows the right clothes to wear, and he nearly beat me in a race across the meadow last week."

"And I'm guessing you put him on the faster horse," the earl shot back.

Patrick's laugh was unexpectedly hearty. "He's got you, Edward. You might as well confess you were trying to make me look good."

"It would be much better for everyone if Edward modeled himself after Patrick," the viscount stated heatedly.

"Edward and I are perfectly content with each other the way we are."

Patrick's comment angered Cyril still more. "It's a pity the rest of us can't feel equally content."

"Daphne has promised to play a Brahms intermezzo," Eden said, trying to defuse the increasing tension. "I'm going to turn pages. Edward can open the pianoforte. Patrick, will you fetch an extra branch of candles?"

"A very neat diversion," Edward whispered to Eden when they were both at the pianoforte, "but it's a wasted effort. It's always like this between my father and me." He glanced at Daphne. "Do you think she's too upset to play?"

Once seated, Daphne seemed to forget everything but the music. The signs of strain faded from her face and the tension left her shoulders. By the time she had played through the first theme, she was completely relaxed.

Daphne played so beautifully, Eden was jealous even though she knew she didn't have the talent or the willingness to practice the long hours required to play well. It was more fun to listen. Besides, it gave her an opportunity to observe Edward. While Patrick seemed to be enjoying the music, Edward's eyes glazed over. Eden wondered what he would have chosen to do this evening if he'd been free to decide for himself. She also wondered what could be distracting his attention from the woman chosen to be his wife. If this were Texas, Daphne would tell him to get lost and turn her attention to Patrick. Having been prepared to dislike Edward, Eden was finding her attraction to him disconcerting and a bit mystifying.

A hissed "*Now!*" from Daphne jerked Eden's attention back to the music and she quickly turned the page. She muttered an apology, but Daphne was concentrating on the music just as steadfastly as Edward's attention was attuned to the thoughts hidden behind his mask of formal politeness. Eden would have given a new bridle to know what he was thinking.

Daphne's performance ended with well-merited applause. Edward managed to rouse himself long enough to congratulate her. When Patrick asked her if she didn't believe the music of Brahms was more beautiful than that of Wagner, the discussion moved beyond Eden's interest and Edward's apparent knowledge.

"Are you a great lover of music?" he asked Eden.

"I enjoy it," she said, "but I don't know enough to follow half of what Daphne and Patrick are saying." The discussion soon involved Alastair, Cyril, and Charlotte, leaving Edward and Eden to gravitate to where Jake and Isabelle were seated.

"Tell me about your farm," Jake said to Edward, who launched into a discussion of livestock breeding, soil preservation, and investment in new ideas.

"You ought to come to Texas," Isabelle said when Edward complained of fields being too wet for spring planting. "We count ourselves lucky if we get enough rain to keep the grass green through the summer."

"Tell me about Texas," Edward said to Jake.

Isabelle got to her feet. "If you get Jake started on Texas, he won't stop. I'm going up. How about you?" she asked Eden.

Eden would have liked another chance to talk to Edward, but he looked so eager to hear about Texas, she decided to wait. "I believe I will," she said and got to her feet.

"Would you like to go riding tomorrow?" Edward asked, his eyes on Eden. "I mean all of you. I'd invite Daphne, but she dislikes horses," he added a little self-consciously. "I like to go before breakfast. There aren't many riders out that early."

"I stay as far away from horses as I can," Isabelle said.

Jake also turned him down.

Eden's excuse was, "I don't have proper riding clothes. Besides, I've never ridden sidesaddle."

Mystified, Edward asked, "How do you ride?"

"Astride like you, and I wear trousers." Eden nearly laughed at the shocked look on his face. "You don't think I'd ride around our ranch with my skirt flapping in the breeze, do you? It would catch on some bush, tree limb, or cactus, and I'd be jerked out of the saddle."

"It doesn't look nearly as shocking as it sounds," Isabelle assured him. "And it's much more practical."

"I'm sure it is," Edward said. "Apparently our English women don't have as much courage as Texas women, but that's no reason for you to deny yourself the pleasure of a ride."

"Nice recovery," Jake said, then laughed at Edward's increased discomfort.

"Are you sure you won't be uncomfortable with me riding astride?" Eden asked Edward.

"Of course I won't. You're my cousin."

Eden couldn't tell whether he really meant what he said, or whether he was merely being polite. These English had a way of concealing their inner thoughts and feelings that would be the envy of any poker player.

A sudden grin transformed Edward's expression. "Maybe you'll start a new fashion."

"More likely a scandal," Eden said, wondering if he was laughing at her or with her. "Maybe I shouldn't go. I don't want to upset your parents."

"We've already upset them by being here," Isabelle said. "Go riding if you want."

"I can't wait to see how a Texas woman handles a horse," Edward said. "Now I'd better say good night to Daphne. She and Patrick will talk about music half the night if I don't stop them."

The difference between the brothers was striking. Patrick said very little about himself, but he hid nothing. At first glance Edward appeared to be just as open, genuine, and approachable, but it hadn't taken Eden long to decide much of it was an act he'd perfected over the years. The real Edward Davenport was hidden well out of sight.

The stable boy was too well-trained to allow his face to show he was startled by Eden's riding attire. Edward was less reserved.

"That ought to raise a few eyebrows." Eden couldn't tell whether he was shocked, amused, or had simply expected a Texan to do something outrageous.

"My skirt is long and the boots are high," Eden pointed out. "My lower limbs are completely hidden from view."

"Your calves aren't. That ought to cause a few tulips of fashion to lose their habitual hauteur."

Ignoring him, she asked, "Where's Patrick?"

"My little brother isn't fond of getting up at dawn. He went back to sleep after I woke him. Maybe he'll catch up with us."

"Then I guess I'm stuck with you," she said with an arch smile.

Ignoring her jibe, Edward helped her into her saddle, mounted himself, and then they walked their mounts out of the stable yard and toward the park.

It was difficult for Eden to keep her horse at a walk

through the streets and narrow paths that led to the park. The weather was wonderful, ancient trees shaded their path, she was mounted on a good horse, and she was in the company of an exciting man. Her body hummed with energy. It took an act of concentration to pay attention to the small talk Edward employed to fill the time. She didn't really care who lived in which house, what had made them famous or infamous, or how London had grown so crowded Edward felt unable to take a deep breath until he was back at Worlege. She wanted to set her horse into a gallop, to feel the wind whipping around her face, to feel the muscles of the horse move beneath her.

"Here's the bridle path," Edward said as they crossed a road and reached a dirt path through the trees. "We're supposed to go no faster than a canter. But it's early enough that we might be able to get away with a short gallop."

Eden had never seen anything like it . . . a wide, dirt path snaking through a lush green park in the middle of a city of more than four million people. It made Jake's assertion that the Hill Country was becoming too crowded sound foolish. She urged her mount into a trot and then a slow canter. They passed two riders, one of whom—a young woman in a tight-fitted black riding habit with a small hard-top hat and a black veil covering her face—stared at Eden in open shock.

"Can we gallop?" Eden didn't really mind being stared at, but if she was going to attract attention, she wanted it to be for her riding, not her clothes.

"As long as we keep a sharp lookout for the police. Just don't go full out. I've already been ticketed for galloping in the park."

"I thought the aristocracy scorned all rules but their own."

"That may be true in their private lives, but the rules for public behavior are rigid and unbending. Things became worse after Prince Albert died and Queen Victoria went into perpetual mourning."

"Maybe any policeman who catches a glimpse of my calves will be too shocked to remember to ticket you."

Edward looked at her in mild disbelief. "Are you always like this?"

She laughed. "I'm being very well-behaved, even though this dawdling pace is just about to kill me." They rounded a bend in the bridle path, which opened out into a straight-away of nearly a half mile. "Can we gallop now?"

Chapter Three

 $\mathcal{E}$ dward checked to make sure no policemen were hiding in the shrubbery. "Very well, but only to the end of the straightaway."

Eden pushed her mount into a gallop a few strides ahead of Edward. "Last one there has to rub down the horses." They rode the length of the straightaway together, each urging the other to try harder. Very ungallantly, Eden thought, Edward finished a length in front.

"No fair," she called to him as they slowed their mounts to a canter. "Your horse is faster."

"He has to be. I weigh about five stones more than you."

"I can't help it if you're an overgrown beanstalk."

"I'll have you know I'm considered a fine figure of a man."

"Is that what Daphne thinks?" When Edward's smile disappeared and his face turned to a rigid mask, she realized she'd ventured into forbidden territory. What had happened to the energetic, open, laughing man she'd raced against just moments ago?

"It's not something Daphne would remark on even if she thought it."

"What's wrong with saying someone is a *fine figure of a man*?" Eden was trying to understand English behavior, but she thought such reserve was carrying things to a ridiculous extreme.

"It would be improper for a lady to make such a statement," Edward explained. "It implies a want of delicacy, of the refinement a gentleman looks for in a wife."

She refrained from saying that was the most ridiculous statement she'd ever heard, but it was a struggle. She tried to catch his eye, but he refused to meet her gaze, paying more attention to the flowers in the beds that lined the bridle path than to her or his mount, which tossed its head restlessly, eager for another gallop. "From the way you and Daphne act when you're together," she said, "an American would think you didn't know each other. A Texan would think you did and wished you didn't."

He turned toward her abruptly, his expression tight and noncommittal. "What would a Texan do?"

"Not everyone would do the same. Some—"

"What would *you* do?"

He was angry, challenging her, ready to criticize behavior he deemed unsuitable.

"I'd smile when I saw the man I loved coming toward me, be glad I was the focus of his attention, that he wanted everybody to know he believed I was the most important person in the room. I'd want to touch him, have him touch me, even kiss me. I'd want him to tell me I was beautiful, to make me *feel* beautiful even if I wasn't. And I wouldn't hesitate to let people know I liked the way he looked."

Edward's expression remained unchanged. "We marry for very different reasons in England. We—"

Eden ruthlessly interrupted him. "And after we married, we'd share every part of our lives. I wouldn't hesitate to work by his side just as he wouldn't refuse to help in the house if I were sick or caring for a child. His happiness would be my happiness, his worries mine also." Eden wanted to say a lot more, but Edward looked away.

They rode without speaking for several minutes, the silence broken by the plop of their horses' hooves in the heavy sand, the chirping of birds looking for food in the grass, the rustling leaves in the treetops. Eden could almost imagine the city of London had disappeared, leaving them alone in a cool, pleasant glade somewhere in the countryside.

She wondered how Edward could be so energetic and vital most of the time, yet stiff and lifeless when he was with Daphne. The only explanation she could find was that Edward didn't love Daphne and didn't want to marry her.

Edward finally broke the silence. "You don't understand. You couldn't without being born and raised here."

Eden was so relieved he'd finally spoken, she didn't challenge him. "Explain it to me."

He appeared reluctant but finally relented. "People like me have a responsibility to the family, to the people who depend on us, to the country if you will, to preserve our way of life. To do that, it's necessary to put others before oneself. We marry for practical reasons. Consider it a social contract if you want, but it's for the benefit of everyone, not for personal reasons."

"Can't you do both?"

"I suppose it's possible, but I don't know anyone who has."

"Don't you want to love the woman you marry?" Eden couldn't imagine spending the rest of her life with a man she didn't love. She'd rather be an old maid.

"It's more important to respect one's wife, to have a common social and cultural background. That will provide a solid basis for a long-term relationship." Edward looked away, studying the trees again. "Love is a fickle emotion that can change as often as the seasons."

"Then it's not love." Eden wanted to shake him, make him look at her. "My parents have been married for more than twenty years, and they're still in love."

"They're an exception."

"Then I have ten brothers, a sister, and a passel of in-laws who're all exceptions. Love is not merely physical attraction, Edward."

He turned to face her, his mouth compressed, his eyes hard. "Then what is it? According to your father, you have a unique variety in Texas."

Eden held back her sharp response. She'd forced Edward

to defend a system she was convinced he didn't believe in. Something was wrong between Edward and Daphne. If she could do anything to change that, she couldn't let this opportunity slide by.

"It helps to have similar social and cultural backgrounds, but real love is strong enough to overcome differences. My parents are a perfect example. Love is also physical attraction, sometimes so strong it's difficult to think of anything else. But you *do* think of something else. Though looks fade, the person you love will still be there, more worthy of love than ever."

"How can that be?"

Did he sound merely skeptical, or did she detect a hint of hope?

"You love a woman for what she is, what she does, what she means to you. In the beginning it may be that you just feel happy being with her, thinking about her. But as you get to know her better, become a part of each other's lives, you reach a point when you can't imagine being without her. That doesn't mean you'll always agree. It *does* mean you'll do your best to find common ground because your need for her in your life is greater than any difference of opinion."

"I don't think that's possible," Edward said.

"I know it is, because I've seen it in my family."

"I mean for me. My family is on the verge of bankruptcy. If I don't marry Daphne, our creditors will strip us of everything that isn't entailed, everything that doesn't have to stay with the title. Daphne wants a title, my family needs money, so we agreed to marry. Everybody gets what they want."

"What about love?"

Edward's expression was opaque. "What about it?"

"I would be miserable knowing someone had sacrificed their happiness for me."

Edward had opened his mouth to reply when his attention was caught by a rider who had just come onto the bridle path about forty yards ahead. A child of around six or seven was astride a big, rawboned horse that was fighting his rider's control. "Children aren't allowed to ride in the park alone."

"Why isn't someone with him?" Eden asked.

The child's horse, having pulled the reins from the child's hands, turned off the bridle path and into the park itself.

"I'd better stop them before the horse becomes completely unmanageable." Edward believed every boy ought to learn to ride as soon as he was able to stay in the saddle, but he was adamant that children needed proper supervision and a suitable mount until they had proved their skills. He angled his own mount onto the grass and set him into a fast canter.

The situation up ahead was getting worse. The boy had regained his hold on the reins, but the horse was throwing its head from side to side with such force, the jerking nearly pulled the child from the saddle. In an apparent effort to bring the horse under control, the boy hit it with his whip. Giving vent to an infuriated snort, the horse reared. The boy again lost his hold on the reins, and took a desperate grip on its mane. When the horse came down, it took off across the park at a gallop.

Edward turned to Eden, who had brought her mount alongside of his. "He's headed toward a rock wall."

"He looks big enough to jump it safely."

"There's a twenty-foot drop to a road on the other side. If he jumps that wall, they'll both be killed."

Edward drove his mount at a furious gallop over the uneven ground, around trees, benches, and over the gravel paths that crisscrossed the park. He jumped his mount over a broad border, putting him in the same part of the lawn as a woman with two small children. Though he wasn't close enough to pose a threat, the woman started screaming.

If that woman were from Texas, she wouldn't be such a fool, Eden thought as she jumped her horse over the same border.

The children watched the two horses thunder by, their eyes wide and staring, with no attempt to heed their nanny's screams to run to the safety of her arms before they were trampled to death.

"I'll lift the boy out of the saddle," Edward called to Eden. "See if you can keep the horse from killing itself."

Edward brought his horse alongside the runaway, but it shied abruptly in Eden's direction.

"Come up on his other side," Edward directed. "Let's see if we can pen him between us."

Eden brought her mount up alongside and held it on a straight course even though the boy was on a bigger and stronger horse. Edward leaned over and put his arm around the boy's waist. "Let go of the mane. I've got you, and the lady will get your horse."

The boy was too frightened to release his grip. Leaning dangerously far out of the saddle, Edward tightened his hold on the boy and lifted him up. The moment the boy's bottom left the saddle, he twisted around and threw his arms around Edward. In the process, the boy's hat fell off, and lengths of dark brown hair fell to the child's waist.

The boy was a girl.

To keep her from slipping out of his grip, Edward pulled the child into his lap. The little girl felt small and fragile in his arms. He couldn't imagine how anyone could have thought she would be able to control a horse big enough to be a hunter. Using his knees and one hand on the reins, he was able to bring his own mount to a halt. Eden caught the runaway and headed it in their direction. "Where's your groom?" Edward asked the child.

The little girl hung her head. "I don't have a groom."

"Who came with you?"

"No one." Her answer was spoken so softly, Edward could barely hear it.

"Does anyone know you're here?"

She shook her head.

A slow burn started in the pit of Edward's stomach. What kind of parents could be so unconcerned about the whereabouts of their children? Where was the stable boy? Such a small girl couldn't mount by herself.

"What is your name?" Edward asked. "Do you know where you live?"

"I'm Valentine Cordelia Baldwin," the girl answered. "I don't know where I live, but I can—"

"Get your hands off my daughter," a man shouted. "If you've harmed her, I'll see you hang."

Edward looked up to see a red-faced, overweight man, who appeared to be in his forties and had obviously dressed in haste, pulling up a horse whose withers were flecked with lather.

"She lost control of her horse, and it ran away with her," Edward explained.

"I saw him." The sound of a woman's voice caused both men to turn. "He spotted her when she was on the bridle path," said the nanny of the two small children, "and took off in pursuit. And that woman"—she pointed to Eden, who was leading the runaway horse—"is helping him."

"Of all the stupid stories I ever head, this is the most ridiculous," Eden informed the nanny. "If you hadn't been so busy screaming like a fool, you would have realized the horse was out of control and we were only trying to rescue the boy."

"Girl," Edward said, lifting the child's long hair for Eden to see.

"Girl?" She confronted the man. "What kind of father are you to allow a child barely old enough to be out of the nursery to take a badly trained horse out alone? Don't you realize she could have been killed if Edward hadn't rescued her before the horse tried to jump that stone wall?"

"He can jump walls twice that height," the man said.

"There's a twenty-foot drop to a road on the other side," Edward informed him.

The man blanched.

"Hector wouldn't do anything I told him," Valentine said to her father.

"How did you saddle and mount that horse?" Edward asked.

"I told Kenny that Papa wanted to take an early morning ride. I made him let me sit on Hector while he saddled my pony. But I didn't wait for Papa. I wanted to show him I was too big for a pony."

"Instead of saddling another horse and following her, the idiot groom came running into my bedroom while I was still asleep," Mr. Baldwin explained. "I didn't even have time to dress properly."

"What's going on here?"

They all turned to see a policeman approaching.

"I have a report of an indecently clad woman galloping in the park."

"So you rescued this man's little girl?" the policeman asked after Edward had explained.

"Yes. Now if that's all, we'll be going."

"I still have this report of galloping in the park."

"How else was I going to catch the horse before someone got injured?"

"It's not about you," the policeman stated. "It's about a woman."

"We were on the bridle path when we saw the horse go out of control," Eden explained.

"They came galloping straight at my charges," the nanny reiterated. "I was so frightened, I couldn't move."

Between the policeman's disapproval of Eden's riding habit and the charge of galloping in the park, Edward's chances of getting off without being hauled before a magistrate were looking slim. He was relieved when Patrick rode up.

"What's going on?" his brother asked.

All the explanations were repeated. There was nothing the policeman could do about Eden's mode of dress because none of her limbs were exposed. And there was no question about Valentine's rescue.

"My brother has explained they were galloping to rescue the child," Patrick said. "Surely that's sufficient reason to ignore the rules this once."

"You've already had one citation for galloping in the park," the policeman said to Edward. "The magistrate isn't going to take it kindly if you're brought up before him a second time."

"I should think the magistrate would be more likely to give my brother a commendation," Patrick pointed out. "It's not every heir to an earldom who would risk his life in such a manner."

"I'll do my best to see I don't get caught galloping in the park again," Edward said to the policeman. He glanced at Eden in time to see her hide a smile. "Now, we'd better take Valentine home. I'm sure her mother is anxious to know she's safe."

Eden handed Hector's reins to Mr. Baldwin and brought her horse alongside Edward's. Patrick pulled up beside the policeman, effectively separating him from Edward. With Mr. Baldwin leading, the party rode out of the park. Valentine resisted all efforts to convince her to ride with her father or Eden.

"She's comfortable where she is," Edward said. "Why should she move?"

"Because you're a dangerous man," Patrick said with a sly smile. "Even our honest policeman thinks so."

The policeman had the grace to blush.

It amazed Edward that the policeman might think him dangerous. He was a responsible, law-abiding citizen. Well, he broke little rules, but only once in a while. He honored his parents, loved his country, worked hard, and had never been involved in a scandal. He had no illegitimate children, had never been in debt, didn't drink to excess, and was a

man of his word. Still, there was something about him that
made people look at him askance.

"I don't understand how parents can be so careless of their
children," Edward said to Eden as they were leaving the Bald-
wins' house. "I wouldn't be surprised to find that half the time
the girl's parents can't be bothered to know where she is. I've
got Sam Kellaway and his wife, Ginny, as nice a pair as you'll
find anywhere and the best farmer on the estate, trying to
have a baby for more than ten years. Ginny breaks into tears
every time one of her friends gets in the family way. I'd like to
take the girl and give her to somebody who'll care about her."

"You ought to talk to my mother," Eden said. "She took
on eleven orphans and convinced my father to adopt all of
them."

"Eleven!" Edward couldn't imagine having eleven brothers and sisters.

"All declared incorrigible and unmanageable. Now they're
married and giving her all the grandchildren she could ever
want."

"I don't know anything about children, but Edward is a genius with them," Patrick said. "You ought to see him with the
little ones in the village. They think he's Father Christmas."

"That's because I give them treats," Edward said, uncomfortable with Patrick's praise. "The little tykes don't have
much."

"That's why he and Father are always fighting," Patrick
said to Eden. "Edward makes sure the tenants have enough
for a decent living."

"Why shouldn't they?" Edward demanded. "It's their hard
work that puts money in our pockets."

"You don't have to convince me," Patrick said. "I was just
explaining you to Eden. All she's had a chance to see is that
you're an irascible country boy who hates London and
hasn't got the good sense to propose to a beautiful woman."

"You don't have to convince me Edward isn't the misfit he's made out to be," Eden said. "Now, I was invited to ride with two charming gentlemen. If you two can't stop picking at each other, I'll ask that nice policeman to accompany me."

They managed to have such a delightful ride, they were late for breakfast. Edward always enjoyed being with Patrick, and Eden was the kind of woman a man could relax and have fun with. She didn't demand special treatment or that he watch his tongue or his manners. It was almost like being with another man, except she wasn't the least bit like a man. Altogether, it was the best morning he'd spent in a long time.

Edward didn't need to see his father's expression to know he was in trouble. The viscount got up early for breakfast only when he was too angry to sleep, and Edward had no doubt he was the object of that anger. There were times when he was ready to give up his claim to the title, retire to some distant corner of England, and raise horses. Today was a perfect example.

"I expect you to take Daphne for a ride in the park," Cyril announced the moment Edward walked through the door.

Edward headed for the coffee without a glance at his father. "She doesn't ride."

"I know that," the viscount replied, his tone sharp and unpleasant, "but her father has bought her a splendid carriage with a matched pair of chestnuts so society can see his daughter with her future husband."

Saying he'd lost his patience completely, Cyril demanded to know exactly when Edward intended to propose to Daphne. Every objection Edward advanced, every reason he gave to delay, was met by the flat statement that Daphne and her family had been expecting the proposal for weeks, and her father was beginning to feel ill-used. He also said the Davenports' financial situation had reached a critical stage and if they didn't receive an infusion of cash soon, they could all be hauled off to debtors' prison.

"I don't understand why you haven't jumped at the chance to make such an advantageous marriage," his father stated. "Her father is so rich he could have held out for a man with a title already in hand. I know she's not of our class, but she's been well-trained and won't embarrass you."

"It's not that," Edward had said. "We're too different. I need time to see if we have enough in common to be man and wife." He hadn't intended to say that, but he couldn't stop thinking that Eden didn't expect anyone to sacrifice their happiness for her. His family was demanding it.

"Don't talk rot," the viscount had said. "You don't have to see her any more than necessary to father children. She's no fool. She won't expect fidelity."

"That's not the kind of marriage I want."

"It doesn't matter what you want. It's what the family needs. If you don't propose immediately, I'll ask the earl to cut off your allowance."

Edward had very few personal needs and spent most of his allowance on the estate. But before he could take a deep breath to respond, his father delivered a devastating threat, one Edward hadn't anticipated.

"In addition, I'll ask the earl to bar you from having anything to do with the estate or the tenant farmers. You will not be allowed to stay at Worlege or in the village."

Edward should have known something important had happened when Alastair spent several hours the previous day closeted with the family solicitor. Apparently, the family debts had piled up until they were out of options. His marriage to Daphne was their only means of survival.

Chapter Four

$\mathcal{E}$dward hated the afternoon ritual of ladies riding through the park at a dawdling pace accompanied by brothers, admirers, or unfortunate future husbands. The heat only made it worse. At Worlege he would have enjoyed cool breezes from the forest or the river, but in London there was no breeze. He rode next to the open carriage, where Daphne and Eden had parasols to protect them from the sun. The brim of his hat wasn't nearly as effective.

The passing of several hours hadn't provided Edward with any solution to his problem. The heat and the walking pace just aggravated his already ragged temper. He still planned to wait until they went to Worlege to ask Daphne to marry him. His father would need time to convince his great-uncle to put pressure on him, but their worsening financial situation meant the earl would soon be willing to do whatever was necessary to force Edward to marry Daphne.

It was impossible to be angry with Daphne. It wasn't her fault the Davenport family was far more interested in spending money than in making it. It wasn't her fault she was very pretty and the only child of a rich and ambitious father. She'd been trained to think marriage to a title was the greatest success she could have as a woman, had been taught not to expect love from her husband, not even fidelity, possibly not even real kindness. It wasn't her fault she'd been turned into a proud, hard woman who looked at life as a simple equation—money plus a title equaled success. It wasn't her fault she disliked horses, was even a little afraid of them. He was glad Patrick had agreed to ride with them. His obvious enjoyment of the ride had caused Daphne to unbend a little.

"It would be impossible for us to enjoy a ride like this in Texas in July," Eden was saying to Daphne. "You'd faint from the heat."

"I'm feeling a little faint as it is," Daphne said in a complaining tone. She hadn't been any more anxious for the outing than Edward and had been a little out of temper from the moment she left the house and climbed into the oversized carriage. Edward didn't know how she would manage at Worlege. He couldn't face the prospect of living in a London town house for the rest of his life. Nor did he feel he could honorably ask her to marry him if he intended to spend most of the year away from her. His father might not care how he treated her once they were married, but he intended to treat her honorably.

"A slow trot," Edward instructed the coachman, relieved to be able to move his own restive mount out of a walk. "It will create a gentle breeze to cool you off," he said when Daphne looked uneasy.

Patrick rode on the other side of the coach, next to Eden. He gave every appearance of being content with the dawdling pace, which only made Edward feel more guilty at his own impatience. Why couldn't he be more like Patrick?

A notion struck him. Did Patrick like Eden? Why did that thought annoy him? Eden seemed just as interested in Patrick. Did she think he might marry her, or was she merely engaging in an enjoyable flirtation with an attractive man? Edward didn't care that her grandmother hadn't married the earl, but the viscount would.

He wondered why these thoughts had popped into his head and refused to go away. He tried distracting himself by talking to Daphne, but she knew nothing about the subjects that interested him—or he the subjects that interested her.

How could he spend the rest of his life married to a woman he couldn't talk to?

"I never ride in the park," Daphne was telling Eden. "It's too much trouble to get the carriage and horses out. Then there's the question of an escort. Edward is up at Worlege all the time, and Papa is too busy."

"All I have to do at home is lasso a horse and saddle up."

"You saddle your own horse?" Daphne asked, aghast.

Edward couldn't tell whether she was more appalled by this unprecedented behavior or that Eden was courageous enough to get that close to a horse.

"I have since I was strong enough to handle a lasso," Eden said.

"What's a lasso?" Daphne asked.

"It's a rope with a loop at the end that you throw over the horse's head when you want to catch him."

"Why would you need to catch a horse that's in a stall?"

"Our horses run loose in a corral. It's like a big pasture. When you need a horse, you have to catch it. Sometimes they'll buck a little before they settle down."

Edward was too entranced by the vision of Eden astride a bucking horse to give much notice to Daphne's look of incomprehension. He found the notion of keeping horses in a corral strange, but could imagine the fun of picking out the mount he wanted before wading in among the horses to lasso it. He'd never seen a lasso, but he had no trouble visualizing one, hearing it sing through the air. It made his blood quicken just to think about it. When they got to Worlege, he'd ask Eden to show him how to handle a lasso.

"You'll have to stop telling stories about Texas, or Edward will follow you back," Patrick said with a laugh.

"Lassoing my own horse and having him buck a little sounds like a great way to start the day," Edward said, uneasy that Patrick could read his mind so easily.

"Tell that to Dad when it's winter and the horses are particularly fractious," Eden said. "He'd be happy to have you lasso them for him."

"Don't say that," Patrick teased. "He'll think you're offering him a job."

"I couldn't live in Texas," Daphne said in a repressive manner. "I wouldn't know what to do."

"Patrick is only teasing me," Edward said, ignoring Daphne's pique. "I'd probably be as lost in Texas as you."

"But you wouldn't be foolish enough to go to Texas." Daphne's tone implied that no one of breeding would go to a place such as Texas.

Hoping to change the subject, Edward said to Eden, "I appreciate your confidence that I could lasso a horse, but I have many limits, one of which is not knowing what to do with my feet when I'm on the dance floor."

Patrick began recounting instances when Edward's admirable physicality failed to help him navigate the intricacies of some dance and the inevitable commentary it drew from the ranks of the dowagers. Since Edward knew he wasn't a good dancer, and had no desire to become one, he was able to laugh along with them.

"In Texas we like our dances slow, so the man can hold the woman in his arms and she can rest her head on his chest," Eden said.

Patrick looked surprised, Daphne horrified. "Do ladies participate in those dances?" Edward asked, intrigued.

Eden threw him a challenging look. "*I* participate in those dances."

"I thought the waltz was a bold dance," Patrick said, "but it sounds like you Americans have gotten the jump on us again."

"We admire your traditions," Eden said, her gaze still firmly fixed on Edward, "but we prefer less regimented lives."

"How do you know what's acceptable, what's proper?" Daphne asked.

"Each person gets to decide on his—or her—own," Eden replied.

"I can't imagine you ever doing anything improper," Patrick said.

But Edward could. He sensed from the beginning that Eden Maxwell had a very unusual idea of what was suitable for women in general and herself in particular. He'd never had a model of the kind of woman he wanted for a wife, but now he did. Eden cooked the food her brothers ate, rode the horses they rode, and did the work they did. She would work beside the man she married, not stand apart from him. She would expect him to earn his living, not siphon it off the work of others. She would be a partner, not a possession.

That was the kind of wife he wanted, but it was the kind of wife he would never have.

Along with the title he would inherit came the responsibility of upholding the dignity of the position as well as responsibility for the people who depended on him for their livelihood . . . his and Patrick's future families, the families of their tenants, and the people of the village of Green Moss. It was his duty to marry Daphne Bidwell and use her fortune to insure the future of everyone who depended on him.

The taste in his mouth was bitter.

He looked at the two women in the carriage and wondered if they had anything in common other than their gender. For seventeen years Daphne had been trained to be the wife of a titled aristocrat. She knew how to dress, how to carry on a conversation, how to dance, and the rules of society.

Eden, on the other hand, had an extensive education, and was used to making her own decisions. She would never ignore the feelings of other people, but she wouldn't allow them to dictate her actions.

It was a shock to realize she had more freedom than he did.

The sound of laughter brought him out of his brown study.

"I wish I could have seen the young man's face," Patrick said.

"I never could have spoken to a man like that," Daphne said.

"You would have if you'd been brought up by my mother," Eden said. "There's not a man alive she's afraid to tackle. She still lights into Dad from time to time. One minute they're in an all-out argument, and the next they're holding hands or kissing and hugging."

Edward couldn't imagine that. Though his father told people Charlotte was a perfect wife, he couldn't recall him holding her hand except to help her into or out of a carriage. He had never seen them kiss or hug. He was certain Daphne would have a fainting spell if he tried to kiss her. He'd never stopped to consider whether he would like it. The idea was simply too far out of his experience to have occurred to him. Daphne made him feel that he was with a china doll, perfect in outward appearance but hard and brittle. Eden was the kind of woman who was mentally tough yet capable of being gentle. Though she'd obviously been brought up well, she wasn't reluctant to show her feelings or deny the effects of a strong physical attraction.

The concept of a lady who was also willing to show her feelings was so new it took his breath away. He told himself to stop thinking about the absurd and the impossible and to concentrate on Daphne. She was his future.

"I hope you're looking forward to going to Worlege," Edward said to Daphne.

"Of course. I'm anxious to see your home."

She said that as if she was preparing herself for an uncomfortable, possibly distasteful, duty.

"Mrs. Jessop has written down the names and addresses of all the families I should visit," Daphne informed him. "I asked her to make up a list of historical sights, too."

Edward felt his hope wane. He loved hunting, but Daphne said the sound of guns shattered her nerves. He cared nothing about the historical sights her companion might recommend. She said she could spend a whole afternoon wandering about an old ruin. He hated the routine social calls, small dinner parties, and impromptu dances that were the sum total of a city-bred lady's social calendar.

"What kind of historical sights are you talking about?" Eden asked.

"Old churches, ruined abbeys, or decaying castles. Nearly everything in London is pulled down the moment nobody wants it anymore, but Mrs. Jessop says no one bothers about ruins in the country."

"That's because it's too expensive to pull them down for the little bit of land under them," Edward explained. "We don't have any ruins at Worlege. But if we did, I'd rather spend the money on a new stable, cow barn, or livestock pens than shifting a pile of old stones about."

"What an unromantic attitude," Eden exclaimed.

Edward couldn't tell whether Eden was teasing him or was shocked by his attitude. She was the most puzzling woman he'd ever encountered.

"Mother would never have any new curtains or Father a new hunter if Edward had his way," Patrick said with a laugh. "We'd all go threadbare so the livestock could live in luxury."

"He sounds like my father," Eden said. "He always has his eye on more land or a new bull. If there's anything left over, Mama can have a new dress."

Edward could tell from the way Eden's mouth was curved in a grin, she was teasing him as well.

"Mrs. Jessop says the best investment a woman can make is in her clothes," Daphne said with a seriousness that squelched the laugh in Edward's throat.

How could anyone think clothes were that important? He never wore jewelry and thought of clothes merely as something to keep him warm or preserve his modesty. He was relieved when the drive through the park came to an end and it was time to escort Daphne home.

"Will you be at the ball tonight?" Daphne asked Edward when the coach stopped at the front door of her father's house and the footman came out to help her down.

"I'll make sure Edward is there even if I have to dress him myself and drag him all the way," Patrick said.

Daphne's smile seemed forced. "Don't make him go if he doesn't want to."

Edward would be at the ball because it would be an insult to Daphne to stay away, but if he made the sacrifice of marrying her, it would be to save Worlege, not for the family.

The next day, Eden was relieved when the train finally reached the village of Green Moss. She could barely contain her excitement at finally getting to see a real English country house. She laughed inwardly to think how jealous some of her schoolmates would be. They'd looked down on her because she came from Texas.

Patrick had been his usual cheerful self during the journey. Between the two of them, they'd struggled to keep Daphne entertained and distracted from her complaints about the crowded station, the heat, the noise, and the smell. The viscount kept saying how disappointed he was at having to leave London until the earl put an abrupt end to his complaints by saying they were leaving because he couldn't afford to keep the house open any longer. Isabelle was telling Charlotte some of the things she'd like to do and see before they returned to America. Jake said he didn't care as long as he didn't have to dance.

Eden turned to Edward to find him staring at her in a vaguely unsettling way. It was as though he were watching, waiting for her to do something. Only Eden didn't know what it might be.

"We don't keep a lot of conveyances at Worlege," Edward explained to Isabelle when it came time to leave the train. "I thought you might prefer to ride with my parents and the earl. Daphne and Eden can go in the open coach. Jake can ride with Patrick and me."

"If I had known you were having horses brought, I'd have changed into my riding clothes," Eden said.

"I'm not about to let you near a horse after you've been closed up in this train for hours," Isabelle said. "You'd head cross-country and I don't know when we'd see you again."

"Okay, but Patrick has to take me for a ride before breakfast tomorrow."

"If he manages to wake up," Edward said.

"I don't sleep late in the country. I hope your parents will join us," Patrick offered gallantly.

"Jake might, but I don't go near a horse unless I have to," Isabelle declared.

The bustle of getting everybody and the luggage off the train and headed toward the various vehicles took up over a quarter of an hour. "How far is it to the house?" Jake asked once he was astride a heavily muscled bay.

"A little over six miles," Edward said.

"I hope you're not expecting me to prance alongside these carriages the whole distance. I'll go crazy."

"Ask Edward to ride with you," Eden suggested. "Patrick can stay with us." She thought Edward flinched at her suggestion, but she couldn't be sure.

"Patrick can ride with your father," Edward said. "It's my duty to stay with Daphne."

He could have said he *wanted* to stay with Daphne. Better still, he could have said he couldn't bear to think of leaving her, but he'd said it was his *duty*. Eden didn't know what Daphne had been taught to expect of her husband, but Eden was rapidly coming to the conclusion *she* could never marry an Englishman. She didn't know what they used for blood, but she assumed it could be replaced by icy water and no one would know the difference.

"If you're going to accompany us, you'll have to stop scowling," Eden said.

"I'm not scowling," Edward protested.

"Call it what you want, but it's a disapproving look."

"I've been wondering if you had a toothache," Patrick said.

"Are you still upset about having to go to the ball last night?" Daphne asked.

Edward had done his best to put all memory of that miserable evening out of his mind. Good manners had dictated that he dance with both Daphne and Eden, but the inadequacy of his performance had been underscored by the way Patrick whirled both women around the ballroom. It hadn't helped when the viscount had very audibly commented on the contrast.

Edward was visibly annoyed. "I don't have a toothache, and I've forgotten about the ball. I'm just not used to having so much company at Worlege.

"You'd better go join Eden's father," Edward said to Patrick. "From the set of his jaw, I expect him to head off down the road any minute. We don't want him to get lost."

"My father doesn't get lost in the thousand miles of wilderness between his ranch and Santa Fe," Eden said. "I doubt he'll have any trouble on your estate." She hadn't meant to sound so abrupt, but she was tired of the belittling comments.

"I'm sure he'll be fine," Edward said, "but it would be rude to abandon a guest at the train station."

Eden wasn't sure how the tenor of their conversation had become so strained, but she was relieved when Patrick wheeled his horse and rode off to join her father. The coach had already left. As their carriage pulled out of the station, men were still piling baggage into two wagons.

Any lingering tension disappeared quickly once the carriage left the station. Daphne seemed almost as bemused as Eden at the village of Green Moss.

The buildings were all built of stone and came right down to the street with almost no sidewalk. Chimneys rose high above the slate or tile roofs, with vents protruding in groups of three or more. The narrow street was cobblestone, which rattled the coach and caused sparks to fly from the horses' shod hooves. A stream that ran through town was spanned by a stone bridge so narrow the sides nearly scraped the carriage. They had hardly entered the village before it ended abruptly and they were in the countryside.

Here, a smattering of stone cottages sat well apart from each other. Their front yards were fenced off by low stone walls or what looked like sticks woven together by wire to keep the livestock out. Small areas of grass were bisected by beds of rich, black dirt spilling over with a riot of blooming flowers. Beside or behind each house was a garden as neat as the yard. Rows of vegetables alternated with beds of herbs. Espaliered fruit trees and vines heavy with grapes were grown against the garden walls to protect them from the wind and to provide the benefit from the radiated heat during the night.

Livestock—cows, pigs, goats, or horses—were kept in pens and fields behind the houses. Even when they couldn't be seen from the road, their presence was evident by smell.

Then there were the sheep. Eden didn't think she'd ever seen so many. Low stone walls wound over the hills and down into the valleys, dividing the land into a patchwork of green. The river wended its quiet way through the crevices of the land, trees along the banks looking even taller because of their isolation. Eden hadn't realized how few trees she'd seen until she rounded the shoulder of a hill and entered the cool shade of a forest.

"This is the home wood," Edward explained. "It was much larger when my ancestors used it as a hunting ground. There are still a few deer in the wood. Some foxes and badgers, too."

Eden was used to the trees in the Hill Country, but those were dwarfed by the size of the oaks and hemlocks that formed a thick canopy overhead. Birds called from the branches above. Nothing moved through the shadows but a pair of noisy squirrels more interested in chasing each other than in storing food for the winter. Eden had barely accustomed herself to the forest when they emerged from the shadows and into the bright sunlight. She would have thought the wide sweep of lawn that led up to Worlege would make the house look less overwhelming, but the house seemed to reduce everything around it to insignificance. The main block and the two connecting wings covered the whole of the hill on which they had been built. The soft grey stone glistened in the sunlight, the windows shone gold. She could see why Edward had been so eager to return to Worlege. The setting was magnificent, the near silence magical.

"Welcome to Worlege," Edward said.

"It's so large," Eden said.

"The original house wasn't this big," Edward explained. "The earl's older brother enlarged the house about fifty years ago. Nobody could figure why. He didn't have any children, the present earl wasn't married, and my grandfather had only one child. If Patrick and I fail to produce a male heir, the estate will go to distant relations. My father becomes apoplectic just thinking about it. He was greatly relieved when my mother gave birth to me after four miscarriages. It's the private belief of half the village that he married a second time to have a spare."

"You and Patrick appear to be very healthy," Eden said. "I think the Davenport line is safe."

As they drew closer, the house loomed so large, Eden could begin to understand how Edward could feel he was owned by Worlege instead of the other way around. The house sat on the hill like a magnificent queen on her throne, welcoming her subjects and accepting their homage.

As they proceeded up the carriage drive toward the house, Edward gave them a brief history of Worlege. The concept of remodeling and enlarging a house several times was new to Eden. In Texas, folks simply moved out of the first and built another one. In a rapidly changing place like

Texas, it was hard to think of a house that had been around before the first English settlers came to America.

When they reached the manor house. Edward helped each of the women down, then escorted them up the few steps. Eden entered the main hall and came to an abrupt stop.

This was even more impressive than the London house. Marble columns rose to support a domed ceiling about forty feet above. A classical painting in soft but rich pastels covered the inside of the dome. Massive paintings hung on the walls between the columns. In front of them rose a staircase broad enough for six men to ascend abreast. Behind it a hallway running the length of the house gave access to the public rooms.

"We can wait in the drawing room until Mother or the housekeeper comes to show you to your rooms."

Eden said, "I feel like I need a map so I won't get lost."

"It's not that complicated. The housekeeper will be happy to answer your questions."

"I can talk with her later," Eden replied. "Patrick can show me the house for now."

"No, he can't."

Chapter Five

$\mathcal{E}$den looked at Edward in shocked surprise. He'd been in an uncertain mood all day, but this abruptness wasn't like him.

"I didn't mean that the way it sounded." Edward looked flustered. "Patrick is probably showing your father the stables. After that, Jake will want to see our breeding bulls. He may not be up to the house for some time."

Eden didn't know what was bothering Edward, but she was going to ask him point-blank as soon as she got a chance to talk to him alone.

"I'd be just as interested in seeing the stables and the breeding stock as Dad," she said. "I work on the ranch, too."

"You'll have to forgive Edward," Daphne said. "English ladies don't work, so I'm sure he has trouble remembering that you do."

It was clear from Daphne's tone that Eden had slipped another notch in her estimation, but she refused to pretend to be something she wasn't. "I help my mother in the house or ride out with Dad to take care of the cows."

"I can't imagine that." Daphne's smile implied no *lady* would.

"Then it's fortunate you don't have to," Eden said, a sharp edge slipping into her voice. Rather than continue a conversation that could only be unflattering to both her and Daphne, Eden turned her attention to the house. She couldn't understand why anyone would want three drawing rooms and two dining rooms. She did, however, begin to understand the cost of owning such a house.

"I didn't know Worlege was so impressive," Daphne said, her habitual hauteur less evident.

"Worlege is not large compared to some," Edward said, "but it *is* roomy."

Eden would have described it as barnlike, but that would have been misleading. She didn't know anyone who owned a marble barn.

Edward could barely suppress a sigh of relief when the housekeeper came to escort Eden and Daphne to their rooms. He sank down onto a sofa and tried to calm his irritated nerves. Was he only imagining things, or was Eden taking every opportunity to be alone with Patrick? More to the point, why was he trying to prevent it? Patrick was a grown man able to take care of himself. Eden had made it plain she was going back to Texas, that she could never live in England. It was inconceivable that Patrick would live anywhere else.

So why couldn't he ignore the situation and let it go away on its own?

There was no indication Patrick was in danger of falling in love with Eden. He showed more interest in Daphne, which was just as well. Since they would soon be members of the same family, it was important they be able to get along. Patrick would live at Worlege until he married. And unless he married an heiress, he'd probably live there for the rest of his life.

Eden showed a genuine fondness for Patrick, but it didn't appear strong enough to turn into something more serious. Still, Texas women didn't do anything like English women. How would Eden fall in love? What kind of man would appeal to her?

He would have to be a strong, confident person. Eden wouldn't respect a man who let her run over him. But neither would she put up with a man who tried to dominate her. It would be a partnership. Edward had never thought of marriage as an equal partnership. As far as he knew, no one in England did. He wasn't sure how an equal-partnership marriage was supposed to work, wasn't sure it *could* work, but he liked Eden's willingness to discuss anything with him, even argue with him, when she disagreed.

Then there was the matter of preparing food as well as working the ranch with her father. The wives of his tenant farmers were responsible for every aspect of the home, but they didn't go into the fields to work alongside their husbands or participate in making the decisions about the farm or the stock. That was exclusively the privilege and responsibility of the husband. The lines of duty were clearly drawn and no one crossed them.

But Eden would. Rather, she would simply refuse to admit they existed. That would be impossible for Patrick to accept. He was English down to his core. Edward was, too, so why did Eden's attitudes and behavior intrigue him rather than alienate him?

He was glad Eden was such an accomplished horsewoman. He was looking forward to engaging in a few spirited races. English women sometimes took part in fox hunts, but they never engaged in anything that could be interpreted as a competition with men. Would proper etiquette require that he let her win or that he never pass her? He wasn't sure of that answer, but he was certain Eden wouldn't accept such a solution. She'd want to win on her own merit or not at all.

He liked Eden's spunkiness, her toughness, her refusal to consider anything off limits or beyond her abilities, her belief that she was the equal of anyone, even a man. At the same time, she was as pretty as any London debutante. Her dance card at the ball had been filled within minutes after he'd escorted her off the dance floor.

She had a feminine quality he found hard to define. All of his feelings about women—his ideas of what was feminine, what was beautiful, what was proper, what was desirable—had been drawn from women like Daphne, yet he found Eden more attractive, more appealing in that special way a woman is appealing to a man.

Edward groaned and got to his feet. All this thinking was giving him a headache. Besides, it was useless. Everything in his life had been laid out for him long before his birth. He wasn't going to change English society, the people, or his role in it. It would be better for everyone if he stopped stalling, asked Daphne to marry him, and got on with his life. So why didn't he?

He didn't want to believe Eden had anything to do with his continued resistance. Though he admired her and was attracted to her, he couldn't imagine being married to such a woman. She would upset the balance of his life. It was better for everyone that she would soon go back to Texas.

Thinking of Texas caused his longing to escape the constraints of English society to flare up again. Eden was proof that the stories of the freedom of the American West weren't exaggerated. If Eden could be allowed so much freedom, surely a man could do anything he wanted, *be* anything he wanted.

Determined to put all thoughts of Eden and of running off to America out of his mind, he left the drawing room and headed down the hall, intending to go to the stables. What he needed to clear his head was a good gallop. But later, as he rode a powerful bay gelding down one of the farm lanes at a brisk canter, he couldn't stop wondering about the man Eden would choose for her husband, and whether that man would be anything like himself.

"You're an even better rider than I thought," Edward said to Eden as they were walking from the stable to the house the next morning.

"Just because I beat you?" She couldn't stop a laugh. The race across the recently cut meadow had been exhilarating. "Your horse was carrying about eighty pounds more than mine. I wouldn't let getting beaten by a couple of lengths bend you out of shape."

Edward was grinning from ear to ear, as they would say in Texas. Eden had always thought he was attractive, but he looked particularly handsome this morning. His clothes were well-worn, but they fit his muscled body like a glove. The wind had whipped his hair out of its carefully groomed shape while his eyes sparkled and his body radiated energy.

"I'm not upset," Edward said with a laugh that backed up his words. "I can't wait to tell Patrick a woman beat me on Crusader when he couldn't."

"Don't you dare," Eden replied. "I'm sure the poor boy has had enough of standing in your shadow."

Edward's expression softened. "Patrick never misses a chance to tell everyone how wonderful I am."

"Well, I wouldn't say you're wonderful," Eden said, a sly smile on her lips, "but you're not too bad."

"I'm surprised they haven't run you out of Texas," Edward said with a laugh. "You have a way of cutting a man down to size."

That thought stopped Eden in her tracks. Was she so critical that men stayed away from her? She had begun to wonder why at twenty-one she hadn't met a man she'd consider marrying. "I do expect a lot of men, but I've got some very fine examples in my family to measure them against."

"Don't worry." Edward's expression had become closed. "Even with your expectations, you'll find lots of men eager to marry you."

"The man I marry will have to love me, not my money. I want love, not a merger of assets."

Maybe she shouldn't have made such a sharply worded reply, but she didn't get a chance to amend her statement. As they entered the house, they were met by the butler, who informed them that the viscount was in the breakfast room and asking for Edward. "I don't think he slept well," the butler said.

"That's a euphemism meaning he's in a rotten mood," Edward translated. "He doesn't like Worlege." Edward's footsteps on the wood floor echoed down the long hallway. "He says the birds make so much noise, it's impossible to sleep." They could hear Cyril's querulous voice even before they entered the breakfast room. "I often have breakfast in the village when the family is at Worlege."

Eden could see why.

"Where have you been?" the viscount demanded the moment they entered the room.

"Eden and I went for a ride." Edward headed straight for the sideboard without looking at his father.

"They invited me to join them," Patrick said from his place at the table, "but I decided to stay in bed."

"You should have taken Daphne," the viscount said.

"She doesn't like horses," Edward reminded his father for the umpteenth time.

"Then you should have offered to take her in the buggy."

"She said she wanted to sleep late," Eden told the viscount. "She was tired after the train ride."

Stymied, Cyril angrily attacked his breakfast.

"Have my parents had breakfast yet?" Eden asked Patrick.

"They were down earlier," Patrick told her. "Your mother and mine are comparing notes on how to preserve fruits. I think your father was headed to one of the farms to see a bull Edward told him about. He likes the idea of going back to Texas with a better bull than the one your brother Chet has."

Daphne's entry into the breakfast room caused a small stir. Patrick jumped up to help her with her food and then seated her at the table between him and Eden. Cyril remained sitting at the head of the table. Edward drank coffee from his position by the window.

The viscount turned his angry gaze on Edward. "What entertainment have you planned for Daphne this morning?"

"I have to work," Edward replied. "I—"

"There's nothing that can't wait," the viscount said, interrupting his son.

"I've been away for more than a week," Edward objected.

"Potter has been here," the viscount pointed out.

"Potter handles the accounts." Edward gazed at the remains of his coffee rather than his father. "He doesn't know anything about the crops, livestock—"

"He would if you didn't get in his way," Cyril said. "Let him deal with hay and turnips. Daphne needs your attention."

Daphne looked up from her breakfast. "I'd prefer not to spend the morning bouncing over muddy roads in an uncomfortable buggy looking at crops and animals I have absolutely no interest in."

"I had planned to ask Daphne to ride into the village this afternoon," Edward explained.

"I have no desire to be introduced to the rustic way of life," Daphne announced, "or people with whom I cannot possibly have a thought in common."

"At least *she* knows what's due the family's position," the viscount growled. "You should leave everything to Potter."

Edward struggled valiantly to hold on to his temper. "If I did that, the family would be living in cramped quarters on one of our small holdings instead of spending half the year in London."

"The family appreciates everything you do for us." Alastair had come into the breakfast room in time to hear the last remark.

"It's what he *hasn't* done I'm complaining about," Cyril said.

Daphne quietly continued eating her breakfast, apparently unconcerned that she was the center of an argument.

"I'll take care of my business in my own way in my own time," Edward said from between clenched teeth.

"But it's *our* business," Cyril thundered back.

"We've got the morning already planned," Eden put in,

hoping to ease the tension in the room. "Patrick has promised to give Daphne and me a tour of the house and grounds."

"Edward can show Daphne the house," the viscount stated firmly.

"I prefer Patrick," Daphne said. "Edward barely knows a Gainsborough painting from a Turner."

"Why can't you leave things alone?" Edward asked.

"I would if you would stick to your business," his father shouted.

"That's what I intend to do right now."

Edward put his coffee on the sideboard and walked out of the room, ignoring the viscount's shouts that he return.

Unable to stand any more, Eden abandoned her breakfast and left the room, too.

"He doesn't mean half the things he says." Patrick had followed her. "He's just worried about money."

"Then he shouldn't spend so much," Eden snapped.

"He doesn't know how to live any other way."

"He still has no right to treat Edward the way he does."

"Yes, Edward was really upset. Would you talk to him?"

The request surprised Eden. "You ought to do that."

"He's had to listen to me too often already. He likes and respects you."

Eden wasn't sure about that, but she was worried about Edward. It had to hurt to have your father constantly berate you, especially in front of the whole family. "Where would he have gone?"

"To the stables. He always goes for a ride or to one of the farms when he's upset."

"Tell my parents where I've gone when they come in," she said.

On the way to the stables, she tried to think of something to take Edward's mind off what his father had said, but she couldn't think of anything except ways to drown the viscount or suffocate him in his sleep.

"To my way of thinking, he's headed for the village," the groom said as he saddled a horse for Eden. "He's most likely in the pub right now."

After getting instructions on a shortcut to the village, Eden set out at a fast canter. A few minutes later she spotted Edward sitting his horse alongside a field, staring at a group of grazing sheep. A swiftly flowing stream ran between the road and the field, noisily threading its way between smooth rocks and exposed tree roots. He looked up when he heard her approaching, but his expression didn't change.

"Did Patrick send you to make sure I didn't throw myself in the river?"

"I was worried about you. I don't understand how your father expects you and Daphne to fall in love when he constantly sets you against each other."

Edward gave her a long-suffering look. "Haven't you learned that titled aristocrats facing bankruptcy can't afford to waste something as valuable as marriage on something as insubstantial as love? We have to marry for advantage—social and political but especially financial—so we can preserve our position in the world."

The bitterness in Edward's voice saddened Eden. "Nothing is more substantial than genuine love. I see it in my parents every day."

"Then they're very lucky." He gathered up his reins. "I'm going into the village. You'd better turn back."

"I'll go with you."

"I'm going to the pub."

"I've seen men drink. I wouldn't blame you if you got drunk. How can you stand your father?"

"He can't help himself. He doesn't have any idea how to live without money."

"Do you?"

Edward's look turned thoughtful. "I've never had to try, but I don't want all the things my father finds so necessary."

"What's important to you?"

They kept their horses at an unhurried walk. Edward was reluctant to begin but soon was talking about the land, the stock, the tenants, their families, the village, his plans for the future, things she was certain he'd wanted to share with his father. He talked about the children like they were his own, about the tenants like they were family. He knew their names, their interests, and their troubles.

"Why haven't you asked Daphne to marry you?" Eden asked when he finally fell silent. "That seems to be the main reason your father is angry with you."

"She's only the latest reason he has to be unhappy with me. He used to brag about me, tell people how good I was with horses, how well I could ride or shoot. He didn't pretend I was perfect, but I think he was satisfied with me."

"What happened?"

He shrugged. "I grew older and started to have different ideas and interests. Meanwhile, Patrick grew into exactly the kind of son he wanted. I used to try to get him to at least consider my opinions, but he never would. Finally, I gave up and just did what I thought was right."

"Is that why you haven't asked Daphne to marry you, because you don't think it's right?"

Edward gazed straight ahead. "I had always hoped to marry someone I could talk to, who would be my friend as well as my wife. My family wants Daphne for her money, and her family wants the title I'll inherit. I keep trying to say the words, but they won't come out. I'm hoping she will find something at Worlege that would give us at least one thing we could share."

Eden pictured Daphne as she'd last seen her, a haughty beauty disdaining all around her, and doubted she and Edward would ever have anything in common.

As they approached the village, an old woman emerged from one of the stone cottages. She looked a little unsteady on her feet, her gaze a little unfocused, but when she saw Edward, she waved and came toward the fence that encircled her yard.

"Who's that?" Eden asked.

"Mrs. Bright. My old nurse," Edward said with a smile that drove away the last of his gloom. "She knows all my secrets, the family secrets, too."

"I can't wait to meet her."

Chapter Six

Eden couldn't imagine having someone other than herself take care of her own children. Everyone in her family felt the same. Maybe it was the lack of such close sharing that had caused Edward and his father to be so distant.

"Are you the young lady Edward's going to marry?" the nurse asked when they brought their horses to a stop just outside the rose-covered wall that enclosed her home and small garden.

Eden chuckled at the startled look on Edward's face. "No, ma'am. I'm a distant cousin come to visit for a few weeks."

Surprised, the nurse subjected her to close scrutiny before turning to Edward. "Your father swore he'd never let those relations set foot in Worlege."

"Miss Maxwell is American. She's not one of *those* relations," Edward assured her. "My father would still take a gun after them if they came near Worlege."

"He doesn't need to worry about them inheriting the place," the nurse assured him. "He took care of that long ago."

Something about the way she said it caught Eden's attention. There was an element of disapproval or maybe something stronger. The old woman had obviously been drinking something besides her morning tea. Her eyes were clear and her gaze penetrating when she looked at Eden, doting when she looked at Edward, but her hands were unsteady and she leaned against the wall for additional support.

"What do you think of your English relations?" the nurse asked Eden.

"I like Edward and Patrick very much. The earl and Charlotte are okay, but I'm not very fond of the viscount. He's too hard on Edward."

"He's not really—" Edward began.

"Don't try to wrap a pig in clean linen," the nurse scolded Edward. "I've known your father longer than you. So you like Edward," the nurse said, turning back to Eden. "I bet you'd like to know what he was like as a little boy."

Eden thought she could see tears come to the woman's eyes, but she couldn't be sure. Women her age, especially when they'd been drinking, sometimes had leaking eyes. "I'd love to hear about him."

"You come by some morning by yourself, and we'll have a nice little chat," the nurse said to Eden before treating Edward to a fond smile. "He was the most energetic little boy, always just where he shouldn't be, full of questions I had to answer, and always determined to have his own way."

"Apparently nothing has changed," Eden said with a laugh.

"When are you going to bring that young lady you're going to marry?" the old nurse asked Edward as she pushed herself away from the wall.

"How about this afternoon?"

"Bring her in time for tea."

She turned toward her house and made her way slowly across the lawn and inside without looking back.

"You mustn't believe everything she'll tell you about me," Edward said as they went on toward the village.

Eden laughed. "I intend to believe every tale of mischief. Then I'll tease you mercilessly."

"I don't mean that. She tends to imagine things that make me sound better than I am."

"I think that's sweet," Eden said. "All my parents remember is what I actually did. My brothers are only too happy to corroborate everything they say."

"You can't fool me. Your parents adore you."

"And I adore them," Eden said. "They sent me away to school, maybe hoping I'd meet some nice young man and get married, but I couldn't wait to go back to Texas." Though sometimes she wondered if she'd done the right thing. As much as she loved the Hill Country, her future there was looking increasingly bleak.

Her depressing thoughts were banished when the village came in sight. A shout went up from somewhere, and over the next few minutes a gaggle of children poured out of cottages and from lanes to converge on Edward, all pelting him with questions.

"We're having a fête champêtre up at the house next week," Edward explained. "The whole village is invited."

"He's promised us games and prizes," one of the boys said.

"And food," another added.

"I want to ride a horse," one of the girls said, only to be informed by several boys that there'd be an insurrection if she got to ride before they did.

The ragtag parade followed them into the heart of the small village but began to disperse when mothers started appearing with orders—and a few cuffs around the ears—to remind them of neglected chores.

One of the women came up to Eden. "My name's Nellie Melsome. My husband, Peter, is one of the earl's tenants," she said. "Unless I miss my guess, Mr. Edward is headed for the tavern to have an ale and talk to the bunch of worthless men who'll be there. It's not a fit place for a lady," she said good-naturedly with a twinkle in her eye. "Why don't you have coffee with me?"

"Yes, go on," Edward said. "Nellie loves to gossip about what's going on up at the house."

"There hasn't been much to gossip about in ages," Nellie said. "I hope that's about to change with your prospective bride coming to the house for a visit."

"Nothing is private in Green Moss," Edward said.

"Not when all the servants are related to someone in the

village," Nellie explained to Eden. "It's just sharing with family."

"It's being damned nosy," Edward said without heat.

"Come on," Nellie said to Eden. "He'll be a lot more friendly once he's had his drink and a chance to talk about pigs and turnips."

Eden allowed herself to be led to a small house in a row of small houses. The cottage had little, low-pitched rooms, but it was neat and clean.

"My mother is staying in bed this morning," Nellie said, "so you only have to put up with me."

Eden settled in the tiny parlor while Nellie talked to her from the kitchen. Before long she had coffee and a plate of cookies set down before her.

"Now tell me about the latest argument between Edward and his father," Nellie said as she settled into a chair opposite Eden. "Don't look so surprised. Everyone knows Edward never comes to the tavern after breakfast unless his father has been at him again."

Eden was in a quandary. The woman obviously had Edward's approval, but that didn't mean he wanted her to be privy to everything that happened up at Worlege.

"It was about him marrying that young heiress, I warrant." Nellie took a swallow of her own coffee. "You don't have to tell me if it makes you uncomfortable. I'll have the whole conversation in a couple of days. The servants can hear the viscount all the way to the kitchen."

"I wish he wouldn't abuse Edward," Eden said, unable to hold her tongue. "Edward's very conscious of his responsibilities, but he's also concerned about making the right choice for Daphne."

"That's Edward all over," Nellie said. "He'd find things would go a lot easier if he'd just think of himself like the rest of that lot does."

"I don't think the earl mistreats him," Eden said. "And Patrick is very fond of him."

"The earl's not a bad man, but he's old school. Patrick tries, but the viscount won't listen to anyone except the earl. Is that heiress the kind who'll make him a nice wife or the kind that'll be more worried about her new dress than her husband?"

Eden didn't feel she could say anything that wouldn't ultimately get back to Edward and his family. "I haven't known her long enough to make that kind of judgment." Anxious to change the subject, she said, "The children seem to be looking forward to the fête."

"They've been talking about it since last year," Nellie said, following readily. "After the viscount canceled the last one, we were afraid there wouldn't be another, but Edward said the children couldn't be disappointed this time."

"I can't imagine the lengths he must have had to go to to convince his father to change his mind."

Nellie huffed. "He didn't. Edward's paying for the whole thing. At first the viscount even refused to let Edward use the grounds, but the earl put his foot down."

"Have Edward and his father always had so much trouble getting along?"

"It's not Edward. He could get along with the devil." Nellie's answer was forceful and defiant. "The viscount should adore that boy. Edward's hard work is the only reason they've got a pot to piss in."

Over the next twenty minutes Nellie showed Eden a side of Edward she'd only begun to suspect. She'd known he loved the estate and was concerned about the welfare of the tenants. She didn't know that as a teenager he'd taken over running the estate from a thieving manager because his father had no interest and his great-uncle didn't know how. She didn't know he took a personal interest in every tenant family, even going so far as to secure apprenticeships for several boys, an academic scholarship for Nellie's son, jobs when they were too old for school, and medical attention when tenants were sick. She didn't know he was helping Sam Kell-away buy land so the tenant could own his own farm.

"You make him sound like Santa Claus and a genie with a magic lamp all rolled up in one."

"I don't know anything about genies or magic lamps, but at one time or another he's done something for every family in Green Moss. We're looking forward to the day when he inherits the title."

Eden was afraid they were in for a long wait. The earl was in good health, and the viscount looked barely old enough to have a twenty-five-year-old son.

"I can understand, but I can't wish my grandfather dead," Eden said.

"Who's wishing the earl dead?" Edward asked from the doorway. He was so tall and broad-shouldered he filled the opening.

"We were just saying we wished your great-uncle a long life and good health," Eden said.

"Me, too," Edward said. "I like the old buzzard. Besides, he occasionally agrees with me. He actually gave me some money to buy a small tract of land last year. My father had been planning to spend it on a new carriage."

"What would he need with a new carriage?" Nellie asked. "He's hardly ever here."

"Exactly what the earl said. Now, I'd better take Eden away before you fill her head with any more nonsense about me."

"I was only telling her the truth," Nellie insisted.

"The truth as you see it." Edward's smile was kind and his eyes were filled with genuine fondness. "Ever since I helped her boy Hubert to a place in a public school, Nellie has tried to turn me into a saint. I keep telling her I did it to get the boy out of my hair."

"I can just see that now," Eden said.

"If you'd seen how my father reacted to Hubert prowling over the estate making lists of ways to run the place more efficiently, you'd know why I had to get rid of him. Now I have to get you back so you don't miss your tour with Patrick."

"I'm sure Daphne will be glad of your return," Eden said when they were on their way back to Worlege.

"I have to work. I've already let my temper cause me to waste too much time."

"I don't see how you can think of spending time with your fiancée a waste of time."

"I'm trying to get Worlege out of debt so Daphne won't think I'm only marrying her for her fortune."

"Well, you are, aren't you?"

Edward's hands tightened on the reins until his horse tossed his head at the pressure. She couldn't decide whether she felt sorry for him because he was caught in a web and couldn't find a way out, or frustrated with him for not taking control of his life. She was startled to realize her concern for him had developed into something much warmer. She had to rein in her feelings immediately. That was a dead end for both of them.

"I'm not as insensitive as you think." Edward's voice was tight, his gaze remaining straight ahead. "I haven't yet asked Daphne to marry me, because I have to know she won't be miserable stuck in the country for the rest of her life."

"What will you do if she hates Worlege?"

Edward's laugh was devoid of humor. "Disappear and let Patrick inherit the title."

"Does he have an heiress who wants to marry him?"

"Heiresses never waste themselves on younger sons. What's the point of having all that money if it can't buy you a title?"

Eden couldn't understand this concept of *buying* and *selling* titles that involved buying and selling people as well. Edward might say it was an equal bargain, but the way she saw it, all the advantages belonged to the man. "I think what you're doing is barbaric."

"What would you have me do? Refuse Daphne so her father can sell her to someone who really does only want her money, who will waste her fortune on gambling and other women?"

"That doesn't have to happen. There's no reason she—"

"This is not America. It's not Texas. Daphne has no control over what happens to her. She belongs to her father just as much as his money does. And if he wants a title for his cash, he'll get it one way or the other. And once she's married, only an act of the House of Lords can grant her a divorce."

"I don't understand."

"That's just it," Edward snapped. *"You don't understand.* I belong to my father just as Daphne does to hers. I can run away, but I'd still be the heir. Taking care of my family and everyone who depends on us would still be my duty. Everybody in Green Moss depends on Worlege. If we go under, what happens to them?"

The hard line of his jaw, the way he compressed his mouth, told Eden that Edward wasn't willing to discuss the situation any more, but he was right about one thing. She didn't understand. She'd *never* understand how a father could sell his daughter for a title. What did it mean to be the wife of an earl? Daphne would live in a big house and go to fancy parties, but she already lived in a big house and went to fancy parties. She would be a member of aristocratic society, but would she really belong? Money could buy her the title, but it could never buy her acceptance.

Eden knew what that meant. It had prompted her brothers to come back to the Hill Country and into the circle of the family that loved them without conditions. Zeke and Hawk had held out the longest, but not even Arizona was willing to give full acceptance to an ex-slave and a half-breed Indian. Eden couldn't imagine English society would be any more accepting of Daphne. The only possible reason for attempting to break into such a closed society would be because she was marrying a man she loved so much that acceptance didn't matter.

But Daphne didn't love Edward and he didn't love Daphne. Try as she might, Eden couldn't see much satisfaction in the marriage for either of them.

"It was so nice of you to invite Edward and me into your home," Daphne said to the tenant they were visiting. She picked up her skirts, holding them close to her body, as if she were afraid they would come into contact with dirt or vermin on Sally Hopkins's carefully swept floor. "Edward holds you and your husband in great regard," she said, turning toward him and smiling.

"Not nearly so much as we think of him," Sally said. "We don't know what we would have done this past year without his help."

"Edward knows his duty," Daphne said.

Edward felt as if he were taking part in a play in which everyone knew their lines, had rehearsed the scene, and were now playing it out to perfection. There was nothing real here. In desperation he picked up Sally's youngest, a little girl of two with enormous blue eyes and stringy blond hair that bore no evidence of the thorough brushing her mother had probably given it that morning. He tickled her ribs and was rewarded with shrieks of laughter.

"You'll spoil her, sir," Sally said.

"She's a baby," Edward said. "All babies should be spoiled." He knew he had been in the beginning.

Daphne stared at him with a look of total incomprehension. She'd been trained, he realized, in the role of mistress of a large house with an attached estate. She'd been taught she would occasionally have to visit tenants and their families. She *hadn't* been taught they were real people just like her, that they had feelings and ambitions and a sense of self that deserved respect. She had been taught they were fixtures in her world, to be dealt with as one would any other belonging. She would never have thought of taking one of Sally's children into her lap.

"She'll expect the same attention when you come back," Sally warned Edward.

"I'll be happy to oblige," Edward said as he handed the child to her mother. "Remind Joe I need to talk to him about the north field. I looked at it again today. It needs to lie fallow another year."

"We need the income," Sally said. "How are we to feed five little ones without that field?"

"You'll have income from the extra hay. With another year of good manuring, it ought to come back strong."

"Is that the way you treat all your tenants?" Daphne asked when she was back in the carriage.

"Is there something wrong?" Maybe he was only imagining the disapproval in her voice, but he wasn't imagining the confusion on her face.

"Mrs. Jessop says one should ignore servants, that one should act as though they don't exist."

It took Edward a full minute to control his temper sufficiently to keep him from saying something rude and hurtful. It had been a really difficult day. On top of his father's abuse at breakfast, it seemed a dozen things had gone wrong in his absence. It had taken all of his self-control to act as though he wanted to spend the afternoon driving Daphne around the estate. He had hoped the tenants' friendliness would ease her constraint, but she was as stiff now as she had been at the first cottage. She couldn't understand why he was interested in anything outside the main house.

"My tenants aren't servants," Edward said. "They're more like partners. I own the land, they work it, and we share the profits. Without them, Worlege wouldn't exist."

Daphne's face was blank. She didn't understand what he was talking about.

"It's the same with the servants," he added, plunging ahead. "Worlege isn't like London, where you hire servants for the season. Our servants have families in Green Moss. Some families have worked at Worlege for generations. When they retire, they stay here. I don't ignore people who work for me. It's important that they do a good job. When they do, I let them know. It builds loyalty and pride in their work."

He could tell from Daphne's expression that this was a concept missing from her education, but Eden would understand. She'd talked with the groom who cared for the horse she rode, complimented him on keeping the equipment in such excellent condition, even threatened to take the groom back to Texas with her. The man had grinned like a Cheshire cat. The next time Eden went for a ride, Edward was certain her equipment would sparkle like new.

He shouldn't have been surprised by Daphne's attitude. His own family was the same. Only Patrick had begun to understand what Edward knew instinctively. Edward wondered why he himself was so different. Why did he love the land? Why did he feel excited to see a field of wheat gleaming golden in the summer sun, the ripening heads of grain bending and twisting in the breeze that rippled across the field? Yet the addition of a new carpet or a set of china went unnoticed. Why was he more interested in people like Sally Hopkins and Sam Kellaway than any titled aristocrat? Why would he rather spend the evening in the village pub discussing what to plant in which field than attending a fancy ball in London?

"Mrs. Jessop says a lady must preserve her dignity at all times," Daphne said. "I hope you don't expect me to visit these people on my own."

"I don't agree with Mrs. Jessop," Edward snapped. "I don't find my dignity is so fragile it needs to be preserved at the expense of others."

He was sorry as soon as the words were out of his mouth. Daphne acted cold and aloof, but he wondered if she might not be feeling a little unsure and afraid. She had been

brought up to believe her beauty and wealth—not any in-
trinsic worth of her own—were all that made her an acceptable wife for an earl. By marrying Edward she would step up
into a class where every deed, word, and gesture would be
noticed and judged. She was probably afraid any relaxation
in the behavior she'd been taught would render her unfit.
Considering all that, was it fair to expect her to be any different, to act like Eden?

Maybe he should ask what Daphne wanted. Even though
it had probably been drilled into her that she must rigidly
control her feelings, there had to be something she wanted
from her husband besides a title. He'd been trained from
birth to do his duty, but he had a whole list of things that
were important to him, things he wouldn't compromise on.
Surely she must feel the same. Edward turned to Daphne
and asked, "Do you love me?"

Chapter Seven

"Why would you ask such a question?"

Daphne's startled expression reinforced his suspicion that she'd been taught never to expect love in marriage. "Eden says she'd never marry a man she didn't love, who didn't love her," Edward explained. "I wondered if you felt the same."

Daphne drew herself up in a manner that reminded Edward of the disapproving matrons he'd encountered in London. "I should hope that as we become better acquainted, we will grow to have a sincere regard for each other." She might as well have been repeating a lesson she'd learned by rote. There was no emotion, no feeling in her voice or expression. "Mrs. Jessop says love is an unstable passion that distorts a person's perspective and understanding of what is important."

"Eden believes in love," Edward said. "Do you think *her* perspective is distorted?"

"I would never wish to speak unkindly of your relations," Daphne said, looking more like an imperious dowager than ever, "but Eden and I have very different ideas of what is suitable for a lady. I know very little about America and nothing about Texas, but what they do there would never be acceptable in English society. She doesn't care if people approve of what she does." Daphne practically shuddered. "I should hope I would never become indifferent to public opinion."

"So you think it's wrong to love your husband or be loved by him?"

Daphne looked as if she'd been asked a question that wasn't supposed to be on the test and was uncomfortable because she didn't know the answer. "I can't say it's *wrong* to love your husband." She enunciated *love* as though it left a bad taste in her mouth. "I've never been afflicted by that emotion. It's much better to admire and respect the person you marry so you can entrust your life, your fortune, and the lives of your future children into his hands."

Edward believed that, too, but he wanted more than admiration and respect. He wasn't sure what he wanted in a wife, but he knew it wouldn't find it with Daphne. He was equally certain she wouldn't find what she needed from a husband in him.

"Would you think less of me if I said I hoped my wife would love me?" For a moment Daphne looked at a loss for words and Edward hoped she'd say what she thought instead of what she'd been taught to think.

"Mrs. Jessop says you're an admirable man, that I'm fortunate my future will be in your care. My father assures me your character is well-formed, and you'll be a credit to your family."

"Then Mrs. Jessop and your father haven't been listening to *my* father."

He sounded like he was whining rather than merely weary of the constant battle of wills. What he couldn't comprehend was why his father's dislike of him had grown until it bordered on hatred. He could understand why Patrick was favored, but the viscount acted as if Edward had committed a sin of such magnitude there could be no forgiveness.

"I know I shouldn't say this," Daphne began. "I've tried very hard not to feel this way—"

Edward's pulse went from a trot to a gallop. Was Daphne going to say she didn't want to marry him? He was surprised to find his most prominent feeling was one of relief. Freed from the obligation of courting Daphne, he would be able to devote all his energy to Worlege and the people who depended on it. He could spend the entire year on the estate, putting money into buying new land, improving the old.

"Mrs. Jessop will say I'm a very foolish girl," Daphne began, "but I cannot live in this place." The sweep of her hand indicated the sprawling house behind them. "I was *not* raised to be a farmer's wife."

Abruptly, Edward was confronted with an entirely different vision, one of his father's rage over the broken engagement, his being cut off from having anything to do with the management of the estate, the family sinking into bankruptcy, and him being sent away from Worlege. It was the only home he'd ever known, the place he loved above all others. There had to be a compromise.

"I would never require you to live at Worlege all the time," Edward said. "Naturally we would move to London for the Season."

"That would still mean spending the greater part of each year here," Daphne pointed out. "I know nothing about crops and find farm animals disgusting. I want concerts and parties, neighbors closer than six miles away. I have nothing to say to your tenants or people in the village. How could I? We don't inhabit the same world."

Edward suppressed a sharp retort. Daphne had never before been outside of London and had been taught to look down on people she considered beneath her. She'd never had an opportunity to meet these people, get to know them, realize they were often more worthy of her respect and admiration than members of her own class. That wouldn't happen in the few days that remained of her visit. It would take time, time he would have only if he found a compromise they could both accept. "There would be no need for you to accompany me to Worlege every time I came. Your presence would only be required a few times each year."

Daphne thought for a moment. "I don't see how that

would change the way I feel, but I'll ask your mother what would be expected of me."

Edward was ashamed of himself for feeling relieved. He should have been more concerned for Daphne's happiness. He should have been more concerned for his own integrity; he'd never guessed the extent to which he was willing to compromise to win security for his family. Instead, all he could think was that he'd been given a little more time to try to find a solution to this seemingly insoluble problem.

Edward turned to Daphne as they approached the house. "Don't say anything until we talk again." He was certain his father was at one of the windows, watching every gesture, wondering if Edward had finally proposed.

"I won't." After a moment of silence, Daphne said, "Patrick says no one knows more about the estate than you. He's depending on you to make the estate so profitable you can increase his allowance enough for him to marry." Her expression turned pensive. "Eden says he's a fine figure of a man, that she doesn't see why some heiress hasn't snapped him up already."

Now it was Edward's turn to be thoughtful. He knew Daphne would never have used a phrase like *fine figure of a man* without attributing it to Eden. At the same time he hadn't been aware Daphne had paid any attention to Patrick. Edward brought the carriage to a stop in front of the house. "No one knows better than I how fortunate I am to have Patrick as a brother, a friend, and an advocate." It surprised him Daphne thought so as well.

Eden was relieved the evening had gone so smoothly. Cyril was angry that Edward hadn't used the afternoon ride to propose to Daphne, but Patrick had changed the subject whenever it became awkward. Edward and Daphne seemed more comfortable with each other. Apparently they'd found a way to work out some of the differences between them.

"Will you play for us again this evening?" Charlotte asked Daphne when they finally got up from the table after dinner.

"I'm sure Edward is tired of hearing me play." It sounded like a challenge.

"Certainly not," Edward replied. "I'll even turn your pages."

Charlotte smiled, and the viscount looked a little less grim. "I think you should see about having her instrument brought down to Worlege," he said to Edward. "It's much superior to ours."

"There are other decisions that need to be made first," Edward replied.

"What decisions?" the viscount snapped.

"To begin with, what piece Daphne will play for us this evening."

Eden wished she could stuff something in the viscount's mouth. He seemed to look for opportunities to berate Edward. Jake and the earl took advantage of the move to the music room to disappear. Eden decided she'd had enough of watching Edward dutifully concentrate his attention on Daphne. The falsity of it irritated her. She turned to Patrick. "It's such a beautiful evening, I'd love to sit on the balcony. If you leave the windows open, we can hear Daphne. Would you join me?"

Edward looked annoyed, but Charlotte gave Isabelle a wink, and Patrick's almost imperceptible look of surprise changed into a smile of acceptance.

"We don't have anything like this in Texas," Eden said to Patrick as she moved to the balustrade that overlooked the garden behind the house. "It would burn up from too much heat and not enough water." The landscape in front of the house was laid out in formal beds of precise dimensions. In contrast, the garden behind the house was filled with shrubberies that formed backdrops for deep borders of flowers, and alleys that directed the eye toward statues or alcoves ideal for passing a quiet summer afternoon.

Patrick told her how much his mother had enjoyed planning and expanding the garden over the years. "It has become her main interest at Worlege. She misses it when we go to London."

"So Edward isn't the only one who prefers the country."

"We all love spending time at Worlege," Patrick said, "but going to London is like going to a party."

"From the way your father complains about Edward's love of Worlege, you'd think he hated the country. Why does he dislike Edward so?"

"He doesn't dislike Edward. He—"

"Don't waste your breath. I've seen and heard him. I think it's very courageous of you to defend Edward."

Patrick didn't respond immediately, just gazed out over the garden. "Edward is three years older than I am." Patrick spoke without turning back to Eden. "Old enough to be a big brother but not so old he wanted nothing to do with his little brother. He took me riding when our father said I was too young. He took me swimming before my mother would let me go near the reflecting pool alone. He told me all the secrets of surviving boarding school, drilled me in the games so I'd never be left off a team, and made sure I knew which boys to trust and which to avoid. The one time I got in debt playing cards, he settled it out of his own allowance. I would do anything for him."

"Could you help Edward learn how to handle your father?"

Patrick shrugged. "Mother and I have tried, even the earl has intervened on occasion, but nothing seems to make any difference. Father's even said he wished I'd been born first."

"I don't suppose that's so unexpected. You are more like your father than Edward."

"Maybe so, but Edward doesn't deserve to be ill-used because of it. So he prefers working at Worlege to parties in London. So he wants to make sure he and Daphne can get along comfortably before he asks her to marry him. So he spends his own money on a fête for the village children. Those are all good things. I don't understand why Father acts like he does."

The piano stopped and the sound of polite applause floated out to the balcony.

"We'd better go inside," Patrick said.

She still had a few more questions. "What if Edward thought Daphne was in love with somebody else?"

"He'd set her free at once."

"Even against your father's wishes?"

"Nothing could make Edward marry a woman if she loved someone else."

Eden wondered if Daphne felt the same way. "What if Edward fell in love with someone else?"

"Edward would never allow himself to do that."

Maybe, but Eden didn't think any man had that kind of command over his emotions, not even one of these cool, controlled, and frustratingly stubborn Englishmen.

Charlotte was doing her best to encourage Daphne to play again after a short rest. Isabelle was less enthusiastic. The viscount's expression had become almost civil since Edward had devoted himself to Daphne all evening.

Edward didn't mind piano music as long as he wasn't expected to listen to a lot of it, but he was more curious as to what Patrick and Eden were talking about on the terrace. He hadn't been so involved in turning the pages that he had failed to notice they'd moved beyond earshot. Nor could he ignore his reaction to their being alone on the terrace. He'd been angry. Well, maybe not angry, but he hadn't been happy when Patrick was so quick to follow her. He hoped Patrick wasn't developing a soft spot for Eden. She was the wrong kind of woman for his brother. From what her mother had said, Eden had to be at least twenty-one, virtually an old maid by English standards. Patrick had never been strongly attracted to any one woman, but tonight he was showing signs that Eden might have changed that.

Patrick was a very conservative, very conventional young man, exactly the kind of husband every father would want for his daughter. He would never embarrass her with tactless behavior or by flaunting a mistress, and he wouldn't run through her money. He would give her several children, a stable home, and a respectable position in society. But as much as Edward liked and admired Eden, he knew she would never make a traditional English wife.

She would be far better suited for a misfit like himself.

"What?" He'd been so caught up in his own thoughts, he hadn't realized Charlotte was speaking to him.

"Eden's mother says she has a pretty voice. Why don't you ask her to sing? Daphne can play for her."

"I never play as an accompanist," Daphne said, clearly annoyed at being moved out of the spotlight, "but I will if Patrick sings, too. He sang for us when he showed us through the house."

Edward moved from his position next to the piano. "I'll tell them the good news." The bottom had dropped out of his stomach when he'd realized Eden was better suited to him than Patrick. It wasn't simply a matter of comparison. He *liked* the notion of being paired with Eden. He could see her as the wife of the country squire he wanted to be, riding at his side over his acres, taking an active interest in everyone who worked for them, and offering him the companionship and understanding he'd previously found only in his brother.

Whereas he couldn't visualize Daphne as a lover, he had no trouble seeing Eden in that role. The thought made his body swell, a condition that would soon be visible if he didn't get himself under control.

"Your mother tells us you have a lovely voice," he said as he approached Eden and Patrick. He was relieved when neither of them looked uncomfortable at his approach. "So my mother has summoned you to sing."

Eden made a wry face. "Doesn't Charlotte realize she has to make allowances for motherly pride?"

"And Daphne has requested that Patrick join you. Apparently you were so ill-advised as to perform for Daphne," he said to his brother.

"It was just a country ditty," Patrick objected. "It was funny and I thought she'd enjoy it."

"I suppose there's nothing to do but go inside and get it over with," Eden said, standing up.

Edward followed them into the house, irritated they could joke and laugh in a way that was impossible for him and Daphne. The realization cast a pall over him. He didn't pay much attention to Eden's spirited assertion that she had an average voice and that only a mother's partiality would think otherwise. He didn't hear any of the lively discussion over what song they would sing or who would sing which part. He didn't care that they would have to wait while Jake and the earl were summoned to hear the performance. Not even his father's caustic comments penetrated the barrier that had sprung up between him and everybody else. All he could think about was the dreadful, stifling, stultifying formality that would exist between him and Daphne and how it fell so short of the laughing, teasing relationship Eden had with him and with Patrick. He wanted that for himself, and he wanted it with Eden.

That was an even more shocking thought. When had his interest in Eden grown to such a level and why hadn't he noticed it? He wasn't an idiot. He hadn't thought he was completely out of touch with his feelings, yet he must have been.

Whether he was infatuated with Eden or with his vision of what his life could be with her, she'd shown him that the kind of life he wanted was possible. In the past, he'd tried to make himself into the kind of man he was supposed to be, to think like that man, to want to *be* that man.

In a few short days, Eden had destroyed all of that.

"Edward, are you going to turn pages, or are you going to stand there like a fence post?"

Edward snapped out of his reverie to find Eden staring at him with a questioning look. "I was just waiting for you to decide what you are going to sing."

"We've already decided that. Daphne is waiting for you to turn pages."

They had chosen a romantic duet. Edward hadn't known they had such music in the house. He had to watch as Eden and Patrick sang to each other as two lovers would, smiling and sighing, even holding hands at one point. He wanted to knock their hands down, push them apart.

Eden jabbed him in the ribs and he woke up enough to turn the page.

He glanced around the room. Charlotte and Isabelle were watching their children with besotted gazes. Jake and the earl seemed to be enjoying the playacting. Edward couldn't understand why the viscount looked like he had indigestion. This was exactly the kind of evening they frequently endured in London. Edward was the only one who had a right to be unhappy, because he'd always hated evenings like this. He'd rather talk about rotating crops, repairing fences, even the maintenance of pigpens.

He had to admit that Eden did have a nice voice. It wasn't powerful, thank God, just the right size for a salon. He wouldn't mind Patrick's singing if he'd stop looking at Eden like a lover mooning over his sweetheart.

This time he managed to turn the page before anyone poked him in the side.

How many verses did this song have? It wasn't an opera, but it seemed to go on forever. No one appeared to mind but him and his father. Something they could finally agree on.

When Eden and Patrick started on the fourth verse, Edward was tempted to grab the music and rip it to shreds, but this was one of those folk songs that told of a deep yet tragic love. He was going to have to listen to the bitter end whether he liked it or not.

Finally, at the end of the seventh verse, the lovers were parted, the young woman near death, and the young man ready to join the army so he could die in battle and be joined with his lover in a place where they would never be parted. Charlotte and Isabelle had tears in their eyes. Jake and the earl applauded enthusiastically; the viscount remained stoic in his position by the window. Edward breathed a sigh of relief, grabbed the music and put it away before anyone could ask for a second song.

"That was a lovely performance," the viscount said, his expression at odds with his words. "With such an appropriate setting, I think it's the perfect time for Edward to propose to Miss Bidwell."

Chapter Eight

Edward had known his father would do practically anything to get him to propose to Daphne, but he hadn't been prepared for something as brazen as this.

"Cyril!" Charlotte exclaimed. "This is quite improper."

"It's not the usual method," the viscount virtually snarled, "but Edward seems unable to accomplish it on his own. I hoped he might have more success surrounded by his family."

Edward overcame his shock sufficiently to respond to the anger exploding through his body. "You couldn't wait for me to handle it on my own so you thought you could embarrass me into proposing in public. Well, you're wrong on that score, as you have been on so many others."

"I'm not wrong in thinking you aren't respectful enough to do your duty."

"It's my *duty* to protect the woman I ask to be my wife. Daphne and I have been talking about—"

The viscount interrupted impatiently. "What's there to talk about? You get married. She has your children and manages your household. You take care of her fortune and see that the family retains its place in society."

"You might want to continue this conversation in private," Isabelle said, beginning to get up.

"Stay," the earl said. "You're part of the family."

"Have you ever stopped to consider how this situation might look from Daphne's viewpoint?" Eden demanded of Cyril.

Her interruption was so unexpected, the viscount was speechless.

"You don't see her as a person with feelings or any right to personal happiness. You talk about her as though she were nothing but a bag of money to be offered to the highest bidder."

"This is none of your concern!" the viscount thundered.

"As my grandfather just pointed out, I'm part of his family."

"No daughter of a bastard has any right to an opinion of my actions," Cyril snarled.

"Sit down, Jake," Isabelle said when her husband jumped up from his chair. "If you have a problem with my birth, take it up with the earl," she said, addressing the viscount. "If you think a title protects you from the scorn of others, you're a fool. You're one of the most detestable men I've ever known. It's hard to understand how you could have fathered two such remarkable sons. I can only assume they take entirely after their mothers."

Isabelle rose with a calm majesty Edward would have thought couldn't have been acquired by anyone below a duchess. It was obvious where Eden had gotten her sense of self-worth.

"Jake and I are going to bed. It's time we bring our visit to a close. Charlotte has asked me to help with the fête. We'll head back to Texas after that."

Jake rose but he walked over to Cyril. "If you ever insult my wife or daughter again, I'll knock the words back down your throat. You look down on me because I'm nothing but a Texas cowboy, but not even a lying, thieving, murdering Texan would insult a good woman. For all your fancy clothes, big houses, and holier-than-thou airs, you're nothing but horse droppings. You're lower than a snake's belly."

The snake's belly was a new term to Edward, but he had no doubt what the horse droppings comment meant.

"See what happens when you bring people like that into

the house," the viscount said to the earl. "I told you they'd—"

"Shut up, Cyril," Alastair said. "It's a sad day when a bunch of Texans show more class than a titled Englishman."

Eden was relieved to be out of the house and on her way to visit Edward's old nurse. After last night's explosion, breakfast had been uncomfortable even though Edward had eaten before anyone came down and Daphne had asked for breakfast in her room. Eden's parents had eaten their breakfasts as if this morning were the same as any other. Everyone else was stiff and nearly silent for fear of saying something that would cause tempers to flare again. Charlotte had watched her husband with a fearful eye, while Patrick had barely taken two swallows of his coffee before excusing himself.

Eden and Patrick had gone for a ride before breakfast, but they'd avoided talking about the previous evening. Instead, Patrick had asked her what she would do when she returned to Texas. It surprised Eden that her future sounded so unexciting. She knew she didn't want to remain in England. It would be impossible for her to assume the subservient role Englishmen expected of their wives. Even if a rebel like Edward had been willing to give his wife more freedom, society wouldn't allow it. He'd be better off in Texas.

That thought had caused her to laugh out loud, prompting Patrick to ask what was funny. She'd told him Edward ought to go to Texas, where he could farm all he wanted. They'd had an amusing half hour imagining Edward trying to become a Texan.

But now, as she headed alone to the village to visit with his old nurse, she didn't think those images were funny. She was going to miss Edward. She really liked Patrick, but her feelings for Edward were different. She just couldn't decide what they were.

She couldn't help comparing the lush green of the

landscape she was riding through to the gold and brown of the Hill Country during summer. Here, a narrow stream meandered through a pasture where cows grazed in grass up to their knees. Willows lined the stream, their long limbs trailing in the cool, green water. Water lilies— or hyacinths, she wasn't sure which—dotted the placid surface with splashes of white, yellow, and purple. It was easy to see why Edward loved this land.

Edward was big and gruff. He didn't know how to handle his father or the social world that had tried mold him, but he had an integrity that wouldn't allow him to demean other people. He liked and respected people of all classes and was willing to use his own money to help those he felt deserved and needed a helping hand. He was more concerned with his responsibility to the land than the money it produced, saw Worlege as a home rather than a badge of his rank and privilege. And he'd welcomed Eden into his family despite the circumstances of her mother's birth.

She understood it was his duty to make a profitable marriage for the benefit of the family. She also understood Daphne was willing to accept the marriage because it would give her the title her father so desperately wanted. As far as she was concerned, however, none of that mattered because Edward and Daphne didn't love each other.

Why did that thought upset her so? She'd be heading back to Texas in less than a week and would never see Edward again, would probably hear from the Davenports only on the occasion of the earl's death—if the viscount allowed anyone to communicate with the illegitimate side of the family. Still—she splashed through the stream where it crossed the road—she felt sorry that the circumstances of Edward's birth would force him into a life that was not what he wanted. She was thankful her parents had given her and her brothers the freedom to do what they wanted. All Isabelle wanted was to have her family close enough to see the grandchildren grow up. All the viscount cared about was money to support his personal pursuit of pleasure.

As she neared the village, its cottages growing closer together, she told herself to stop worrying about English society. It had been that way for hundreds of years. She couldn't live by its rules, but she shouldn't belittle those who did. She asked herself again why she was going to see Edward's old nurse. She had no real reason for this visit. Still, she was curious as to why the viscount seemed to dislike Edward as much as he loved Patrick. She couldn't understand why a man wouldn't love a son as dedicated to his duty as Edward.

Duty. It had always been an important part of her life, the life her parents had built for their family. In Texas it meant parents and children were expected to support and respect each other. Since being in England, however, she had started to dislike the word. Here it meant Edward was forced to do what his father wanted regardless of his own wishes.

She was relieved to reach the nurse's cottage. Her own thoughts were giving her a headache.

Mrs. Bright was delighted to see her, inviting her to sit in a small garden behind the cottage. The well-tended beds spilled over with flowers and herbs, their heavy perfume scenting the afternoon air. Eden hadn't learned to appreciate the taste of strong tea, but could tolerate it as long as it was laced with cream and sugar.

"I was hoping you'd come to see me again," the nurse said when they were settled. "You seem like such a spirited young woman. Not at all like our English girls."

"I'm not sure that's a good thing," Eden said. "Women like me can cause a lot of trouble."

"Better to cause trouble than be afraid to open your mouth." The old woman took a big swallow from a cup Eden guessed contained more than tea. "I'm very glad you've come to Worlege. I was afraid Edward was going to marry that self-important girl he brought to see me."

"I'm not here to marry Edward or anyone else," Eden said.

Mrs. Bright's gaze narrowed. "You don't like him?"

"I like him very much."

"Then why don't you marry him?"

Eden laughed to cover her embarrassment. "Edward isn't in love with me and I'm not in love with him."

"He's not in love with that stiff-necked girl, either. She wouldn't sit down when she came here, acted as if she was afraid she'd get fleas. Hardly said a word."

Eden sobered. "Edward says people of his class don't look for love in marriage, that it's much better if they respect each other." The nurse used an unfamiliar expression, but Eden was certain it was profane.

The old woman spat a mouthful of gin-laced tea into a nearby bed of jasmine. "That's the viscount's doing. He used to think the sun rose and set on Edward. But as soon as the boy was old enough to have his own opinions, the viscount turned against him. Now he expects him to act the dutiful son and marry so he can have pockets full of money to waste on himself and his own son."

"What do you mean by *his own son?*" Eden asked.

Mrs. Bright looked startled, used putting on the kettle for fresh tea as an excuse to escape into her cottage. Her cup was full when she returned, but she brought no fresh tea. Eden wondered what was so serious that she had to fortify herself before she could talk about it.

The old woman launched into a long description of Edward's life growing up, how he gradually went from being the hope of the house to being treated like a dirty secret, how he'd been confined to Worlege, never allowed to participate in the family activities until it was time to drag him up to London to find a wife with enough money to shore up the sagging family fortune.

She replenished her cup twice during the recital. "I took the viscount to task about it many a time, but he'd just tell me to mind my own business and keep what I knew to myself."

"What *do* you know?" It was apparent the nurse had said more than she'd intended. "Is it something that can help Edward? I haven't known him very long, but he's miserable."

The nurse's voice was dull, her expression losing its animation, her body beginning to sag. "Ever since he was a little boy, he's known it would be his responsibility to take care of the family."

"I thought you loved Edward," Eden said, angry the old woman would avoid a direct response. "I thought you cared what happened to him."

"I love him like my own son," the nurse said, firing up, only to look old and defeated once again. "Why do you think I drink so much? It's the only way I can forget."

"Forget what?" Eden asked.

Mrs. Bright stared into her cup without speaking.

"Will you be party to forcing Edward to spend the rest of his life in a loveless marriage? Do you want him to raise his own son like the viscount did?"

"Edward would never do that. He's not like the viscount."

"Not now, but once he's forced into this marriage, he'll be the same. Anything for duty. It'll happen all over again."

"It won't."

"Of course it will. Blood runs true from father to son."

"That won't happen because he's not the viscount's son!" Shocked by her own words, Mrs. Bright raised horror-stricken eyes to Eden. "I never would have said anything if I hadn't met that girl he plans to marry. She hates everybody in Green Moss."

"What do you mean, Edward isn't the viscount's son?" Eden asked, utterly uninterested in the nurse's opinion of Daphne.

The nurse deflated like a soufflé that had been pulled out of the oven before it was done. "I don't know who his father is, but the viscount's late wife wasn't his mother."

"Does Edward know?"

"Nobody knows but his mother, the viscount, and me."

The two women sat in silence for several minutes. Eden didn't want to think of what would happen to Edward if this information became public. It wasn't just a matter of being illegitimate. He had assumed a role that wasn't his by law, something that would ruin him if it became known.

"Something terrible must have happened for the viscount to take the risk of raising a false heir," Eden said.

The nurse's laugh was bitter. "The man has suffered for his trickery. It has galled him terribly to see another man's child keep his legitimate son from taking his proper place in society and knowing it was all his own doing."

"What happened?" Eden asked.

Mrs. Bright bolstered her courage by replenishing her cup yet again. "The viscount's first wife had two miscarriages and a stillborn son before she conceived the last time. The viscount was determined nothing would keep her from carrying this baby to term, so he came to Worlege, barred all visitors, and let it be known he wasn't leaving until his heir was born. Cyril has a much younger sister. She was only eleven when their father was killed in Crimea, and it affected her mind. She refused to marry any of the men who offered for her and took a lover who abandoned her when she told him she was carrying his child. Determined no scandal would attach to the house of Southampton, Cyril brought his sister to Worlege and kept her locked away. Only two people, he and I, were allowed to see her. The child was to be sent to an orphanage as soon as it was born."

Eden could only imagine the viscount's fury when he learned the earl was bringing his own illegitimate daughter to London and planned to introduce her to society.

"As luck would have it, the viscount's wife and sister were brought to bed on the same night. His wife delivered a stillborn son, his sister a healthy boy. Certain by this time his wife would never bear a living child, the viscount was faced with the possibility that a hated branch of the family would inherit after him, so he took his sister's child as his own.

The stillborn babe was buried in secret, and his sister was sent away to start life over in a more prudent style."

Eden wouldn't have believed even a man as evil as the viscount would do something like this. "Doesn't Edward's mother care what happened to him?"

"Having the circumstances of Edward's birth become known would hurt her just as much as it would the viscount. She married a wealthy businessman and has a family of her own. Everything might have worked out if the viscount's wife hadn't died and he hadn't married again. When Patrick was born, Cyril was caught in his own trap. The more different from him Edward became, the angrier he got, until he couldn't bear to look at Edward. He kept Patrick in London so he wouldn't turn out like Edward."

"If they rarely saw each other, how did Patrick and Edward become such good friends?"

"The earl and the viscount spend so much money in London, they have to retire to Worlege for several months every year. That's when Patrick got to know a big brother who could do all the things a younger brother longs to do. Edward was delighted to have a companion and anxious to teach Patrick everything he knew. Patrick doesn't resent being the younger son and has always tried to make things easier for Edward.

"I shouldn't have said anything," the nurse said. "I was just so mad at the viscount for trying to force Edward to marry that awful girl, I couldn't mind my mouth." She looked down into her cup. "And too much gin. I've tried not to think about what's happening, but when I saw how much he liked you, saw how unhappy he is, well . . . No good could come from people knowing the truth, so I've had to stand by helpless and watch what that man did to Edward."

"But you could have freed Edward from the burden of his responsibility to the family," Eden pointed out.

The nurse's eyes blazed. "Freed him to be put in an orphanage, to be sent to a workhouse, to be thrown out without a penny to his name!" She took a big swallow from her cup. "I couldn't do that to the boy. Besides, he'll be a good earl one day. Better than any of the three who've come before him, I can tell you."

Much against her will, Eden acknowledged the force of the nurse's argument. Regardless of the burden he had to bear, Edward would undoubtedly prefer it to the reputation of an impostor.

"You won't say anything, please," Mrs. Bright begged. "No telling what the viscount will do if he finds out."

Eden longed to tell Edward, but what would it achieve? He'd still be in the same position but with knowledge that would make it even more difficult to fulfill the role destined for him.

No, she wouldn't say anything. It wasn't her place.

His father would be coldly furious when Edward announced he wasn't going to ask Daphne to marry him. He and Daphne'd had another conversation that afternoon in which Daphne had made it plain she believed the life Edward wanted was beneath her. "I was trained to be a countess or a duchess," she'd insisted, and nothing he'd said had made any difference. When she'd referred to his old nurse as *that drunken old crone*, he'd quit trying. His stomach felt queasy when he thought of debtors pounding on the door around the clock, but the family would have to figure something out. After all, it wasn't his spending that had put their future in jeopardy.

He had wanted to go through this only once, so he'd waited until everyone was gathered in the music room after dinner. The viscount looked like he might fall into an apoplectic fit. "This is impossible!" he shouted once he'd calmed down enough so his words were actually understandable. "I won't allow this to happen. Daphne's father won't allow this to happen."

"You don't understand. Daphne doesn't want to marry me," Edward explained.

Momentarily shaken, the viscount took a different line of attack. "Have you thought of what this would mean?" he asked Daphne. "Have you considered what your life will be when you go home, face your father, and explain you don't want to marry Edward? Have you thought of what people will say when they hear you came down to Worlege and left without becoming engaged? They'll be certain we found something wrong with you, and no protests to the contrary will make any difference."

"Daphne knows it will be uncomfortable," Edward said, "but she's willing to endure it."

He'd been concerned about what would happen to her, but she'd said she was willing to face her father's wrath. "I'm his only child," she'd said. "He wants a title in the family so desperately, and he can't get it without me." She had said he might increase her dowry to make her even more attractive to potential suitors.

"Have you tried to change her mind?" Cyril demanded of Edward.

"No."

His father condemned Edward's morals, his integrity, his sense of values, his neglect of duty, his intelligence, and his lack of interest in all the important things in life. When his words appeared to leave Edward unaffected, he shouted, "I wish you had died at birth."

Hearing those words threw Edward off balance. "That's not a surprise," he replied when he'd had a moment to recover. "You've made it very plain most of my life that you wished I'd never been born."

"You have no idea how much!" the viscount thundered.

"No, because you've never said why you hate me, why you tried to bury me at Worlege. How did you expect me to fit into a world I'd never been part of?"

"Are you sure you want to follow this course of action?"

the earl asked. He seemed puzzled and disappointed, but he didn't appear angry

"I realize it's my duty to marry well," Edward told his great-uncle, "but Daphne and I are so different, we'd make each other miserable."

"That's nonsense!" the viscount shouted. "She could live in London and you could stay at Worlege."

"Edward made that offer," Daphne stated in cold tones, "but I refused."

Turning to Eden, the viscount shouted, "This is your doing! And yours, too," he said, turning to Jake and Isabelle.

"If I had some part in showing these young people the importance of love, I'm glad," Isabelle said, not the least bothered by the viscount's rage.

"This would never have happened if you hadn't gone to Texas," Cyril shouted at his uncle.

"Actually it's your fault," Edward said. "Because you kept me away from London, I learned to value different things, to want a different kind of life. I don't want to be part of a society that cares more about money and position than about people."

"You won't have to worry about that!" Cyril shouted. "I'll disinherit you. I'll cut you off without a penny."

"You can't disinherit him," Alastair said, "and I'm the one who gives him his allowance."

"Get out of my sight!" the viscount shouted at Edward.

"I'm always ready to oblige you, Father." Edward turned to Daphne. "I'm sorry to leave you, but Patrick will see you safely back to London."

"Edward, you can't—" Patrick began.

"Sorry, little brother, but I already have." Without looking back, he turned to leave.

"Wait!"

Eden didn't know what she was going to say when she called out to Edward, but he didn't stop. Headed toward the stables at first, he changed course and turned into the gardens. Eden caught up with him at the far end of the reflection pool.

"Your father doesn't hate you," she said when she reached him. "He's just angry."

It was hard to describe Edward's expression when he looked up. She could see pain, resignation, even relief. She longed to reach out, to offer him comfort, but she knew he wouldn't accept it. Something about this cold, wet climate bred a reserve that denied the need for emotional comfort.

"If he doesn't hate me, why does he look at me like he wishes I was dead? I tried to be the kind of son he wanted, but nothing I ever did was good enough." He looked around him. "I used to love this place. Now it's become a duty that will twist and bend me until I yield."

"You could leave."

His sigh was long and heartfelt. "I can't. It's my duty to find a way to restore the family fortune. After my great-uncle and father die, I'll be responsible for Patrick and his family. When I die, I'll pass that responsibility on to my son." He groaned. "That's another part of my duty, to have sons to insure the continuation of the line. I wish there were some way I could get out of it."

"Can't you give up the title?"

He sighed again. "Patrick would never let me. He would go to his grave thinking he'd ruined my life. I couldn't do that to him."

"What would you do if you could give it up?" Eden asked.

"I can't, so why tease myself thinking about it?"

"But if you could, what would you do? Where would you go?"

"Maybe I'd go to your American West." His expression turned serious. "I know a man from Scotland who spent a year out there and can't wait to go back."

"Why would you go to America?" Eden asked, stunned by his answer.

"Because people there don't care about titles. I could be anything I wanted and nobody would care." The excitement faded from his eyes. "Instead, I'm bound by duty to stay here."

"What if you weren't bound by duty?"

Edward shrugged, shook his head.

Eden felt as though she were balanced on a precipice. Her next words would decide Edward's future success or failure. It petrified her to know she had so much power over someone else's happiness. She didn't want that power, cringed inwardly at the thought of using it, had no idea where to begin or what to say. She wished the nurse had never told her, but she had and there was no way Eden could escape that knowledge. If she didn't tell Edward, it would prey on her mind forever. If she *did* tell him, she would forever bear the responsibility for having divulged something that had the power to shatter his world.

When it came down to it, she had no way of knowing whether telling Edward would cause greater happiness or greater pain. She thought she understood Edward, but she didn't understand English society or why Edward would feel constrained to uphold values he didn't believe in. Nor could she understand why the earl and viscount could continue to spend money on useless frivolities when they knew doing so would force Edward to make a distasteful marriage. Their behavior was unfair and supremely selfish. It was her sense of outrage at the way the viscount had treated Edward that decided her. He had a right to know, a right to make the decision for himself.

"You aren't bound by duty," she told him. "You can leave or stay. The choice is up to you." Then she told him everything the nurse had said. She was only halfway through when the look on his face made her wish she could take back every word. He seemed to collapse inwardly, withdraw into himself until he shrank in size. She continued, halting between sentences, hoping he would say something, anything, instead of staring at her with empty eyes. When she was finished, silence hung between them.

"You've killed me," he said finally. "It would have been kinder to use a gun."

She'd given him his freedom only by destroying his world. Without another word, he turned and disappeared into the night. It was useless to call after him; it would be cruel to go after him. Why had she thought she had the right to tell him what his beloved nurse had kept from him for twenty-five years?

She made her way back to the house, which loomed before her like something overwhelming and slightly menacing. It was a home, a monument to the human spirit. Yet it could be a prison to crush the human spirit. She didn't know whether she'd done the right thing by telling Edward or not. Patrick met her as she returned to the house.

"Where's Edward?"

"I don't know."

"Did he say where he was going?"

"No."

"Do you have any idea?"

"I don't think even Edward knows."

Edward shook Patrick gently until he woke.

"Thank God you're back," his brother said when he'd rubbed the sleep from his eyes. "Where did you go?"

"I went to see my nurse."

"What for?"

When Edward told him, Patrick looked stricken. "It can't be true."

"It explains why your father hates me. It explains the enmity between him and his sister."

"Even if it is true, it doesn't change anything."

"It changes everything," Edward said. "I'm leaving."

"The earl will never let you go."

"He won't know until I've gone. Now listen closely. I have a lot of things to tell you and not much time."

Edward put his hand over Patrick's mouth to stop his protests. He told him of his plans for the estate and that Peter Melsome was the best person to help him manage it. He explained his arrangements with the tenants and detailed their strengths and weaknesses. He covered the village of Green Moss and the children who depended on him. He insisted that Patrick hold the fête as planned.

"My one regret is that I have to leave you," Edward said. "You're the best brother any man could have."

"You were," Patrick said through his tears. "Never me."

They embraced.

"When will I see you again?" Patrick asked when Edward stood to leave.

"This is good-bye," Edward said and walked through the door.

Chapter Nine

Texas Hill Country

$\mathcal{E}$dward sat across the table from Zeke and Hawk Maxwell. He didn't know what kind of family he'd expected Eden to have, but finding that Zeke was a black man and Hawk a half-breed Indian was different from anything he'd imagined.

"You're not what we were looking for when we advertised for a man with experience working with horses," Zeke said. "I've never been to England, but I'm sure it's different from Texas."

"That difference is the reason I'm here," Edward replied.

"That may be," Hawk began, "but—"

"Let me tell you why I want this job," Edward interjected. "After I'm done, if you still want someone else, I won't say another word."

Edward had never had to ask for a job. He didn't really know how. There was no influence he could bring to bear, no power or prestige he could use to sway these men's opinion if they turned him down. They were in essence the lords of their own land and could do what they wanted. That was how it had been in England, only he'd been the lord, not the supplicant. This wasn't the only job that would give him the opportunity he was looking for, but it was the only job available with anyone in Eden Maxwell's family.

Despite being nervous, he was amused by the various expressions that crossed Hawk and Zeke's faces as he told his story. When he'd first met these men, he'd gotten the impression they were more impassive than any Englishman. But as soon as he started talking about Jake, Isabelle, and

Eden, their reserve melted. They were amazed, shocked, amused, disbelieving, even laughed aloud.

"Is all this true?" Zeke asked when Edward was done.

"Every word."

Zeke looked at Hawk and they nodded. "I don't know if you can do a lick of work," Zeke said, "but we'll hire you even if you do talk funny. You've got to buy some new clothes though. You look so much like a dude, not even the horses will pay you any mind."

"When can you start?" Hawk asked.

"I'm ready now," Edward replied.

Edward glared at the bunk that was his bed, his place of rest. It was hard enough for a man who'd grown up with his own suite of rooms and a personal servant to get used to living in a bunkhouse with two other men, but to expect a man who'd slept in a huge four-poster bed hung with velvet curtains to actually *rest* in that confined space was ridiculous. But then he still had a hard time believing he was in America. It was more like a long, unending nightmare. He'd come to Texas because he'd believed it would offer him a different life. At times, such as when he attempted to organize his clothes inside a bedroll and saddlebags, he wondered if he was up to the challenge.

Learning he wasn't the legitimate heir to the Earl of Southampton had staggered him. He hadn't been exaggerating when he'd told Eden she'd killed him. The man he'd thought he was, the man he'd tried to become, had ceased to exist. He'd had no choice but to leave England.

He'd had enough money to get him and his stallion Crusader to America, but not even English pounds worth almost five American dollars each could last forever. Trying to find a job had turned into a humiliating experience. If his clothes and accent didn't prejudice people against him, his lack of job skills or experience disqualified him from even such lowly jobs as store clerk or bank teller. He'd never mucked out a stall or pitched hay. It was daunting to discover that twenty-five years of living had qualified him to do nothing useful.

He knew what he wanted to do. He wanted to own his own ranch and breed the fastest horses in Texas, yet how could he do that when he didn't know how to run a ranch, much less have the money to buy one? Seeing the advertisement in San Antonio for a race with a ten-thousand-dollar purse to the winner had offered a possible solution to one of his problems. He only had to figure out how to get a job so he could learn how to run a ranch while he trained Crusader for the race.

That was when he'd decided to look for a job with someone in Eden's family.

He had refused to let himself believe he was doing it because of his attraction to Eden . . . or because he was furious at her for destroying his life. He was still a distant relation, so if anyone were likely to overlook his lack of experience, the Maxwells would. He was relieved when he'd heard about the opening at Zeke and Hawk's ranch. At least he knew something about horses.

Still, he'd come within a hairsbreath of not getting the job. It wasn't until he'd told them Eden had exposed the secret of his birth that they'd actually shown any willingness to listen. They hadn't seemed likely to hire him until he said he meant to win the race in San Antonio. Zeke had said Eden expected to win the race with her mare, that he'd get a kick out of seeing her get some real competition. By the time Edward had put Crusader through his paces and promised to let them breed to him if he won the race, they were ready to give Edward the job.

He dropped down on the bunk, still surprised there was no give. The cotton-stuffed mattress was hard and the board underneath was inflexible. He resolutely forced himself not to think of his down-filled mattress, the spacious room that had contained his clothes, or the luxury of a personal servant to anticipate his every need. After having washed in the horse trough and hung his personal linen on the corral pole to dry, such luxury seemed a foolish waste. He was looking forward to the freedom to be himself, but learning to be a Texan would come at a high price.

"I'm not sure I should stay with Josie and Suzette unless they ask," Eden said to her mother. "It'll soon be time for the children to go back to school. I've been gone so long, they've probably forgotten everything I taught them."

"We weren't gone that long," Isabelle said, not taking her gaze from the biscuits she was making.

Junie Mae turned her attention from the pork loin she was stuffing. "It seemed like it. Everybody said so."

"What you mean is they enjoyed not having me butting into their business and wished I'd stayed away longer."

"I didn't mean any such thing," Junie Mae said, unsure how to treat Isabelle's remark. Even after three years, she wasn't accustomed to Isabelle's blunt sense of humor.

"The children will enjoy having another month off," Isabelle said, turning back to Eden. "This fall weather is too nice to spend inside a classroom."

Eden finished slicing the peaches intended for a cobbler and washed her hands. "I didn't think Hawk and Zeke had planned to set up their ranch here for another year or two."

Isabelle reached for a biscuit pan. "They didn't have much choice when Josie and Suzette got pregnant at the same time. They couldn't find a decent doctor in Tombstone. The physicians there only know about bullet wounds and broken limbs."

"They could go to San Antonio," Eden suggested.

Isabelle looked up from her biscuit dough. "Don't you want to help your brothers' wives?"

"I don't want to make them think they're being treated like invalids. Josie won't take that well."

"Then don't do it. How many people will be at dinner tonight? Do you think I have enough biscuits?"

"You never make enough biscuits," Junie Mae said. "I swear, sometimes I think the men will get into a fight over who gets the last one."

Her mother's biscuits were famous throughout several counties, but Eden was too agitated to get into a discussion about biscuits. It wasn't that she didn't want to help Josie and Suzette. She'd been out of sorts ever since getting back from England. When Patrick had told her of his brother's abrupt departure, guilt for telling Edward about the circumstances of his birth had weighed heavily on her heart. The upheaval caused by his disappearance only added to her distress. It was underscored when the fête turned into a dispirited affair. Some of the children broke into tears when they heard Edward was gone. Before day's end, she'd had to go back to the house to keep from breaking down in public.

"You won't have to stay more than a month," Isabelle told her daughter. "If the babies haven't come by then, I'll go."

Eden wasn't sure that was the best plan. Everybody loved her mother. Hers was the iron will, the passionate love that had bound the family so strongly that separations of years and thousands of miles hadn't broken the bonds. Yet it was that very strength that tended to overwhelm people. Josie and Suzette were still trying to get used to being part of such a huge family, still trying to get used to being in Texas rather than Arizona, still trying to get used to being married, being a wife, and expecting a child. A live-in mother-in-law might be more than they could handle.

"If you move in with them, Dad will move in a couple days later," Eden said. "That ought to send them back to Arizona on the first train they can find."

Isabelle finished loading the biscuit tray and reached for another. "You don't have to go," she said, "but you haven't been in very good spirits lately. I was hoping a change of scenery would help you feel better."

How could she feel better when she'd destroyed a man's life? *You've killed me. It would have been kinder to use a gun.* Edward's words echoed in her head a dozen times a day. She'd deprived a man of his birthright. He was right. She *had* killed Edward Davenport, future Viscount Wentworth, future Earl of Southampton. Wherever he went, whatever he did, he would never be that person again.

Edward hadn't told the earl or the viscount the reason behind his decision; he'd just left a letter formally renouncing any claim to the title. She wondered if Edward would talk to his mother, if he'd want to get to know her and his half brothers and sisters. She wondered if he'd demand to know the name of his father, want to know what the man was like, want to get to know him.

Most of all, she wondered if he would always hate her for destroying his life.

"Zeke and Hawk are competing with Luke to see who can breed the fastest horses," Eden said to her mother. "I wish they could see Edward's Crusader."

"I doubt the boys are interested in Thoroughbreds," Isabelle said, busily cutting out biscuits. "They don't make good cow ponies."

Eden tried not to think about Edward or his horses, but dozens of images bombarded her during the day and invaded her dreams at night. At times she wondered how a month of her life could outweigh the rest of her twenty-one years.

"They won't care about that," Eden said. "They just want the honor of breeding the fastest horse."

She wondered what had happened to Edward. What he was doing. If he was okay. She supposed she'd never know, but she'd made Patrick swear to write to her if he heard from his brother. She needed to know he was okay.

"When do you think I should go?" Eden asked her mother.

"Why not tomorrow? Junie Mae and I can take care of everything here."

A school room full of children would keep her from brooding about what she'd done, but spending a month with Zeke and Hawk might be fun. The two men had never been big talkers, but Josie could make up for both of them.

"I'll take both my horses so Dad won't have to worry about them," she said. Exercising them along with helping Zeke and Hawk with their horses would give her something to do. Maybe she'd stay for a while after the babies were born. With so many nephews and nieces, she was practically an experienced mother.

That was something else that bothered her. She'd never been in a hurry to marry. But going to England had upset all her expectations of the future. Now men she used to find attractive and interesting bored her. Things she used to do had lost their excitement. Even the Hill Country seemed colorless, lifeless, too familiar. She'd never considered marrying an Englishman, but she couldn't get Edward out of her mind. Worse, she'd started comparing other men to him. Her mother would say it was a sign she was in love. Eden thought it was more likely a guilty conscience.

Spending a month at Hawk and Zeke's ranch could be just what she needed to shake herself out of her depression. She barely knew Suzette and Josie. And being with her two most unusual siblings was always fun. Well, maybe not the *most* unusual. Luke and Chet had been gunfighters, Pete had impersonated a dead man, and her sister Drew had been a sharpshooter in a Wild West show. Like his adoptive parents, Matt had such a reputation for taking in strays, they found him instead of the other way around.

She was a schoolteacher, just about the most ordinary thing a woman could be. And her ambition was to be a wife and mother, the *most* ordinary thing any woman could be. She'd never attract the attention of an intriguing man if she remained hidden away on a ranch. Maybe she should have stayed in England.

She had caught Edward and Patrick's interest, but they preferred women who'd been brought up to be obedient, unquestioning, and faithful. Eden was intelligent, educated, attractive, and intellectually curious. She wasn't afraid of horses, and she knew how to cook. She could dance, carry on a conversation with old ladies without embarrassing herself, and she knew which fork to use. She'd never managed a house the size of Worlege, but she could have learned. She could play the piano a little, sing a little more, and endure both the opera and ballet, though she'd really rather not. Her father could even give her a dowry, if he decided to do something that ridiculous. What was so terrible about her?

She had to stop thinking like this. She sounded exactly like Daphne, focusing all her attention on marrying a man with a title. She didn't want to live in England, and she had no interest in a title. She wanted to marry a Texan and stay in Texas. Why, then, couldn't she stop thinking about Edward?

Because you ruined his life.

If she could only go back and . . . go back and do what? If there were some way to change what had happened, maybe she could stop thinking about him, stop feeling so guilty. But even if she'd known where to find him, there was nothing she could do. She was the last person he would want to see.

"I think I will go tomorrow," she said her to mother. She took a dish from the cabinet for the peaches. If this visit didn't help to get her mind off Edward, she'd come up with something else. She had to stop feeling guilty about a man she'd never see again.

"I know you don't need anybody to take care of you," Eden said, dicing a potato and putting the pieces in a pot of boiling water, "but it's me or my mother."

Suzette, a French Canadian who had married Hawk, had been pleased Eden had come to stay with them, but Josie—

Zeke's very beautiful wife—wasn't so happy. She liked being pregnant, but she hadn't become accustomed to being a housewife. She still cherished memories of dancing for cheering men desperate for a glimpse of a beautiful woman. Suzette had made the transition from dancer to wife without a hitch.

"What are you supposed to do here?" Josie asked.

The three of them were preparing supper for Zeke, Hawk, and the ranch hands, including the new man they'd hired recently. Eden had taken over any work that had to be done while standing so Suzette could sit down as much as possible.

"Nothing in particular and everything in general," Eden told Josie. "You know Mama. Any woman expecting one of her grandchildren has to be kept under surveillance."

The three women laughed. "I'm glad you're here," Suzette said. "I'm not doing as well as Josie, so she's had to take on some of my work." She had finished setting the table and had sat down to rest a moment.

"Is something wrong?" Eden carried a bowl of fresh corn to the table. It would probably be the last of the season.

"No. I just don't have much energy."

"Is the coffee ready?" Josie asked. "I heard the men ride in ten minutes ago."

"Don't get up, Suzette." Eden didn't pause as she removed a dozen smothered pork chops from a pan. "Josie and I have everything under control."

"Speak for yourself," Josie said. "Suzette is not the only one about to contribute to the population explosion around here."

"How are the men coping with becoming fathers at their age?"

"They're standing over us like mother hens," Josie said.

"If Hawk asks me once if I'm okay, he asks me once an hour," Suzette said. "I was actually relieved when they hired a new hand who's never worked on a ranch. They've had to spend more time with him lately than with us."

"Why would they do that?" Eden took the biscuits out of the oven. Hers weren't as good as her mother's, but no one refused them.

"I'm not sure," Josie said, bringing the coffee to the table. "They've got something up their sleeves, but they won't tell us what it is."

Josie looked at Suzette and winked. Eden found it incredible that two women could get along as well as they did. It was fortunate, since their husbands had been best friends for more than twenty years. She wasn't sure anyone could think of Hawk or Zeke without thinking of the other.

Eden put the biscuits in a bowl wrapped in a towel to keep them warm. As she turned to set them on the table, Zeke, Hawk and the three ranch hands came through the doorway. The next instant the bowl landed on the floor with a loud clatter, sending biscuits rolling around the room.

The third man through the door was Edward.

Chapter Ten

*G*ood Lord, Eden!" Zeke hollered. "You dropped the biscuits."

Zeke and Hawk fell to their knees to scoop up the food, but Eden didn't move. Her heart was thumping in her chest so hard she felt faint. She opened her mouth to speak but no sound came out.

"Are you okay?" Josie asked.

"Of course she's not okay," Hawk said. "Didn't you see her drop the biscuits?"

Eden didn't answer Josie or Hawk; she just gaped at Edward, who stared back at her without expression. "What are *you* doing here?" he demanded.

"You know each other?" Suzette asked, looking from Eden to Edward and back again.

"We met when she was in England." There was no censure in Edward's words. He picked up a biscuit that had rolled up against his boot. It was still hot so he tossed it into the bowl Josie was holding. "She didn't appear to like anything she found there."

"What are *you* doing in Texas?"

Having gathered up the biscuits, Hawk turned to Eden and Edward. "If you two are going to fight, you'll have to wait until after supper."

"We're not going to fight," Edward said. "We have nothing to say to each other."

"I have lots of questions," Eden contradicted.

"As I recall, you also had a lot of opinions."

Eden couldn't blame Edward for being angry with her. She had done a terrible thing when she'd divulged the secret of his birth.

"Let's eat," Hawk said. "You can work this out between you later."

"It's not necessary," Edward said.

"It is if you two are staying here," Josie said. "I've got enough to worry about without having an undeclared war on my hands."

"There's no war," Eden said. "I just want to ask Edward some questions."

Eden didn't have any appetite, and it irritated her to see Edward eat like he didn't have a worry in the world. As the meal progressed, she felt increasingly frustrated. She wasn't used to being unable to do anything about a situation. She reminded herself it had been her penchant for *doing something about a situation* that had gotten her into this mess in the first place.

"How long have you been here?" she asked, unable to wait until after supper. She could keep her mouth closed about as well as she could stop breathing. It was becoming more apparent every day she was her mother's child.

"We moved back while you all were in England," Zeke answered.

"I think she was talking to me," Edward said.

"We've only been back a month," Eden said. "You must have left the same time we did."

"I don't know when you left."

"Will you go back to Worlege?"

"I have no reason to go back."

"I get the feeling there's something I don't know," Josie said.

"It's not important," Edward said. "A matter of a misrepresentation, but it's all been set right."

"How—" Eden began before she realized he couldn't answer that question without divulging his secret. "Never mind."

"What did you boys do today?" Josie asked. Her look

said she was tired of a conversation in which she could have no part.

The ranch hands remained silent while Hawk launched into a discussion of their horses, the various qualities each of them exhibited, and how they hoped to capture these qualities in future foals or breed them out. "Edward thinks we ought to concentrate on speed. He says Thoroughbreds are where the real money will be in the future."

"The Thoroughbred is the ultimate horse," Edward explained. "His sole purpose is to run faster than his competition."

"Will many people want such a horse?" Josie asked. "I haven't heard of much racing in Texas."

"There were some great North-South match races before the war," Eden said. "Now that Texas has recovered from Reconstruction, people are interested in racing once again. I'm entering Black Cloud in the race in San Antonio next month. Dad says she's the fastest horse in Texas." Eden noticed that Hawk and Zeke were looking at Edward rather than at her, and Edward was studiously ignoring her. "What?" she asked. "Did I say something wrong?"

"No," both of her brothers replied, but the way they looked at Edward implied they knew something she didn't.

"Come on, what is it you know that I don't?"

Edward lifted his gaze. "I plan to enter Crusader in the same race."

Edward's hands traveled down Crusader's legs, looking for swelling, or any indication the horse wasn't in perfect health. Training a race horse in the Texas Hill Country wasn't like training one in England. There were few straight stretches here and the ground was littered with stones and cut by depressions from rainwater runoff. But his horse needed to learn to handle the rough terrain to have any chance at defeating horses that had been bred and raised in this area, horses like Eden's Black Cloud.

Edward wasn't sure how he'd made it through the meal without losing control of his tongue. He had known he'd run into Eden one day—he'd *planned* on it—but he'd intended it to be after he'd had time to become acclimated to this new country . . . after he'd won the race. Seeing Eden when he walked into the kitchen had nearly caused his legs to go out from under him. He'd never been prey to such contradictory emotions. Despite the conflicts that had enveloped him from time to time, he'd always been in control of himself. He didn't feel that way now.

He knew it wasn't fair to be angry at Eden. Though she'd been the one to tell him about the circumstances of his birth, she had done it to free him, to give him a chance to live his own life. He *was* deeply and profoundly angry at his so-called father. When the viscount had decided to substitute one child for another, he hadn't cared how this might someday affect everyone else. His only concern had been his own pride. He *would* prevent a distant and despised cousin from inheriting the title after him. And he *would* force everyone to bow to his will.

Crusader nudged Edward's side. "Looking for a treat?" he asked. He took some sugar out of his pocket. "No apples until later in the year. No carrots at all. The ground is too rocky to grow them." Crusader seemed satisfied with the sugar. Edward couldn't say the same for his one and only meeting with his mother.

Even before he'd visited her and endured her copious tears of remorse, he could understand her dilemma. An unwed mother with a meager dowry had stood no chance of a decent marriage. He could also appreciate the pressure her brother had brought on a frightened and lonely woman to lend herself to his plan. Having then made a successful marriage and being possessed of a growing family of her own, she would have jeopardized her future and the future of her family to recognize Edward now.

So he had sent a letter to the earl renouncing the title

and had left England. As far as everyone was concerned, he'd simply disappeared. Only Patrick knew the reason. His brother had been so angry, he'd threatened to expose his own father, but Edward had made him see that wouldn't do anyone—including Edward—any good.

He didn't blame his nurse for revealing the secret. She'd always loved him, had been the one to comfort him when he couldn't understand why he was never allowed to be with his father, why he was always hidden away while Patrick was taken everywhere. She'd invented many fanciful reasons, some of which he'd actually believed, until he was old enough to accept that his father wanted nothing to do with him. Now he understood why the old woman had turned to gin. It was the only way she could endure seeing how the viscount treated him and knowing she could do nothing to change it.

Edward moved away from the shadows of the barn, a flimsy structure compared to the stable at Worlege. Made of wood rather than brick and stone, the stall walls were only head high to allow air to circulate. He was certain snow would blow in during the winter. He intended to build much more substantial stables when he had his own ranch.

The person standing in the way of that goal was Eden.

He couldn't imagine why the nurse had revealed to Eden a secret she hadn't divulged to anyone else in twenty-five years. It must have been a shock to Eden to realize he was illegitimate. Not that she could throw stones, considering her own mother's birth. Still, she probably looked down on him. He knew everyone in England would, which was part of the reason he'd left. He had done nothing wrong, but would spend the rest of his life suffering because others had.

And he wasn't the only one who'd suffer. He hoped to have a family someday. If he'd stayed in England, it would have been impossible to protect his children from the jibes of friends who didn't understand how deeply such things could hurt. Dammit, why couldn't Eden have left things as they were?

He supposed he ought to be thankful to her. If he had stayed in England as the heir, he would have become a sleepwalker in his own life, going through the motions without feeling or caring. Eden had told him the truth to free him from his father's tyranny. What she hadn't been able to do was offer him another life. She'd destroyed the person he was without helping him create a new one.

So he had come to Texas to do it himself.

He walked over to the corral. More than half a dozen horses stood in a loose group along the fence, their heads hanging low, sleeping standing up. Zeke had explained that these horses had spent much of their lives out in the open, where they were prey to wolves and cougars, a kind of large cat Edward had never seen but imagined was something like a lion without manes on the males. These horses couldn't afford to sleep lying down. The time it would take them to get to their feet might mean the difference between life and death. This was just one of the many differences he had to get used to.

The women here were different, too. Though he thought they were allowed so much freedom it was virtually impossible to remain ladylike, he was attracted to the character the women developed as a consequence of that freedom. Despite her amazing energy and forceful personality, Eden remained remarkably feminine.

That was the crux of his dilemma. While he was angry at Eden for destroying his life, he was strongly attracted to her. He tried to convince himself it was purely physical, but he knew he was fooling himself. After having unwittingly spent his life living a lie, he was determined to stick to the truth regardless of how unpalatable it might be. And liking Eden Maxwell was very unpalatable.

He turned at the sound of footsteps to see Eden approaching. He would have preferred to avoid her a little longer, but this meeting was inevitable.

"I didn't expect to find you here," he said when she joined him at the corral fence.

"You couldn't have been any more surprised than I was. I've never come so close to fainting."

"I can't believe that. You're a very strong woman."

"The kind of woman you don't like."

"I never said that."

"You didn't have to. You were brought up in a society that values women only for their looks, wealth, social standing, and their ability to produce an heir."

"That doesn't mean I feel the same way."

She turned her gaze to the half dozen horses congregated in the shade of a large maple with heads down, their swishing tails the only movement. The quiet calm of the evening was at variance with the turmoil showing on her face. "I suppose not, or you wouldn't have refused to marry Daphne." She turned back to face him. "But you don't like strong women."

"English women aren't weak. They have to know how to manage a large household, be responsible for the welfare of an estate's tenants, and take the lead in civic activities."

"All suitable activities for a woman, but suppose she wants to own and manage her own property, wants to run the estate herself."

"She wouldn't know how."

"Because men like you would have kept her confined to doing fancy needlework and learning how to paint or play the pianoforte."

"Why are you attacking me?" Edward asked, surprised by the force behind her word; the angry spark in her eye was visible even in the fading evening light. "You've never had to put up with such restraints."

"No, Americans don't believe in imprisoning their women."

"So you think letting a woman do anything she wants, *think* anything she wants, is preferable."

"We have minds as well as men. Why shouldn't we be allowed to use them? It's preferable to being a piece of property owned by your husband." She leaned back against the corral fence and faced him. "Daphne's father expected her to accept the first offer she received from a titled gentleman. In exchange for the title, that gentleman will get Daphne's money. What does Daphne get?"

"A husband, a position in society, and the allowance her husband gives her."

"Her husband gives her," Eden repeated. She kicked an offending rock into some brush. "You make her sound like a child."

Edward was trying to control his temper, but it was getting increasingly difficult to moderate each word before it came out of his mouth. Eden had always been independent, but now she was acting like the entire English social structure, which she obviously despised, was his fault. Didn't she remember he'd disliked it, too? Besides, he was the one with the right to be angry. Nobody had destroyed her life. She was back in Texas as sassy and independent as ever. And just as pretty.

"If anyone here has a right to be angry, I do," Edward declared. "I'm not the one who divulged a secret that had been kept for a quarter of a century."

"I didn't do it to hurt you," Eden insisted. "You were miserable. Your father was forcing you into a marriage you didn't want and making you feel responsible for Worlege, all in the name of duty. I figured if you knew you weren't really his son, you wouldn't feel duty-bound to do everything he wanted. I had no idea you'd disappear."

"What did you think I'd do?" Did she have no idea what she'd done, how it had affected him? "Did you think I was the kind of man who would cling to a title that wasn't mine? Did you think I could live with myself knowing I'd cheated Patrick of his birthright?"

Eden bit her lip. "I didn't think of all that. I was just thinking of you. I never said . . ." She turned her back to him. "I wouldn't have said a word if I'd thought anything like this was going to happen."

"What did you think would happen? I could have gone berserk and attacked the viscount. I might even have been angry enough to shoot him."

"I was just trying to help," Eden protested. "It made me furious to see the way your father treated you."

Could he be mistaken—the gathering dusk made it hard to be sure—but were those tears glistening in Eden's eyes? He moved closer. "Why were you so angry? I could take care of myself."

"It didn't look like it to me. Every time you tried to stand up for yourself, he'd hit you over the head with your duty to the family. I was just trying to give you a way to fight back."

Edward didn't know what got into him, but the next thing he knew, he'd taken Eden in his arms and was kissing her.

Chapter Eleven

Edward released Eden and practically threw himself in the opposite direction. "I'm sorry," he said, horrified. "That was unforgivable."

Eden's emotions were in such a confused tangle, she couldn't sort them out. She'd never expected Edward would kiss her. That he'd done it against his better judgement was obvious. That he had done it at all was earthshaking. How much she liked it and wanted him to do it again was frightening. "For heaven's sake, Edward, this is Texas, not England. A girl expects to be grabbed and kissed a few times in her life."

"I don't know why I did that," Edward said.

He didn't have to act like it had been a horrible mistake. She *had* been kissed several times before, but she'd never felt lightheaded, breathless, anxious to do it again.

"Maybe you were so surprised I was trying to do something nice, you forgot yourself," she suggested, moving toward him.

"As long as I'm working for your brothers, it would be very improper for me to do such a thing."

Even in the gathering dusk, she could see Edward looked miserable. It was impossible to remain excited with him acting as if he'd committed the worst social crime in history. "You just kissed me. That might be the same as a pledge of marriage in England, but this is Texas. If you don't kiss a girl a couple of times, she'll think you don't like her."

He stiffened, his eyes glazed over. "Are you that free with other men?"

Eden bristled. "Just what do you mean by *free?*"

Edward shook his head. "I don't think I'll ever get used to America."

Eden smiled to cover her disappointment, to ease his worry he'd done something unforgivable. "I don't know why you kissed me, but I'm going to take it as thanks for trying to do something nice for you. Now tell me what made you decide to come to Texas. I would have thought it would be the last place you'd go."

It was strange to see him struggle for an answer. He was such a big man, so strong and capable, it was hard to understand the devastation caused by learning the circumstances of his birth. Being born out of wedlock wasn't a good thing in Texas, nor was it the end of the world.

"I thought of Australia first."

Edward seemed to have recovered his composure, but Eden was sure he wouldn't soon forget he'd kissed a woman who wasn't his wife. It would take him a long time to shed the straitjacket Victorian society had imposed on him.

"I wanted someplace where people were more concerned with the future than the past, where there was no burden of duty hanging over my head. I wanted to be free to discover who I am, what I want . . . free to choose who I want to be responsible for. I'm not sure I'll ever learn to accept that I'm a bastard, but at least I have the chance to start over."

"That still doesn't explain why you came to Texas."

One of the horses had come over to the fence and pushed his head between the bars. Edward absently patted his forehead. The gelding rewarded him with a bump in his ribs. Eden didn't know whether it was the sound of their voices or the animals' jealousy over the attention one of their number was receiving, but the other horses were slowly ambling in their direction.

"According to you, I could do everything in Texas I couldn't do in England. I figured if there was one place where being a bastard didn't matter, this was it."

Eden had been leaning against the fence patting the neck of a sorrel mare, but his last remark caused her to straighten up. "We don't use that word in our family."

"What do you call a child whose parents abandoned him?"

"A kid who needs a home and somebody to love him. My parents adopted eleven orphans, my brother Matt, five fatherless kids. My sister Drew took in three orphaned girls. Junie Mae and her three-year-old son live with my parents. He's a sweet kid even though his father was a jerk." Edward appeared to be having trouble accepting that fatherless children weren't automatically pushed to the fringes of society. "Forget about your birth. What do you want to do? You don't know how to run a ranch. And you don't know a thing about cows until you've tried to wrestle a longhorn to the ground."

"What would I do that for?" Edward asked in confusion.

"Lots of reasons, but as long as you work for Zeke and Hawk, you'll only have to lasso horses."

Edward looked grim. "I can't do that, either. The other men laughed at me when I tried, but I *will* learn."

Their laughter must have hurt his pride. In England, nobody would dare laugh at the heir to an earldom.

The buckskin gelding kept butting Edward with his head. He wanted a treat and was irritated none had been forthcoming.

"I'll work with you if you want. There's not much I hadn't learned to do by the time I was six." It had taken a lot of courage for Edward to come to Texas and ask for a job as an ordinary ranch hand. It couldn't be easy for a man accustomed to giving orders to take them. Or to work with Hawk and Zeke, who probably made fun of him to his face. Going to England had been a severe culture shock to her, but coming to Texas had to be worse for Edward. He had cut himself off from the only society he knew.

"I feel like an idiot," Edward said, his English control slipping. "It's humiliating not being able to do things a woman can do."

"Why?" Eden asked. "I've been doing them for years. You've never even seen them done."

"It's just humiliating," Edward grumbled.

Male pride. She supposed it was a good thing, but why couldn't men be satisfied with being bigger and stronger than women? Did they have to feel they could do everything better? "My grandmother didn't want to leave England, but she was able to make a good life for herself and my mother. You'll do the same."

Edward turned to the pinto that had taken the buckskin's place. "That wasn't the only reason I came to Texas. I was so angry at what you'd done, I was determined to find a way to make you suffer as much as I had." He looked up, turned his penetrating gaze on Eden. "I don't feel that way anymore. If I'd had the choice, I don't know if I'd have wanted to know the truth, but it's much better to know it now than to have it come out years from now when I would have a family to be hurt."

"I felt terrible when you disappeared."

"Do you still feel guilty?" Edward asked in a softened voice.

"Yes, but maybe helping you adjust to Texas will help me overcome it. Let's shake on our new relationship." She put her hand out. Edward met it with a blank stare. "You just take my hand and shake it like you would a man," she explained.

"Is this another instance of American women being equal to men?"

"I guess it is."

Edward put his hand out and her hand disappeared in his grip. "I'm agreeing to let you help me, but I intend to catch up."

It didn't make any difference what country men came from, they were all alike. "Then you'd better be really good, because I am."

It felt odd shaking Edward's hand. She couldn't decide

whether it was the feeling of her hand being lost in his powerful grip, or if it was more about the powerful currents that arced between them. It was impossible to be around Edward and not be physically attracted to him. He exhibited too much raw physicality, exuded too much veiled sexuality, for a woman to ignore.

His humanity made him even more attractive. He had a deep love for his brother despite his father's glaring preference for Patrick. His interest in his tenants and their families was genuine. The children's sadness on learning he was gone and wasn't coming back was the kind of testimony that couldn't be bought.

The thing that intrigued her the most about Edward was the contrast between the rigid society that had formed him and the adventurous spirit that had led him to Texas. There were more reasons why she'd never want a man like him for a husband than she had fingers to count them on, but she'd be remiss if she didn't add that she was powerfully attracted to him and liked him a heck of a lot.

She withdrew her hand from Edward's grip. "I'd better get back. If I'm out of sight of a family member for more than ten minutes, they get uneasy. You can't imagine what it's like to have ten older brothers breathing down your neck. It takes a brave man just to ask me to a dance."

"I imagine you can handle your brothers."

"Not as well as you think." She paused. "I'm glad you decided to come to Texas. I hope you'll like it here."

"We'll see," Edward said.

She backed away, then stumbled over a rock she couldn't see, but quickly got to her feet before Edward could help her. She hoped no one in the house was watching. She didn't want to have to explain to Zeke and Hawk how looking at Edward had made her fall on her face.

Remaining at the corral fence, Edward watched Eden walk back to the house while idly playing with the forelock of the sorrel mare that had deserted Eden for him. He couldn't figure out how he felt about this woman. He ran hot and cold, liking her one moment and frustrated with her the next. He still couldn't believe he'd kissed her. He'd never done anything like that in his life. It was contrary to everything he'd ever been taught. At the very least he'd expected her to slap his face.

He didn't have a problem understanding why he liked Eden. A man would have to be blind not to be attracted to her. To say she was pretty was an understatement. To deny that her body caused him to think impure thoughts would have been pointless. When she smiled at him, he could feel himself stand a little taller, throw out his chest a little more. It was foolish, a silly way to show off, but she made him want to accomplish impossible tasks, do something of importance. Daphne had made him grind his teeth in frustration. Most of the debutantes he'd been introduced to made him want to run straight back to Worlege. All Eden had to do was smile at him, and he felt more like a Restoration rake than a Victorian gentleman.

It wasn't simply her looks. She was unique in his experience. She was exciting to be around. A kind of energy poured off her that made it impossible to think of anyone else but her. She was like a magnet, drawing attention rather than forcing it. She knew how to conduct herself and was always tastefully dressed, but she was as unconcerned about her clothes as she was impatient with the rigid manners of society. He didn't know how she managed to maintain her personal freedom without upsetting those around her. He'd tried to do what was expected of him, and all he did was upset people.

Giving the mare one last pat, he pushed off from the fence. It was time to go to bed, but he was reluctant to head toward the bunkhouse. He wasn't used to sleeping in a room with anyone else, certainly not two men who snored. Regardless of how tired he was at the end of the day, he couldn't sleep through the night. Then there was the problem of relieving himself before bed or during the night. There was no indoor privy, just an outhouse! That might have been the biggest single shock he'd encountered since he'd arrived. He doubted he'd ever get used to that.

Nor could he get used to the smallness of the bunkhouse, the minimal comforts offered by the bunk bed, the total lack of privacy or sufficient space to store his belongings. He thought he'd brought only the bare necessities, but as far as he could tell, Finn and Brady, his fellow ranch hands, had no more than two changes of clothes and one set of underwear. Edward was used to wearing more clothes than that by the time he went down to breakfast. His bunkmates constantly made comments about his trunk full of clothes. He supposed the two men were nice enough in a Texas sort of way, but he was still getting used to Texas. Finn and Brady would take a little longer.

"How'd it go with the boss's sister?" Finn was lounging on his bunk, looking through indecent pictures of women. Brady was reading a five-cent Western novel.

"Won't do you any good if she does take a shine to you," Brady said, looking up from his book. "Her daddy ain't going to let her hook up with a fella that talks funny."

"Or who's afraid of an outhouse," Finn added.

Edward's first experience with the outhouse had been at night. An owl hooting just as he was about to sit down caused him to start so badly he'd bumped his head against the door. Finn and Brady hadn't stopped teasing him about trying to run away with his pants around his ankles. It had been all he could do not to employ his greater size and strength to lock them in the outhouse for the night.

"We got to know each other when she was in England. She wanted to know if I had any news about the people she visited."

Edward hadn't told anyone the circumstances of his birth. All he wanted people to know was that he'd come to

Texas to learn how to be a rancher, win a horse race, and buy his own ranch where he'd raise Thoroughbreds.

"Does everybody there talk like you?" Brady asked.

"Does everybody in Texas talk like you?" Edward responded.

He approached his bunk, certain he'd never get a good night's sleep until he learned to be comfortable on a mattress packed so hard it felt solid.

"What's wrong with the way I talk?" Brady demanded.

"You take forever to say anything, and you put so many extra syllables in some words I hardly know what you're saying."

"You don't have to," Brady said, returning to his book. "Texans understand me just fine. It's you they can't figure out. You even ride funny."

Edward was having the devil of a time getting used to the heavy saddles everybody here used, but that didn't compare to the trouble he had with his boots. First he couldn't get them on. Next he couldn't walk in them without feeling as if he were about to pitch forward off his two-inch heels. Then they were so tight he couldn't get the damned things off. He slept with them on the first night. He had been staying at a hotel in San Antonio at the time, or Finn and Brady would have never let him forget it. Somebody should have told him boots were made for riding, not walking, before he spent a whole day walking around San Antonio.

"Texas is different from England," Edward said. "It'll take me a little time to adjust."

"It'll take you longer than that to learn to handle a rope," Finn said and burst out laughing.

It mortified Edward that he couldn't do something common cowhands did with ease, but he refused to be drawn. He was going to learn to handle that damned rope. He would get used to a Western saddle and remember to ride everywhere when he wore boots with heels as high as those of an English woman. And one day, he would have the last laugh, because he would be the one to own his own ranch.

He wouldn't be working for anybody and he wouldn't be sleeping in a bunkhouse or using an outhouse.

"All things in due time," he said to Finn as he started to undress.

That was something else. Why did Texans have to wear clothes so tight they threatened to cut off a man's circulation as well as damage his manhood? He wrestled his boots off and put them in the corner. After removing his shirt and pants, he folded them and put them on top of his trunk. He would dearly have loved to put on a dressing gown— something he'd previously considered an essential part of his wardrobe—but he didn't need Finn's amused glances to tell him that doing so would cause both men to roar with laughter. They already called him *duke*. He figured it wasn't meant as a compliment.

"The laundress doesn't come until next week," Brady said. "Maybe you'd better wash your shirt in the horse trough. It ought to dry by morning."

They still laughed about Edward washing his personal linen after wearing it for three days, but there were only so many privations Edward was willing to endure, and soiled linen wasn't one of them. On chilly days, Finn and Brady wore something they called long johns. They looked like what some men in England wore during the winter, but they smelled like something left out in the stable yard.

"I already did it," Edward said. "It's hanging on the corral fence."

"I hope one of the horses doesn't decide to make a meal of it," Finn said.

"It's goats that eat clothes, not horses. Your American horses aren't kin to goats, are they?"

Finn didn't like it when Edward turned his barbs back on him, but Edward wasn't about to let two scrawny cowboys get the better of him.

"You'll think they're kin to gazelles when you try to beat

them with that long-legged nag of yours," Finn said. "I bet Eden's horse can run circles around yours."

Edward hadn't seen Black Cloud run, but he'd been impressed the moment he saw the mare in the corral. "I'll take my chances," he said to Finn as he folded his frame into the bunk that was three inches shorter than he was. "I've got to have better luck than I have with this bunk."

"Brady's and mine are just fine. It must be you."

"I can't help it if Americans are sawed-off little runts."

Brady's book closed with a snap about the time Finn's pictures hit the floor. "Americans aren't runts," Brady growled. "Wait until you see Sean. He'll make two of you."

"I thought Sean was Irish."

"All of us were something else a little ways back," Finn said, "but we're Americans now."

Edward settled into his bunk, resigned to having his feet hang over the end. He wondered if anybody would say the same about him a year from now.

"We ought to work our horses together," Eden said to Edward as she brought a bowl of steaming grits to the table and set them in front of Hawk. "It'll get you used to losing to Black Cloud."

Edward eyed the grits with disfavor. A blob of butter in the center was quickly turning to a golden liquid. "That's a good idea. Crusader needs somebody to make him stretch his legs."

"What about Chief?" Josie asked Hawk. She helped herself to grits and passed them to Suzette, who waved them away.

"He's too valuable as a stud to risk racing," Hawk replied. "You should keep that in mind with Crusader," he said to Edward. "He's a fine-looking horse."

"He has to win some races before anybody will be willing to pay more than a few dollars to breed to him," Edward said. At the moment Edward was more concerned about his breakfast than Crusader's future at stud. Except for coffee, there wasn't much on the table he recognized. He was afraid to touch the grits. Fried ham was acceptable, but he was more used to mutton chops or rump steak. He talked himself into eating the sausage without asking what might be in it. The scrambled eggs were questionable, especially after he learned they were often cooked with beef brains, but if he didn't eat them, there wouldn't be much to keep him going until supper—the American term for dinner. He welcomed the sight of bacon and thick fluffy biscuits even though he was more used to toast, but who drank milk? He missed his tea and marmalade. This American jam wasn't the same.

"You'll soon get used to the food," Hawk said when Edward passed on the grits. "I did, and that was after spending thirteen years living as an Indian."

There was no end to the incredible stories that surrounded Eden's family. Compared to the Maxwell clan, his entire family was one great big yawn.

"If you'll saddle my horse, I'll meet you as soon as I help Josie and Suzette clean up," Eden said to Edward when breakfast was coming to an end.

"You go on," Josie said. "We can clean up."

"And let my mother find out I was gallivanting all over while you two were washing dishes? You do remember my mother, don't you? Isabelle, the tyrant who rules the lives of everyone within a hundred miles?"

"Your mother is the kindest woman I've ever met."

Suzette appeared to have trouble getting to her feet. Edward didn't know anything about women having babies, but he didn't like what he saw.

"She is as long as you do what she wants," Hawk said, helping his wife up from her chair. "Why do you think Zeke and I spent twenty years getting shot at rather than living at home?"

Edward excused himself, left the house, and headed for the barn. He took his time saddling the two horses. He used

Eden's Western saddle on Black Cloud, but he used his lighter English saddle on Crusader because that was what he'd use when he raced.

"I didn't know English lords knew how to saddle their own horses."

Edward turned to see Eden headed toward him. He was prepared to be struck yet again by her wholesome beauty, the energy that radiated from her, but he wasn't prepared for the jump in his pulse rate. He had to remember that she was now the competition. If he didn't concentrate, he could end up watching that lovely backside finish the race in front of him.

"Ex-English lords don't have any choice. By the way, I didn't tighten the cinch. You'll fall off, crack your head, and be unable to race against me."

He wasn't sure he'd ever get used to Eden's laugh. It wasn't just that it was deep and full-throated. There was an honesty, a spontaneity, that was foreign to a man who'd grown up in a society where every detail of one's life was studied and calculated to create the maximum effect. Eden acted on her feelings and pretty much didn't care what anyone else thought. He could hardly imagine such freedom. Learning to be a Texan was like learning to walk all over again.

"I plan to sabotage your saddle," Eden teased, "but just enough to cause you to slow down."

"I'll bed down with my horse and saddle. Sleeping on straw can't be any worse than that bunk."

Eden laughed again and a thrill shot through him. Who could have believed that a laugh could be sexy? No proper Englishman would refer to a lady as sexy, but that's exactly what Eden was. Maybe these Texans had it right. There was no use denying the obvious. He smiled to himself. Getting used to being a Texan might be fun.

"Wait until you spend the night in a bedroll on rocky ground," Eden said. "You'll wish you were back in that bunk."

Edward had never spent a night anywhere except in a warm, dry bed. He couldn't imagine why any sane man would sleep outdoors.

"Time to get going," Eden said. "Give me a leg up."

Chapter Twelve

*T*here went his pulse again. English women never exposed more than the tips of their shoes, yet Eden nonchalantly placed her foot in his clasped hands, exposing her leg from the knee down to the calf where it disappeared inside her boot. He'd enjoyed several liaisons over the years, but they'd been about releasing sexual tension so he could get his mind back on his work, about attending to a bodily function that was natural and healthy. His interest in Eden was far more complex; so complex, in fact, he couldn't say exactly what it was. Being around her had an effect on him that being around Daphne had never approximated.

"Has anybody shown you the training trail Hawk and Zeke are building?" Eden asked as they rode out into the sunlight.

Edward had yet to get used to the Texas sun. There was no morning fog as in England, no mist to rise from the meadow or the lake, no chill in the deep shadows of the forest, no feeling of being slowly brought to consciousness and gently coaxed awake. No, this sun was pushy, sometimes rude. It came bursting over the horizon like a nanny bustling in to rouse a reluctant charge from bed, the sky as bright and clear as it would ever get, and the heat spearing one's skin like hundreds of hot needles.

"Zeke told me about the trail, but I haven't had time to use it."

He'd only been working for Zeke and Hawk a week and was still trying to get his bearings. He'd expected to have more time before seeing Eden again, more time to understand his attraction to her. He understood basic attraction, but where had the intensity come from? He had to stifle an urge to reach out and touch her. Would she object? Was touching, like kissing, something Texans were allowed to do with impunity? Maybe, but he couldn't trust himself to stop there, and no matter how liberal they were in Texas, there were certain rules that held no matter where you were.

"I'm not sure how practical it will be for us," Eden was saying. "They only use it to train pleasure horses, the kind rich men and women ride to show off."

"Just like they do in London," Edward said.

"I suppose so."

"Do you disapprove?"

"Not really. Different people take pleasure in different things."

"What do you take pleasure in?" He was shocked as soon as the words left his mouth. He would never have asked Daphne such a question.

"I'm not sure what kind of pleasure you mean." Eden had cocked her head at an angle. She looked at him from under lowered lashes, a half smile hovering on her lips, her attention only partly on her mount.

"I meant anything, everything," Edward answered, embarrassed that his thoughts had taken a particularly provocative turn.

Eden turned her attention to a low-hanging branch that protruded into the trail. "Lots of things."

Edward wondered if he was only imagining that she sounded slightly disappointed.

"I enjoy teaching my nieces and nephews. I have fourteen now, with that many more coming. I enjoy riding, especially when I get to race, but nobody will race against Black Cloud. Sometimes I enjoy cooking, but I have to be in the mood or have an occasion to cook something special."

"You didn't seem to have any problem with breakfast this

morning, and it was pretty much the same thing Josie and Suzette fixed before you got here."

She made a wry face. "You asked about pleasure, not work. Only an Englishman would think the two were the same."

"What else?"

"I like going to parties, dances, picnics, just about any kind of fun get-together, especially if I'm with a man whose company I enjoy."

"Are there a lot of men whose company you enjoy?"

The demon of jealousy was a bothersome thing, though why he thought he had any right to be jealous was a question he couldn't answer. Eden had indicated she liked him but not in a special way. Sometimes he felt she did, the times when she looked at him out of the corner of her eye or when he would look up and find her staring at him, but he couldn't be sure. American men and women had a different way of showing interest in each other. He knew the rules in England, but he had no idea how things were done in Texas. That was one more item to add to his list of things he wanted to learn quickly.

"Not a lot, but enough to have a good time," Eden said. "Dad encourages me to talk to lots of different men, but I think he's really trying to keep me single. He says I'm too young to be married."

Another difference. In England, she would practically be an old maid. "Do you want to be married?"

"Yes, but only to the right man. You're mighty serious this morning. Why?"

"Everything is so different here. Even sitting down to breakfast."

Eden's peal of laughter caused a pair of birds to burst from the arching branches of a pecan tree ahead. "You looked at the bowl of grits like you were afraid of it."

"It looked disgusting."

"It's only ground corn. Josie said you liked corn bread

once she convinced you to try it. Grits aren't much different. A little salt, pepper, butter, gravy, whatever you like to season them, and they're wonderful. You'll have to try them."

"Maybe." That was the most he could promise. They had reached an open area where flooding from a shallow river had left sandy deposits along the banks.

"This trail is about a half mile long," Eden said. "It's not perfect—you still have to watch out for an occasional rock or tree root—but it will give the horses a chance to stretch their legs and work up a little speed."

The trail was nothing like the carefully laid-out race courses or meticulously maintained training tracks in Newmarket, England. It would be a miracle if Crusader didn't end up with a strained ligament.

"Come on," Eden said when Edward hesitated. "I know this isn't what you're used to."

"It looks dangerous."

"Not to horses that grew up running on even rougher ground."

"Crusader has never run on anything like this."

"Then it's time he learned."

Eden didn't wait for him to make up his mind. She clucked to Black Cloud and the mare moved into a slow gallop. Edward knew he should be watching the mare, studying her stride, trying to determine her speed and stamina, but all he could think of was seeing Eden with her rear end up in the air. How was he supposed to concentrate on a horse when he had that to look at?

Tearing his eyes away from Eden, Edward urged Crusader into a trot, a canter, and finally a slow gallop. The horse tugged at the bit, wanting to catch up to the horse and rider ahead of him, but Edward wasn't willing to go any faster until he'd ridden the full length of the course. He couldn't risk an injury, even a slight one. Crusader was his one chance to win enough money to buy his own ranch. He would never go back to England, not even if he had to use an outhouse for the rest of his life.

"What do you think?" Eden asked when he reached the end of the course. She'd arrived far enough ahead to have turned around, and was waiting for him.

"It's not as bad as I feared. I'll see if Zeke and Hawk will give me some time to work on it. Maybe I can trade that for training some of their horses. I know all about pleasure horses. That's how half the horses at Worlege were used."

Unlike Eden, he'd never thought using horses for pleasure was a waste. Maybe that was because she'd grown up needing horses for work. He supposed most ranchers couldn't afford to keep separate plow horses, dray horses, riding horses, hunters, and even racehorses. Then there were ponies for children and matched pairs to pull one's carriage or phaeton in the park. He'd never stopped to consider whether all these horses and the expense they entailed were necessary. It was just part of the life into which he'd been born.

"Are you ready for a good run?" Eden asked.

"Whenever you are," he answered, but he wasn't planning to race all-out. Crusader wasn't ready for a hard gallop. Besides, he didn't want to embarrass Eden by beating her today.

Crusader had a fast start, but Eden's horse sprang away with the quickness of a hare and was two lengths ahead before Crusader hit full stride. Edward expected to catch up quickly but was shocked to see Eden's lead lengthen until she was four lengths ahead at the end of the trail.

"That wasn't bad," she said when she pulled up, "considering you must weigh eighty pounds more than I do. Black Cloud will leave your horse in the dust if you don't get a jockey who can make weight."

Edward had considered hiring a jockey, but he knew Crusader better than anyone, knew how to get the best race out of him. Still, he'd never beat Black Cloud carrying that much extra weight. The mare was much better than he'd expected. One hundred years of importing horses from

England into Virginia and New York had improved the American racehorse. He just hadn't expected the improvements to have reached down into Texas.

"Why don't we jog them back, and do another run?" Eden suggested. "Quarter-horse blood gets Black Cloud off the starting block first, but Crusader is pretty fast."

Edward's competitive blood was up. "All this traveling has gotten him out of condition for running."

"He'd better get in shape quickly. People in San Antonio train all year for this race. Some even buy a horse especially for it."

What Edward had thought would be a sure thing was beginning to look uncertain. Having reached the end of the trail, they lined their horses up and started together. Eden still finished ahead of Edward. He would have to get a jockey. He wouldn't have a chance otherwise.

He hated losing the opportunity to race against Eden. He had a strong need to prove himself to her and to everyone at the ranch—maybe even the entire Maxwell family. He was certain they believed he was little more than an effete aristocrat who was playing at being a rancher and would probably head back to England as soon as some bronco dumped him on the ground or he got jerked out of the saddle trying to lasso a steer that was in no mood to cooperate. They didn't realize he had no options. He had to succeed. He didn't have a home to go back to.

And in order to succeed, he had to find a way to beat Eden and Black Cloud.

"We always go to San Antonio about a week before the race," Eden was saying as they rode back toward the ranch house. "Mama likes plenty of time to shop. They have stock shows the same week, so Dad and the boys are busy looking to see if there's anything they want to buy. You'll want to go with them."

She was pleased with Black Cloud's morning workout.

The mare had finished second in the race last year, and Eden was sure she'd have won if not for the poor performance of her jockey. This year she had every intention of convincing her father to let her ride. The question in her mind was whether Black Cloud could beat Crusader.

"I don't have money to spend," Edward said. "Everything depends on my winning the race."

Edward had covered it well, but she could tell he was shocked and dismayed that Crusader hadn't beaten Black Cloud. The mare was fast and had plenty of stamina, but at equal weights, Eden feared Crusader would beat her mare.

"You don't have to buy anything, just look at what's being offered. It'll give you an idea what people want and what they're willing to pay for it. Didn't you go to stock shows in England?"

She listened to his description of the county fairs he'd attended, but her attention snapped when she noticed a mare and foal wading into the river a short distance ahead. Edward must have noticed at the same time. "That's one of your brothers' horses. I didn't know they let them roam free."

"They don't," Eden said. "Every horse is kept behind barbed wire, in a corral, or in the barn. I don't know how they got out."

"That's the Morgan mare. I saw Finn take her to her pasture."

"That's the most expensive horse they own," Eden said. "We have to take her back."

Having gained her freedom, the mare wasn't ready to give it up. She splashed through the shallow river and bounded up the far bank. When Eden and Edward followed her, she played hide-and-seek among the bald cypress, mountain cedar, elm, pecan, and oak trees that lined the banks of the river, her six-month-old colt following nimbly in her wake. Twice she managed to avoid Eden's lasso, once by turning sharply and once by ducking her head.

"You're not going to catch her that way," Edward said. "Lasso her colt and see if she'll follow."

Not being as acquainted with the ways of humans as his mother, the colt didn't notice the lasso until it settled over his head. His efforts to rid himself of the noose were so frantic Eden began to worry that he might injure himself. He was a nearly perfect colt, and she knew Zeke and Hawk couldn't afford to lose him. She had just about made up her mind to let him go when Edward called out that he'd gotten a grip on the mare's bridle.

"You can let the colt go," he said.

It took all of Eden's skill to get the rope off the bucking, fighting youngster. Having been caught, the mare stood quietly, nuzzling her colt to reassure him.

"I've got to learn to handle a lasso." Edward had tied his rope to the mare's bridle. "I would have been helpless if you hadn't been here."

"You'd have figured out something," Eden said.

"Maybe you ought to ride with me," Edward said. "Finn can do the cooking and cleaning."

Eden laughed. "I don't think Suzette would agree to that. She's not very fond of Finn."

"Neither am I," Edward said, "but I hardly know him."

"Texans don't like people they think look down on them. Your aristocratic background is a red flag to people like Finn. You can change your clothes, but you can't change the way you speak or your inbred attitude of command. I'm surprised Zeke and Hawk hired you."

"It took some doing, but I won them over with my knowledge of horses. And a promise to let them breed to Crusader after he wins the race."

"What will you do with the money *if* you win?"

"I'm not sure. It's not enough to buy the land I need, but I can't buy stock until I have a place to keep them."

"Maybe Dad or one of my brothers will let you use some

of their land until you can find a way to get the rest of the money you need."

"I'm going to use all the money I have left to bet on the race," Edward said. "Hawk said I could get really good odds since nobody knows anything about Crusader."

"But you could lose," Eden warned. "Somebody is bound to bring in a horse from New Orleans. It was an outside horse that beat Black Cloud last year."

"I have faith in Crusader. Besides, it's the only way I'll ever get enough money to have the ranch I want and be able to buy good stock."

Eden started to suggest that he ask his family for money, but she suspected Patrick had already offered and Edward had turned him down. She didn't know how much the escaped mare he was leading had cost Zeke and Hawk, but they'd banked their earnings for twenty years before they had enough to buy horses and land. Edward wasn't willing to wait that long.

"I'm going to do my best to beat you," she warned him.

His smile was surprisingly warm. "I wouldn't expect anything less, but will your father let you ride?"

"He will, but he won't like it."

After the way her jockey had misjudged the race last year, her mother would make certain of it. Isabelle didn't like horses any more than she liked cows, but she liked an incompetent jockey even less. She swore he must have been paid off. Eden wouldn't have been surprised if that was true. Despite the size of the purse, the real money was in bets on the race. Several hundred thousand dollars would change hands.

As they left the cover of the trees along the riverbank and the ranch house came into sight, Eden was surprised to see her father's horse at the house. It wasn't unusual for him to visit the various family ranches, but he'd have had to set out at the crack of dawn to have reached Hawk and Zeke's ranch this early in the day.

"I don't know that horse," Edward said.

"It's Dad's." Eden urged her mount forward. She had a feeling something wasn't right. Her father and brothers, along with Finn and Brady, were in deep conversation under the large walnut tree next to the corral. When they saw the mare and colt, the group broke up.

"What are you doing with that mare?" Zeke appeared poised between anger and confusion.

"We found her down by the river," Eden told him. "I don't know how she got out."

Hawk was already running his hands over the mare's body. After giving the colt a similar going-over, he said, "They don't appear to be hurt." He turned to Finn. "Did you make sure to fasten the gate?"

"Sure. I slid the bar through and put the chain on it. They didn't get out through the gate."

"I don't think she could jump the fence," Hawk said. "I know the colt couldn't."

"I'll see if I can figure out what happened," Zeke said. "Brady, you and Finn take the mare and colt and put them in the corral. I'll be back in half an hour," he said to Hawk.

"What are you doing here this early?" Eden asked her father.

"We've been having some trouble with stock at several of the ranches," Jake said. "At first we thought it was just accidents, but there have been too many."

"What kind of trouble?" Eden asked.

"Little stuff. Fences down, a cow in a bog, some poisoned by eating loco weed, the kind of stuff that happens all the time, but not all at once. It looks like somebody has a grudge against us."

"Do you think the person is dangerous?" Edward asked.

"No. Probably a hand who got fired and is trying to get back at us."

"You hardly ever fire anyone," Eden reminded him.

"People can still have grievances," Edward pointed out. "It happened to me at Worlege."

She kept forgetting Edward had occupied a similar position to her father's. Did she want to forget his past because it separated him from her or because of her part in his losing it?

"I'll tell the boys to keep a close eye out," Hawk said. "I doubt the mare's escape has anything to do with what's been happening on the other ranches. We haven't had any trouble here."

"The horses need to be rubbed down and cooled out." Edward reached for Black Cloud's reins. "I'll take care of both of them."

Eden didn't let go of the reins. "Daddy says a good cowhand takes care of his own horse. That way he knows he can depend on his mount when the time comes."

"You don't trust me?" Edward asked.

"That's not the point. I take care of my own horse. Do you want me to take care of Crusader, too?"

"I can't let a woman care for my horse."

"I'm going to see how Suzette's doing." Hawk could sense a fight brewing. "She was feeling rotten after breakfast. You want some coffee before you head out?" he asked Jake, who appeared equally relieved to depart before the storm broke. They both knew how Eden would react to anybody telling her she couldn't do something because she was a woman.

"Are you saying I'm not good enough to care for *your* horse?" Eden demanded.

Edward looked disconcerted. "Of course not."

"That's what it sounded like."

"An Englishman would never expect a woman to curry her own horse, much less his. Not because women are incapable," he added quickly. "It's considered improper to require a lady to care for her horse in any manner."

Eden's temper started to cool. Another difference between England and Texas, another time when Edward didn't realize his words had offended her. She wondered if it was possible for him to learn to live in Texas. She wouldn't be surprised to see him turn around in a couple of weeks and head back to England. Still, if he went back, he'd have to divulge a truth that would destroy his family's reputation. She knew enough of his character to know he couldn't do that to people he loved, or even to people he didn't.

"I know you want to raise horses," she said, "but what kind of horses? Who will buy them? What kind of prices will they bring? Is this the best part of the country, or should you go to someplace like Virginia or Kentucky?"

They had walked their horses to a corral in a grove of trees by a creek that flowed into the Medina River. They led them up a chute that connected the corral to the barn on the hillside, above the reach of periodic floods.

"I thought I knew exactly what I was going to do," Edward said, "but now that I'm here, I'm not sure."

Standing under the shed, they unsaddled their horses and washed them down with buckets of water drawn from a cistern fed by a pipe from the creek. They rubbed the animals dry with soft cloths, then walked them in a sunny pasture behind the barn to let the sun finish drying them.

"I still want to breed Thoroughbreds," Edward said, "but I love that Morgan mare. I saw some other horses in New Orleans I liked, too, Tennessee Walkers."

Eden smothered a smile. His enthusiasm was incredible, but he would soon learn he couldn't do everything and succeed.

"I have an idea I believe will be important in the future," Eden said, "but I can't get anyone to agree with me."

"What's that?"

The horses had cooled down and started to graze. They released them into their corrals and headed back to the barn.

"The only true Texas horse is the cow pony. Rich people have Thoroughbreds, fancy saddle horses, even Tennessee Walkers, but everybody, young or old, male or female, rich or poor, can own a cow pony. Each person thinks his pony is the fastest, the most agile, the best cutting horse. A good cow pony won't bring as much money as a Thoroughbred or a good riding horse, but you can sell a lot more of them."

"If it's such a good idea, why isn't anyone in your family interested in doing it?"

"Most of them are too busy with cows to be interested. Bret's wife, Emily, and I are the only two interested in this kind of competition, so the men say only women are interested in *playing* with a working horse. They think we'll ruin them for real work."

"Would you ruin them?"

"Of course! Who would risk a show horse chasing after some loco steer who'd just as soon gore him, then throw you on the ground and stomp you to death?"

Edward laughed. "It looks like you just proved their argument."

"Maybe I did, but you're missing the point. When a woman buys an everyday dress, she wants to make sure it looks nice on her, but she's more concerned about how it functions. When she buys a really nice dress, she's also concerned about how it functions, but she's more concerned about how it looks on her, so she's not going to expose it to the hazards of everyday life. It's the same with cow ponies for work and for show."

"We do pretty much the same in England. We keep hunters who eat their heads off most of the year just for the few weeks when we go fox hunting, but no one begrudges the expense."

"Exactly," Eden exclaimed. "Are you interested?"

"Will you help me?"

Chapter Thirteen

$\mathcal{E}$den didn't know how to answer. It wasn't that she wasn't willing to help Edward breed cow ponies for show. She just wasn't sure what he meant by helping. Besides, her teaching responsibilities wouldn't leave her much time. She couldn't travel every day from the schoolhouse to Hawk and Zeke's ranch and then back again.

"You really ought to talk to Emily. She knows more about training cow ponies than I do."

"I don't know Emily. I don't even know where she lives."

"I can arrange for you to meet her at my house."

"I thought you'd want to help me."

"It's not that I don't want to help you."

"Then what is it?"

She was going to tell him about the logistics, how it wasn't possible to be in two places at one time, but she had a nagging feeling that wasn't the only reason she was holding back. She didn't want to admit it, but she liked Edward more than was good for her. The fact that she knew he liked her, too, only made things worse. They weren't good for each other for too many reasons to catalog, not that she expected Edward to stay in Texas for long. She didn't know where he'd go or what he would do, but she was certain he'd be gone before the end of the year.

"We can work around that," Edward said after Eden had explained the problems caused by distance and time.

"How?"

"I don't know yet. I've just been here a few weeks. I don't

even know how to find your house, but we could work out something. Besides, you have a responsibility to help me." He said it with a sheepish grin.

"How do you figure that?"

"It was your description of Texas that convinced me to come here instead of going to Virginia or Kentucky."

"If you'd been planning to concentrate on Thoroughbreds, you *should* have gone to Kentucky or Virginia."

"But I didn't," he pointed out, "and it's your fault."

Even if she could have convinced herself she'd had nothing to do with his choosing Texas—she hadn't thought her descriptions were that numerous or that enticing—she knew she was directly responsible for his decision to leave England. That alone carried a heavy load of responsibility.

"Okay, I agree to help, but I'm not making any promises. Now I need to get back to the house and you need to get to work."

As they walked to the house from the barn, Edward plied her with questions about cow ponies and the kind of things people liked to see in competition. She'd been gathering information all her life, but she hadn't realized she knew so much about the bush league circuit until now. Before they reached the house, she was becoming excited about the prospects.

"That mare's escape wasn't an accident," Hawk announced as soon as they entered the house where he, Zeke, and her father were gathered. "The fence was cut." Josie was making more coffee, but Suzette was absent, which Eden found unusual. Suzette liked to be near Hawk as much as possible.

"That doesn't make any sense," Eden said. "Why would somebody cut the fence but not steal the mare or colt?"

"It makes about as much sense as what's been happening at the other ranches," her father said. "It seems like somebody's got a grudge against the whole family."

"That must be it," Hawk said. "Zeke and I haven't lived

here for twenty years, so they can't have anything against us. It's pretty much the same for Luke and Pete, but we've all been hit."

Eden wasn't pleased to think someone had a grudge against the family, but she didn't see much to get upset about. "I'll leave this to you. Where's Suzette?"

"Lying down," Hawk said. "She wasn't feeling well."

"I think I'll check on her."

"Don't wake her up if she's sleeping," Hawk said. "She hardly gets any rest at night."

Suzette was sitting up in bed when Eden eased the door open and peeped in. "Are you okay?" she asked as she advanced into the room.

"I don't know," Suzette said with a wan smile. "I've never been pregnant before. All I have to go by is Josie, and she doesn't feel the same way."

Suzette didn't look sick, but she looked tired, as if she'd worked too hard and rested too little. "You ought to see Ward," Eden suggested. "He's delivered every baby in the family."

"I've already seen him. He said if I didn't start feeling better soon, he wanted me to go into San Antonio so I'd be close to a hospital."

"Does he think something is wrong?" Some of the wives had suffered small problems during pregnancy but nothing serious. After both Hawk and Suzette had given up on ever having their own family, Eden hated to think anything might happen to this child.

"He said he couldn't be sure, but he thought all I needed was plenty of rest. Hawk practically stands over me every time I get out of bed. I'm glad you're here. Maybe now he won't be so anxious."

"Stop worrying and go to sleep." Knowing Hawk as she did, Eden was certain he wouldn't stop worrying until the baby was safely delivered.

Over the next ten minutes, as she watched Suzette sink

into a peaceful slumber, she couldn't help wondering if this would ever happen to her. She'd always assumed she'd get married and have a family, but it had never happened. Her mother said she was being too picky; her father said she was being sensible; her brothers didn't care who she married as long as they approved of him. Eden figured that stipulation alone guaranteed she'd never marry.

She wondered if Edward would ever find a wife, settle down, and raise a family. If he didn't, it would be one more thing to add to her load of guilt. Why had she ever assumed she knew what was best for someone else?

She hadn't done a spectacular job with her own life. She would be twenty-two on her next birthday, was living at home, had no prospects for a husband, and no plan to find one. The logical thing would have been to move to San Antonio or Dallas, or better still, Galveston—New Orleans if she got really desperate—but she hadn't wanted to live so far from her family. She had missed them terribly when she was away at school. Her schoolmates had made it clear her family wasn't like any they'd ever heard of, but Eden was convinced there was more love among her adopted siblings than among any of the natural siblings her schoolmates complained of so frequently.

And now she was responsible for Edward being a virtual orphan, looking for a home, a place to start over, a way to discover who he was and where he belonged. She wondered if her family would take him in as well. Maybe they'd made a start by giving him a job, but she didn't know if she wanted the family to do anything more. Her feelings were so mixed up with guilt, it was hard to know what she wanted to do or why.

She shook her head to clear it. She needed to remember she was here to help Suzette and Josie. Once they had their babies, she'd go home and start teaching school. It was possible she would see Edward only a couple of times after that. In a few months, he'd be more comfortable and wouldn't need to depend on her, or he'd be so miserable he'd go back to England. Either way, he didn't fit into her future. It was time to stop thinking he might.

Eden didn't like training Black Cloud by herself, but the cut fence had changed everybody's routine. Hawk and Zeke wanted constant patrols of every field, pasture, corral, and enclosure on their ranch. Because of Suzette's condition, Hawk refused to be more than a few minutes from the house. Zeke wouldn't go much farther. That meant Edward, Finn, and Brady had to be in the saddle the minute breakfast was over. Edward got up before dawn so he would have time to train Crusader before breakfast. Eden wasn't free to leave the house until she'd cleaned up after breakfast and made supper plans.

Maybe she was just nervous after the wire-cutting incident, but she couldn't shake the feeling someone was watching her. Since Black Cloud was the favorite for the race, it wasn't unreasonable to think one of the competitors would send someone to spy on her. For some owners, there was more at stake than money. There was the pride of winning, of being able to brag that you owned the fastest horse in Texas, and if there was anything Texans had plenty of, it was pride.

She wondered how Edward was coming along with Crusader and if anyone in San Antonio realized they ought to be watching him, too. She had only run against him one morning, and though Black Cloud had won easily, Crusader was carrying about eighty extra pounds and Edward hadn't put him into a hard gallop.

A movement in the trees up the hillside caught her eye. It was hard to tell at this distance, but it looked like something large and white was deep in the trees. The hair rose on the back of her neck as she stared at the spot, trying to decide who or what might be up there. Some rocks looked white when the sun was on them at just the right angle, but she was convinced this wasn't a rock. Still, she couldn't see any movement.

She was probably worrying for nothing. She was on Maxwell family land. And everyone in the area was well aware that her brother Luke had been one of the most feared gunfighters in the West before he married two years ago. It would be foolish to imagine he'd lost his skill or his bad temper in that short period of time.

She ought to be thinking about Suzette. Her sister-in-law seemed to be losing strength each day. Ward said there was nothing wrong he could fix; just to watch her carefully and let him know if anything unexpected happened. Eden didn't know what that meant any more than Josie, Hawk, or Zeke. None of them had ever been around a pregnant woman before. Eden wished her mother had been the one to stay, but everyone agreed Eden was the best choice. Except Eden herself. Nobody had asked her.

Out of the corner of her eye, she caught a movement among the trees. This time she was certain someone on a pinto was up in those trees. She tried to remember if Hawk and Zeke had any pinto riding stock, but she'd never paid any attention to their regular horses. She was tempted to put Black Cloud into a canter, even a slow gallop to get home sooner, but she told herself to calm down. It could have been Finn or Brady going back to the ranch. She had never had occasion to do more than exchange a short greeting with either of them, so there was no reason to expect they would come down out of the trees to ride with her. And if it was someone checking on Black Cloud's workout, they wouldn't want to be seen, nor would they pose any danger.

She was still a mile from the house when a horseman suddenly emerged from the trees. She was so startled, she tensed in preparation for a quick escape.

"I was hoping to catch you before you finished working Black Cloud," Edward said. "I like to keep track of my competition."

It took Eden a moment to calm her racing pulse. Edward was riding one of the ranch's horses—a roan, not a pinto. There *was* a mystery rider in the trees.

"Then you'll have to stop disappearing after breakfast."

"I've been riding fence all morning." Edward brought his mount alongside Eden. "I'm on my way to report to Hawk before heading over to help Bret. Someone cut his fences, too. Zeke says we'll be riding fence for the whole family until we catch whoever is doing this."

"Did you see anyone in those trees?" Eden pointed to where she'd last seen the mystery rider.

"No. Why?"

"There was someone on a pinto up there just before you showed up. I thought it might be Brady or Finn."

"Brady's riding a dun today. I didn't see Finn mount up. Did you get a look at the rider?"

"No. I just caught a glimpse of the horse in the trees. I expect it's someone spying on Black Cloud. I told you some people buy horses just for this race. Maybe they're trying to figure out how good the horse has to be."

"Do you think he'll do anything to you or your horse?"

"This is about winning a race, not eliminating the competition."

"Sometimes that's the easiest way to win a race. Certainly easier than trying to buy a faster horse."

Eden had always felt invulnerable on Maxwell family land, but these cut fences had proved their defenses were not impenetrable. Somebody was finding a way in and back out again.

"I'll take a look," Edward said.

Eden waited on the trail while Edward rode up into the trees. She watched as he rode along what appeared to be a rough trail following the ridge. A moment later he vanished.

"Someone's been up there more than once," he said as he rejoined her. "Maybe as many as three or four times. I'll ask Brady and Finn if they ever use that trail, but it would hardly make sense since this one is better."

It looked as if someone had been spying on her from the beginning. She wasn't sure everyone in her family even knew she was helping Suzette and Josie. How would strangers know? She'd never realized until now that being surrounded by family didn't guarantee complete protection. It wasn't a pleasant realization.

"Did you find any signs of trouble?" she asked Edward.

"Not a thing. No signs of other riders, either."

"Do you think it's some kid cutting fences just for fun? There's not a lot for young people to do out here."

"I couldn't say. You know Texas better than I do."

"I have a way to help you learn the lay of the land that's more fun than riding fence all day."

"I don't trust you when you grin like that. Is it going to hurt?"

"Probably. I'm inviting you to a dance. I expect it'll be my feet that will hurt."

"You know I can't dance," Edward protested. "Why would you invite me?"

"Because you'll never learn to dance if you don't try. Besides, you've done nothing but work since you got here. It's time you had a little fun."

"If you think going to a dance will be fun for me, you don't know me very well."

Edward couldn't remember when he'd felt more uncomfortable. He should have stayed as far away from this barn dance as possible. The dance wasn't actually being held in a barn but on some hard ground illuminated by a dozen lanterns suspended from poles that served to mark off the dance area. Crowds of gaily dressed men and women milled about, greeting one another with shouts, embracing each other with an enthusiasm unmatched in Edward's experience, and generally creating an atmosphere that in England would be found only in all-male company gathered at such sporting events as a boxing match or a game of cricket.

"We've got a good crowd," Eden said, clearly delighted by the milling throng. "It's going to be a great dance."

Maybe for a Texan, but for Edward nothing about it was great, normal, or enjoyable. To start with, he wasn't wearing his own clothes. Eden had assumed, correctly as it happened, that he intended to wear the kind of clothes he would have worn in England. After giving him a look that said she had very little appreciation for his intelligence, she'd raided Hawk and Zeke's closets for something suitable. Over the protests of all three men, she'd laid out what she said was a suitable outfit for a young man going to his first country dance. Edward felt more like he was dressed for a Wild West show than a social event.

He was wearing a clean white shirt—she'd personally washed and ironed it for him—along with a dark blue silk vest and a silk bandana to match. Zeke had yelped when she'd raided his possessions, but Josie had told him not to be selfish, that there was no reason Edward shouldn't use them if Zeke wasn't going to the dance. Her husband had given several reasons why his property rights ought to be respected, but Josie had swept them aside. Eden then raided Hawk's closet for a pair of wool pants and a new hat that Hawk hadn't yet had a chance to break in. All that Edward was wearing of his own were his boots and his underwear.

"Is that the music we're supposed to dance to?" Edward asked, pointing with gathering horror at the collection of foreign-looking instruments making very unmusical noises.

"It's the best band around," Eden assured him.

The scraping sound coming from the violin and the

metallic twang being drawn from what looked like a guitar with a round body seemed to refute Eden's statement. If this was indeed the best band around, it was clearly going to be harder to become a Texan than he'd expected. Nobody had told him tone deafness was a requirement.

"What is there to drink?" Edward asked.

"Punch for the ladies, beer for the men. You'll want to have the punch."

"Why would I want to do that?"

"Because you can't dance when you're drunk."

Considering that the dancing was going to be done to the accompaniment of instruments that reminded him more of the squealing of an ungreased wheel or the shrieking of metal against metal, he thought being drunk might be the only way he was going to get through the evening.

The band started playing a song. At least he figured it was *supposed* to be a song because the discordant sounds were coming together in some sort of pattern. He didn't recognize the melody the squawking violin was playing, but it repeated itself so many times before the song mercifully ended, he worried he might have the jingle running through his head for several days to come. The one thing that encouraged him to think the evening might not be so terrible was that nobody danced, nobody appeared to listen to the music, nobody even tapped their feet. They kept right on talking, laughing, and lining up for beer and punch until Edward's spirits began to improve. It didn't hurt that he was starting to get inquiring glances from some of the women. Eden had assured him that friendly kissing was permissible, even encouraged. If the women staring at him were any indication, ogling attractive members of the opposite sex was equally acceptable.

Rather than let him stand around and watch, Eden dragged him into the crowd and began to introduce him. The moment he opened his mouth to acknowledge an introduction, he got startled looks, amused grins, and a few sassy remarks. He finally just nodded.

"I'll get us something to drink," he told Eden.

He didn't like the looks of the punch. A taste confirmed his suspicion. He poured it out on the ground.

"Make that a beer," he said, ignoring the disapproving glance of the woman serving the punch but winning a grin from the guy passing out the beer.

"That stuff will addle your stomach," the guy said. "I don't know how the women stand it."

"It's very good for you," the woman argued. "We combine fruit juices with a little bit of white wine to make it interesting."

The guy made a face that caused Edward to smile, remembering some of the terrible punches English women were forced to drink for the sake of propriety.

By the time he found Eden again, the dancing had begun, but he intended to postpone his humiliation for as long as it would take him to drink his beer. One of the young men he'd been introduced to earlier came over to them.

"May I have this dance?" he asked Eden.

Eden cast a questioning glance at Edward.

"Sure," he said to Eden. "I'll just drink my beer."

As he drank, he observed the dance they were doing. It bore little resemblance to anything Edward had ever done or seen done. He took another big swallow of his beer, realized it was gone, and went for another one. By the time he returned, the dance had ended and Eden was looking for him. "Did you enjoy the dance?" he asked.

"It was okay, but I'd rather dance with you."

"I can't do what you're doing."

"It's called square dancing. It's a lot like country dancing in England."

It didn't look like it to him.

"All you have to do is listen to what the caller says. If you don't know how to do the movement, just watch everybody else."

Apparently Eden had forgotten he'd already been watching everybody else and he still couldn't figure out the movements. "I need to watch some more."

Eden had no trouble finding partners. She had danced with three different men before he'd begun to recognize some of the steps. He'd had three beers and was feeling maybe the dancing wasn't quite as complicated as he'd first thought.

He got as far as *Honor your partner.* After that things went downhill in a hurry. He couldn't even figure out what the announcer was saying in time to do it. Watching the other dancers didn't help. By the time he'd figured out how to do the step, the announcer had shouted something else and they were off on a different movement.

"That wasn't bad for the first time," Eden said as he staggered off to the sidelines. "A couple more dances and you'll have it."

A couple more years, maybe, but his feet were doing nothing recognizable as dancing tonight.

"I'll get you some more punch," he said and hurried off despite her insistence she didn't want anything to drink. Maybe she didn't, but he did.

For the next several dances, he was forced to watch her whirl around the dance floor with a different partner each time. Several women tried to coax Edward into dancing, but he steadfastly refused. He had no desire to endanger his limbs or batter his self-esteem on another square dance, but he didn't mind if the women stayed and talked to him while he watched Eden and her various partners. It irritated him that he couldn't be the one she was smiling at and being held by, but the number of women interested in him proved he could attract attention, too. He was talking to a very attractive young woman when the band unexpectedly launched into a slow dance. He looked up to find Eden, but she had already been claimed by a cowboy he'd never seen before.

"This is a nice slow dance," the young woman said. "Do you think you could handle it?"

Edward had explained he was from England and didn't know anything about Texas dances.

"All you have to do is shift your weight from one foot to the other like you're walking very slowly around the room."

Edward wasn't sure he could handle even that, but he was getting tired of watching Eden dance with nearly every un-attached man in the place—and they all seemed to be unat-tached. "I'll give it a try, but I'm warning you to look out for your toes."

"I'm sure my toes will be quite safe," the woman said with a giggle.

It went a lot better than he expected, even though he spent more time looking at Eden than concentrating on his feet. Slow dances in Texas really were like walking slowly around the dance floor. He couldn't figure out why people bothered with that complicated square dance stuff. You couldn't flirt, you couldn't talk, and you were separated from your partner more often than not. And when you were with your partner, you had to keep your mind on what the archfiend of a dance caller was going to think of next.

He preferred holding a woman in his arms, having her lean against him and rest her head on his shoulder. "I like this kind of dance," he said, wishing he was the one holding Eden in his arms instead of that cowboy. The man was too damned handsome for Edward's comfort. "Why doesn't that fiddle scraper play more of them?"

The woman laughed. "They will as the evening goes by. Folks have a lot of energy when they first get here, but after a while they just want a nice friendly dance with a pretty girl or a handsome guy."

Was that why Eden was dancing so close to that cowboy? He was undoubtedly the best-looking man at the dance. Edward was unprepared to see Eden stand on her tiptoes and kiss the guy on the cheek. He was incensed when the cow-boy laughed and kissed her back.

Edward tore his gaze from the lighthearted couple. "Can

a woman dance with any man she wants to?" he asked his partner.

"Pretty much, unless she's got a steady."

"Do you have a steady?"

The woman lowered her gaze. "Not at the moment."

He paused, looking over at the happy couple. Why couldn't that be him? He felt a sharp stab of jealousy but quickly quelled it. "Are you looking to get friendly with some guy?"

"If the right guy happens along."

More than anything he wanted to wipe the smug look off that cowboy's face and show Eden what she was missing. Jealous that Eden had never kissed him like that, he ratcheted up his resolve, tightened his arm around the woman, pulled her to him, and kissed her on the mouth.

Chapter Fourteen

Things happened quickly after that.

The woman emitted a kind of gasp and pushed Edward away. Then a hand gripped his shoulder, spun him around, and he saw a fist coming at his face. Trained in boxing from the time he was eleven, he had no trouble blocking the punch, but before he could ask the guy what was wrong, several hands shoved him off the dance floor so roughly, he nearly lost his footing.

"He must be drunk," he heard someone say.

"I don't care. That's no reason to push himself on Carrie."

"Who the hell is he?"

"Some English dude trying to pretend he's a cowboy. We ought to teach him Texas cowboys are real particular about the way people handle their women."

Edward recovered his balance and turned to find himself facing a group of angry men. He wanted to explain he'd let his jealousy over Eden get the best of him, but he had the feeling they weren't going to accept that explanation. Besides, he couldn't admit to jealousy in front of Eden. That would be tantamount to admitting he loved her. He heard a movement behind him and turned.

"Are you crazy?" It was Eden. "Were you trying to start a fight?"

"You kissed that cowboy," Edward protested, pointing to the handsome man, who appeared to be curious but not angry, "so . . . I guess I just, well . . ." he stammered.

A dead silence came over the people gathered around.

Then someone laughed. A second person laughed, then a third until the whole group was virtually doubled up with laughter.

"That's her brother, you fool," someone said. "She's allowed to kiss him."

"She's got so many, you can't blame the man for missing a few," someone else said, which brought on another wave of laughter.

"I'm Will Haskins," the man said, introducing himself to Edward and offering his hand. "I take it you're the Englishman I've heard so much about."

Nearly paralyzed from embarrassment, Edward managed to take Will's hand. "Edward Davenport. Sorry to create a disturbance. Now if you'll excuse me, I'd better go. I'd be grateful if you could see Eden home."

Edward plunged off the dance floor and into the shadows that surrounded it. He didn't know where he was going or what he was going to do. It didn't really matter as long as he could get away from those laughing faces. It seemed he didn't know any more about how to behave in Texas than he did in England.

"Wait up."

Edward didn't stop. Eden was the last person he wanted to face just now.

"I'll keep following you, so you might as well stop."

"Why? So you can laugh at me like everybody else?"

"I'd never laugh at you."

He couldn't see Eden's expression, but there was no trace of laughter in her voice. "When I said it was okay to give a woman a friendly kiss, I didn't mean just any woman," Eden said.

"How am I supposed to know when it's okay and when it's not?"

Eden averted her gaze. "Why did you kiss her?"

Edward felt the heat returning. How could he tell Eden how he felt without saying too much or too little?

The answer seemed to dawn on her because she let out a breathy, "Oh . . ." She ducked her head, to hide a smile no doubt. "It would be okay to give *me* a friendly kiss because we came to the dance together." She looked up. "For tonight, at least, people will see us as a couple."

"So I really *do* have to like the woman, she has to be someone special, before I can give her a friendly kiss." They had walked away from the crowd for a little privacy. Eden sat down at one of the tables set up for couples who weren't dancing, but Edward was too agitated to sit.

"Is kissing that important to you?" she asked.

"That's not the point. It's—"

"If you've got to kiss somebody, you can kiss me."

Her words weren't what stopped him in his tracks. It was the look on her face. He couldn't begin to say what it meant, but it made him extremely uneasy. "Won't people think I'm a cad to be kissing two different women only minutes apart?"

"They'll think we had a lover's spat and are making up."

Lover's spat. Why had she used that phrase? They were friends, he liked her and thought she was very attractive, but neither one of them had ever said anything about love, and yet he had thought about it. He did want to kiss her. He'd found it very enjoyable before. What kind of kiss did you give a woman when you were making up from a lover's spat? English couples didn't have lover's spats. It sounded like something that would be beneath their dignity. Thoroughly confused, Edward decided to throw caution to the winds and rely on instinct. He took Eden in his arms and kissed her firmly on the mouth.

He got more than he bargained for. Just the experience of holding Eden in his arms was enough to blow his English cool out of the water. She wasn't stiff or unyielding; she wasn't wrapped in yards of thick material and held together by a corset; she didn't appear to care about her hair or her makeup. Most important of all, she returned his kiss.

He could see why the English had a rule against this kind of kissing.

He'd reached the age of twenty-five without having any idea what was lacking from his life. The English weren't generally a people who went in for much kissing. He decided that was a serious oversight. If every Englishman could experience what he was experiencing right now, there'd be a cultural revolution. It was unfair that Texans got to hold women in their arms while Englishmen were limited to holding hands and an occasional arm around a waist. He'd have to write Patrick and let him know what he was missing. It was his brotherly duty.

Kissing a hand or cheek was a poor second to kissing a woman on the mouth. Lips were a wonderful thing. They were soft, moist, pliable, and they could kiss back, something not even the most magical hand could do. They tasted wonderful, too. It was hard to say exactly how it worked, but they were warm and inviting and Edward decided this was something he could do all night.

Apparently Eden wasn't equally captivated. She broke the kiss and moved out of his embrace. "We should go back to the dance."

Edward wasn't sure his legs were steady enough for anything more than holding him up. He didn't know why this kiss with Eden was so different from before, but this was like a whole new experience. Was he different, or perhaps Eden? Maybe it was a matter of knowing he was free of the duty to marry for money, that he could marry any woman he wanted . . . or even fall in love?

"What?" he asked, because Eden was looking at him as if something were wrong. Did his expression tell what he was thinking, what he was feeling?

"You look upset," Eden said. "I didn't mean you *had* to kiss me. I just thought—"

"I wanted to kiss you." The words were out before he could stop them. Now she was looking a bit uneasy.

"It's usual to save the friendly kiss for the end of the evening when we're saying good night. It's a way to say you had a good time and would like to do it again sometime." She averted her eyes, watched dancers coming off the dance floor. "A kiss at any other time generally means you and the person have developed a special relationship."

"What kind of special relationship?" They needed rules in Texas. *Special relationship* didn't tell him enough. He wanted to know what it meant, exactly what he could and couldn't do.

"That's hard to say. It could mean a lot of things."

No doubt about it. They needed rules. "What kind of things?"

"Well, generally it means you like each other enough that you don't want to go out with anyone else."

"What do you mean, *go out*? Why wouldn't you want to leave the house?"

"Oh, Edward." Eden turned to him with a smile that made him want to kiss her again. "We use the same words, but we might as well be speaking a foreign language."

"Try again." He was afraid she wouldn't explain and would thereby cut him off from any future kisses. "I'm trying to understand. I really want to understand."

"*Going out* just means going places together like this dance, a picnic, to church, even riding. It means you enjoy spending time with a person and you want to be with that person instead of anyone else."

Going out was a strange way to say you'd fixed your interest on a particular woman. It was even more unusual than *being sweet on someone*. If the rest of Americans talked the way Texans did, he wondered how they ever understood each other.

"I enjoy dancing and riding with you more than anyone else. Does that mean we're *going out*?"

"Edward, you don't *know* anyone else."

"I know Carrie, and I know I like kissing you better."

Eden turned the color of a plum. He wasn't sure whether that was good or bad. Daphne had never blushed or showed any emotion at all.

"I think we'd better leave the rest of this discussion for later," Eden said. "The band is playing a slow dance."

"There's no point in going back. I can't dance. Certainly not the way Texans do."

"You danced with Carrie."

"I just walked around the floor. It was nothing like what you and your brother were doing."

"Will is a marvelous dancer. You could be, too, if you would just try."

"I'm not going to embarrass myself again."

"We don't have to go back. We could dance right here."

No trees stood between them and the dance floor, but they were separated from everyone else by the shadows. Feeling less exposed to ridicule, Edward let his desire to hold Eden in his arms overcome his reluctance.

"Once you get comfortable," Eden said, "you'll start dancing without even realizing it."

There was little chance that would ever happen. Two left feet would always be two left feet—but he discovered he could dance. He even began to like it. Dancing gave him a chance to hold Eden in his arms. It looked like a lot more dances were in his future. Now if he could just figure out the protocol for kissing.

"I'll put the horses up," Edward said when they drew near the house.

"I can take care of my own horse."

"You've already proved that, but allow me the chance to play the English gentleman while I can still remember how."

Eden couldn't decide whether she was relieved or disappointed the evening was coming to a close. It had been far more exhausting than she would ever have imagined, the biggest drain of energy being emotional. She had liked Edward almost from the first, but with the expectation he would soon be married and she would never see him again, the attraction hadn't gone any further. When Edward turned up in Texas without a wife and determined to win the race in San Antonio, buy his own ranch, and settle down in America, everything had changed.

It didn't hurt that his new clothes emphasized his body in a way that his old clothes never could. Except for Will, he was the best-looking man at the dance. Carrie hadn't been the only woman giving Edward covert, and overt, glances all evening. Eden was certain several women envied Carrie and would have been delighted to have been in her place when Edward had kissed her.

She wasn't sure what she'd felt was envy, but she was certain it was pique with a bit of jealousy thrown in. Edward had come to the dance with her. No other woman had a right to try to attract his attention or his interest as long as she was within sight. Eden hadn't danced with any man more than twice, and she'd only slow-danced with Will. Every woman there understood that was reserved for somebody special. It had never occurred to her that Edward would attempt to kiss anyone; she'd certainly had no inkling that she would react the way she had.

"This square dance stuff was easier than I thought," Edward said as their horses came to a halt in front of Zeke and Hawk's ranch house. "I didn't think I'd like trying to learn it, but I did. Do you think we could go to the next dance?"

Eden couldn't help smiling. "What changed your mind? All the pretty women smiling at you?"

Edward grinned sheepishly. "You can't always tell why a person's smiling, but I've made up my mind not to let that bother me. If I'm going to learn to be a Texan, I expect there'll be a lot of times when I'm laughed at."

"Zeke and Hawk must think you've got a lot of potential, or they'd never have hired you. It took Finn the better part of six months to convince them he could handle the job."

Edward dismounted and tied his horse to the hitching post. Eden decided that since he wanted to play the English gentleman tonight, she'd let him help her out of the saddle. He cast her a questioning look when she didn't dismount on her own, then burst into a smile when he realized she was waiting for him to help her down.

Eden was used to men who could lift her from the saddle without any apparent effort, but it felt a lot different when Edward did it. Her breath caught in her throat, leaving her a little breathless when he set her on the ground. She turned to walk toward the porch, but his touch on her shoulder caused her to turn back.

"You said the end of the evening was the right time for a friendly kiss," he reminded her. "You said it was a good way to say you enjoyed the evening and would like to do it again."

She couldn't deny her own words, but she could deny that any kiss between them would simply be friendly. There was a lot more between them now. The kiss at the dance had shown her that. "We've already had a kiss tonight."

"Is there a limit? You only get one a night? Or one a week? Is there also a restriction on how long the kiss can last? You'll have to forgive me if I'm asking stupid questions, but the rules keep changing." Sounding more angry than confused, he released her and took a step back. "If you don't want to kiss me, all you have to do is say so. Even spoiled, arrogant English aristocrats don't force themselves on unwilling women."

"It's not that."

"Then what is it? I don't understand."

"Any kiss between us would be more than friendly."

"Is that so bad?"

"It's not bad, but it's not a smart thing to do. It would be very easy to let you kiss me more than once, but that might lead us to imagine there's more between us than just friendly kisses."

"Would that be terribly wrong?"

Her stupid heart was on the verge of becoming involved, and she couldn't allow that. There were many reasons why falling in love would be a mistake, the most important one being she was certain Edward wouldn't stay in Texas. If he won the race, he'd have enough money to go wherever he liked and buy a place of his own. Even if he didn't win, he'd soon decide Texas wasn't the place for him. No, she couldn't allow him to kiss her again.

"You shouldn't be more than friendly with a woman like me," she said to Edward. "I'm bossy, opinionated, determined to do anything I want just because I want to do it, and I don't give a fig for anyone else's opinion. You've got more than enough to worry about, working for Hawk and Zeke and preparing for the race."

"I managed an entire estate from the time I was in my middle teens," Edward replied. "I oversaw the home farms, all the tenant farms, made arrangements for everything that involved the people of Green Moss, established a new breeding program for all our livestock, and still managed to finish my education. Why do you think I can't handle riding fence and training just one horse?"

Why did she keep forgetting Edward had far more life experience than she did? His entire family had respected his talent, with confidence in his ability to manage the many economic elements that supported their lives. Why could she not be equally confident? Because if she did, she might not be able to control her heart.

"It's not that. We're just not right for each other. It wouldn't work."

"In that case, one more kiss won't hurt."

She should have pulled back, pushed him away, but

craven coward that she was, she simply gave in and let him take her in his arms. He made no pretense that this was merely a friendly kiss, that there was nothing behind it other than appreciation for a pleasant evening. His arms closed around her like bonds to hold her captive . . . like an invitation to merge with him. His mouth took hers with hard yet inviting lips that tempted her to join him in celebration.

She couldn't resist.

Her arms closed around him and she rose on tiptoe to meet his kiss, to match him in intensity, in an attempt to wring as much emotional fulfillment as she could from the few seconds she would have in his embrace. She knew it was foolish, even futile, but that only made her cling to him more desperately, made her close her mind to the future and concentrate on these few precious seconds.

What was it about Edward that made him so different from every man who'd held her in his arms, who'd kissed her, who'd tried without success to touch her heart? What was it that, despite their differences in background and culture, despite knowing any future relationship was impossible, made her open her heart to the risk of being hurt? She couldn't answer that question any more than she could explain why his touch, his smile, his mere presence could make even the most boring moments exciting. She wanted him to hold her so long and so tight she would never forget the feeling of his arms around her.

He released her much too soon. She didn't want to let go, to lose the warmth and comfort of his arms, the heat of his body pressed against her, the curling warmth of desire she could feel all the way down to her toes. It was like being torn away from the source of life itself.

"That wasn't too terrible, was it?" He looked and sounded as shaken as she felt.

"It wasn't terrible at all. That's the problem."

She turned and ran inside before he could see her tears.

* * *

Eden didn't like the jockey the moment Edward introduced him to her.

"He's the best one available," Hawk whispered to her so the young man couldn't hear.

"The best jockeys were signed up months ago," Zeke added, "but the boy has a good reputation."

Everybody, including Finn and Brady, had taken time to watch Crusader's first workout with his jockey, but she was more anxious to see how Crusader would do without Edward's weight. Unless one of the other owners bought a horse specifically for this race, Crusader was the biggest obstacle to her winning. The only problem she could see was that he had the high-strung temperament so typical of Thoroughbreds.

Edward had shortened the stirrups because the jockey was about a foot shorter than he was, but the jockey wanted them even shorter. He rode in the style that was becoming increasingly popular in America, standing up and leaning forward in short stirrups. That put the jockey's weight forward over the horse's shoulders where it was easier to carry. Edward gave the jockey a leg up into the saddle and stepped back.

Crusader sidestepped off the trail, then abruptly shied away from a tree. He tossed his head from side to side when the jockey tightened the reins.

"He seems awfully skittish," Hawk observed as Edward walked over to join them.

"He doesn't like strangers," Edward said. "I'm the only one who's ridden him in more than a year."

"If you're going to turn him into a racehorse, he's got to get used to people," Hawk said. "You can't carry your jockey around with you."

"He'll never win anything worthwhile carrying your weight," Zeke said.

"That's the only reason that man is on his back right now," Edward said.

It was beginning to look like Crusader and the jockey had taken a dislike to each other. The jockey was trying to teach the horse to stand still with his head pointed straight down the trail. Since all races used a walk-up start, it was crucial that a horse learn to stand headed in the right direction. Otherwise, he could lose many valuable lengths at the beginning of a race.

"Jog him a little bit," Edward called out to the jockey. "Give him a chance to get used to you."

The jockey let up on the reins, and Crusader took off like a shot.

"Not like that," Edward shouted, but the jockey was already trying to rein Crusader in and the horse was fighting him every step of the way. The boy finally got him stopped, turned around, and headed back to the start of the trail.

"He's got to stop fighting the jockey, or he'll use up too much energy," Hawk said.

Eden knew Edward was fully aware of just how much energy Crusader was using. He rode the horse every day, knew all of his quirks, his strengths, and his shortcomings.

"Try the start again," Edward called to the jockey.

Things went a little better this time. Crusader was still restive, but he only backed up instead of turning around or tossing his head from side to side. He did try to pull the reins from the jockey's hands, but when that failed, he seemed to calm down a bit.

"Walk him forward like you're coming up to the starting line," Edward called.

Crusader moved forward in a straight line but didn't stop until the jockey pulled hard on the reins. Eden winced involuntarily because she knew that had hurt Crusader's mouth and would make him even harder to handle.

"That's enough," Edward called. Eden could hear the

anger in his voice. "Work him a half mile. Start when I drop my arm."

The jockey eased up on the reins. When Crusader calmed down, Edward dropped his hand.

Rising up in the saddle, the jockey let out a loud shout and brought the whip down in a rapid tattoo on Crusader's left hindquarter.

Chapter Fifteen

"Stop!"

Edward's shout was drowned out by the thunder of Crusader's hooves as he raced down the trail at a hard gallop, the jockey bending over his neck and hitting him with the whip at regular intervals. Crusader ran the entire distance fighting the jockey for control.

"There was no reason to hit him like that," Eden said to Hawk. "The jockey doesn't even know what the horse can do yet."

"That's how most jockeys ride, especially when leaving the start in a big race."

"If he does it again, Edward will send him back to San Antonio so fast he won't know how he got there." She would have done the same had anyone punished Black Cloud like that.

They watched as Crusader reached the end of the trail and the jockey fought to turn him around. He came back at a slow gallop. Edward went to meet them. Eden couldn't hear what was said, but she could tell Edward and the jockey were arguing. Edward turned and beckoned to them.

"What does he want?" Eden asked Hawk.

"I think he wants you."

Eden pointed to herself, and Edward nodded.

When Eden reached them, Edward told the jockey to dismount, and took hold of Crusader's bridle to calm the horse. "I want Eden to show you how to ride a horse you've never been on."

"I've ridden in more than a hundred races," the jockey said, outraged.

"I don't care if you've ridden a thousand," Edward snapped, still patting the restless animal. "You don't know how to ride my horse. Maybe your style works on mules. I don't know. I've never tried to ride one. Now get down."

The jockey slid to the ground and stalked off about ten feet. Edward took a few more minutes to soothe Crusader before he turned to Eden. "Let me give you a leg up."

Eden swallowed a protest. She had never ridden Crusader and had no idea if he would respond to her any better than he had the jockey. She wanted to ask Edward a hundred questions, any one of which would defeat the whole purpose of showing the jockey how to ride an unknown mount.

Eden settled in the saddle. The stirrups were a little short for her—she was taller than the jockey—but she decided not to change them. She gathered the reins and patted Crusader on the neck to reassure him. Edward let go of the bridle and stepped back.

"Bring him up to the line and get him to stand still," Edward said to her.

"He doesn't have to stand still," the jockey said, "just stay pointed in the right direction."

Employing everything she knew to calm a restive horse, Eden brought Crusader up to the line Edward had drawn in the sandy soil. The horse tossed his head when he felt the reins tighten. Eden kept a steady but gentle pressure until he finally settled down. Edward moved beside the sullen jockey and raised his hand.

"When I drop my hand, shake the reins at him and give a shout."

Eden didn't remember Edward shouting when they'd raced together. Would Crusader respond to such a loud noise? Would he respond to a woman's voice? She didn't have time

to worry. Edward dropped his hand, and she followed his instructions exactly.

Crusader bounded forward with a speed she'd only associ-
ated with cow ponies. She'd barely gotten her balance when
he was in full stride, pounding down the trail as if he hadn't
run a half mile just minutes ago. Eden was used to fast
horses, but she'd never been on one with such a smooth
stride. It was almost like sitting in a rocking chair as his
hooves glided over the ground underneath her. Crusader
didn't want to stop at the end of the trail, but again gentle,
steady pressure slowed him down enough to turn and begin
to canter back toward Edward.

"That's how it ought to be done," Edward said to the
jockey when he helped Eden dismount. "Do you think you
can do it?"

Eden walked back to rejoin Hawk and Zeke. Together
they watched the jockey remount Crusader. The horse remembered his previous treatment and it took a while to
calm him down, but finally the jockey brought him up to
stand at the starting line. This time the jockey did exactly
what Edward said, and Crusader bounded away as before.

"He's not running as fast for him as he did for you," Hawk
observed.

The jockey was riding hard, not urging as Eden had done.

"He's expecting that whip again," Zeke said.

Eden didn't know if that was the case, but Crusader
fought being pulled up, and he fought coming back to the
starting line.

"I wish Edward hadn't put you in the saddle," Hawk said.
"I'm afraid showing the jockey up has made him your enemy."

A hand on her shoulder woke Eden out of a sound sleep.
She opened her eyes to see Zeke standing next to her bed.

"I hate to wake you, but Suzette has had a really bad
night. Hawk has decided to take her into San Antonio until

she has the baby. He's already sent Brady over to Ward's house to ask him to meet us there."

Eden struggled to get the cobwebs of sleep out of her brain. "What's wrong?"

"Nothing, we hope, but we're not doctors." He laughed. "If she were a horse, we'd know what to do."

"Does she need any help packing?"

"Josie is helping her."

"Then you don't need me getting in the way."

"I'm taking Josie, too. All four of us are going."

Eden sat up in the bed. "Is Josie having trouble?"

"No, but she doesn't want Suzette to be alone."

Eden didn't understand how Suzette could be alone if Hawk was with her, but it was none of her business if Josie wanted to keep Suzette company. For all Eden knew, Josie could be just as worried as Suzette about having her first child.

"You've got to go home," Zeke said.

Eden shook her head to clear the last of the cobwebs away. "Who's going to look after the men?"

"They can look after themselves."

Eden threw back the covers and reached for her robe. "Since when did you know three men who could be in the kitchen without one of them burning down the house?"

"They can cook over a campfire. Hawk and I did it for twenty years."

Eden put her feet in her slippers and stood. "Until he came here, Edward had never even been in a kitchen unless he was visiting one of his tenants. He'd starve before he figured out how to boil water."

Zeke turned to leave the room. "He can eat what Finn and Brady eat."

Deciding she didn't have time to dress properly, Eden buttoned her robe and followed her brother. After making sure neither Josie nor Suzette needed her help, she told her brothers she intended to stay at the ranch until they returned.

"You can't do that." Hawk didn't look at Eden when he spoke but kept his attention on his wife. "Jake won't let you."

"I'm not a child. I can take care of myself."

"You don't have to convince us," Suzette said with her sweet smile, "but I expect your parents will have something to say about that."

"They won't know," Eden said.

"Hawk sent Edward to tell them that we're leaving," Suzette said. "Your father will be here shortly."

Eden didn't intend to be bundled off home like a little girl. Her parents had given her a job to do, one she intended to see through to the end.

Hawk handed Suzette down the steps and helped her mount up. They'd decided traveling by horseback would be more comfortable than bouncing all the way to San Antonio in a wagon. "Whatever you decide is okay with us."

As Eden watched them disappear down the trail—Finn was going along to bring the horses back—she was already cataloging her reasons why it would be best for her to stay at the ranch. She had no intention of telling anyone the most important reason. She hadn't quite admitted it to herself yet.

"You can't stay here," her father said. "Your mother wouldn't hear of it."

"If Mama had been that upset, she'd be here herself."

Anticipating that her father and Edward would be hungry, Eden had prepared a late breakfast for them. Edward flashed a smile of genuine appreciation, but her father had been only slightly interested in food.

"Your mother went to stay with Pete and Anne for a few days. With the twins starting to teeth early, and Mary Anne determined to get her hands on everything within reach, Anne has her hands full."

"Stop trying to make me go home to take care of you," Eden said, pouring her father some more coffee. "Junie Mae can't do enough for you."

"Junie Mae is a fine woman, but she's not you or your mother."

"Then you'll just have to suffer until Mama gets back." Eden sat down with her own cup of coffee. "It'll do you good. You've had it soft for a long time."

Jake spent the next five minutes explaining to his daughter why running a ranch wasn't easy even for a young man, not that Jake would admit to being old.

"If it's such a hardship, why don't *you* come stay with *me?*" Eden suggested. "You could make sure the boys are taking proper care of Hawk and Zeke's horses." Eden was pleased to see the twinkle in Edward's eyes.

"I've known you for a long time, young woman," Jake said with a deep laugh, "and I know when you're trying to get something by me." After a couple of kidding exchanges, Jake turned serious. "You can't stay in this house alone with all this stuff going on at the ranches," Jake said. "We've had more cut fences, more dead cattle, and one of Sean's barns was set on fire. He lost most of his hay for the winter."

"Do you have any idea who's doing this?" Edward asked.

"None," Jake said. "The family lives so close together, practically all the land is Maxwell land for miles around. We can't figure out how the men are getting in and out again. It's a chilling thought to believe several people are involved, but the attacks are too far apart for it to be a single person."

"Do you know why they're doing it?"

"They seem to be trying to annoy us more than anything else. And it is *us* because they've hit nearly every ranch in the family."

Eden remembered thinking that someone had been spying on her earlier but decided not to mention it. She was certain it was the owner of another racehorse.

"I can't have you stay in the house by yourself," Jake said. "Someone could break in while you were asleep."

"Then one of the men could stay here with me. What about you, Edward?"

Edward choked on his food.

"Why did you choose Edward?" Jake asked.

"You know him better than Brady, and Finn won't be back until tomorrow." Eden hoped her father couldn't tell her stomach was turning somersaults, or that she'd dropped her hands into her lap because they were shaking too much to pick up her coffee. "You wouldn't mind, would you?" she asked Edward.

He washed his food down with a swallow of coffee before answering. Eden wondered if he was giving himself time to come up with a graceful way to refuse.

"Where would I sleep?" he asked. "I'd feel uncomfortable sleeping in either Josie or Suzette's beds."

"They wouldn't care," Eden said. "If it really bothers you, I'll sleep in one of their rooms, and you can have mine."

"I don't think that would be much better," Edward said, his voice tight, his gaze fixed on Eden and avoiding Jake.

"Then you could sleep on the couch or use your bedroll," Eden said. "It doesn't matter as long as you are in the house."

Jake looked from one to the other. "Am I missing something here?"

"I'm not the best person for this," Edward said. "I don't know much about Texans yet."

"You don't have to know much," Jake said. "If anybody breaks in, shoot first and ask questions later. If they can't answer, well, they should have knocked first." Jake's gaze focused on Edward. "You're not going to go all funny on me, are you? I know you English are peculiar about the way you treat women, but just use your common sense. If you have any questions, ask Eden. She'll know what to do." Apparently thinking the situation had been resolved, Jake got to his feet. "I'd better be getting back. I don't want Junie Mae having to hold supper. Scott likes to eat with me."

Not having Will to spoil any longer, her parents had

turned all their attention on Junie Mae's son. Scott was such a sweet little boy, it was hard not to make much over him.

"Are you sure you're okay with me staying here?" Edward asked.

"Are you afraid of Eden?" Jake asked. "Because if you've got something in mind, you ought to be."

Eden was stunned to see Edward flush. "I was asking if *you* were worried I might have something in mind."

"Not a bit. You're so tied in knots by your gentlemanly principles, you'd strangle before you laid a finger on her. You also know if you tried anything, there'd be more than a dozen Maxwells ready to cut your heart out."

"Dad!" Eden didn't think Edward had a cowardly bone in his body, but there was no need to threaten him with the entire family.

"Just making sure he knows the score," Jake said. "Now I'll leave you to decide where you sleep. If I were you, I'd take Josie's bed. That woman likes to be comfortable." He patted Eden's shoulder, and left.

If Eden hadn't been so irritated at her father, she'd have been amused by the look on Edward's face.

"Your father has a lot more faith in my *gentlemanly principles* than I do," he said.

"Were you thinking about seducing me?"

"No, but I was thinking about another kiss."

The twinkle was back in Edward's eyes. Eden could feel answering butterflies in her stomach. "Dad wasn't talking about kisses. We like our men to be a little forward. It lets us know they're really interested. And if any man asks my father if he can marry me before he finds out what my feelings are, he won't get the answer he's looking for."

Edward's smile grew broader. "It's a good thing you didn't grow up in England. You'd have been utterly miserable."

"I'd have run away like you did."

That was the wrong thing to say. The wounds were too recent, too deep. She might complain that her life was going nowhere, but Edward must feel his life had nowhere to go. She stood. "Do you want something else to eat?"

"I've had plenty." He stood without any thought of taking his plate to the sink. He might be in Texas, but he still thought like an English gentleman.

"If you see Brady, tell him I'll have supper ready about six," Eden said as she picked up the plates. "If he can't be back by then, I'll save him something."

"What if I can't be back?"

"Then you'll both have a cold supper. I don't intend to be cleaning up in the kitchen at nine or ten o'clock."

"In England I didn't eat dinner until eight. If I went to a ball, we'd have supper after midnight."

Eden poured some warm water from the stove in to the sink with the dirty dishes. "Well, this is Texas, and *supper* comes early. If you aren't in bed long before midnight, you'll never be in the saddle at dawn."

Edward took a last swallow of coffee. "Are you trying to be as tough a boss as Zeke and Hawk?"

"We're all Maxwells. We learned from the same man."

Edward handed her his cup. "I guess this is good practice for running your own ranch."

She didn't want to think of the day her parents would be dead and she'd inherit the Broken Circle, nor did she want to think she would still be unmarried without children of her own. That vague feeling of disorientation, of wandering about without a destination in view, threatened to settle around her, but she shrugged it off. What she couldn't shrug off was the feeling that Edward was stepping back, moving away from her rather than closer. Had his kisses been nothing more than a friendly way of saying he enjoyed her company? They hadn't felt that way, but now that the two of them were alone, it felt like he was putting distance between them.

"I don't know what my future holds, but I don't intend to run a ranch. I'm not even sure I want to be a rancher's wife," she confessed.

"I'd better get going," Edward said, making no comment on her admission. "With Zeke and Hawk gone, there'll be more than enough work for the three of us."

"You are going to come back to sleep in the house, aren't you?" Eden wasn't afraid of being in the house by herself, but it might be her best chance to see if this attraction between them could develop into anything beyond the physical.

"Are you sure you'll be comfortable with me in the house alone with you?"

"Why wouldn't I be?"

"If this were England, you'd be ruined unless I married you the next day."

"Reputations aren't so fragile in America, especially when it's generally conceded that the lady in question can take care of herself. Really, Edward," she said when she saw him hesitating, "you have to remember this isn't England."

"I know that, but—"

"But you don't want to sleep in the house."

"It's not that. I'm just not comfortable."

"Well, this is part of learning to be a Texan. There's lots more discomfort ahead."

His sudden smile was unexpected. Then she realized it wasn't a smile. It just looked like one. It was more of a grimace.

"You're enjoying this, aren't you?" he said.

She was horrified to realize he thought she enjoyed making fun of his discomfort. "Of course not. Maybe I'm doing it wrong, but I'm only trying to help you realize it's easier to be a Texan than you think. You just have to be more natural, to be more yourself."

"To be more myself." He appeared surprised. "That's the first time anyone has asked me to do that. I've always been told I needed to be more like Patrick."

"I liked your brother, but I prefer you just the way you are."

"Really?"

"I thought you knew that."

"I hoped, but I never believed it. Except for Patrick, no-body else ever has."

"I guess that's why I like Patrick. He has good taste."

He paused, looked hard at her as though trying to read her inner thoughts. "You really want me to stay in the house with you?"

"Yes, I really do."

The next pause was even longer. "Okay," he said, and nonchalantly walked out the door.

She turned back to the sink, her mind on Edward rather than her rapidly cooling dishwater. What was the reason for his reluctance? Up until now he'd been more than willing to spend time with her. She didn't understand why he should suddenly get cold feet. If he wanted a chance to kiss her, then staying in the house was the perfect opportunity. She could only assume that although he'd found it compara-tively easy to shed the yoke of duty to his family, he was having a much harder time unlearning the training that had been bred into him since birth.

Eden decided to do everything she could to help him. She liked the English Edward, but she suspected she'd like the Texas version even more. There was only one way to find out.

Her dishwater had gone cold, but she hardly noticed.

Edward couldn't decide whether he was too much of a snob or whether Finn and Brady were complete jerks, but he couldn't like them. Brady was bad enough by himself, but he was even worse when Finn was around. The latter was presently describing, for Brady's envious enjoyment, how he'd spent his night in San Antonio. Since it involved pass-ing so many hours in the arms of three lust-driven women that it would have been impossible for Finn to get any sleep, Edward was inclined to be skeptical. Brady drank in every word, periodically punctuating the recital with exclama-tions of frustrated animal hunger.

"You'd better hurry and wash up," Edward said, impatient to have the recital come to an end. "Eden said dinner, I mean supper, would be ready at six."

Finn turned to Edward and said with what he assumed was an English accent, "Then dinner will just have to wait."

Edward decided it would be better to ignore Finn. The man had never liked him and made no attempt to hide the fact. Since their work kept them apart most of the time, it had been fairly easy for Edward to stay out of his way.

Using the small mirror on the wall next to the bunkhouse door, Edward finished combing his hair, then turned away.

"Who are you trying to look so pretty for tonight?" Finn asked. "I haven't heard tell of any dances."

"I'm trying to *look pretty* because it's common decency to make sure you don't smell like your horse when you come to the table, or look like you've been dragged through a bush backward. Did I say that right? I don't want to appear *too English*."

"He's just kidding you," Brady said to Edward, obviously a little nervous at the antagonism between the two men.

"No, I'm not," Finn nearly snarled. "I hate the limey's guts. He waltzes in here without knowing his ass from his head, and expects everybody to kowtow to him."

"I don't expect to be treated any different from anybody else," Edward said. "But I hope people will withhold judgment until I've had a chance to prove myself."

"You'll never prove yourself as long as you can't handle a rope."

"It's on a long list of things I need to learn. Now, I'm headed to the house. It's almost six."

Finn made some parting remark, but Edward dug his heels so deeply into the rocky soil he wasn't able to hear most of it. He supposed he'd have felt the same as Finn if some American had come to England and expected to be handed a job right away without having any qualifications or previous experience.

"Where are Finn and Brady?" Eden asked when Edward entered the kitchen.

"They're coming." He hoped they were, but the smells enveloping him were so mouthwatering, he didn't care if they never showed up. He couldn't remember any meal in England smelling this good. "What did you cook? It smells wonderful."

"Nothing special," Eden said, a big smile lighting her flushed face. "Just some baked ham, potatoes, beans, fresh peaches, and hot biscuits with butter."

He couldn't decide which aroma was more enticing, the ham or the biscuits, but it didn't matter because he intended to enjoy plenty of both. He wondered why a plain meal on a Texas ranch could seem more appetizing than a banquet table in London. The sudden explosion of a door being thrown open caused him to whirl around, seeking the reason for the unexpected noise.

"Bring on the victuals," Finn shouted as he headed for the chair at the head of the table. "Everything had better be good and hot." With that he yanked the chair out from the table and dropped into it. "What are you waiting for?" he demanded when Eden didn't move. "Get a move on. I don't like to wait."

Chapter Sixteen

Edward had never been one to act without thought. That wasn't consistent with his heritage or his responsibilities. Now, however, those restraints were off, and before he realized it, he'd crossed over to Finn and hauled the man up from the chair by the front of his shirt.

"You'll speak to Eden with respect," he growled, his nose only inches from Finn's, "or you'll cook your own supper." Edward was aware that his size dwarfed Finn—the man's toes barely touched the floor—but he wasn't about to let any errant sense of fair play cause him to back down.

"I didn't hear neither Hawk or Zeke set you up to give orders," Finn growled back. "I've been here longer and I've proved myself. You can't do a damned thing."

"One thing I can do," Edward said, "is fight with my fists. I'll be more than happy to *prove myself* should the need arise."

Edward could understand bad manners—all sorts of men were afflicted with them—but what he couldn't understand was the hatred he saw deep in Finn's eyes. He hadn't done anything to inspire such enmity and couldn't imagine Eden had, either, yet Finn was filled with a bitter anger at something or someone.

"A lot of good that will do the horses," Finn scoffed, too angry to back down. "If anyone should be giving orders, it's me."

"As far as I know," Eden said, interrupting, "neither Hawk nor Zeke felt it was necessary for anyone to give orders. Each of us has our own work. If any orders need to be given, I'm sure my father will be more than capable of giving them."

"But he's not here, is he?" Finn asked in a voice that taunted rather than inquired. "How's he to know what needs to be done?"

"I believe Eden is more than capable of keeping her father abreast of what's going on here."

"*Keeping her father abreast*," Finn repeated in mockery. "My, you sure do talk mighty fine. I can almost see you in a wig and knee breeches, bowing and scraping before some godless whore in silks and satin."

Edward was as shocked by the image Finn had of him as he was by the venom in his voice. "What you think of me isn't at issue here. This is about treating Eden with courtesy and respect. If you can't do that, get your own meals."

The hatred in Finn's eyes didn't abate, but Edward's grip on his shirt had tightened until his feet threatened to leave the floor. "I'm sorry I spoke so roughly," Finn said to Eden. "I didn't get any sleep last night. It was a long ride into San Antonio and back."

Edward didn't know how Finn had the gall to make such a statement after his stories about how he'd spent his night in San Antonio, but he figured it was pointless to press Finn any further. He hoped Hawk and Zeke would consider replacing the man as soon as possible. He might be a top hand, but he was too filled with hate to be trusted. "Eden will take the seat at the head of the table," he said to Finn and Brady. "We'll take our customary seats."

The atmosphere at the table was so strained, Edward would have been willing to forego eating just to escape, but he didn't want to leave the man with Eden. He doubted the ranch hand would attempt to harm her, but he was impatient for Finn to leave the house. It was a relief when Brady pushed his chair back from the table, thanked Eden for supper, and got up to leave.

"I guess I'll be taking my leave as well," Finn said, getting to his feet with exaggerated slowless. "Miss Maxwell, the quality of your cooking is exceeded only by the extent of your beauty." Turning to Edward, he said, "Don't wake me up when you come to bed. Some of us have real work to do."

Edward's hands balled into fists he longed to send smashing into Finn's insincere face, but he forced himself to ignore the man's words. He didn't take a full breath until the kitchen door closed behind Finn.

"Why does he dislike you so much?" Eden asked.

"Because I exist," Edward said. "I don't know whether he thinks your family favors me unfairly or whether he resents that I own a horse like Crusader, but he has disliked me from the beginning." Edward hadn't paid too much attention to that at first. Being an aristocrat had made him the object of disfavor with lots of people, but this was the first time the situation had become so personal.

"I never feel comfortable around him," Eden said as she began to clear the table. "I feel like he disapproves of me."

"Why would he?" Edward had never cleared a table in his life, but it suddenly occurred to him that if he wanted to become a Texan, he probably should learn. It felt strange at first, but Eden didn't blink, just said, "Set the bowls on the counter. I'll put the food away."

"Do you save what we don't eat?"

"Of course. Why wouldn't I?"

He didn't know, but now that he thought of it, no dish ever came to the earl's table a second time. If it wasn't eaten by the family, some of the servants ate it or it was fed to the livestock. Texas ranchers didn't have servants. Nor did they have several farms as well as a whole village to keep them supplied with an endless quantity of food. Learning to be a Texan seemed more challenging every day. The more he learned, the more he realized he didn't know.

"I just never thought about it," Edward said.

Eden laughed without turning back to look at him. "Of course not. You were the heir. The cook might have talked about what to do with leftovers with your stepmother, but she'd never have mentioned it to you."

"I never talked about food."

"Neither does my father. He pays for the food and expects it to appear magically every day."

Watching Eden put away the food and begin to wash the dishes made Edward realize there was a great deal of work involved in preparing meals. He'd attended dozens of banquets and lavish dinners without once giving a thought to the time and effort that went into the preparation of the food or setting the table. It shocked him to realize how little he'd valued the efforts of the men and women who enabled his family to live at leisure and in luxury. Maybe this was the reason Finn disliked him so much. Had he been acting as if he expected everything to be done for him, as if what he wanted was more important than what anyone else wanted?

He'd been so focused on preparing Crusader to win the race, he hadn't paid attention to anything except learning how to do his job. He didn't know how he related to Finn and Brady. Did he think he was better than they were? If so, did it come across in the way he acted toward them? His whole life he'd been taught to believe he was better than anyone who wasn't also an aristocrat, that he was owed courtesy and deference just because he was who he was. But who was he really?

He was a bastard, and that meant practically everybody was better than he was.

"Do you think I'm a snob?"

The question appeared to have caught Eden by surprise. She turned, a questioning expression on her face, her brow creased. "No. Why did you ask? Did Finn say something?"

"I was taught to be . . . arrogant, that I was better than anybody who wasn't in my class."

"I never thought you were a snob." Eden wiped her hands, prepared to give him her full attention. "You never acted like that toward me."

"But we were all of the same class in England."

"I wasn't."

"The earl treated you as an equal. The rest of us just followed suit. Now I've got all the training and experience but not the pedigree."

Eden turned back to her dishes. "No one cares about pedigree in Texas. You are what you make of yourself. Even if you were the earl himself, you'd have to start over here. Now stop worrying and decide where you're going to sleep. Dawn comes mighty early."

She didn't have to tell him. He'd been getting up early for years, but early in England wasn't the same as early in Texas—by about two hours. At least he didn't have to worry about midnight balls or evenings at the opera. All he had to worry about here was a day spent in the saddle and the pleasant ache of a well-used body.

"Would you like some fresh coffee?" Eden asked.

His first response was to say he'd prefer a brandy or a cognac. "Coffee sounds fine. Should I take some to Finn and Brady?"

"I expect they'll make their own. Go on into the front room. I'll be done in a few minutes."

He felt a little guilty leaving before she had finished her work, but he barely knew what he was supposed to do around the ranch when he was on horseback. He had no idea how to handle himself in a kitchen.

It made Eden sad to see Edward caught between two worlds and not feeling he belonged in either. It wrung her heart to see him try so hard to mold himself into his idea of a Texan. Despite the accident of his birth, he was an aristocrat through and through, and that could prove an insurmountable barrier to his staying in Texas. He never spoke of his family, but she knew he missed Patrick. The brothers had been each other's best friend. Edward hadn't been able to make any real friends in Texas. Here Hawk and Zeke were his bosses, Finn and Brady kept their distance, and he barely saw anyone else. He must feel lonely, isolated, cut off from everything he knew and loved.

"Will you race Black Cloud against Crusader tomorrow?" They'd been sitting quietly in comfortable armchairs, each lost in thought, so his question surprised her.

"I thought you didn't want to train him that hard."

"I want to try him with the jockey, to see how he acts in a race."

"The jockey or Crusader?"

"Both."

She thought he was more worried about the jockey. Crusader was an easy horse to ride.

"I'd be glad to ride against Crusader, but don't get angry if I beat him." She'd said that to tease him, but he didn't smile.

"You won't beat him if the jockey can get the best out of him."

Eden didn't argue because she was afraid Edward might be right. Black Cloud was a proven success, but Crusader practically bubbled over with promise. Still, she had every intention of winning that race. After last year's bungled competition, Black Cloud deserved it.

She should probably have asked her father for some of his brandy. Men like Edward weren't accustomed to drinking coffee after dinner. They weren't used to eating Texas-style food either. She was probably lucky he didn't have indigestion.

They fell into another comfortable silence. She liked the quiet, the feeling of companionship that didn't require words. For all of his energy and drive, there was a quiet about Edward that was comforting and reassuring. Maybe it came from his lifetime as an entitled member of the privileged upper class, but Edward was the only man she knew who could relax without losing his sense of power. Even twenty-five years of uninterrupted success hadn't taught her father how to do that. It was something to marvel at . . . and enjoy. Not that every woman wanted a man who would sit across the room from her without saying a word.

Her thoughts startled her. *Did she want this man?* That's what it sounded like, what it felt like, but was she sure? Their whole relationship had been off-center from the beginning. Before she'd ever met him, his family was certain she'd come to England hoping to squeeze something out of the earl. Then there had been the problem of his anticipated engagement to Daphne. And once Eden and Edward had managed to become friends, she'd confronted him with the facts of his birth, and his whole world had fallen apart. Now he was in the last place she'd expected him to be— Texas—trying to become what was virtually impossible—a Texas rancher.

Did she feel responsible for him? In a way. Could that be why she felt this connection to him? Maybe. But she was very much afraid that it had more to do with wanting him. When had that happened? Just now when he'd shown vulnerability, or had it been there all along without her realizing it?

It hardly mattered when it had happened, just that it had. What was important now was what she was going to do about it, and right now she didn't have the foggiest notion.

She reached for her empty coffee cup. "I think I'll go to bed. Can I get you some more coffee?"

Edward, shaken out of his reverie, looked down at his cup half full of cold coffee. "I haven't finished what I have."

"Give me your cup."

"I'll take it."

"Thanks, but I have to wash them and clean out the coffeepot." He wouldn't know how to do either.

"You make me feel so useless."

"Your job is to make sure the bad guys don't get me while I'm asleep. I'm happy to make the coffee in exchange."

"I still don't think I should be alone in the house with you. I wish one of your brothers were here."

"Well, they aren't. As a distant relation, you're the next best choice."

"I don't feel like a relative, not even a distant one, and I don't want you to think of me that way either."

The force behind his words caught Eden by surprise . . . and caused a shiver of excitement to sizzle down her spine. He'd risen from his chair and stepped close to her.

"A relative wouldn't be allowed to kiss you the way I want to kiss you."

Eden put down her coffee cup before she dropped it. Maybe the electricity between them had existed all evening, but if so the voltage had leaped astronomically with that one sentence. His words asked a question that was duplicated by the look in his eyes. Edward wasn't talking about a friendly kiss. His look said *I want you.*

"Kiss me?" She was surprised her voice sounded so weak and tremulous. She'd never been one to be shy around men.

Edward came closer. The expression on his face was one of great solemnity, as though he was about to make a life-changing resolution rather than simply enjoy a good-night kiss.

Before she could consider what that look meant, Edward took her in his arms. She wanted to lose herself in his kiss, to cling to him so closely, hold him so tightly, she could feel part of him. She wanted the kiss to go on and on, for Edward to stay with her until she felt she had finally gotten enough of being held by him, of being kissed by him, of being made to feel vibrantly alive and infinitely desired.

Until she could get used to the feeling she'd finally found where she belonged.

The end of the kiss was gradual, Edward's leave-taking slow. It took a moment before she could begin to loosen her hold on him. It was even longer before she felt she could stand without holding on to him.

"I don't want to go to bed, but I'd better," Edward said in a strained voice.

"We both should," Eden replied with an equally awkward tone. "We have a lot to do tomorrow." Yet at the moment she couldn't think of a single thing, proof her brain had stopped functioning.

"I've decided to take your father's suggestion and sleep in Hawk and Josie's bed."

She didn't want him that far away, but if the way she was feeling right now was any indication of her true feelings, then no place could be far enough for her to feel cut off from him. It didn't make sense, but she felt that even if he went back to England, a part of her would go with him. That thought was like cold terror slicing through to her heart. "I'm not worried. I trust you." She tried to sound casual, but she was certain her voice betrayed her.

Edward stepped back from her. "I think I trust me, too, but I've never been in a house alone with an attractive woman."

She wondered why men thought they were the only ones faced with temptation. Surely he must realize she was as attracted to him as he seemed to be to her? "Should I brace a chair against the door?" She couldn't repress a smile, was relieved when Edward answered with its twin.

"I promised your father I'd keep you safe. I've never gone back on my word yet. I don't intend to start with you."

She wondered if he was referring to her heart? If so, he'd already been caught napping. She needed time alone to sort through her thoughts, to figure out just what her feelings were and how deep they ran. If they were what she thought, she had to find a way to keep Edward from going back to England.

"Then I'd better say good night." She turned and walked quickly to her room. If he had attempted to kiss her a second time, she might not have been able to let him go.

Unable to get comfortable, Edward tossed from one side of the bed to the other, but his discomfort had nothing to do with the bed and everything to do with Eden. She fascinated him, and that fact alone was petrifying. She was nothing like the English women he'd grown up expecting to marry. And although that was good in many ways, it was just as hazardous in others. Even though he hadn't enjoyed the role of heir to an exalted title, now he was a man without a country, without a society he understood and felt comfortable in. He was strongly attracted to Eden and couldn't stop himself from thinking of a relationship that went beyond mere friendship, but the thought of what he had to learn, the changes he had to accommodate before he could consider such a relationship, staggered him. He didn't want to contemplate what Jake would say to the idea of having a former lord as a son-in-law. Jake thought the privileged class was useless, bloodless, and had no positive value to society.

Sighing in frustration, Edward stacked all the pillows behind him and sat up. Through the window he caught a glimpse of the deep blue sky and stars that looked like pinpricks of light shining through a velvet canopy. The unseen moon bathed the landscape with a silvery sheen that made the buildings and trees look like part of a dreamscape, so still and quiet it was hard to believe the scene would burst into motion at the rising of the sun.

Against such a setting, his thinking of a future that included Eden didn't seem impossible. There would be difficulties, but he'd spent his life overcoming difficulties. This was just one more, a big one for sure, but still just one more. But when he tried to picture his future, he came up hard against brutal reality.

When he visualized a house, he saw an English house. When he imagined how they would live, their friends and the things they'd do, he realized he'd Anglicized everything. That included the food they'd eat, even the clothes she'd wear, the way she would speak. He didn't need anyone to tell him such an eventuality was impossible. Eden was in her natural setting. If there was any possibility of a future between them, he would have to be the one to change.

But could he build a future here to offer her? She was the beautiful daughter of a wealthy and powerful rancher. He was certain there were many rich men who'd be only too happy to take her out of Texas and settle her into a home staffed by servants, to give her things he'd never be able to give her. All he had to offer was the possibility that his horse would win enough money to enable him to buy enough land to try to start a ranch.

Try to start a ranch.

What kind of future was that for a woman like Eden? He didn't even know if she would be willing to live on a ranch. She preferred Texas to England, but that didn't mean she preferred the rough life of a rancher's wife to that of the wife of a wealthy man, living in Galveston, New Orleans, or Charleston. Some American millionaires were building spectacular homes that they filled with furnishings rifled from the fabled castles and mansions of Europe. Some of the mansions he'd seen when he arrived in New York made Worlege look shabby by comparison. What could he offer Eden to rival that?

It didn't take any intelligence to know the answer was nothing. When he looked at himself objectively, he wasn't better off than Finn or Brady. If Crusader failed to win the race, there wasn't a chance in hell he could have a future with Eden. He'd be better off if he went further west. That was an easy way to disappear without a trace. It would certainly be easier than staying in Texas and watching her fall in love with someone else.

He tossed aside the extra pillows and lay back down. He refused to feel sorry for himself. He was young, healthy, had a good mind, and a wonderful horse. His future was still ahead of him, but that couldn't keep him from thinking of the past, mostly of Patrick. Did his brother ever wonder what was happening to him, or was he simply too glad to be the heir to care? Did the viscount ever regret what he'd done? Did anyone in England care that he was gone?

Edward had a bad feeling about the workout even before the jockey mounted Crusader. Though they'd worked together several times since that first day, and the jockey had learned how to handle Crusader more effectively, Crusader's dislike of the jockey hadn't abated. He'd been calm and inquisitive while Eden saddled Black Cloud, but the moment he set eyes on the jockey, it was obvious his acceptance didn't extend to that young man.

"He appears eager to race," the jockey said, a rare smile replacing his usual frown. "That's good."

Edward didn't consider it *good* that his jockey couldn't distinguish between eagerness and antipathy. How was the fellow supposed to get the best out of Crusader when he had no understanding of the horse? A chuckle distracted him, and he turned to see Finn sitting on the ridge above the trail, seemingly more interested in seeing the two horses race against each other than he was in doing his work.

"He's not eager," Edward told the jockey. "He's uneasy. He remembers that you've whipped him."

"How can he win the race if he won't be whipped?" the jockey asked.

"You can get more out of him without the whip. You just have to learn how to do it. He likes to run. He likes to win."

"He hasn't so far," the jockey said. "I'm beginning to think I'm on the wrong horse."

"You just do what I say, and you won't have to worry," Edward said.

He contrasted the contentious relationship between him and the jockey, and the jockey and Crusader, with the calm that reigned a few yards away where Brady helped Eden saddle Black Cloud and get her ready for the workout.

Putting aside his worries for the moment, he finished saddling Crusader, checked the girth to make sure it wasn't too tight, then let him trot at the end of a long rope to loosen up his muscles.

"I can warm him up jogging to the start," the jockey said.

"I know, but he likes the long rein. It calms him."

The jockey looked skeptical, while up on the ridge Finn seemed to think the tension below was amusing. Try as he might to think the best of the man, Edward was sure Finn was hoping something would go wrong.

"Take your time letting him settle into stride," Edward told the jockey as Crusader trotted placidly in a circle around them. "I don't care if he's behind Black Cloud the whole way the first time down. Crusader is bred for stamina. He'll catch anything ahead of him in the second half of the race."

The race would be a single two-mile heat. There had been some talk about shortening it to a mile and a half for next year, the distance of some Thoroughbred races in Kentucky and Long Island, but they were for three-year-olds. Crusader was five and Black Cloud was seven.

"American horses are built for speed," the jockey said. "If he gets too far behind, he'll never catch a horse like Black Cloud."

"Just ride him the way I asked."

The jockey didn't say anything when he mounted, and even though Crusader acted up, the young man was calm and relaxed during the warm-up. Some of the tension left Crusader, but Edward knew the horse didn't trust the jockey. He could see it in Crusader's eyes.

"Okay, line up."

Edward raised his arm high as the black mare walked up to the starting line and stood perfectly still. The jockey brought Crusader up at a nervous walk, the horse tossing his head, trying to pull the reins from the jockey's grip. There was no point in waiting until Crusader calmed down. Edward lowered his arm and the horses were off.

Chapter Seventeen

Black Cloud was in the lead after a couple of strides. Crusader was bigger and more powerful, but it took him longer to reach his full stride. By that time Black Cloud was several lengths ahead. Could Crusader win the race if he gave that much distance away at the start?

"He's not going to win any money from the back of the field," Finn said.

Edward had climbed the ridge so he could see the horses as they raced to the end of the trail. He didn't believe Crusader had lost any more ground, but it was impossible to tell at this distance.

"He has plenty of time to catch up," Edward said to Finn.

"Have you ever seen that black mare finish a race?" Finn asked, sounding angry. "She doesn't back up."

"She won't need to. Crusader will catch her."

The turn didn't go well. Black Cloud slowed down, gradually came to a stop, turned in a tight circle, and was off running in a couple of seconds. Crusader fought the jockey's attempts to slow him, actually reared before he turned. By the time he was back into stride, he'd lost about ten lengths.

"You ought to be glad there are no turns in San Antonio," Finn said.

The jockey had changed his strategy from attempting to keep Crusader relaxed and running in his best stride to pumping hard to get him to make up the lost ground.

"Ease up, you fool," Edward muttered under his breath.

"How many times do I have to tell you Crusader responds best to steady encouragement?"

"He's riding like all jockeys do," Finn said. "Once the race is half over, they go to the whip."

Crusader had stopped trying to catch the black mare and was using his energy to fight the jockey, who resorted to the whip. Too disgusted to utter the curses that came to mind, Edward watched helplessly as Crusader fell farther and farther behind. "He's an idiot!" Edward raged as he strode down the hill toward the trial. "A complete moron would have ridden better."

Eden and Black Cloud reached Edward well ahead of Crusader.

"I think Black Cloud is the fastest horse in Texas," Eden said, "but she's not that much better than Crusader." She'd finished more than twenty lengths ahead.

"It was the jockey," Edward said. "Crusader fought him the whole way."

"What are you going to do?"

What could he do? There was no other jockey available. "I'll talk to him again. Maybe if I speak very slowly and use little words, he'll understand."

Eden didn't think that would solve the problem. Edward didn't either. He was even less hopeful about being able to keep the anger and contempt out of his voice.

The first words out of the jockey's mouth when he rode up to Edward were, "You'll never make a racehorse out of this nag."

Edward took a hard hold on his temper and asked more calmly than he'd thought possible, "Why?"

"He doesn't want to race. He doesn't even want to be ridden."

Edward took hold of Crusader's bridle and tried to calm his horse. "Maybe you should follow instructions and see what happens?"

"It wouldn't do any good. He'll never get close enough to

Black Cloud to see her shadow. He's a good-looking nag, though." The jockey slid from the saddle. "You ought to sell him to some dude looking to breed pretty riding horses and get yourself an animal that can actually run."

"He can run," Edward said from between clenched teeth. "I've been on him enough to know."

"I've been on more horses than you've seen in your life," the jockey said. "If I can't get it out of him, it ain't there."

Edward wasn't sure what was the final straw. Maybe it was the jockey's cocky attitude. Maybe it was the little man's colossal ego, which made it impossible for him to realize he had no ability to communicate with this horse. Maybe it was the disgusting way he spat on the ground, but Edward had had more than enough of this pint-sized ball of ignorance.

"You're wrong," he stated with quiet authority. "I've ridden Crusader against Black Cloud, and even with my weight, he was only beaten by two lengths. You know very little about horses and nothing about how to get the best out of Crusader. I don't know how you came by your reputation, but you're lucky that owners haven't realized you're incompetent. I can only assume your mounts have been so terrified of you, they've run as fast as they could to get you off their backs as soon as possible. In any case, you're fired."

The jockey had a lot to say; so much in fact, he stalked behind Edward for several minutes, shouting.

"This has been a very interesting morning," Finn said after the jockey had stormed off. "I can't wait to see what you do for the second act."

Edward stifled a sharp reply. He had to work with Finn. No point in antagonizing him even if Finn seemed determined to drive him to it.

"I'm glad you got rid of that jockey," Eden said when she joined Edward in walking their horses, "but what are you going to do for a rider?"

"Maybe I'll ride Crusader myself."

"He'll never beat Black Cloud carrying your weight."

"He won't beat a milk wagon with that jockey riding him. At least with me in the saddle, he'll give a good account of himself."

"But he won't win, and you need the winning purse."

Seeing his hopes crashing before his eyes made Edward feel desperate. He couldn't go back to England. Neither could he continue to trade on the Maxwells' hospitality, being paid to do a job he was only beginning to understand. If he didn't win, he'd have to find another place to make a life for himself.

"What are you going to do?" Eden asked.

"I don't know."

"Maybe I could ask Drew to ride him for you."

Edward had never met Eden's sharpshooting sister, but he knew it had been years since she'd worked in the Wild West shows. Besides, she had a husband, three daughters, and a ranch to take care of.

"Crusader is my horse, so finding a rider for him is my problem. You and your family have done more than enough for me already. I should never have imposed myself on you."

Eden's expression changed abruptly, and she looked away. "I'm glad you did. I've never forgiven myself for telling you about your birth. I was a fool not to see it would ruin everything instead of helping. I've never stopped being sorry."

Edward put his hand under her chin and lifted her head up until she had to look him in the eye. "It was a terrible shock, but I'm glad you did it. The viscount was miserable knowing he'd maneuvered his only son out of his rightful position in the family. Patrick will make a far better earl than I ever would. As for me, I now have the answers to a lot of things I never understood. It may take a while, but I'll end up being happier not trying to be somebody I'm not."

"But I drove you from your family with nothing but a horse to show for all those years of hard work. And I led you to believe coming to Texas would make up for everything. How can you forgive me for that?"

Edward couldn't hold back a smile. "You never made me think Texas was anything but a good place to start over, a place where not knowing my father's name wouldn't be held against me." He didn't tell Eden he'd come to Texas because of her.

"Has it been?" Eden asked.

"Your brothers gave me a job when I didn't have any real qualifications, and your father has faith I can protect you from whoever is threatening the family. You have done everything you could to help me with Crusader. Now it's time for me to stand or fall on my own."

"But without a jockey—"

"That's for me to worry about," he said, cutting her off. "You have your own horse and your own race strategy to plan."

It was hard to keep his distance from her when she looked up at him as if he were so much more than a novice cowboy trying to figure out how to do a job that was about as far from what he'd expected his life to be like as Texas was from London. If there was the remotest chance his future would include Eden, he had to come up with a jockey who could ride Crusader rather than fight him. He would wait until they went to San Antonio. Maybe some horse would turn up lame, and he could hire the jockey.

"I've got to get Crusader back to the barn," he said. "Your brothers have been very kind to give me time to train him, but I have a job to do."

They fell into step as they walked back toward the ranch. Their talk turned to the mundane topics of daily living, but being with Eden was never mundane to Edward. She was becoming more and more necessary to him, even as he was becoming more and more aware of the distance between their stations in life. Unless he could win the race, it would be too wide to span.

* * *

"What are you going to do with your horse today?" Finn asked Edward as they were finishing up breakfast.

"Train him as usual," Edward replied.

"What's the point when you don't have a jockey?"

Eden didn't know Finn as well as she knew some of the other hands who worked on the Maxwell ranches. For one thing, he'd been hired while she was in England. If Suzette's pregnancy had been without incident, she might never have had occasion to decide she disliked him. Hawk said he was a good hand, but the way Finn treated Edward was more than enough to cause her to dislike him.

"I have until about an hour before the race to find one," Edward told Finn. "I intend to ride him until we get to San Antonio. If I can't find a jockey, I'll ride him myself."

"You'll never win," Finn said.

"Why do you say that?" Eden asked.

"Every jockey in the race will do his best to see he doesn't. It would ruin their reputations if a spindly-legged foreign horse won carrying an amateur as big as Edward."

Eden was aware of the competition between the jockeys as well as the owners, but she'd never thought of them as a threat. "What would they do?"

"Anything they could to make sure Edward didn't win." Finn paused. "No, that wouldn't be good enough. They'd have to make sure he didn't finish the race. They wouldn't want him to beat any of them."

"I've ridden in roughly run races many times," Edward said.

"In England against people like yourself," Eden pointed out.

"Don't think all Englishmen are gentlemen," Edward said. "Some of the most unscrupulous men I know are titled aristocrats."

Eden had asked Edward to wait while she finished putting the breakfast things away so they could go to the barn together. She'd hoped Finn would have gone out to work by now, but he and Brady had stayed to finish extra cups of coffee.

Finn said the extra chill in the weather made him especially appreciative of the warmth of the kitchen. She was of the opinion that he was taking advantage of Hawk and Zeke's absence to go easy on his work. Finn didn't feel he ought to have to go to work before Edward did, but it wasn't her place to say anything. Hawk and Zeke would have more than enough to say when they got back if they believed any of the men had been slacking off.

"Rinse your cups before you leave," she said when she was ready to go.

Finn jumped to his feet and rinsed his cup almost before the words were out of her mouth. "I don't want to miss the show," he said with the toothy grin she disliked.

"What show?"

"Gentleman Edward astride Spindly Legs."

"He's an excellent rider," Eden said, tired of Finn's attempts to provoke Edward. "I rode with him many times in England." Determined to give Finn as little opportunity as possible to reply, Eden hurried from the house.

Some mornings in the Hill Country were particularly invigorating, and this was one of them. The weather had turned cool without being cold, the humidity had dropped, and a welcome breeze came out of the west. The drying leaves rustled on the trees, a promise that in a few weeks the ground would be thick with them. A clear sky forecast a brilliant day and a night full of stars. If it were not too cold, maybe they'd sit on the porch after supper. It was about the only time during the day that she and Edward had to themselves.

She'd always thought the barn Zeke and Hawk had built was a substantial building. It wasn't until she'd seen the stables at Worlege that she realized the barn here had been intended only to keep the horses out of the worst weather, not protect them from the elements altogether. Large openings under the eves provided plenty of fresh air while keeping out wind and rain. Divided by a wide aisle with six stalls on each side, the barn was the largest on Maxwell land. It was intended primarily for mares around foaling time and any horses needing special care or attention.

She was surprised when she didn't see Black Cloud's head sticking out over the stall door. Having spent the first years of her life in the open, the mare was always anxious to leave the barn. Crusader, in contrast, was usually lying down.

"Wake up, sleepyhead," Eden said as she approached Black Cloud's stall. "I can't have you picking up Crusader's lazy habits."

"He's just saving his energy," Edward said, defending his horse.

"It won't do him any good," Eden said. "Black Cloud will—"

She broke off when she saw the mare standing in the back of the stall, her weight resting on three legs, swinging her head slowly from side to side. Eden opened the door and entered the stall. When the mare didn't come to her immediately, she knew something was wrong. She patted the mare on the neck.

"What's wrong, old girl? Are you feeling out of sorts this morning?"

The mare nickered softly but didn't move.

"Don't you dare come down with colic. We've got a race to win." She took hold of Black Cloud's halter, intending to lead the mare from the stall. The mare didn't move, didn't put her weight down on the left foreleg. Eden looked down.

That's when she saw the blood.

Chapter Eighteen

Her gasp brought Edward to Black Cloud's stall at a run. "What's wrong?"

Eden had sunk to her knees on the hard ground, looking at the long gash that ran down the back of Black Cloud's foreleg. The blood had coagulated and become matted with hair and straw.

"She must have cut herself on one of her shoes." Even as she uttered the words, Eden knew that was unlikely. Horses injured themselves running or working, not lying down in their stalls.

"Bring her out of the stall where I have enough light to look at it," Edward said.

Black Cloud wouldn't run in the race—Eden had known that as soon as she saw the blood—but that wasn't important. She just hoped the injury wasn't crippling. She didn't think she could stand to put the mare down. She stood, took hold of the halter, and held her breath when she tugged. She shuddered with relief when Black Cloud followed her out of the stall, favoring her leg only slightly.

Eden led the mare the short distance down the center of the barn through the swinging double doors into the morning sunlight. Edward was right behind her with Finn and Brady only a few steps away. Brady looked staggered, but it was impossible to tell what Finn was feeling. For Eden, fear for her horse was paramount. There would be other horses and other races, but there would never be another Black Cloud.

The moment she brought the mare to a halt, Edward bent down, lifted the injured leg, and looked at it.

Eden watched over his shoulder. "I can't imagine how she did that with one of her shoes. Could it have been a nail?"

Edward looked up, anger in his eyes. "She didn't do this to herself. Somebody cut down the middle of the tendon sheath with a knife. A little more, and you'd have had to put her down."

Nausea nearly overcame Eden. She couldn't imagine why anyone would do such a thing to Black Cloud. Even though her horse was the favorite to win the race, she couldn't convince herself one of the other owners would have hired someone to eliminate the competition. Worst of all, she'd slept soundly in her bed while someone had stolen into the barn and incapacitated her horse. "Can we save her?"

Edward's expression softened. "The injury isn't as bad as it looked at first, but she'll never race again."

"I don't care about that," Eden said, nearly weeping with relief. "I just don't want to lose her."

"You'll have to be very careful with her, but I'm sure she'll live to give you many speedy colts. Maybe one of them will win that race for his mama."

Eden spent the next hour helping Edward clean the wound and bandage it. Finn searched for clues as to who had attacked her horse. She sent Brady to the Broken Circle to tell her father there'd been another attack.

Despite the brightness of the early morning sun, a cool breeze rustled the leaves of a nearby grove of oak, ash, and sycamore trees. A pair of wrens and a warbler fluttered about scratching for food while a field mouse darted among the dry grass, his little cheeks bulging with seeds. Several horses in the corral had pushed their heads through the fence rail, more interested in the possibility of a treat than in the drama surrounding Black Cloud. It seemed incongruous to Eden that anything so terrible could have happened against this pacific backdrop. "I don't understand why we didn't hear anything. Dad says a horse is a perfect watchdog and will let you know when strangers are about."

"Only the ones that keep some of their wild nature," Finn said. "You pen a horse up in a barn, teach it to be handled by anybody who comes into the barn, and before long it accepts the presence of strangers as readily as you or me."

Eden hated to admit that Finn knew more about her horse than she did, but Black Cloud could be ridden by anyone, handled by anyone. She was a perfect racehorse. And that had nearly cost her her life.

"I want you to be on the lookout for anything that seems unusual," Eden said to Edward and Finn once Black Cloud was back in her stall. "I don't know who did this or why, but I saw a man watching me from the ridge several mornings ago. I didn't think much of it because of the race, but this may be part of the attacks that have been happening to nearly all the Maxwell ranches."

Finn adjusted his hat. "I'd better be getting to my work. I don't suppose your father will like finding me sitting around twiddling my thumbs." He looked at Edward. "I expect you'll be here when he comes. You still have to exercise your horse."

"That can wait until tomorrow," Edward said.

"No, it can't," Eden said. "Even one missed day will slow him down."

Finn leered at Edward. "He doesn't have to be as fast now, does he? He just lost his most serious competition."

Hot chagrin burned through Eden when Finn put into words the thought that had flashed into her mind after Edward so expertly diagnosed the injury. Even if he could have left his room without her knowing, he had too much integrity, too much love and respect for horses to do such a thing. "You can't possibly think that Edward—"

Finn's leer deepened. "Of course not. An English gentleman would never sink to anything as low as that. Besides, with him sleeping in the house, I expect he couldn't leave his room without your knowing." Finn paused. "He did stay in his room, didn't he?"

Eden couldn't believe Finn could be suggesting what he *seemed* to be suggesting, but apparently Edward had no doubt.

"You say one word disparaging Eden's reputation, and you won't have to wait for one of her brothers to make you regret it."

"I'd never disparage Miss Maxwell," Finn said. "It's just that you seem to know an awful lot about tendons."

"Edward would never do anything so cruel and underhanded," Eden said.

"A man never knows what he's capable of until he is brought to the point where he believes he has no other choice." Having delivered himself of that thought, Finn turned and left.

"You can't believe that I—"

"Don't be ridiculous," Eden assured Edward. "Finn is just trying to cause trouble." Despite being certain Edward would never attack her horse, she couldn't ignore the fact that Black Cloud's injury provided the perfect solution to his problem. She shook her head, ashamed of her thoughts.

"I'll withdraw from the race," Edward said. "If Finn believes I would injure Black Cloud so I could win, other people will think the same thing. As he pointed out, it's obvious I'm the one who benefits."

"What about all the other owners?"

"They aren't living on the ranch with access to Black Cloud any hour of the day. They aren't so familiar to all the horses that they could walk into the barn with no sound beyond a welcoming nicker. They probably don't know enough about a horse's anatomy to be able to cut into a tendon without severing it. They haven't just lost their jockey and their best chance to win the race."

Another person might have said Edward was building a case against himself, but just looking at Edward's rigidly controlled features was all Eden needed to know he was innocent. Having been brought up in a society where personal honor was more binding than the law, he was practically stiff with mortification that his integrity should be questioned.

"I know you wouldn't hurt Black Cloud. Everyone else will feel the same. Now quit worrying about it and start thinking about finding a jockey for Crusader. With Black Cloud out of the race, I'm certain he can win, but you've got to find a jockey."

"I'll ask around when we get to San Antonio. Maybe one of the other entrants has had to drop out and his jockey will be available."

Eden cast one last look at Black Cloud to make sure she was okay. She was furious that anyone would attack an innocent animal for any reason, but she was relieved the injury would heal. She studied Crusader as Edward led him out of the barn. She loved her mare, but Crusader was a magnificent animal. Greyhoundlike with long slim legs and a red chestnut coat that gleamed like gold in the sunlight, he was a sight to cause any horse lover to catch a breath. If he could win the race and sire colts like himself, Edward might one day have one of the most important horse ranch in Texas. With a last look at Black Cloud, she followed them from the barn.

Eden held Crusader while Edward saddled him. The horse was playful this morning, grabbing at the reins much like a dog biting at a stick. "He's in a good mood this morning."

"He probably knows I fired that jockey. I wouldn't put it past him to have acted up just to get rid of him."

Eden laughed and patted Crusader's neck. He responded by nudging her in the chest. "You make him sound awfully crafty."

"Crusader's first owner was a brutish man who thought the only way to get the best out of an animal was to break his spirit. Crusader fought back so hard, the man used him as a bet in a race. I won and got Crusader along with a nice draft mare for Worlege."

Eden could tell from the awkward silence that followed that the loss of Edward's home and family still hurt. It said a lot for Edward's strength of character that he'd been able to find a direction, develop a plan, and put it into action. Still, there had to be a hole in his heart. She wished there were something she could do to make up for it. But the only thing anybody could do that would mean anything would be to help him win the race.

"He's not going to like having my weight on his back," Edward said as he checked the girth to make sure the straps were tight.

"Let me ride him." The words were out before Eden thought. "He's familiar with me. This way he won't have to adjust to your weight, then adjust again to a new jockey."

Edward turned to her, relief and gratitude in his eyes. "Are you sure?"

"Of course. Now that Black Cloud is out of the race, I'll be pulling for Crusader." And by pulling for Crusader, she was pulling for Edward.

"You have no idea who could have done this or how he got on the ranch without being seen?" Jake asked the three men standing before him.

"We were all asleep," Finn said.

"The horses didn't make a sound," Brady added.

"I couldn't have heard them over your snoring if they had," Finn said.

"We've been over every foot of the ranch without finding anything to tell us who it was or how he got here," Edward said.

Eden had seen her father upset and angry many times, but she'd never seen him look defeated. He strode about the big sitting room of Hawk and Zeke's house like a bear in a cage.

"The bastards are like ghosts," Jake exploded. "It's the same every time. They seem to know the ranches as well as we do, so they get in and out without being caught or leaving a trace. None of the boys can figure out who's doing it or why."

None of the damage had been serious enough to affect the stability of the ranches, but after years of feeling safe, the family was finding this sabotage as frustrating as it was infuriating. It had gotten so bad, Luke was coming back from Arizona ahead of time. No one in the family actually spoke the words, but the feeling was percolating below the surface that the situation might turn into a gun war. Having Luke in Texas was their best insurance that wouldn't happen.

"If you can figure out why it's happening, you'll be halfway to figuring out who's doing it," Edward said.

"I didn't know you were trained as a policeman, too," Finn said, his voice more oily than usual.

"It's common sense," Edward said, visibly struggling with his temper.

"Let us listen and learn," Finn said. "We're lucky to have a master among us."

"Stop acting like a moron," Jake snapped. "If you can't stop baiting Edward, clear off and look for a job someplace outside of Texas."

Eden smothered a smile when Finn subsided abruptly. Jake was the grizzled old bear of the Maxwell clan, but he had lost none of his strength or the sharpness of his claws.

"There's more than one person involved," Jake stated. "The attacks are too far apart and require too much specific knowledge to be pulled off by just one man. I don't know whether it's a group of men working together or several men hired by a single person. I favored the latter theory at first, but now I'm not sure."

"Why?"

"These men know too much to be strangers brought in from the outside."

"Are you saying it's some of our hands?" Eden asked.

"It has to be, even though most of them have been with

us for several years. I've told the boys to pay close attention to every detail. If there's the slightest question about anything, don't let it go until you have an answer."

"We still don't know why they're doing it," Eden said.

"No, and until we do, I don't want you to leave this house."

"I only go outside to ride Crusader."

"I don't want you doing that."

"Why? Nobody's after me."

"They went after your horse."

"I think Black Cloud was injured by one of the other owners in the race."

"All the more reason for you to stay inside."

"They'd only go after Crusader, not me."

"I want you to—"

"Dad, I'm only riding the horse for a few minutes each morning."

"If your father thinks you ought to stay inside," Edward said, "then you—"

"I won't be forced to hide like a prairie dog in its hole because some crank has it out for the family," Eden stated. "I know you're only being protective, Dad, but you can't tell me my mother would have locked herself away in the house until the trouble was over."

Jake's angry scowl turned to a smile as he emitted a rumbling laugh. "Your mother would insist on being in the middle of the fight. She'd have had nothing but scorn for anyone who did otherwise."

"Then you understand why I have to do the same thing."

Jake turned to Edward. "It's up to you to look after her. She's just like her mother, and everybody knows I never could corral that woman."

"Now that that's settled, what do you intend to do?" Eden asked her father.

"Go home and do some thinking. I have a gut feeling this is directed at me. But rather than attack me directly, they're attacking me through my children. I need to think back over the last twenty-five years to see who I might have made so angry they're still carrying a grudge. You two had better get back to your work," he said to Finn and Brady. He turned to Edward when the two men had left. "You make sure nothing happens to Eden. Sleep with your bedroom door open. I don't want a mouse to cross the floor without your knowing."

"Do you really think these attacks are directed at you?" Edward asked.

"I don't know, but if they are, the two most obvious targets are Isabelle and Eden. I can't watch them both, so Eden is your responsibility."

With a smile on his face and his heart filled with optimism, Edward watched Crusader thunder down the trail, his stride long and powerful, with Eden crouched over his withers like a burr caught in his mane. Rid of the jockey he hated, Crusader had responded by running every bit as well as Edward believed. He would have been happier if he still had Black Cloud to measure Crusader's progress against, but he felt confident his horse had improved his time by several seconds in the week Eden had been riding him. Crusader liked Eden. He nickered when she came into the barn and would stand perfectly still during saddling if she talked to him. Most important of all, he responded to her encouragement with bursts of speed that amazed Edward. Only injury or colossal bad luck could keep him from winning.

Once Crusader slowed, Eden turned him and jogged back toward Edward. "That was his best run yet," she said, breathless but brimming with excitement. "He really stretched out that last quarter mile."

Edward looked at the watch in his hand. What he saw there amazed him. "He was nearly a second faster than yesterday. You can get more out of him than I can."

"He's a smart horse," she teased as she patted his sweating

neck. "He probably figures if he's sluggish when you're on him, you'll let me ride him."

Edward felt some of his enthusiasm wane. "I hope he doesn't like you so much he won't run like that for anyone else. He won't have much time to get used to a new jockey."

Eden avoided Edward's gaze as she slid from the saddle. "I don't see any reason why I shouldn't ride Crusader in the race." She looked up, hurried on when she saw Edward was about to object. "There's no point in his having to get used to anyone else."

"That's impossible. Your father will—"

"What if Crusader hates the new jockey? You won't have time to keep trying jockeys until you find one he likes. There might not be any good jockeys available. You said I can get more out of him than you can."

The same thought had occurred to Edward several days ago. He'd tried without success to put it out of his mind. Even if he had been certain he could find a new jockey, he doubted he could find anyone better suited to Crusader than Eden. He offered to take the reins, but Eden shook her head.

"I'll make sure he's thoroughly cooled down before I put him in his stall. It doesn't take two people to walk him out. Besides, you need to get to work."

With trouble at several of the family ranches and everyone needing to spend as much time as possible in the saddle, Eden had started taking care of Crusader. "I promised your father I wouldn't leave the house until you were inside," Edward said.

Everyone in the family had moved as much stock as possible to nearby fields to make supervision easier. But even though every available person was in the saddle from dawn to dusk, they didn't have any better idea who was committing the vandalism or why. The numerous grandchildren, who had previously been free to go from one ranch to another, had been ordered to stay close to home. Isabelle said she doubted anyone would be foolish enough to attack a child, because even a fool had to know that would bring the wrath of every person in five counties down on their heads. Jake said there were lots of people stupid enough to stick their head in a noose and pull the rope.

"I promised your father," Edward told Eden.

"Is that the only reason you're staying?"

The tenor of the conversation had changed so quickly it almost gave Edward whiplash. Trying to avoid saying too much while hoping not to say too little, he said, "I always enjoy being with you. I just feel guilty about not putting in as much time in the saddle as Finn and Brady."

"You don't have to worry about that. Dad says I'm your first priority."

Edward was sure Jake hadn't meant that the way Edward would like it, the way Eden seemed to be implying.

"What are you going to do after you win the race?" Eden asked.

Another jolting change in the conversation. "Buy a ranch and hope to have enough money left to buy a few quality horses." He didn't know if Texans would be as anxious to compete against each other as Englishmen, but he'd already figured out they were as competitive and full of pride as any of his countrymen.

"I have some money if you need a partner." Eden turned from Crusader, looked up at Edward. "You'll need someone to help train your horses. Naturally you'll issue challenges and organize races to showcase your horses. People will pay more for a proven winner. You'll need someone to ride the horses, too, someone who knows how to get the most out of them."

Edward would love to have Eden as a partner, but what he had in mind was much more than a business relationship. He hoped Eden knew his interest in her went beyond mere friendship, but he couldn't say anything, *do* anything, until he had the means to support a wife. "What about your teaching?"

"I wasn't planning to do that forever." She looked away. "Just until I got married."

What responsible, loving, *wealthy* father would allow his daughter to marry a man who couldn't name his father, couldn't claim his mother, and was without financial resources? If she were really in love, Edward had no doubt Eden wouldn't hesitate to marry against her family's wishes, but he couldn't in good conscience put a wedge between Eden and her parents. She had no idea what it was like to be without family, but he did. "Your parents wouldn't like you living very far from them."

"They sent me to school in Pennsylvania. They had to know there was a possibility I would fall in love with someone up there."

"I can't see you living far from your family," Edward said. "You're all so close." He couldn't imagine what it was like to have a family of more than two dozen who'd do anything for you. Some nights the loneliness he suffered was almost enough to make him consider going back to England. Eden was the reason he never considered it for long.

"I wouldn't want to be so far away I couldn't see my parents fairly often, but my husband would be my family."

"Is that why you insisted you could never marry an Englishman?"

"I said I could never marry and *live* in England because I couldn't accept the way women are treated there. I never said I wouldn't marry an Englishman. If I did," she added as a qualification, "I didn't mean one who'd left England."

Edward's heart beat a little faster, but he was so conscious of his inferior position, he'd been careful not to say anything that could be interpreted as an offer of marriage. Now Eden had put the issue squarely on the table between them. The next move was up to him.

"You can't be unaware that I've always had a considerable fondness for you," Edward began, "but I haven't felt I was in a position to say anything."

Eden muttered something under her breath that sounded perilously close to a curse. "Will you stop being such a *gentleman!*" Her voice was so emphatic, Crusader tossed his head. "Sometimes you are so English I want to shake you. In Texas, if you like a girl, you say so. My father had no ranch and no money when he fell in love with my mother. Yet he married her and adopted eleven orphans."

"I do like you," Edward said. "Surely you know that."

"I'd know it a lot better if you showed me."

Edward wasn't so English he couldn't recognize an invitation. He had, however, hoped that when he finally got to kiss Eden the way he wanted, it would be under different circumstances. Not even a cold-blooded Englishman could think having Eden preoccupied with a thousand-pound horse, a couple of flies buzzing around, and the sun beating down on their heads was romantic. And as he thought he might manage it, a drop of perspiration rolled down between his shoulder blades. Still, he had been in Texas long enough never to waste an opportunity when it presented itself. He took Crusader's reins from Eden and tied them to the low-hanging branch of a tree. Then, taking her in his arms, he kissed her.

Experience had shown him kissing Eden in friendship was a great improvement on kissing her hand or cheek, so he expected kissing her with real feeling would be still better. He'd underestimated the difference.

The simple act of having her melt into his arms caused a weakness so profound he trembled. It was no hardship to tighten his arms around her, no penance to pull her closer. It was nearly more than he could stand when she slipped her arms around him, rose up on tiptoes, and returned his kiss with a heat more than sufficient to melt his English reserve.

From somewhere deep inside him emerged a man Edward didn't recognize. A man who, with a growl that sounded primitive, enveloped Eden in a crushing embrace, ravaged her mouth with the savagery of someone on the edge of starvation, staked his claim to her, and defied anyone to challenge him. Caught between two versions of himself, Edward yielded to instinct.

Instinct told him Eden wanted him as much as he wanted her, that she was unafraid to make that known to him, that she—

"I doubt Jake had this in mind when he asked you to protect his daughter."

Chapter Nineteen

The sound of Finn's harsh voice was more startling than a bucket of cold water. It took all of Edward's control to gradually release Eden from his arms rather than fling her from his embrace and guiltily jump away. He struggled to formulate a response that would prevent the situation from turning ugly while letting Finn know that whatever happened between him and Eden was none of his business.

"What are you doing here?" Eden demanded before Edward could get his feelings under control.

"My horse got a stone wedged in his hoof so tight I couldn't get it out. I'm walking him back." The horse, a pinto with black, white, and brown markings, favored his left foreleg.

"Then you'd better get him to the barn," Edward said. "If you don't remove it soon, he'll be worse off."

Finn eyed them with a look Edward could only characterize as malevolent. "I couldn't reconcile it with my conscience to leave Miss Maxwell alone with the likes of you," Finn growled at Edward.

"I'm in no danger from Edward," Eden assured him. "I never have been."

"Nevertheless, Miss, I—"

"What Edward and I choose to do is none of your concern," Eden said. "You needn't worry about my safety. I'm well able to take care of myself."

"No woman is able to take care of herself with a varmint like him around," Finn spat at Edward. "He comes in here thinking his funny talk and fancy horse make him better than the rest of us, pretending to be a gentleman so he can take advantage of unsuspecting females like you."

"He's not taking advantage of me," Eden insisted. "I *wanted* him to kiss me."

"That's exactly what I mean," Finn declared. "He's used his fancy talk and dandified ways to confuse you."

Some instinct warned Edward there was something wrong with this conversation. Despite Finn's words, despite the hate-filled looks he directed toward him, he couldn't shake the feeling that Finn disliked Eden more than him. That made so little sense, he decided it was just another instance of his being unable to understand Texans.

"I haven't done anything of the sort," Edward said to Finn. "I wanted very much to kiss her. If anyone has been bewitched, it's me." He looked down at Eden and was rewarded with a smile. "I have been from the moment I saw her."

"I wonder how her ma and pa will feel about this?"

"My parents like and trust Edward," Eden told Finn. "Now, I have to finish cooling out Crusader, Edward has to get to work, and you have to get that stone out of the pinto's hoof."

For a moment, no one moved. "You go on," Edward said to Finn. "I'll catch up after Eden and I finish talking about Crusader."

"You weren't doing any talking when I showed up," Finn reminded him.

Edward thought it best to make no reply.

"What are you gonna do if that pretty horse of yours doesn't win?" There was so much malice in Finn's voice and expression, Edward wondered if he'd do something to make sure Crusader didn't win.

"He's going to win," Eden said. "He's even better than Black Cloud."

Surprised, Edward looked at Eden.

"I hate to admit it," she said, "but I've ridden them both and Crusader is faster."

"Only because you're riding him," Edward said. "He does things for you he never did for me."

"I wouldn't go congratulating yourselves just yet," Finn snapped. "The race is still a ways off."

Edward wondered what Finn meant by that, but he'd turned and headed toward the barn, the pinto limping along behind him. "I don't trust that man," Edward said to Eden.

"Forget about him. He talks a lot, but he's harmless."

Edward wasn't so sure, but he was more concerned about Eden than he was about Finn. "You promise to stay inside after you finish with Crusader?"

"I'll promise if you hurry back. I'm anxious to pick up where we left off."

Edward felt the same way but doubted it was a good idea. A man could be expected to control himself only so far, and he was feeling perilously close to the edge.

"I want to get a fast workout from him today," Edward said to Eden. "I don't want to concentrate so much on his stamina that I dull his speed."

"No worry about that." Eden gave Crusader a couple of pats on the neck. "He's always quick off the mark." She had become very fond of Crusader. He was beautiful, spirited, easy to handle, responded eagerly when she asked him for more speed, but was equally willing to settle into a slow gallop. She had ridden a lot of horses in her life, but none generated the excitement she felt every time she rode Crusader.

"Yes, he's faster than he ever was for me," Edward said.

"That's because I don't weigh as much."

Crusader might object to the extra weight of Edward's manly build, but Eden didn't. She never tired of watching the play of muscles in his shoulders, feeling the power in his arms when he lifted her effortlessly into the saddle each morning. She'd been used to saddling up and riding out without help from anyone. But Edward believed a gentleman should help a woman mount her horse, so she let him.

The poor man was having enough trouble making the transition to Texas. No point in making it more difficult for him.

"I don't want him to run hard the whole length of the trail," Edward told her. "Push him for a quarter of a mile, then canter the rest of the way. When you turn him around, do the same again."

She coaxed Crusader up to an imaginary line and brought him to a standstill. Edward wanted to practice beginning the race as often as possible. Crusader had learned to stand still while remaining alert, his ears twitching from front to back, eager for the signal to run.

Edward dropped his hand, and Crusader sprang forward at Eden's signal.

Crusader didn't have Black Cloud's quickness off the starting line, but the surge of muscles beneath his gleaming chestnut coat gave Eden a sense of bottomless power. The cool morning breeze, still heavy with moisture from an overnight rain that glistened on blades of grass and dripped from the sodden leaves of gnarled and stunted oaks, brushed her flushed cheeks and whipped Crusader's mane into a flag of flame. The thud of his hoofs on the yielding sand was like a muffled roll of thunder. Tree trunks, overhanging branches, and glimpses of the nearby stream rushed by with ever-increasing rapidity until they formed a seamless kaleidoscope of form and color. Eden didn't want to slow Crusader to a canter after a quarter of a mile, but she respected Edward's knowledge of how to train him to be at his best on the day of the race.

"Time to relax, fella." Eden spoke softly to Crusader as she tugged gently on the reins she held in gloved hands. "You'll get to do it again in a few minutes."

He resisted only a moment before shortening his stride and allowing himself to be reined down to a fast canter. He tossed his head a couple of times and swished his tail from side to side, but these were the only signs that he objected to following her instructions.

"You're the best," she said as they neared the end of the trail and Crusader slowed to a trot. "Do you think you could like Black Cloud enough to father her babies?"

Crusader blew through his nostrils. Eden couldn't tell whether that was a *yes* or a *no.*

"Think about it," she said as she brought him to a stop and turned him until he faced back up the trail. "You could do a lot worse."

Crusader tossed his head and faced down the trail, his gaze seemingly on the spot where Edward stood waiting for them.

"Are you trying to tell me you can't be bothered with anything so frivolous as love when you have racing on your mind?"

The horse seemed much of the same mind as its owner. Though Eden enjoyed Edward's kisses, she wanted more. She wanted to know what was in his mind and heart, to hear the words so she wouldn't be forced to guess. Her feelings for him had developed into something much more than liking, but she had held back from telling him. Such reluctance was untypical of her. She was more likely to be too free with her opinions. Maybe she was holding back because she wanted him to be the first one to put it into words. Maybe she hesitated for fear he didn't feel the same and she would end up with a broken heart. Maybe she—

The jangle of metal caused by Crusader impatiently tossing his head drew Eden's attention from her thoughts. In the distance Edward signaled with a broad sweep of his arm. It was time to finish the workout and get on with the rest of the day. Both of them had a lot to do. She gathered the reins and leaned forward in the saddle. Just as she did, she felt something whiz by her head, followed by the sharp crack of a rifle.

Somebody had shot at her and Crusader.

Chapter Twenty

The sound of a second shot destroyed what was left of the morning quiet. Eden tumbled from the saddle and rolled off the trail onto the creek bank. Birds erupted from the branches overhead, their indignant squawks a protest against the destruction of their sylvan calm. She was relieved to see Crusader rapidly disappearing down the trail.

Hunkering down out of sight, Eden waited, motionless and silent. She had no way of knowing if the rifleman had left or was waiting for another chance. Since two shots had failed to hit such a large and easy target as Crusader, she could only conclude that the shots were meant for her. What mystified her was why anyone would want to shoot her.

Kill her!

Someone had already put Black Cloud out of action. If they were trying to win the race, why hadn't they attacked Crusader rather than her? Edward could find another jockey, so eliminating her wouldn't eliminate Crusader. Besides, she couldn't imagine that anyone wanted to win the race badly enough to kill. Now nothing made sense.

Unwilling to cower in the shadows any longer, Eden raised her hat in the air to see if it would draw fire. She hadn't heard a horse leave, but the sound would have been covered by the noise of Crusader's mad gallop back to the ranch. When nothing happened, she rose up on her hands and knees. Still quiet. Certain the gunman had left, she got to her feet, brushing the leaves from her clothes. She had a few scratches on her legs and was certain the sharp pain in her left hip would mean she would be left with a large purple bruise. She had no idea whether this shooting was part of the attacks on the ranches or something separate, but an attempt on her life meant other members of the family could be in danger. Everybody had to be warned.

The distant sound of a galloping horse growing louder told her Edward was coming to see if she was hurt. Hopeful that the gunman had disappeared and wasn't waiting for her to emerge from the trees, she approached the edge of the trail, using the protection of the broad trunk of an ancient bald cypress. She scanned the ridges beyond the trail but could see no one. She stepped out from behind the tree when Edward brought Crusader to a bone-jarring halt.

"Are you hurt?" Edward practically leapt from the saddle. Once satisfied she wasn't hurt, he took her in his arms. "What happened?"

"I'm not sure," Eden said, glad to be in the comforting circle of his arms. "Someone shot at us twice, but I don't know whether he was shooting at me, Crusader, or just trying to scare us out of the race."

"What civilized person would do such a thing?" Edward exclaimed.

"It's *especially* the civilized person who would do something like that," Eden explained. "A real cowhand has too much respect for a horse to try to hurt one."

"What about hurting you?"

"No Texan would hurt a woman." Eden could tell Edward wasn't convinced, but she'd lived in Texas all her life and had never once felt unsafe around any man, even strangers.

"There's nothing that can protect you from a black-hearted villain who's determined to kill you. We need to get back to the ranch right away."

Eden didn't like the feeling of vulnerability Edward's words conjured up. She'd spent her whole life feeling protected, safe, able to go wherever she wanted without fear of danger.

"I can't put you in the saddle and take a chance on your

being a target," Edward told her as he released her from his embrace. "Walk on the side of Crusader nearest the creek so no one can see you." He crossed around Crusader and started to lead the big horse back toward the stable. Normally the high-spirited animal would have tossed his head and tried to break into a run. But having run a half mile at a hard gallop, Crusader didn't object to walking, though he still tossed his head impatiently from time to time.

"Once I feel sure you're safe, I'll ride over to tell your father what has happened," Edward said to her from the other side of the horse.

"Don't make it any more than it was," Eden implored, "a possible attempt to scare you into withdrawing Crusader from the race."

"I'm not sure that's all there is to it," Edward said. "You can't forget the attacks on the other ranches."

"I don't think they're connected," she insisted. "The shooter is probably the same person who nicked Black Cloud's tendon."

"No matter who the shooter was or why he did it," Edward told her, "I'm taking you back to the ranch and you're staying inside until your father decides what to do."

Eden kicked at the loose sand underfoot in frustration. Once her father heard what had happened, he wouldn't be satisfied until she was under lock and key. "I'm not going to be shut up like a prisoner."

"We'll let your father decide what to do," Edward said. "He knows a lot more about Texas than either one of us."

Eden knew her father was likely to lock her in her bedroom and order every able-bodied man to stay in the saddle around the clock, rifles at the ready. She didn't know how she was going to accomplish it, but she was determined to keep that from happening.

"I won't be locked up."

Eden faced her father, an unbecoming flush in her cheeks

and a tightness about her mouth. Edward wasn't surprised she wanted to take part in discovering who had shot at her. She hadn't hesitated to face down her parents as well as a couple of brothers who used to be well-known gunfighters. Edward found it difficult to believe two such soft-spoken men as Chet and Luke could have been hired gunmen. The contradictions of the West continued to baffle him.

"How can we protect you if you insist upon making yourself a target?"

"All the protection I need is for people to know that Luke is back," Eden reasoned. "Let him ride out with me a couple of times and nobody will come near the ranch."

"It's been a long time since I used a gun in a fight," Luke reminded Eden.

"It's only been two years. Nobody's memory is that short."

Edward wondered if gunfights were anything like duels, which had been outlawed in England for more than a hundred years.

"You've got to be more careful," Eden's mother said. "You could be putting others in danger as well."

"Would you have let Dad lock you up when the rustlers tried to steal his herd?" Eden demanded of her mother.

"You know I wouldn't," Isabelle responded with a guilty laugh. "I wouldn't have spoken to him for a month if he'd tried."

"Then you know how I feel," Eden replied. "I won't let some coward who doesn't have the courage to show his face or state his case make me hide like a scared little girl."

"I'm not asking you to *hide*," Jake said to his daughter, "just take reasonable precautions."

"Which in your mind means not going out of the house."

This family confrontation fascinated Edward. Nothing like it would have happened in England. A daughter would never have spoken to her father as Eden had. She would have silently acquiesced to any decision he made. Had she been foolish enough to object, she would have been bundled off to some remote family estate until she learned to mend her ways. Charlotte would never have publically taken issue with the viscount no matter how much she disagreed with him. And the brothers would have taken their lead from their father.

These Americans operated quite differently. Jake was clearly the head of the Maxwell clan, but he was no despotic ruler and his decisions didn't go unchallenged. What Edward found so hard to believe was the way they worked out a group decision that everyone agreed to follow *even though they might disagree with it.* He couldn't conceive of the viscount letting any member of the family take an action he disagreed with, and then supporting them in it.

"So what do you propose to do?" Jake asked Eden.

"I can't stop training Crusader for the race. If that's what the attack is about, then I want to do everything I can to make sure he wins. I'll leave it up to you and the boys to decide the best way to do that."

Though it could mean the end of his dream, Edward couldn't endanger a whole family just so he could win a race. There would be other races, other chances to win the money he needed to start life over again on his own terms. "I'm going to withdraw Crusader from the race," he said. "There'll be no need for Eden to train him or Luke and Chet to put themselves in danger." He had expected some polite objections before they accepted the easy answer. What he hadn't expected was vociferous objections from everyone present.

"But it would solve the whole problem," he said when he finally managed to get someone to listen to him.

"You don't know that," Eden said. "This could be about Dad, about the family, or about me. We don't know what it's about."

"Withdrawing Crusader would eliminate one possibility," Edward insisted.

"This is a Maxwell problem," Jake said, "not your responsibility, so I won't let you withdraw Crusader." He glanced at his daughter and smiled. "Eden says he's faster than the mare. Since I bred Black Cloud, I'll take it as a personal affront if you let some inferior horse win a race she would have won."

Edward tried to make further objections, but his heart wasn't in it. There would be other races, but none with this much purse money. He could keep working for Zeke and Hawk as a regular cowhand and wait until next year, but his feelings for Eden wouldn't allow him to wait that long. Just as he knew he couldn't wait a whole year before telling her how he felt about her, he knew he couldn't say a word as long as he was penniless. He had too much pride to declare himself to Eden when his entire inheritance consisted of one unproven Thoroughbred.

"Okay, but only if we can work out a plan that insures Eden's safety. I could never forgive myself if she got hurt because of me."

"If she gets hurt, it'll be because of that stubborn streak she inherited from her mother," Jake said.

"Combined with the one she got from you," Isabelle added.

"Is it any wonder she's impossible?" Chet said to Edward.

"Don't try to tell me either you or Luke ever backed away from danger," Eden challenged her brothers. "I'm just following your example."

"God help us," Luke moaned.

"Stop wasting time and come up with a plan," Isabelle said.

"There's no need for a plan that will only expose Eden to danger," Edward said. "I can ride Crusader for his workouts."

"You weigh close to a hundred pounds more than I do," Eden pointed out. "He needs to be trained for speed, not carrying weight."

Once that option was disposed of—Eden didn't bother to listen to his rationale—there weren't a lot of variables to consider. Crusader could only be trained in the open, and the only suitable surface available was the training track at Zeke and Hawk's ranch.

"At least I can warm Crusader up and cool him down after the workout," Edward said, determined Eden wouldn't overrule him this time. "That would cut the time she's vulnerable down to less than half an hour. Fifteen minutes most days."

As expected, Eden objected, but she was forced to give in when everyone sided with Edward. She didn't take it well, but when her father pointed out that putting herself in needless danger also endangered the brothers who were trying to protect her, she begged Luke and Chet not to think she didn't love them.

Chet gave her a hug. "We know you do, but like everybody else in this family, you hate it when you don't get your way."

"So it's decided Chet and I will patrol the hillside along the trail until the workout is finished," Luke said. "After that we'll do anything we think might yield some clue as to what's going on."

"Do what you think is best," Jake said. "You're better at this than I am."

"Are you sure he's not coming down with something?" Chet asked Isabelle, a big grin on his handsome face. "I've never heard him admit *anybody* could do anything better than he could."

"He's so worried about Eden, he's not himself," Isabelle said. "After this is over, he'll have forgotten he ever said it."

Everyone laughed, but Edward could feel the undercurrent of tension that permeated the room. Nobody had liked the attacks when they were limited to cut fences, poisoned cattle, or a burned barn, but all those things could be replaced. The attack on Eden had changed the complexion of the problem. Someone was out for revenge. What else could have prompted an attempted murder?

"I don't know what I could have done to make anyone so mad they'd go after Eden," Jake said.

"I don't know, either," Isabelle said. "You've led a virtually blameless life since you adopted the boys." She ignored Jake's groan. "But anyone harms so much as a hair on the heads of my children or grandchildren, you'd damned well better shoot them in the gut. I want them to suffer as much as possible before they die."

Edward had never known anyone as loving as Isabelle, but there was a steely look in her eyes that warned him she could be a dangerous and implacable enemy. Her shoulders were squared, her spine straight, her body leaning forward from the waist. Energy and determination virtually sparked the air around her. Jake and the boys might be the brawn that had built the Maxwell empire, maybe even the brains, but it was clear Isabelle's was the heart that bound this wildly disparate collection of humanity into a single unit that wouldn't stop to count the cost before coming to the defense of any member who was threatened. The viscount thought marrying for money was the way to protect a family, but money could never have forged such strong bonds, such a sense of duty or self-sacrifice. The Maxwells had no family tradition to uphold, no social position to maintain, no reputation to keep burnished. They had come together by chance, drifted away in search of their individual destinies, come back out of love.

Edward wanted that for himself.

"What do you want me to do?" he asked when the men had finished discussing possible ways of discovering who was behind the attacks and why.

"All three of you can help most by doing your jobs. Zeke and Hawk's property is in as much danger as anyone else's. I'm going to ask the boys to start riding with their guns. It's been nearly twenty years since we had to do that on Maxwell land. I never thought it could come to this again."

After further discussion, it was decided Chet and Luke would spend the rest of the day studying the layout of the ranch to decide how best to protect Eden. It was only a week before everyone would be leaving for San Antonio. They felt sure they could protect her that long.

"It'll be fun telling Eden what to do," Chet said.

"You did that the whole time I was growing up," Eden retaliated.

"But you never listened."

"What makes you think she'll start now?" Luke asked. "She's already talked her way into riding that horse."

"She'll listen," Edward said. "If she insists upon endangering herself, I *will* withdraw Crusader from the race."

"Maybe that's not such a bad idea after all," Jake said. "Then Eden could come home because there'd be no reason to stay at the ranch. I'd feel a lot better if you were where I could watch you."

"You could come stay with us," Eden suggested. "Bring Mama, too."

Isabelle paused a moment before replying. "I think Jake and I should stay at the Broken Circle. It's where the family knows to find us if anything goes wrong. You're a grown woman. You don't need anyone telling you what to do. I'll worry, but I'll still be worrying even when you're married and have a house full of children to look after."

"Two will be enough," Eden said with feeling.

"If you can find a man to put up with you that long," Chet challenged.

Eden glanced in Edward's direction. "Who's to say I haven't already found one?"

Edward could feel himself flush. He was certain everyone in the room suspected how he felt about Eden. He'd have felt better if they'd just come out and talked about it. But no one would speak before he did, and he couldn't until he had enough money to establish himself.

"If there's nothing else to discuss, I'd better get in the saddle," Edward said. "Finn already thinks I'm not doing my share of the work."

"If he's got a problem, tell him to talk to me," Jake said. "On second thought, maybe I'd better speak to him."

"I'd rather take care of my own problems." Edward glanced at Eden. "I'm told that's the Texas way."

"Independence is fine as long as you don't carry it too far," Jake said.

"You're a fine one to talk," Isabelle retorted. "You were trying to round up and brand a whole herd of cattle as well as fight off a bunch of thieves when I met you, and you didn't have a single person to watch your back."

"I knew you and your ragtag band of cutthroats were on the way," Jake teased. "I only had to hold out until you got there."

Isabelle and the boys recounted one incident after another when Jake had acted against advice, and he responded by saying success had proved him right. Even when they argued against his criterion for success, Edward could see the love those brothers had for the man who'd given them a home when everyone else had turned their backs on them.

It could have been that way for him and the viscount, too. He wouldn't have expected money. All he'd ever wanted was to feel that he belonged, that he was wanted. He could remember when he'd thought he had both, and how terrifying it had been to have them gradually withdrawn. He'd torn himself apart looking for the flaw, the failure, the unsuspected act that had turned his father against him. He'd jumped at the opportunity to manage the estate, hoping success would mean the return of his father's favor.

He understood why the viscount felt he had no choice but to allow an imposter to retain the position that rightfully belonged to his own son, but Edward could have dealt with the truth better than the growing lump of anger and dislike that had come close to hatred. Knowing the secret of his birth would have been a shock, but he wouldn't have hesitated to renounce the title in favor of Patrick. He would have been content to stay in the background at Worlege.

No point in thinking about what might have been. Better to concentrate on his chances for a future in Texas. And the best way he could do that was to learn to be an effective ranch hand so he'd have the skills to manage his own place.

"Abusing Dad is their favorite activity," Eden said with a laugh as Chet, Luke and her mother continued the verbal attack on Jake. "They won't stop for at least an hour. You might as well help me fix supper."

That was something else about Texas. Edward was fairly certain no heir to an English earldom had ever been asked to *help fix supper*. What's more, he didn't mind doing it. He laughed. He'd always said he'd make a lousy earl.

"You don't know how glad I am to be out of the house," Eden said to Edward. "There were times during the last week that I thought I'd go crazy if I had to stay inside one minute longer."

Edward had only agreed to go for a walk with Eden because the moon was hidden by clouds, making it virtually impossible for anyone to see a target in the dark. And first he'd checked the woods around the house to make sure no one was hiding there.

It had been a difficult week for everyone. Edward had been forced to use all his powers of persuasion to keep Eden from doing something that would have caused her father and brothers to restrict her moments even more. He'd exercised a charm he didn't know he had to keep her reasonably content with her confinement.

Luke and Chet had appeared every morning. They had refused to let Eden step outside until they'd made a thorough reconnaissance of the trail. Afterward they'd disappear without explaining where they were going. When Eden chastised them for sleeping out rather than staying at any one of a dozen ranches where they'd have been welcome, Chet said sleeping in a soft bed was a poor way to guard against intruders. Luke said snuggling down in his bedroll made him feel young again. Edward figured Luke was no more than thirty-six, too young to feel old.

"I hope Suzette is doing better," Eden said. "I've never heard Hawk so worried."

The one letter from San Antonio had told them only that everyone had arrived safely and Suzette was resting comfortably. In England, Edward would have expected daily bulletins, but apparently Texans didn't bother to write unless something really important happened: birth, death, or the worst tragedy of all—leaving Texas.

"You'll soon be able to judge for yourself," Edward said.

Eden was irritated she wouldn't be allowed to accompany Crusader and Edward to San Antonio, but Jake had refused to let her needlessly expose herself to danger. When Isabelle agreed, she had no choice but to give in. She was to travel under the watchful eye of her father and brothers while Edward followed with Crusader in two easy stages.

"I'll be glad when this is all over," she said. "I love walking at night, but it's much better in the daytime."

Edward wasn't quite so sure. He still hadn't gotten used to the heat in Texas. The night and early morning were the only times he felt he wasn't about to melt. The trees didn't provide much help, either. In England, forests were so thick they blocked out virtually all sunlight. No matter how hot the day—and the days were *never* as hot as they were in Texas—he could count on finding a shady spot by a woodland stream.

Nearly every stream in the Hill Country had dried up now and the rivers were barely running. The forested land was thinly covered by trees. While this allowed grass for grazing, it failed to provide much in the way of relief from the heat. Eden might think Texas was perfect, but Edward could think of a few improvements.

Even now he was able to see through the wide-flung

branches of oaks and maples to the dark clouds that rolled across the sky. Eden said it was a spooky night. She hooked her arm in his and leaned against him.

"You'll have to protect me from ghosts and goblins."

It seemed incongruous to him that this empty land could contain ghosts and goblins. It was too new.

"It's more likely I'll need to protect you from yourself," Edward told her. "Your father says you're foolhardy. He's worried about you, you know."

"Are you worried about me?"

He didn't need the moonlight to be aware she was looking up at him with an expectant gaze. Despite her father's penchant for showing up at any time, Finn's watchful eyes, and the hours Edward spent in the saddle, they'd spent their few hours together acting like lovers. They'd fixed meals together, talked about their hopes for the future, held hands, kissed. When Edward had told her he couldn't make any promises until he had a future to offer, she'd told him her mother had married Jake and talked him into adopting eleven orphans before he had a roof to put over their heads. That had led to their only fight, but it hadn't stopped him from kissing her good night. He might be English, but the Texas sun had heated his blood until it was uncomfortably hot.

Kissing Eden did nothing to cool him down.

"Of course I'm worried about you," he said, knowing that wasn't what she was really asking. "I still feel guilty about asking you to ride Crusader. It's selfish of me to let you continue to put yourself in danger."

"Nothing has happened all week, and the boys haven't found any evidence that anyone has been back. There haven't been any more attacks on the other ranches, either, so maybe it's over."

He hoped it was, but they still hadn't figured out the reason for the attacks. "Even so, it's best to continue being careful."

"You've been careful all your life. Don't you get tired of it sometimes?"

He was glad it was dark enough to cover his smile. She wouldn't understand that he wasn't laughing at her. He wasn't laughing at all, just marveling at the immensity of the gulf that separated their lives. How could he explain that being the heir to an earldom meant that he wasn't so much a person as the representation of an ideal. It wasn't a life he would have chosen for himself, but he'd been born into it, the rules bred into him even before he was old enough to understand what they meant. While her family had used their resources to make sure she had the freedom to be anything she wanted, do what would make her happy, his family had expected him to order his life for their benefit regardless of his personal feelings. In her eyes that was unbelievable. In England, it was expected.

"I'm not being careful. I haven't been since I left my only home with just a horse and little more than pocket change to come to a country and a state where everything is strange and my accent makes half the people think I'm speaking a foreign language. I took a job I know nothing about, and now my whole future is riding on a woman winning a horse-race. For a man like me, that's sheer insanity." If he had hoped to make her laugh, he failed.

"That's not insanity. You left a situation that was about to destroy you and took with you a great deal less than was rightfully yours. You came to people who you knew would help you achieve the independence you want. As for depending on me to ride Crusader, that was a stroke of brilliant luck. I think you're a very smart man."

"Not smart. Desperate."

She stiffened. "Is that why you pretended to like me, because you were desperate?"

Chapter Twenty-one

$\mathcal{E}$den hadn't wanted to ask that question, but no matter how hard she tried to deny it, she couldn't rid herself of the vague fear he was using her to help him get the ranch he wanted.

"I haven't pretended to like you," Edward said. "I really do like you."

Like was such a pitiful word when what she felt for him reached down to her toes and out to her fingertips. She'd been drawn to him from the time she first saw him, muddy and disheveled from his hurried ride to London, but she hadn't expected the attraction to grow to this extent. Maybe she had confused her feeling with sympathy for his situation, with admiration for his efforts to rebuild his life. Maybe her desire to help him had masked the true nature of her feelings. Maybe her college should have offered classes in what to do when you fall in love with the wrong man. She'd had the courage to bring her feelings into the open. His not doing so didn't mean he'd rejected her, but it felt that way.

"I'm talking about more than *like*." She was determined not to talk around the issue. "You can try to hide behind your English reserve, but you can't hide that you feel something stronger when you kiss me, when you hold me in your arms, even when you look at me."

"Eden, I've told you—"

"And *I've* told *you* I don't care whether you're rich or haven't a dollar to your name. The only thing that counts is what we feel for each other. As long as we have that, we can figure out everything else."

She couldn't understand what was holding him back. Any red-blooded Texan would have been declaring his undying devotion ten minutes ago, not standing here like a fence post trying to figure out how to say he loved her without *saying* he loved her. Was she crazy to fall in love with a man who was so tied in knots he couldn't admit to his own feelings, who had so many conflicting emotions from the last twenty-five years that he might never work through all of them? Probably, but the damage was done.

She wondered if there was something wrong with her, something no one in her family could see but every man noticed immediately. Was she too independent to be lovable? She knew she would be heartbroken if Edward returned to England. She could see her whole life looming before her, always the maiden aunt, the spinster schoolteacher, taking care of others with no one to fill her lonely nights.

"Eden, I've tried to explain—"

"And I've tried to make you understand, I don't care. What we feel for each other should have nothing to do with money or social class."

"It's not that."

"I know." Eden pulled away from him. "It's your pride. You couldn't marry Daphne for her money, so naturally you can't marry me for mine."

Edward took her by the shoulders, turned her to face him even though it was nearly impossible to see in the dark. "It has nothing to do with money."

"Can you honestly tell me you'd feel the same way if you had a ranch and all the money you needed to run it?" she demanded.

"That would be different."

She shrugged out of his grasp. "No, it wouldn't. You're just using money as an excuse. If you really loved me, nothing could stop you from marrying me." A stifled sob came out sounding like a hiccup. He *didn't* really love her. Her future looked more bleak and lonely than ever. If she had to fall desperately in love, why did it have to be with a man who was incapable of emotion, who'd been taught that emotions were dangerous and unreliable? "I promise to ride your horse so you can win your money. Then you can stop pretending feelings you don't have. You probably think I'm just another crazy American from Texas, but I'd take a Texan any day over an Englishman who's as cold as an icicle."

She was running before the last words were out of her mouth. She ignored his pleas to stop, shook off the hand that tried to restrain her. She had to get to the house, to her room. She had to be alone. She would not break down in front of him. She stumbled up steps she couldn't see, through rooms she barely noticed, until she reached the safety of her bedroom. Barely pausing long enough to lock the door behind her, she threw herself on the bed and gave vent to the sobs locked in her chest. She heard Edward pound on the door, call her name, beg her to unlock the door, but she didn't move. She didn't want to see him, to talk to him, to—

A splintering sound brought her up from the bed, her sobs choked off by shock and surprise. She didn't need a light to know the shadowy figure in the doorway was Edward. What she didn't know was what had transformed this cool-blooded English aristocrat into a man angry enough to break through a locked door. Hawk was going to kill him.

"I never pretended to like you," he said in a voice nearly choked by emotion. "It's been all I could do to keep from telling you that *like* doesn't even begin to touch on what I feel for you. When I first met you, you scared me as much as you fascinated me. Then before I could figure out what I did feel, you told me about my birth. I thought I could never forgive you, but when I followed you to Texas, I knew I was only fooling myself. There were other choices I could have made, but all I could think about was you and the promise of the kind of life I could have in Texas. I've *never* been guilty of pretending more than I feel, only of pretending to feel so much less."

He stood there like an exhausted colossus, his shoulders bowed, wrung out by emotions so strong it caused his body to tremble. Feeling a sudden and overwhelming need to see him, Eden lit the lamp on the table next to her bed. The pale yellow flame filled the room with just enough light to allow Eden to see Edward's tortured expression. Knowing how much exposing himself emotionally meant to such a man, her resentment melted and she hoped anew that he was as deeply in love with her as she was with him.

"Come here," she said. "It's okay," she assured him when he didn't move. It seemed ironic she should be the one to say that, but Edward had been hedged in by inflexible rules for so long, he hadn't yet learned to act on his feelings. She had to know what was right for both of them.

He approached the bed slowly, reluctantly. "I shouldn't be in here."

"Why?" She was going to make him answer that question, commit himself to some small extent.

"It's not proper for a man—"

"I don't want to know what other people have told you, especially if it's anything the viscount said. I want to know why *you* think you shouldn't be here."

He didn't move as his gaze traveled from her face down her body and back again. "I shouldn't be here because my thoughts aren't respectful."

Eden struggled not to laugh. "Do you think I'm attractive?"

"You know I do."

"Does kissing me and holding me make you want to make love to me?" Everything rested on his response. Either she would return home knowing she would probably always remain alone—an aunt, never a wife and mother—or he would offer her a love that would last for the rest of their lives. She doubted anyone in her family would approve of her putting that question to Edward, but he was too slow getting around to it for her. She wanted to know . . . no, she *needed* to know.

Edward swallowed convulsively, took an uncertain step forward, then stopped. "How would a Texan answer that question?" he asked.

"Honestly."

"I've always been taught it's disrespectful to look upon a lady with lust in one's eyes."

She longed for him to feel love, not lust. "I can't think of a greater compliment than to be told you're so much in love with me you practically have to sit on your hands to keep from making love to me."

"That's how I feel," Edward said in a strangled voice. "Sometimes it grabs me so hard, I can hardly breathe."

"Why didn't you tell me?" That was a useless question. She knew the answer. All his life he'd had it drummed into his head that his own wants were of no importance unless they served the good of his family. He'd lost his father's love for no reason he could discern other than his own failure to live up to the viscount's expectations. It was a lesson he'd never forgotten. He couldn't allow himself to want anything because it would hurt too much when he lost it. "I love you," Eden said. "I think you love me, but you've never said it. Would it hurt so much to say it just once?"

"I can't—"

Frustration consumed her and she balled her fists, wishing she could escape the feelings that threatened to wash over her. "If you tell me one more time you can't say you love me because you don't have any money, I'm going to . . . I don't know what I'll do, but I'll think of something."

She had no idea what response she expected—she knew what she hoped he'd do—but she hadn't expected him to laugh and look so dazzlingly handsome she wanted to forgive him everything.

Edward walked over to the bed, sank down on it, and

took her hands in his. "I've never felt anything in my life like what I feel for you. I don't know if it's love or insanity, but I can't think of anybody but you."

"Mama says you have to be insane to fall in love with a man. She says no woman in her right mind would do anything that stupid otherwise."

"But your mother loves your father."

"Passionately, but she swears falling in love with him was the craziest thing she ever did."

"And you're your mother's daughter."

"My dad's, too. He said he was just as crazy to fall in love with Mama."

"Well, if two people I admire so much can do it, I suppose I could, too."

"What about me?" she said, firing up. "I'm in love with you."

"I don't admire you." Before she could plant her fist in the middle of his handsome face, he added, "I adore you. You're the most incredible woman I've ever known. I don't know why a thousand men haven't moved heaven and earth to marry you."

When she had a few moments to spare, she'd have to teach him not to wind her up before he said something nice. It was making her dizzy. "A few have tried, but I was waiting for just the right man. It never occurred to me I'd have to go to England to find him."

"Or to me that I'd follow you to Texas."

"Why did you?" Eden asked.

"Didn't you expect me to?"

"You were so angry at me, I thought I'd never see you again."

He leaned back a little. "It's hard to say what I felt when you told me. When I was little, the viscount was so proud of how well I could ride, he bought me a horse for my sixth birthday. The earl thought I was too young to have a horse, but the viscount said I could handle any horse in the stables. I couldn't understand it when things started to change.

I thought it was my fault. Ultimately I decided love didn't last, that one day it just wore out and there wasn't anything left. When you told me about my birth, the only life I knew came to an end, too."

"That didn't mean you had to come to Texas. There must have been lots of places you could have found work in England."

"Not without exposing my past. For twenty-five years I was in line to inherit an earldom. Anybody who could give me the only kind of job I knew, would recognize me. If I managed to find one who didn't, he'd demand references." He smiled as he let his gaze rest on Eden. "Besides, I'd been enticed by the kind of freedom you said I would have in Texas."

"You make it sound like I was offering you political refuge." She was shocked at the trace of petulance in her voice. She'd never been one to expect men to offer her extravagant compliments, but she was honest enough to admit she wanted Edward to have come to Texas because of her. Personal freedom was just an added bonus.

"Do you want me to say I would have followed you anywhere?"

She was appalled he could read her mind so easily.

"I would have. You captivated me that first evening when you advised me against causing dinner to be late. You completed the conquest the next morning when you caught that runaway horse."

"Is that how you see me, a pushy woman who can ride?" Never had her character traits looked so unattractive.

"I thought you had a mind of your own, the strength of character to use it, and the courage to ignore anyone who didn't agree with you."

She'd long struggled with the fact that men didn't seem to be attracted to her for very long, that she was lonely and life was passing her by. She'd never understood why until now. She was a bossy virago, the kind of woman wise men avoided no matter how wealthy or attractive. She didn't want to be that woman. She had thought she was loving, generous, and kind, but she'd been seeing herself through the eyes of her family. She pulled away from him. "I'm surprised I didn't send you rushing to fall at Daphne's feet, begging her to marry you."

Edward recaptured her hands, brought them to his lips, and covered them with kisses. "I thought you were magnificent. I'd given up on finding a woman who could share my life rather than be another dependent in it."

Eden's heart skipped a beat. Edward had never said anything about wanting to share his life with her. She hoped that meant he loved her and wished to marry her, but maybe the reason he hadn't said anything was that he wanted a woman *like* Eden to share his life, not Eden herself. If he'd been that much in love with her, he'd had plenty of opportunity to say so. She didn't know why someone hadn't questioned Edward's parentage years ago. His powerful chest, shoulders, and forearms had nothing in common with the slim, elegant torso of the viscount. Everything about Edward spoke of physical strength, abundant energy, the kind of sexual aura that must have made him seem out of place in a staid drawing room. She was certain many a female had been forced to use her fan quite energetically to prevent a telltale blush from flaming her cheeks at the sight of him.

"It won't be hard to find such a woman," she said. "I know a dozen who'd jump at the chance to marry you. And all of them can ride as well as I can."

Edward put his hand under her chin and raised her head until he could look into her eyes. "I'm not interested in a dozen women. I'm only interested in you."

She'd always considered herself a sensible, rational woman. Right now she didn't feel she was either. Her thoughts were in chaos, and reason had utterly vanished, leaving her prey to a confusing mixture of hope and fear—

hope that he meant what he said, fear she would fail to live up to his expectations. She'd never really cared what people thought of her, so why should one man's opinion throw her into a virtual panic? Especially when that man was an English expatriate with whom she had hardly a dozen thoughts in common. "You never said anything."

"That's because I've got nothing to offer you."

"Will you stop thinking like an Englishman?"

"That's what I am."

"You're a Texan now, and Texas women don't want titles, country estates, or fancy houses in town. All we expect from a man is his undivided love."

"You've got that already."

He pulled her to him and she melted willingly into his embrace. They'd kissed many times, but this time was better because it was far more than a pleasurable exercise between a man and a woman who cared for each other. This time they were acknowledging the love between them, saying that each had found in the other the perfect realization of what they'd been looking for in a partner. It was also the most erotic experience Eden had ever had.

Though she had been kissed by several men in the past, they'd never been more than friendly kisses. There had been no passion, no feeling of being connected, no promise of more in the future. She and Edward had kissed several times, but those kisses had had a kind of innocence, an element of playfulness. Both had been holding back, unwilling or afraid to commit themselves. Now that they had admitted their love to each other, there was no need to hold back.

Any idea that Edward's rigidly formal upbringing had resulted in a lack of sexual experience was quickly routed. The things he could do with his lips and tongue were a revelation. Texas men were more straightforward and aggressive, had a greater sense of entitlement, but Edward knew better what to do with that permission once he got it. Texans were long on energy and stamina. They tended to hit you hard and try to wear you down. Edward's kisses were so inviting, so seductive, she couldn't wait to follow where he would lead.

Rather than merely kissing her lips, he seemed to be feasting on them. He didn't press his lips to hers in one long, passionate embrace. Instead he kissed her a dozen times, tiny touches on her lips, the sides of her mouth. He took her lower lip between his teeth and gently bit it until she couldn't stand it any longer. She tried to capture him, to hold him to her, but he was too strong. When he began to scatter kisses on her eyelids, the sides of her neck, the lobes of her ears, she surrendered, gave herself up to him.

Eden had always believed a woman ought to be an equal partner in everything, but she found it was more enjoyable to let Edward lead the way. She didn't resist when he gently laid her down on the bed. She didn't resist when his kisses on her neck and ears turned her bones to jelly. She didn't resist when the feel of his warm breath on her skin gave her goose bumps. She didn't *want* to resist when his whispered *I love you* made her heart sing with joy.

He didn't resist when she pulled him down to lie next to her. He didn't resist when she kissed him with more passion, more intensity, more love than she thought her body could contain. He didn't resist when she whispered *I love you* back to him. Exhausted by the outpouring of passion, she fell away from him.

"Where did you learn to kiss like that?" she asked. "It certainly wasn't from Daphne."

"Not every English woman is like Daphne." He pinched her cheek. "Some are just as brazen as you."

"I'm not brazen," Eden protested. "I'm just not afraid to let a man know I like him."

"I prefer to think of you as brazen," Edward teased. "It makes you forbidden, and everything is sweeter for being out of bounds."

Eden couldn't stop a laugh. "And I thought you were a repressed Englishman."

"I was," Edward said, giving her a squeeze, "but I didn't want to be. You gave me my freedom, so you deserve a reward."

She leaned on her elbow so she could look into his eyes. "What reward did you have in mind?"

"To kiss you so thoroughly you'll become my slave for life."

"That would be your reward," she said with a chuckle. "What's mine?"

He flashed the grin that inevitably caused her to feel weak in the knees and her muscles to ache pleasurably. "Your reward is to love being my slave."

"That's going to take a mighty lot of convincing. I don't think you're up to it."

The English liked a challenge, and Edward was English through and through. Eden wasn't about to become any man's slave, but she had no objection to letting Edward try to convince her otherwise.

He renewed his assault on her sensibilities with a single-mindedness that would have made her smile if it had not been so intoxicating. She fought against the desire to give in completely, but she was losing ground. No one had ever kissed her with such abandon. She hadn't wanted anyone to, but she couldn't get enough of Edward's kisses. He couldn't hold her tight enough. She luxuriated in his strength, in the feeling of being securely wrapped in the safety of his arms. The heat from his body flowed into hers until she was sure she would melt, until she thought she could stay there forever.

She wrapped her arms around him, amazed she was unable to completely encircle his chest. She pressed against him, allowed him to hold her tight, until she felt their bodies begin to meld. She couldn't get enough of being close to him. She'd often wondered if she'd ever meet a man she could love the way her mother loved her father. She'd wondered if she'd be able to find happiness in Texas or if she'd have to look somewhere else. Now she had the answer to both questions, and the answer to each was the same.

Edward.

She'd follow him wherever he went, but she was convinced he'd been happier here in Texas than in England. She had to find a way to convince him to stay. She'd decide later whether the best way to do that would be to win or lose the race, but right now all she could think about was keeping him in her arms. Nothing had ever felt quite so good.

Edward cupped her face in his hands. "You're so beautiful," he murmured. "I can't imagine why you'd be interested in someone like me."

"Call it my good deed for the month," she said, smiling up at the face that had become an integral part of her thoughts, waking and dreaming.

Edward held her so tightly she could hardly breathe, but she didn't care. She felt that she'd waited all her life to find him. Now that she had, she wanted to make up for lost time. She wanted to experience the love her parents had found, that her siblings had found, and she wanted it now. She didn't object when Edward's hands moved from her face to her shoulders, then down her arms. Her whole body tingled with excitement, with anticipation, with longing for what she could envision only imperfectly, for what she believed to be the ultimate expression of love between two people. She moved closer, a mute invitation for him to do with her as he would.

Edward continued to cover her with kisses while his hands moved over her arms and sides. When she caressed his chest, he responded first with a groan of pleasure, then with a firmer grip on her shoulders as he placed kisses on both sides of her neck. She had never imagined how sensitive her neck could be. She felt herself melting under his assault, gradually losing any desire to retain command over her body or control over what Edward might do to it.

She didn't mean to, but she gasped when Edward's hands

unexpectedly covered her breasts. Before she could explain, he had released her and virtually flung himself from the bed. He gaped at her, apparently horrified by what he'd done. Words of apology poured from his lips, but Eden heard none of them. She only saw the look on his face, a look compounded by self-loathing and fear that he'd lost whatever love she felt for him. She reached out to him, but he backed away.

"I shouldn't have followed you in here," he said, "but I was afraid you were so angry you wanted nothing more to do with me."

When he didn't come to her, she sat up, patting the spot on the bed next to her. "I'm not angry. I'll only be upset if you keep backing away from me."

"If you had any idea what it feels like to kiss you, to hold you in my arms, you wouldn't say that. You're enough to drive a man crazy. I thought I was strong, but I'm not sure I can be responsible for myself."

She patted the bed again. "I can be responsible for both of us."

"If I come near you right now, I won't be able to stop at kissing you or holding you in my arms."

"I don't want you to stop. I want you to make love to me."

Chapter Twenty-two

$\mathcal{I}$t was impossible to gauge the exact effect her words had on Edward. He appeared in turn stunned, amazed, relieved, eager, yet all the while struggling to retain control over himself.

"Do you love me?" Edward asked.

"Yes, with all my heart."

"Do you understand what that would mean?"

"It would mean I love you so much I want to be with you the way every woman wants to be with the man she loves. It would mean I trust you to love me as much as I love you, and I want to spend the rest of my life with you."

"If I cross this room, I may have to fight every male member of your family."

"I'll stand at your side."

The tension gradually left his body and a slow smile spread across his face until his eyes glowed with warmth. "You are truly the most remarkable woman I've ever met. I hate to think of what my life would have been like if you hadn't gone to England."

"And I hate to think of what my life would have been like if you hadn't come to Texas."

"We're about as different as two people can be. Do you think there's a chance for us?"

"A very good chance if we have the courage to take it."

Edward approached the bed. "I do."

"So do I," she responded.

Edward sat down next to her on the bed, took her face in

his hands, and kissed her gently on the lips. Now that Edward had finally admitted his love, Eden wanted to sink into that kiss, to taste every morsel of its sweetness, to make it last forever. Edward loved her and wanted to be with her always.

Edward had other ideas. Though he, too, seemed to want the kiss to go on forever, his hands moved restlessly over Eden's back and shoulders, pulling her closer to him until her breasts were pushed hard up against his chest. She didn't immediately realize he'd been unbuttoning the back of her dress until she felt it begin to slide off her shoulders. The feel of his hands through the thin fabric of her shift sent chills racing to every part of her body, sent the blood rushing through her veins until she felt heat suffuse her skin. She wondered if she had the same effect on Edward.

She stopped wondering when Edward slipped her dress off her shoulders and let it fall around her waist. He eased her down on the bed and covered her shoulders with kisses as his hands roamed over her sides, her stomach, and her breasts. No man had ever touched her that way before. Her sensitivity to his fingertips as they moved across her body was so acute, her shift seemed like no barrier at all. Tremors shook her from head to foot and a pleasurable ache settled between her legs.

Anxious to explore Edward's body as thoroughly as he was exploring hers, she fumbled with the buttons on his shirt until he undid the last of them for her. Without breaking the kiss that seemed to have welded their bodies together, she pushed his shirt off his shoulders and got her first look at the chest she'd only seen in her dreams. Over the course of her twenty-one years, she'd seen many men without their shirts, but she didn't think she'd ever seen anyone except Sean with a chest to equal Edward's. Thick muscles divided his upper chest into halves that joined with powerful shoulders to create the impression of unlimited power. The whole was covered by smooth skin that felt like rich satin as she moved her hand from side to side, luxuriating in the feeling of intimacy it gave her. Ridges of muscle crossed his abdomen down to his waist.

Breaking the kiss at last, she leaned her head against Edward's chest and moved her hands to his back. She loved the play of muscles under his skin when he raised his arms or changed the position of his body. On a few occasions she had noticed that when one of her sisters-in-law let her hands roam over her husband's torso, she'd get a faraway look in her eye. Now Eden understood. Having complete freedom to explore Edward's body was enough to make her surroundings fade into insignificance.

She was brought hurtling back when Edward slipped her shift over her shoulders and exposed her breasts to his touch. She would never have believed her breasts could be so sensitive, but she flinched when he touched her.

Edward froze. "Did I hurt you?"

"No. I'm just more sensitive than I expected."

Edward's touch was feathery, but she still felt like she was about to jump out of her skin. All the nerve endings in her body had come together in one place to amplify every feeling, every sensation, until the pleasure grew so powerful it impacted her whole body. When he massaged her nipple with his fingertips, her body went rigid. When he took her nipple into his mouth, she nearly rose off the bed. She felt unable to breathe, the air locked inside her lungs. He tongued, nipped, and sucked her nipples until she was certain she couldn't stand any more. How could anything feel so agonizingly wonderful?

She was dimly aware of his hands moving gently over her body, touching, probing, caressing. She wanted to do the same to him, but she felt helpless, all the energy drained from her body, all the strength sapped from her muscles, leaving her defenseless before his onslaught. But it was an onslaught her body liked and wanted more of. With no guidance from her near-paralyzed brain, she rose to meet Edward's touch, pressed hard against him, yearned for more, the more that some part of her brain told her was yet to come.

When Edward's hand moved down her side, slid her shift down over her hips, and glided up her thigh, her whole being was suspended. She had known this moment would come, but she still wasn't prepared for the overpowering force of it. Her muscles quivered and her nerve endings were so sensitive, she felt as if her body had become a pincushion. Her heart raced but her breathing nearly stopped. She felt disconnected from her surroundings even though the entire room seemed burned into her brain. Everything was either a contradiction or an exaggeration, and she was incapable of telling the difference.

When Edward's finger slipped inside her, it ceased to matter. She was aware of nothing but her own body, the powerful rings of sensation that began to spread from her center like ripples in a lake. Each successive ripple thrilled her a little more until she floated helplessly on the rising tide of ecstasy Edward was creating inside her. She tried to speak, but only moans of pleasure escaped her lips. She tried to lift her arms, to reach out and touch him, but she could only lie there and ride the waves that rose higher and higher with each movement of Edward's hand inside her. She had expected making love would be wonderful—she'd seen her sisters-in-law whispering to each other while casting amorous glances at their husbands—but she hadn't anticipated anything like this.

She was gradually losing the ability to think, to remember. She could only react to the powerful surges that gripped her body. The greater her need to do something to escape, the more incapable she was of movement. She rose from the bed, a cry of protest lodged in her throat, as the coils tightened around her body until her breaths came in noisy gasps. Her fingers gripped the bedspread beneath her and closed like the talons of a bird of prey. Then just as she thought she must cry out in agony, the moment she'd been waiting for came and she seemed to soar right out of her body.

She was not even aware that Edward was removing the rest of her clothes. Keeping her eyes closed, she thought only of her racing heart, her labored breath, her knotted muscles. She was drained of energy, could think only of her complete satisfaction. She didn't realize Edward had removed his own clothes until she felt the bed sink under his weight and she opened her eyes to see him poised above her.

"This may be a little uncomfortable at first. Just tell me and I'll pull back."

The sight of his engorged manhood sent a quiver of apprehension through her, but she wanted so badly to feel Edward inside her, to feel they were joined, that she refused to let his size worry her. He loved her. He wouldn't do anything to hurt her.

She felt herself stretch as he slowly entered her. When she was certain she couldn't stretch any more, he paused before penetrating deeper. Only when he began to move inside her did she realize there would be no pain, only the wonderful feeling that she had finally become joined to the man she loved.

She wrapped her arms around his neck and pulled him down into a kiss that was filled with a kind of passion she'd never dreamed possible. They had been born to be together. No one else could have stirred such depths of passion, have traveled so deep into her soul. No one else could have made being in his arms, making love to him, feel like a sacred experience.

When the waves came the second time, she rose to meet them eagerly. She let herself be tossed by the sea of love that surrounded her, braved the storm as it broke across her body, latched onto the lightning that illuminated her soul and turned their love into a white-hot flame.

In the same way she rejoiced when the storm broke, the waves receded, and calm settled around her. She now knew the full meaning of love, and that knowledge filled her heart with a joy no words could describe.

On top of everything else he had to live with, now Edward had to deal with the guilt of having made love to a woman he wasn't in a position to ask to be his wife. It didn't matter that he was certain she loved him as much as he loved her. A man of character had a responsibility not to raise a woman's hopes if he couldn't fulfill them. He didn't know a lot about Jake Maxwell, but he'd be surprised if such a successful rancher would allow his only daughter to marry a man without the means to support a wife. Added to that, he was illegitimate, an outcast, and his financial future depended on the fragile legs of one horse: it was a hopeless situation.

He never should have come to Texas. And having done that, he should never have explained to Hawk and Zeke that he'd fallen in love with Eden and needed a job so he could be near her while he learned how to be a cowboy and trained his horse for a race on which he was gambling his entire future. Zeke had laughed, Hawk had looked at him like he was crazy, but they'd given him the job. Yet what had he accomplished besides compromising Eden and putting her life in danger?

He turned his head so he was facing her on the pillow. She looked so peaceful, so beautiful, so utterly desirable. How had he ever thought he'd be able to keep his hands to himself? He should have refused to stay alone with her in the ranch house after Zeke and Hawk took their wives to San Antonio. He should have kept looking until he found someone else to ride Crusader. He should have told Eden he had to keep his distance until he could honorably ask her to be his wife.

Okay, so he'd told her about keeping his distance, but he hadn't stuck to it and he couldn't excuse himself by saying she didn't want him to keep his distance. A man of character would have done it anyway.

He reached out to caress Eden's cheek, then drew his hand back. She looked so achingly lovely, so very nearly irresistible, it took all his self-loathing to keep from waking her, kissing her, making love to her again. Remembering the sweetness of her kisses, the softness of her body was torture. The past several hours had been incredible. They had given meaning to a life that had always felt uncomfortable, often felt useless, sometimes felt like a failure. It seemed too cruel for Fate to snatch it away the moment he found it.

But Fate hadn't given him this past evening. He'd stolen it. He had no right to it. He had to get out of the bed, out of the room. Eden's body lying next to his, her softness only inches away, was too much temptation. Taking care to move slowly, he eased off the bed. Enough light came through the window to enable him to find his clothes. He gathered them up without bothering to put them on and left the room without a backward glance. He wasn't sure he could have forced himself to leave if he'd done so.

Once outside the room, a measure of sanity returned. It was fortunate he'd awakened before morning. If Finn had come into the house and caught both of them leaving the same bedroom, all hell would have broken loose. Getting fired and ordered never to set foot on Maxwell land again would have been the mildest consequence. Members of Eden's family would stand in line to spill his blood.

He reached his room and sank down on the bed, as exhausted from the disgust he felt for himself as by his inner turmoil. He ought to go someplace he wouldn't be a danger to Eden and himself. It disgusted him even more to know he wouldn't leave. He was too weak, too much in love with Eden to think of going anywhere or doing anything that would prevent him from seeing her every day. Her smile made his day worthwhile; her happiness became his. She was the reason learning the secret of his birth hadn't destroyed him. She was the reason Crusader *had* to win the race.

He stood to dress. It wasn't time to get up, but going back

to sleep was out of the question. He could bring in some wood, start the fire, make coffee. Anything to occupy his mind, to keep him busy, to prevent him from going back into her bedroom.

Crusader thundered down the trail, his powerful stride carrying him faster and faster toward the imaginary finish line. Perched low over his neck, Eden urged him on with her hands and voice. Crusader responded with a burst of acceleration that caused his mane to whip across her face, nearly blurring her vision of Edward waiting at the end of the trail, stopwatch in hand, an intent expression on his face. He had been in a strange mood all week, but he had to be pleased with this workout, Crusader's final before they left for San Antonio. Eden didn't need a stopwatch to know the young stallion had never run so fast.

His gaze focused on the stopwatch, Edward didn't look up as they raced by. Eden stood up in the stirrups and pulled gently on the reins to slow Crusader. He didn't want to stop and tossed his head impatiently, but she applied gentle pressure until he began to slow. She was glad he wanted to keep running, but he needed to conserve his energy for the race just a few days away. This workout was just a tightener to keep up his speed and flexibility.

Crusader finally came to a stop. She turned him and headed back to where Edward waited.

Even though the sun had barely been up an hour, it was already hot. Birds that had chirped so noisily before dawn had mostly fallen silent as they looked for a shady spot to perch during the heat of the day. Eden would be inside, but Edward, Finn, and Brady would be in the saddle until dusk. They still hadn't found the man who had shot at her—or Crusader—or the men who had committed the vandalism at the various ranches. Her father had been hopeful they'd be found before the family left for San Antonio, but that now seemed unlikely. As a result, everyone was going to San

Antonio. The children were in a fever of excitement. Faced with spending several days in an unfamiliar city, their parents were busy considering various strategies for corralling the energies and curiosity of children used to roaming virtually at will.

Eden didn't have to look at the smile wreathing Edward's face to know he could hardly wait to get to San Antonio. He planned to place as many private bets on Crusader as possible. He was certain the long odds would enable him to win enough money to buy a ranch . . . or go back to England and buy the farm he'd always wanted. He said he'd never go back to England, but Eden knew what he really meant was he would never go back a failure.

Much to her dismay, Edward had kept a distance between them since the night they'd made love. He'd told her he should never have touched her, that it was inexcusable to compromise a woman he wasn't able to marry. She'd replied as she always did: that money didn't matter when it was a question of true love, but she was gradually learning there was more of England in Edward than either of them had supposed. He wanted the freedom Texas offered, but his values, his code of behavior, had been instilled in him by the aristocratic society into which he'd been born and reared. Money, social rank, and personal honor were integral parts of his thought processes, the criterion by which he made his decisions.

As far as she was concerned, love leveled the playing field.

The feeling that the life she'd dreamed of was slipping away filled her with a growing sense of desperation. It seemed there was always something wrong with her. For some of the local boys it had been her independence and refusal to leave her family. For the men she met when she was in college, it was that she was from Texas. The hurt of being rejected for reasons that weren't her fault wouldn't go away. It wasn't fair, it wasn't right, yet she couldn't do anything about it. Now she was being rejected because of Edward's outmoded morality.

Somehow, some way, she wouldn't let it happen. She loved her family, adored all of her nieces and nephews, but she wanted a husband, her own children. She'd finally found a man who appreciated her independence, who wanted the life she wanted. She didn't need any burst of intuition to tell her she'd never find another man she could love the way she loved Edward. He was the one meant to share her life. All she had to do was find a way to convince him.

"You're a genius." Edward looked down at the stopwatch when she brought Crusader to a stop next to him. "I could never get that kind of run out of him."

Excitement danced in his dark blue eyes. His smile made him look so handsome, Eden felt her stomach turn over. How could she face the possibility that he might return to England? He wouldn't ask her to go with him. She would never fit in there, certainly not as well as he'd acclimated to Texas. In a short time, he'd become comfortable wearing boots, jeans, a shirt open at the throat, and a wide-brimmed hat to keep the sun out of his eyes. Until he spoke, you could almost think he'd been in Texas most of his life. So why wouldn't he want to stay?

"He's still young. You can race him for several more years if you want." Why had she said that? If it was racing glory he wanted, England was the place to be. The English racing tradition went back to the reign of King Charles II.

"All I need is to win enough races to build a reputation. Then I'll put him to stud and race and sell his offspring." Edward was looking at the stopwatch again, shaking his head in wonder. "That's where the money is."

In England. There wasn't much call for Thoroughbreds in Texas. Even the derby they had started a few years ago in Kentucky was an obscure country race compared to the famous derby in England, which drew crowds of several hundred thousand each year. If Edward dreamed of becoming rich breeding Thoroughbreds, he couldn't stay in Texas.

"Your parents will meet us here tomorrow," Edward told her. "Chet and Luke will be with them, but most of the family will follow a few days later." They were going early because Isabelle couldn't wait any longer to see how Suzette was doing.

"Finn and Brady will have their hands full taking care of the ranch, but it won't be for long," Edward said. "If all goes well, Hawk and Zeke will be back soon."

Then it would be time for her to return home and start school. She had no hope of talking her mother into letting her stay to help with the babies. Someone had to teach school, and Eden was the only one qualified. She wouldn't be able to see Edward every day. She wouldn't be able to remind him of how much he loved her and she loved him. She had the terrible feeling that if she were separated from him, he would go back to England and she'd never see him again.

But if Crusader lost the race, he'd be forced to stay in Texas.

It filled her with disgust that she could even think of throwing the race. It would destroy her integrity. She couldn't, she *wouldn't* consider such a course of action. But even as Edward outlined what they needed to do to be ready to leave the next day, the thought wouldn't leave her. She tried to close her mind, force herself to pay close attention to what Edward was saying, but not even her best efforts could drive out the thought.

If Crusader loses the race, Edward will have to stay in Texas.

Eden couldn't remember when she'd been prey to such conflicting emotions. She'd always loved going to San Antonio. It was a beautiful old town with a strong Spanish heritage, a vibrant German community, and a welcome for anyone who wanted to stay for a few hours, a few days, or the rest of their lives. Impressive buildings of brick and stone stood three stories high, sunlight reflecting off their huge glass windows. Most of the family was staying at the Menger Hotel next to the Alamo. The race would finish in the plaza in front of the hotel. The limestone and ironwork edifice was one of the most impressive buildings in San Antonio and the best hotel.

It was late afternoon, but the streets and plaza were comfortably crowded with wagons, carriages, and men on horseback. Crusader was tethered to the back of the buckboard Jake had used to convey Isabelle to San Antonio. She steadfastly refused to ride a horse unless it was impossible to get to her destination any other way.

"It's not as bad as London," Edward was telling Eden, who rode next to him. "London streets are nearly impassable any time of day."

Eden agreed with him, but the noise and crowded conditions irritated her. Knowing the conclusion of the race would mean the end of her time with Edward made her feel worse. That she couldn't stop thinking about throwing the race mortified her. What kind of woman would consider winning a man by cheating?

"Your father can take care of our bags for us," Isabelle said to Eden. "I want to see Suzette as soon as possible."

"I ought to go with Edward so I'll know where Crusader is stabled," Eden said.

"He can show you later. Right now, Suzette is more important."

Eden didn't know what she could do for Suzette that her mother couldn't, but she didn't argue. The messages from Hawk and Zeke had been reassuring, but neither man had conveyed anything beyond the essential facts that their wives had not been hospitalized and the babies had not yet been born.

Eden had stayed at the Menger before, but now that she'd been to London, she had a better understanding of just how elegant the hotel really was. Corinthian columns on marble pedestals rose from the lobby to support the floors above. Garlands decorated the columns, which each bore four lights that flooded the lobby with a warm glow. Plants in large pots and high-backed chairs set against the wall softened the effect of the white walls and columns.

"I want a room facing the square," Isabelle stated. "I intend to watch the finish of the race from the comfort of the roof outside my window, not fighting the crowd on the street below."

"I told Hawk to reserve the front rooms on all three floors weeks ago," Jake said. "The name's Maxwell," he said to the clerk. "I trust there'll be no problem with the reservations."

The flustered clerk ran his finger down the page of the register in front of him. It came to a stop three quarters of the way down and his expression relaxed into a smile. "No problem at all, sir. You have all twelve front rooms."

"Maybe that'll be enough since Hawk and Zeke already have rooms," Isabelle said to Eden. "You can stay with your father and me. The rest will have to settle it among themselves."

Since Matt had seven kids, five adopted, and Drew had six, three adopted, Eden expected there'd be a lot of settling to be done. Pete's and Luke's wives, with five children between them under two, had decided to stay home. Will was bringing his son Riley and Junie Mae's boy, Scott, but Idalou said three-week-old Belle was too young to travel. That still left thirty children if all the older ones came, and seven more couples. The hotel would be overrun with the Maxwell clan.

"Could I have the numbers of the rooms occupied by Mr. and Mrs. Hawk Maxwell and Mr. and Mrs. Zeke Maxwell?" Isabelle asked.

"They're on the back overlooking the garden," the clerk said.

"Come on," she said to Eden. "I have to see Suzette for myself before I can relax. Hawk never tells me what I want to know."

"They're not here," the clerk said. "They left for the hospital early this morning."

Chapter Twenty-three

$\mathcal{D}$id they leave a message?" Isabelle asked.

The clerk shook his head.

"Which hospital and how do I get there?"

"Edward can finish up here," Isabelle said as soon as the clerk had given directions. "Jake, drive me to the hospital immediately."

"Go on," Edward said when Eden hesitated. "I'm sure the hotel porters can help me with the luggage."

The ride was short, but Jake managed to cut off two buggies, nearly run over a wagon, and scare one horseman so badly Eden could see the whites of his eyes. Isabelle was out of the buckboard and inside the hospital before Jake could get the horses tethered. The woman in charge tried to tell her mothers-in-law weren't allowed in hospital rooms without a doctor's permission, but Isabelle marched down the hall opening each door until she peeked inside the third, gave a small gasp, and entered the room. Fearing the worst, Eden hurried after her.

She entered to find Suzette sitting up in bed, nursing a tiny infant, with Hawk at her side looking so bemused Eden was nearly betrayed into a laugh. Hawk, the guy who never lost control, who never showed emotion, had had all the underpinnings knocked from under him by the sight of his wife nursing an infant with her mother's golden hair.

"Say hello to Zoe Maxwell," Suzette said with a tired smile. "After scaring us for the last few months, she came without any trouble."

Isabelle could barely wait for Zoe to finish nursing so she could hold her newest grandchild. In the meantime, she peppered Suzette with questions until she was convinced both Suzette and her daughter were doing fine.

"Where are Zeke and Josie?" Eden asked Hawk.

"In the next room," Hawk replied without taking his eyes off his daughter. "Josie started her labor soon after Suzette, but the doctor said it wasn't going to be quick."

As though to confirm Hawk's statement, a long drawn-out wail penetrated the wall between the two rooms.

"It scares me every time I hear her," Suzette said, "but the doctor says she's strong and doing fine."

"I'll go see." They'd barely left the room when an infant's cry reached them.

"Do you think that came from Josie's room?" Eden asked.

"We'll soon find out."

Josie was glowering at her husband when her mother-in-law charged into the room without knocking. "I *told* Zeke it was going to be a boy. A girl would never have been so stubborn or caused so much pain."

A doctor was checking the baby while a nurse cleaned up the room. It was impossible for a man as dark as Zeke to look pale, but he had lost a lot of color. "We're going to name him Jessie." He looked wrung out, but his voice was still a deep, resonant bass.

"Is he okay?" Josie asked the doctor. "After I've gone to this much trouble to have him, he'd better be perfect."

"You have a healthy son," the doctor said, "with all his toes and fingers. Would you like to nurse him?"

"I guess I'll have to if he's going to grow big enough to get some woman in trouble one of these days."

The doctor looked shocked, but Eden knew Josie talked tough to hide the softness of her heart.

"He's a handsome baby," the doctor said. "I expect he'll have lots of women giving him the eye if he grows up to be anything like your husband."

"Why couldn't I have had a girl?" Josie moaned.

"They're more trouble," Isabelle said, looking over the doctor's shoulder to make sure her grandson was indeed healthy. "If you have a girl, you'll be pacing the floor every evening waiting for her to come in. This young man will be keeping somebody else up at nights."

Having finished checking the baby, the doctor handed him to Isabelle and left.

"It's been quite a summer," Isabelle said, smiling down at Jessie. "Pete's twins, Luke and Will's daughters, and now these two."

The nurse finished tidying up while Eden helped Josie into a fresh nightgown. Once the bed was ready, she climbed in and held her arms out for her son.

"Are you hungry?" Isabelle crooned to the baby. "Your mommy said such terrible things, I think I'll keep you. I like little boys."

Eden moved to where she could see the baby. His big brown eyes never left his grandmother. He looked more like his mother than his father. He would definitely be a heart-breaker when he grew up.

"I like little boys, too." Josie's expression softened when she turned her head to look at her husband. "I already have a big one to look after. I don't suppose a little one will be too much harder."

"Easier but more time-consuming," Isabelle said as she surrendered Jessie to his mother. "Now we're going to leave you alone so you can get some rest before the family arrives. How long does the doctor want to keep you here?"

"That depends on Suzette," Josie said. "I don't want to leave her alone."

"I'm going to sit with her a while. She doesn't look as strong as you. I'll leave Eden to keep you company. Zeke looks about as useless as Hawk."

Eden had always thought it was ironic that such big, confident men as her brothers could be reduced to helplessness by a tiny baby. She wondered if Edward would feel that way.

"Do you know any jockeys who are free to ride?" Edward asked a man who was one of the sponsors of the race now two days off.

"We don't have much call for really good riders of Thoroughbreds around here," the man told him. "The best ones are in New Orleans."

Since it was too late to bring a rider from New Orleans, Edward was limited to those in San Antonio. He'd interviewed two men and rejected both.

"I'll ask around, but you'd be advised to go with whoever has been riding your horse unless it's you." The man paused, his brows knitted before he spoke again. "It's rumored that you already fired one jockey."

"He refused to ride the horse the way I told him."

"Are you a trainer?"

"No, but I've worked with the horse for six months and know what it takes to make him run his best."

"Maybe, and maybe not," the man said. "Jockeys don't pay much attention to owners, who generally don't know what they're talking about. The scuttlebutt is that you don't know much and your horse is a rogue."

It angered Edward that one ignorant jockey could ruin his and Crusader's reputation with just a few words, but it didn't surprise him. His horse was unknown and he was a foreigner. Even this man, who had no reason to care about Edward one way or the other, had turned stiff and a little unfriendly when he'd heard Edward's accent. "He's wrong," Edward said, "but I guess the only way to prove that is to win the race."

"How are you going to do that without a jockey?"

Edward left without telling the man he had a jockey. He just didn't want to use her.

He was still wrestling with his conscience about allowing

Eden to ride Crusader. Eden was convinced her unknown attacker had been trying to take the horse out of the race, but Edward couldn't get it out of his mind that the gunman was aiming at Eden. Someone had already taken Black Cloud out by injury. If the shooter had been after Crusader, why wouldn't he have tried something similar?

Attempting to kill Eden wasn't something someone was likely to do on the spur of the moment. Murder was a serious matter, even in Texas. Now if he'd been the target, that would have been another matter. What was one foreigner more or less? He wondered why people didn't stare when he passed. A glimpse of himself in a store window provided his answer.

He was dressed like every other cowboy in a town full of cowboys. Until he spoke, there was nothing except his height to make him stand out from the crowd.

That provided some comfort. Though he still felt out of place—one month in Texas wasn't nearly enough time to erase the effects of twenty-five years in England—he had begun to feel more comfortable with his surroundings. He knew that had a lot to do with the acceptance of the Maxwell family . . . and of Eden. Which brought him back to his problem of finding a jockey for Crusader. If he didn't, the only way to make certain Eden wouldn't be in danger was to withdraw his horse from the race.

That would mean forfeiting the chance to win the purse money, to win money on bets, money without which he couldn't buy a ranch or ask Eden to marry him. He would have no future. But if Eden did ride and something happened to her, he would not only have no money, no future, but no wife, either. What would he do then?

Return to England? No. That was impossible. He'd work as a common ranch hand before he begged his family to take him back. What place would he have? He didn't know who his father was, his mother didn't want him, and his place in the family had already been taken. He would be a penniless dependent. After having run the estate and been the patron of the village of Green Moss, he couldn't endure the humiliation.

What could he do in Texas with no money? Wait a year for another race? Surely he could find a good jockey by then. But he couldn't keep working for Hawk and Zeke even if they were still willing to give him a job. After having kissed Eden, held her in his arms, made love to her, it would be impossible to be so close and not do something to dishonor himself.

He could go farther west and hope fortune smiled on him. He could race Crusader for side bets. From what he'd heard, there was a lot of money around gold mining towns like Virginia City and Tombstone or sophisticated cities like San Francisco and Denver. Someone would always be willing to back his horse to win. But that would mean leaving Eden. Could he endure that?

His audible curse drew the startled attention of two women who were window shopping. Since the older woman immediately put herself between Edward and the younger one, he could only assume the curse, uttered with an English accent, had convinced the woman he was a very dangerous person, possibly a deranged one.

There didn't seem to be a solution to his problems, but he knew one thing for certain. He couldn't allow Eden to ride Crusader, and he'd have to tell her tonight. He didn't know how to begin. She was going to be angry and argue with anything he said. Maybe he ought to talk to Jake or Isabelle. One of them might be able to—

His chain of thought snapped when he saw a man who looked amazingly like Finn talking to the jockey he'd fired. They were between fruit and vegetable stands in Market Square, a place Edward would never have come near if he hadn't been looking for a jockey. Certain he was mistaken, he hurried on. Finn was back at the ranch with Brady. A few steps later he paused, reconsidered, and turned back. The stranger looked too much like Finn for Edward not to make sure. The two men had moved deeper into the market when Edward caught sight of them again. It was hard to be certain in the crowded aisles.

Working his way around women poring over fruit, dodging children running down the aisles, and moving aside for men carrying baskets or sacks of produce, he worked his way closer to the two men. He didn't want to take a chance that one of them would recognize him, but he had to get close enough to be sure it was Finn.

The two men paused next to a stand of potatoes that were being put into crates and carried away in preparation for closing the market for the day. Edward was able to circle around and approach them from the back. It was too noisy to catch anything they were saying, but he caught an occasional word during lulls in the surrounding noise. The man was Finn. Edward could never mistake that sharp, nasal voice.

Now the question became why had Finn left the ranch after Jake had put him in charge, and what was he doing in San Antonio?

With so many members of the family wanting to visit with each other, it was inevitable that the clan would gradually take over the lobby, front hall, and lounge of the hotel. The women compared notes on the progress of their children while the men talked about the attacks. Children from two to twenty, struggling to hold their excitement within bounds their parents would accept, looked forward to one last holiday before most of them would start a new school year. Everybody was excited to learn that Suzette and Josie had had their babies and were doing well. Hawk and Zeke would be staying at the hospital for the night. Consequently Eden was surprised when Zeke entered the hotel.

She tried not to be amused at Zeke's awkwardness in accepting congratulations from his family on the birth of his son. She was surprised when he hurried over to ask where he could find Buck.

"I don't know if he's here yet."

"I need to talk to him as soon as he arrives," Zeke said.

"Is something wrong?" She couldn't imagine why Zeke needed to talk to Buck. They'd hardly seen each other in years.

"I ran into one of Chet's former cowhands on the way over here. He reminds me of Rupert Reison."

Eden couldn't immediately place the name.

"He's the man who tried to kill Buck and nearly killed Jake instead."

Then she remembered being told about the farmers who'd settled on Jake's land while he was off fighting the war. One of them had followed Jake when he took his first herd to Santa Fe. He'd tried to kill Buck because Buck had found the body of a boy Rupert had beaten to death.

"Buck had more contact with Rupert's sons than I did," Zeke said. "When I wasn't working, Rupert kept me chained in the barn. If that man is related to Rupert—he's the right age to be one of his sons—then something strange is going on. All of those people were farmers. They hated ranchers. I can't think of a single good reason why a son of Rupert Reison would be working for anybody in the Maxwell family."

"You ought to talk to Dad."

"Not until I'm sure. I don't want to upset him for no reason."

They were interrupted by still more family members wanting to congratulate Zeke, so Eden didn't get to ask Zeke any more questions before Buck and his family arrived. The first few minutes were spent in greeting all the adult members of the family and teasing a few of the younger ones, but it wasn't long before Zeke got Buck off to a corner. Eden could tell by the altered expression on Buck's face that Zeke's information had startled him. After a few minutes of hurried conversation, they motioned for Chet to join them.

Moments after that Buck's worried expression gradually changed to anger. Unable to remain in ignorance of what they were saying, Eden worked her way over to them.

"I wasn't sorry to see him go," Chet was saying. "I wouldn't have hired Frank if I hadn't been short of hands. He was an average worker and didn't seem interested in improving. He was a real loner, didn't try to make friends with any of the other men."

"Who are you talking about?" Eden asked.

"The man I saw," Zeke said.

"What do you think is wrong?"

"We don't know," Buck said, "but Rupert's sons were as mean as their father. The oldest one used to torment me, then dare me to tell his father. He knew Rupert would beat me if he thought I'd even spoken harshly to one of his boys."

"What are you going to do?" Eden asked.

"We're trying to decide," Chet said.

"Only thing is," Buck said, "none of Rupert's sons was named Frank. They were Aaron, Abel, and Adam."

A commotion near the door caused Eden to look up in time to see Edward enter the lobby. She waved him over to join them.

"If he had anything to do with the attacks on the ranches, wouldn't he have used a false name?" Eden asked.

"I don't know," Buck said, "but if anybody would poison cattle and burn barns full of hay—"

"Or attack horses with knives and guns," Eden added.

"—I'd vote for a son of Rupert Reison," Buck finished.

"Where's your father?" Edward asked when he reached Eden. "I need to ask him if he knows why Finn should be in San Antonio."

"He can't be. He's in charge of the ranch," Eden said.

"I saw him in the Market Square talking to the jockey I fired."

"Let's see if we can find Frank," Chet said. "I don't like the feeling I'm getting."

"I want to go with you," Edward said after they told him they were concerned about who Frank might really be. "But I need to talk to Jake first."

The three men looked at each other and Eden knew they were thinking Edward was an outsider only tangentially involved in a situation that ought to be kept within the family.

"Take him with you," Eden said when Edward left to find Jake.

"Why?" Buck asked.

"You won't let me go with you, and I need somebody who can tell me what you find."

"We'll tell you," Chet said.

"Only what you think I need to know. Now don't argue. I have a feeling all of this is somehow related."

"How?" Zeke asked.

"I don't know, but I can't believe all these things happening at the same time are merely coincidence."

"If my cowhand really is named Frank Pender, we have nothing to worry about," Chet said.

"And if he isn't?" Eden asked.

"Then I have a lot of questions I want answered."

It was apparent to Edward that his presence was pointless. Eden's brothers weren't overtly rude. They listened politely to anything he said, then ignored his suggestions. Edward was annoyed but figured they were probably justified. He'd been two years old and five thousand miles away when Jake had been shot.

It hadn't been too difficult for Eden's brothers to find Frank Pender. He hadn't tried to hide. No one could have described him as friendly, but he showed no reluctance to answer the questions put to him. He denied any knowledge of the group of farmers who had taken over Jake's ranch. He said he couldn't say whether or not he looked like Rupert Reison, but he'd never heard of the man and wasn't any relation. He said his family came from south of Fort Worth.

He knew enough about the area to convince the men he was telling the truth.

"I quit because I'm thinking of going back home," Frank said. "I don't really like being a cowhand."

"You didn't try hard to learn," Chet told him.

Frank shrugged. "I didn't like it."

"What are you going to do in Fort Worth?"

"My family has a store. I guess I'll work in it."

Edward thought Pender would have to improve his attitude or he'd alienate the customers, but that wasn't his problem. He was more interested in why he thought Frank was lying. The man wasn't likeable, but that didn't mean he wasn't telling the truth. It might have ended there if a young cowhand hadn't recognized Frank and come over to join the group.

"I got tired of being the butt of jokes just because I'm the youngest in the group," the cowhand said when Chet asked him why he wasn't out enjoying himself with the other men. "Besides, I wanted to ask Frank if he had a cousin or something working for Sean."

His words riveted the attention of everyone in the group.

"What do you mean?" Buck asked.

"I saw a guy who looked like the spitting image of Frank a while ago. One of the hands said he worked for Sean. I just wondered if they were kin."

"What's his name?" Frank asked.

Edward had to give Frank credit. He didn't appear to be any more concerned about the answer than he would have about the name of an alley cat.

"Sam Grimes," the cowhand said. "Looks to be close to your age."

"Can't be related to me then," Frank said. "Ain't nobody in my family named Sam. Don't know anybody named Grimes, either."

It was his eyes that gave him away. Everything about his posture, his voice, his facial expression proclaimed boredom, maybe irritation at having to answer so many questions, but his eyes moved too quickly, too evasively.

"Where's this Grimes fella now?" Buck asked.

"Probably still at the cantina. The guy I know said he acts like a prude, but I say he has his eye on a pretty dancer."

"We ought to talk to him," Buck said. "This could be sheer coincidence, but I'd feel better if I could make sure for myself."

"I agree," Zeke said.

"What do you think we ought to do?" Buck asked.

"You go," Chet said to Buck and Zeke. "You two know what Reison looked like. I only saw him when he was dying. I'll stay here with Frank. Be as quick as you can. I'd like to clear this up and get back to the family."

"I don't intend to waste my evening satisfying your family's curiosity," Frank said. "I don't work for you anymore."

"It won't take long. Order anything you want to eat or drink. I'll pay for it."

"I'm not hungry, and I don't drink spirits," Frank said.

Chet eyed him more closely. "I guess I can understand why you couldn't make it as a cowhand."

"I didn't *want* to make it," Frank said. "I could have if I'd wanted."

The two men exchanged a few uneasy sentences, then fell quiet. Chet ordered a glass of sangria. Edward asked for a glass of ale. When they said they didn't carry ale—the waitress had never even heard of it—he settled for beer. Frank insisted he wanted nothing.

Chet asked Edward about England. Ordinarily he'd have jumped at the chance to talk about England, but it was difficult to talk about his life there without explaining his birth. He might have missed the change in Frank if he hadn't turned to order another beer. Frank's eyes had widened suddenly. The next instant he was on his feet running.

Chapter Twenty-four

$\mathcal{E}$dward immediately gave chase. Frank would have gotten away if he hadn't collided with a young couple trying to enter the cantina at the same time he was dashing out. Edward grabbed him by his shirt collar and hauled him backward, but was caught off guard when Frank pulled a knife from inside his shirt and turned to attack him.

The sound of a pistol shot sent screaming patrons diving for the floor and under tables. Frank's knife clattered on the tiles as his scream rose above the noise around him. Edward was stunned to see him clutching a bloody hand.

"I haven't had to do any shooting like that in nearly ten years," Chet said calmly as he approached. "It's good to know I haven't lost my eye."

"You tried to kill me!" Frank screamed.

"If I'd tried to kill you, you'd be dead."

Edward had found it hard to accept that Chet and his brother had been gunfighters. Now, however, the pitiless look in Chet's cold blue eyes along with Frank's bleeding hand made it easy. Neither had to ask why Frank had tried to run. Zeke and Hawk were approaching the cantina with a man who looked like Frank's twin. From the way the fellow was struggling, it was obvious he hadn't come willingly.

"What is your real name?" Chet asked Frank.

"I need a doctor before I bleed to death," Frank growled through his pain.

"That hand won't be of much use to you in the future," Chet said, "but you won't bleed to death."

Zeke and Buck had come close enough to ask what had happened.

"Apparently Frank saw you two approaching with his near double and decided to run before he had to answer any more questions," Chet explained.

"The first time I saw Rupert's two younger boys, I thought they were twins," Buck said. "I'm positive these two are Abel and Adam. The older one was named Aaron."

"Does either of you know where he is?" Chet asked.

Both men disclaimed any knowledge of each other or their older brother.

"Searching San Antonio for him won't do any good," Buck said. "He doesn't look like his brothers."

"Can you give us some idea what he looked like?" Edward asked.

"I guess he'd be close to the same height and build as his brothers," Buck said, "but he had faded brown hair, pale blue eyes, and a nose that reminded me of a hawk's beak. He was mean-spirited and liked picking on everybody. Even the other farm boys disliked him."

Edward had the uneasy feeling that the description ought to have conjured up a picture of someone he knew, but the chance of his knowing the older brother was practically nonexistent. "What are you going to do with these two?" he asked.

"Turn them over to the sheriff," Chet said. "One tried to kill you, and they're both suspected of willful destruction of property, arson, and attempted murder."

"You can't prove any of that," the unwounded brother said.

"Not yet, but now that we know who to investigate, I expect we'll come up with all the proof we need."

Edward decided to let the brothers take the two men to the local authorities. He had to go back to the hotel and tell Eden he was withdrawing Crusader from the race. He was now certain the attack had been on Eden rather than Crusader. He was equally certain the third brother would try to finish what none of the others had accomplished.

Murder Eden Maxwell.

"You can't withdraw Crusader," Eden protested. "He's a cinch to win the race."

"I have no choice," Edward insisted. "It's not safe for you to ride him, and I've been unable to find any other jockey."

"No one is trying to kill me," Eden insisted. "Why would they?"

"Because they think I killed their father," Jake said.

Even though Abel and Adam Reison continued to deny that they were related, using assumed names, or responsible for the attacks on the ranches, everyone was certain they and the missing brother were the culprits. Apparently it made no difference that the Maxwells had given Rupert a decent burial and explained the circumstances of his death to his wife. She had refused to believe Rupert would hire men to steal Jake's herd or that Rupert would try to kill Buck. Jake had lost track of the Reison family after he'd rounded up the last of his cows and moved to the Hill Country. They could very easily have moved to Fort Worth and opened a store.

Whatever their actions and movements, they had learned to be cowhands so they could find jobs on Maxwell ranches and take revenge for their father's death.

"Whatever they're planning is to take place in San Antonio," Edward said. "They want revenge. What better way to get it than to kill Eden?"

"If they wanted to hurt my father the most, they would go after my mother," Eden said.

"The love I feel for your mother is different from what I feel for you," Jake told his daughter, "but they're both equally strong."

"If anybody killed me, you'd be devastated," Eden said,

"but you'd survive. If they killed Mama, you'd go crazy. You wouldn't care what happened to you as long as you hunted down and killed everyone involved."

Jake might have protested if three sons hadn't nodded their heads in agreement.

"So they can't be after me," Eden concluded. "That shot was fired by someone trying to keep Crusader out of the race. Now that he's failed, there's no reason not to enter the race as planned."

"It doesn't matter whether the gunman was trying to kill you or the horse," Edward said. "I'm not running Crusader."

Eden started to argue, but Jake interrupted her. "Crusader is Edward's horse and only Edward has the right to decide what to do. Now that he's made his decision, everyone should respect it."

"Well, I can't respect it," Eden said. "Crusader can win that race easily. That would establish his reputation as a stud horse. How can you give up?" she asked Edward.

"I can't take the chance that you're wrong, that the gunman *is* trying to kill you."

Eden understood the sacrifice Edward was making and loved him all the more for it, but she wanted to bang his head against a wall. This was *her* future he was giving up, setting aside, putting on hold. He had no right to do that without taking her wishes into consideration. And her father had no right to side with him. She was a grown woman. If she was willing to take risks, it was her right to do so.

"I'm not giving up," Edward said. "There'll be opportunities to race Crusader against other horses for bets on the side. And there's next year's race. Crusader will be a year older and even better then."

"A hundred things could go wrong in a year's time," Eden argued. "Crusader could be injured, the race could be canceled, somebody could buy a Kentucky Thoroughbred and bring him to Texas." She stopped, unsure whether to utter the words trembling on her lips. In the end, they fell out on their own. "You could run out of money and have to return to England." It frightened her even to think that. If Edward ever went home, she believed she'd never see him again.

"I'm still taking Crusader out of the race."

Eden didn't argue, though there were hundreds of things she wanted to say. She was the daughter of one of the most stubborn men alive . . . as well as the sister of ten more. She could tell when a man's mind was made up and he wasn't about to change it. But she was her mother's daughter, and she didn't mean to give up. In order to be with the man she loved, her mother had faced cooking for a cattle drive to Santa Fe when she didn't know anything about cows, cattle drives, or cooking. In Eden's mind, one crazy Reison brother wasn't nearly as dangerous as several hundred miles of virtual desert infested with Indians, rattlesnakes, and white men willing to kill to get what they wanted.

She wasn't sure what she would do, but already a plan was forming in her mind. She needed time to think. She couldn't trust anyone to help her. This she would have to do on her own.

"I'm retired," the little man told Eden. "I've already turned down several offers to ride in this race."

"I don't want you to ride in the race," Eden explained. "I just want you to mount up. Then after Edward leaves, we'll exchange places."

"Why doesn't he want you to ride?"

"He's afraid the race will be too rough for a woman." Eden couldn't tell him the truth, or he'd refuse to help her. "I've been riding the horse in training. I know how to get the best out of him. He'll win so easily I won't be in any danger."

The man subjected her to a long, silent scrutiny. "I don't think you're telling me the whole truth."

Eden smiled. "Do you ever know a woman to tell the *whole* truth?"

He laughed. "Only when it suits her purpose." He sobered quickly. "You know I wouldn't do this for anyone but you."

"I know," Eden said without apology. "It's the reason I asked you."

He was silent a moment longer. "You promise me he's not objecting to your riding for any reason except your safety?"

"Every time I argue with him, all he talks about is my safety." She needn't tell the man exactly what Edward was keeping her safe from.

"Okay, but if I get caught, I'm blaming everything on you."

"I'm going to get the blame no matter what happens. Now, here is what I want you to do."

Edward couldn't believe his luck. The most famous jockey in Texas had volunteered to come out of retirement to ride Crusader.

"It's rumored around town that you have the best horse," the jockey had said, "but you can't find a rider."

"I couldn't find a jockey to ride Crusader the way I wanted," Edward had told him.

"Tell me what you want me to do," the man had said.

After a detailed explanation, during which the man never looked bored or inclined to argue with him, the jockey mounted Crusader and did exactly what Edward had asked. Eden could get more out of the horse, but Edward was confident this jockey would get enough to win. He didn't know what providence had provided him with the means of protecting Eden and winning the race, but maybe the gods that had treated him badly for so long had had a change of heart and decided it was time he had some good luck.

"Is there anything more you want to know?" Edward asked the jockey after they'd finished discussing strategy for the race the next day.

"Nothing you can't tell me later," the man said.

"Good. Then meet me here tomorrow at two o'clock. I'll have him saddled and ready to go."

Edward knew he had a big smile on his face as he watched the man walk away. He would win the race, get his money, be able to ask Eden to marry him. Now he had to see how many private bets he could place on Crusader. No matter what rumors might be flying around town, Crusader was an unknown quantity. There would be plenty of people willing to bet against his winning, and Edward meant to keep finding them until his money ran out. Unfortunately, that wouldn't take long.

A nagging voice warned him that good fortune never came without a price, but he'd paid the price, hadn't he? He'd lost the life he'd had in England and survived a crash course in how to become a Texan. He was going to forge ahead, make a new life for himself with Eden at his side. Fortune was smiling on him at last.

"I'm not going," Eden repeated. "Why should I want to watch another jockey ride Crusader to victory? *I* should be on his back, not some retired jockey, no matter how famous he used to be."

"Much of the credit for anything he does belongs to you," Edward insisted. "Without you on his back during training, he might never have trusted an unfamiliar jockey."

"If I were riding him, he wouldn't need to trust an unfamiliar jockey."

"That's enough," Jake said. "I've never known you to be so unreasonable."

"*You* think I'm being unreasonable," Eden said. "I don't."

"I was of two minds until this jockey showed up," Isabelle said. "I hated to see Edward lose his chance, but I couldn't let you take such a risk when we hadn't found the third Reison brother."

"We'll probably never find him," Eden said. "For all we know, he isn't in San Antonio and doesn't even know who I am."

"If he's anything like his father," Jake said, "he's here, he knows, and he won't stop until he's done what he set out to do."

"Or we find him first," Edward said.

Everyone in the family had Buck's sketchy description of what Aaron Reison looked like as a boy. They would be searching for him as they moved around the city, as would the local law officers, but Eden had little expectation they would find him. She couldn't believe the man was trying to kill her. There had been so many opportunities before, hundreds of times when she'd been outside with no protection, when she'd been on Crusader, even on the trip into San Antonio. If she'd truly been the main target, Reison could have attacked her before any of the family realized she was in danger. Considering how the attacks had been carried out, it didn't make any sense that she was the target. *If* the attacks were all attributable to the Reison brothers. They might never know the answer to that question.

"It won't matter what he wants to do as long as I stay in the hotel," Eden said, "so everybody can stop worrying and enjoy watching Edward win the race."

"Eden, you know I didn't want—"

She cut Edward off. "I know you're doing this because of me. I think you're wrong, but I appreciate that you were willing to give up your chance of winning to protect me."

"I should think you would," her father said. "It's not every man who'd give up something like this race for a woman. *Any* woman."

"I'm glad Edward thinks I'm special, but I already knew that," Eden said with a self-satisfied grin. "Now I'm going to stay in Hawk and Suzette's room at the back of the hotel so I won't have to hear any crowd noise from the race. You can send someone to get me when it's over. Don't any of you come trying to talk me into changing my mind. I'm going to lock the door."

It was hard to inject her performance with the right amount of pique when excitement at what she was about to do bubbled inside her. Her parents were going to be very upset—Edward would be furious—but they would forgive her when she won the race and everything turned out just as she planned. Now, all she had to do was get out of the hotel without being seen.

Edward was surprised at how little pleasure he got from saddling Crusader. He should be excited, and he was. He should be happy he had an excellent jockey, and he was. He should be looking forward to a successful future, and he was. Yet he had a bitter taste in his mouth because Eden wasn't in the saddle. No one would know she'd helped train Crusader, that she was as responsible as anyone for his victory.

"He is a beautiful horse," the jockey said. "Are you planning to put him to stud after the race?"

"Not immediately. It might be fun to run him a few more times." If they could find this other Reison brother, Eden would be able to ride him. Maybe not. He wasn't sure she'd ever forgive him for not letting her ride Crusader today.

He still had a nagging feeling that something about Buck's description of Aaron Reison was familiar, though he couldn't figure out how that was possible. Except for Finn and Brady, he didn't know anyone outside of the Maxwell family. No Maxwell had anything to do with the attacks, and Finn and Brady had been on the lookout for trouble as much as anyone else. Which made it even harder to understand what Finn had been doing in San Antonio talking to the fired jockey.

Did Finn think that jockey might know something about who could be trying to eliminate Crusader from the race? Did he think he was more useful in San Antonio now that Eden and Crusader were here rather than back at the ranch? If so, he should have talked to Jake, explained his concerns and what he thought should be done about them.

But that wasn't like Finn. He wasn't friendly or inclined to share his thoughts with someone else. Edward never knew what he was thinking, was often convinced Finn was laughing at him behind that blank gaze. He hated the way Finn would stare at him sometimes, those eyes flat and pale, boring into him like—

That was it! He rarely noticed eyes, but Finn's pale blue eyes sometimes gave him the creeps. He'd ignored his uneasiness because he'd decided it was without foundation, but he remembered Buck's description of the third brother: *faded brown hair, pale blue eyes, and a nose that reminded me of a hawk's beak. He was mean-spirited and liked picking on everybody.* Finn's brown hair had a lot of grey in it and his nose wasn't nearly as hooked as a hawk's beak, but he had pale blue eyes and was certainly mean-spirited. It was hard to believe Finn could be the third Reison brother, but Edward needed to tell Jake and his sons. It would be up to them to decide.

"I'm going to put you up in the saddle a little early," he said to the jockey. "There's something I have to do right away."

"Is everything okay?" the jockey asked.

"Everything is okay with the horse," Edward said. "That's all you have to worry about. I'll see you at the end of the race with the fee we've agreed on."

He barely waited for the jockey to settle in the saddle before heading back to the hotel. The race would begin two miles out of town. Since the horses would use the distance to the starting point as a warm-up, Edward would have time to explain everything to Jake before the race. Then he would go back to the square. If Finn really was the other Reison brother, he disliked Edward enough to include Crusader in his revenge. Edward had no intention of losing his horse. If Finn was in the crowd, Edward intended to find him.

"Did you have any trouble getting away from Edward?" Eden asked the jockey.

He didn't dismount but guided Crusader to the shade of a

sprawling live oak that stood a little way off the road they would be racing down minutes later. Crusader danced in a circle, his gaze on the other horses headed for the starting line.

"He was in such a hurry to leave, he practically tossed me into the saddle. Maybe he thought of something while he was talking to me, but he didn't say."

That bothered Eden because it didn't sound like Edward. His future rested on the outcome of this race. She'd expected him to stay with Crusader as long as possible, relating to the jockey any detail he thought might help him win the race.

"Maybe he wants to make sure he gets a good spot at the finish line." She didn't believe that was the reason. He would be sitting with her parents on the roof of the hotel outside their room. He would have a perfect view of the entire square.

"Are you sure you want to ride in this race?" the jockey asked. "I'm retired, but I can still ride. This is an excellent horse. I would enjoy riding him."

"I'm positive."

Eden couldn't explain why she had to be part of Edward's success. Part of the reason was that she'd been the one to divulge the information that made it impossible for him to remain in England. Winning the race would help give him a new life.

Part of the reason was purely personal. She wanted, *needed*, to have a hand in securing Edward's future. She knew he loved her, but she couldn't dispel a lingering doubt that he still might not ask her to marry him. Edward had a peculiar sense of honor. In his former world, people had been divided into classes based on education, wealth, and most important of all—birth. Since neither of his parents would claim him, he believed he was somehow inferior to her, unworthy of her. Her family's wealth only made the divide deeper and wider.

She insisted on being an equal partner with her husband.

She refused to settle into a *woman's role*. She had nothing against taking care of a house and having children, but she wouldn't be excluded from making decisions that affected the family. She wanted to be consulted when he planned breedings, to help with difficult foalings, to train the horses, to ride them in races. She finally understood that her calling wasn't to be a schoolteacher, despite her fancy education. She wanted to be a rancher, and she wanted Edward to be a rancher with her.

"Do you know the course?" the jockey asked.

"I rode over it yesterday and again today."

"Do you have a race strategy?"

"I had that even before I rode Crusader the first time."

"How will you explain it if you lose the race?"

She laughed. "I won't."

The little man didn't laugh. "This is a serious thing, your riding in the race. There's a rumor going around that the other jockeys are out to make sure Crusader doesn't win. They don't like the idea of being beaten by a foreigner's horse. Once they know you're riding, they'll do anything they can to keep from being beaten by a woman."

"I can take care of myself."

He hesitated. "I have a terrible feeling I shouldn't do this."

"You agreed! You can't change your mind now."

"I probably should, but I won't go back on my word. Promise you'll be careful and take no foolish risks. I couldn't live with myself if something happened to you."

"I'll be fine," Eden assured him. "I know this horse almost as well as Edward does. Now help me mount up. It's almost time to start."

"I know saying Finn could be the third Reison brother sounds far-fetched," Edward was saying to Jake, "but it would explain how Black Cloud was injured and Eden was shot at without our being able to find any trace of an intruder."

"It fits with what the other brothers were doing," Chet said, "working on the inside so they'd have access to and knowledge of the ranches."

"But this would require a detailed plan put into motion years ago," Edward said. "Those men had to learn to be cowhands, had to wait until all three could find jobs on Maxwell ranches."

"Rupert followed us to New Mexico and hired men to steal our herd to cover up his attempt to kill Buck," Jake said. "I could easily see him doing something like this."

"Then they really were after Eden and not Crusader," Edward said.

"That would be my guess, but we won't know until we find Finn and see what he has to say."

"We need to warn Eden," Edward said. "She needs to know to stay away from Finn if she sees him."

"I'll get her," Isabelle said. "I never liked the idea of her missing the race."

Eden's father and brothers still hadn't decided what to do about Finn when Isabelle returned, visibly upset.

"Eden isn't in the room. One of the maids said she saw her leaving the hotel by the back way at least half an hour ago."

Chapter Twenty-five

They began to consider all the possible reasons why Eden might have left the hotel, but Edward was positive there was only one. "She's going to ride Crusader," he announced.

"You already have a jockey."

Edward had always felt there was something too good to be true about a well-known retired jockey seeking him out at the last moment and volunteering to ride Crusader. He had jumped at the chance because it seemed foolish to turn it down, but Eden had lived in Texas all her life. She was bound to know virtually every outstanding horseman in this part of the state. He didn't know what inducement she'd offered the jockey, but he had no doubt Eden had persuaded the man to volunteer to ride the horse, then let her climb into the saddle at the last minute. And Edward had made it easy by leaving the jockey to make his own way to the starting point.

"She wouldn't do that," Jake said. "She knows how dangerous it could be."

Her brothers didn't say anything, just looked from Jake to Isabelle.

"That's exactly what she would do," Isabelle said. "I should have known she was up to something when she refused to watch the finish of the race."

"That's crazy," Jake said. "She knows there's a gunman out there."

"Of course she does," Isabelle said. "Just like you knew

there was a gunman out there when you rescued Buck from being trampled by a stampede. Just like I knew Sawtooth was a killer when I tried to let him out of the corral to keep the boys from running away. Everybody in our family has faced this kind of danger at least once. Why did either of us think she wouldn't as well?"

"Because I thought she was more sensible," Jake said.

"No," his wife corrected. "Because you were too busy worrying about the Reison brothers, and I was too busy worrying about Suzette and her baby to pay attention to our own daughter."

"I'm the one who should have guessed," Edward said. "I knew how much she wanted to ride Crusader, how important winning this race was to her. I should have known she gave in too quickly. Your daughter is the most persistent woman I've ever met."

"And?" Isabelle added, a smile slowly erasing her worried frown.

"And the woman I want to be my wife," Edward added. "Once I know she's safe, I don't know whether I'll want to kiss her or strangle her first."

"I know exactly how you feel," Jake said, looking at his wife. "I've felt like that many times."

"Stop making jokes and decide what you're going to do to protect my daughter and the woman you love."

"We're going to put the entire family on alert," Jake said.

"I'm taking the square out front," Edward said. "I think Finn wants as big an audience as possible."

"You really think he'll attack in front of hundreds of witnesses?"

"I'm not sure he cares what happens to him afterward," Edward said. "I have a feeling revenge is all that matters to him."

"You know him better than any of us," Jake said. "Tell us anything you can to help us identify him."

"He's not like his brothers in any way except build." Edward told them everything he could remember about Finn. "The most distinctive thing about him is his eyes. They're pale blue, cold as ice, and stare at you without wavering."

"What kind of gun will he use?" Buck asked.

"My guess is he'll use a rifle," Chet said. "It would be nearly impossible to hit a moving target with a pistol from back in a crowd."

"How can he hide a rifle?" Isabelle asked.

Edward had been wondering the same thing.

"People use their rifles practically every week, even women, so they're always bringing them in to be repaired or buying a new one," Jake said. "People come into San Antonio so often carrying rifles, nobody thinks much about it. If a man showed up wearing pistols, people would assume he was a gunfighter and notify the police."

"Hawk and I will be in the square with you," Zeke said to Edward. "Buck, too, but Chet ought to stay up on the roof with Isabelle. If he can spot Finn, he'll probably have a better chance of getting a shot at him without hitting anybody in the crowd."

Edward walked over to the ceiling-high window, raised it, and stepped out on the roof. The plaza below looked enormous. How could he find one person in such a milling mass of color? A path through the center of the plaza to the finish line had been kept clear for the horses, but every other square foot was filled with people of every age, talking, laughing, eating, playing. It was a holiday atmosphere down there, yet one person planned to turn it into a tragedy.

And it was up to Edward to find Finn before he could harm Eden.

"What are you doing on Albie Durham's mount?" one of the jockeys asked Eden when she arrived at the starting point.

"There's been a change of plans," she said. "I'll be riding Crusader."

"Does his owner know?"

"I've been riding him in training for the last two weeks," she replied, avoiding the question. "Mr. Davenport realizes I know more about how to ride this horse than anyone else."

"That don't mean you can ride him in this race," another jockey said.

"There's no rule against it," Eden pointed out.

"That's because no gal was crazy enough to think of trying it before," a third argued.

"I'm not crazy, and I'm a good rider. Black Cloud would have won last year if I'd been riding her."

"Then where is she if she's so good?"

"She's recovering from an injury. I thought it best not to push her to be ready for this race." No one had to know she'd been injured so severely she'd never race again.

"You don't belong in this race," the third jockey insisted.

Eden didn't know many of them by name, but she recognized some of their mounts. The first jockey, a cowhand named Murray, was riding a good horse, but only extraordinary luck could enable him to win. The second jockey was riding a horse called Ulysses who was primarily a short-distance runner. Apparently his owner was hoping he could build up a big lead at the start, and hang on the last half mile. The third jockey—his name was Ramon, and he was the one who insisted she didn't belong in the race—was riding a horse called Little Chickadee who was anything but small and birdlike. He wasn't a fast horse, but he had size and plenty of stamina. Eden thought he was the only horse with a chance to beat Crusader.

"You'd better drop out now," Ramon advised. "You never know what can happen in a race."

"I know what *shouldn't* happen." Eden held his gaze. She was determined he would know *she* knew he'd issued a threat and she wasn't backing down. There was a starter to make sure the horses lined up properly at the beginning of the race and a finish-line judge to call the order of finish if the race was close at the end. Other than that, she would be on her own for most of the two miles.

"That's a mighty pretty-looking horse," the rider of Ulysses said. "It would be a shame if anything happened to him."

"It certainly would since he belongs to a member of the Maxwell family." Okay, that was a lie, but she hoped it wouldn't be in the very near future.

"Who are you?" the man asked.

"Jake Maxwell's daughter," Eden replied. "He'd be very unhappy if anything happened to this horse or his daughter."

Eden didn't like to use her family's reputation like that, but she wanted the men to understand that any foolhardy action would have serious consequences for them. She felt better when she saw caution in their gazes, but she wasn't happy when they turned away and formed a group a little distance off. She was certain they were trying to come up with a way to beat her. She'd expected that. She just wanted a fair race.

For the last several minutes Edward had scanned the milling crowd in the Alamo Plaza without seeing anyone who looked vaguely like Finn. People were in constant motion as they waited anxiously for the pistol shot that would tell them the race had begun. He didn't know how he could possibly find one individual in this tightly packed throng. Men hoisted children on their shoulders so they could see better. Others stood on boxes, climbed trees, stood on tiptoes for a better view. How was he to find a man who was of medium height who didn't *want* to be singled out from the crowd?

He stepped back through the window into Jake and Isabelle's hotel room. "I'm going down to the plaza. If I did spot him from up here, he'd be gone before I could reach him."

Isabelle greeted Edward's decision with a nod of approval.

"I'll watch from up here. Even if you don't see him, your presence might scare him off."

Edward doubted his mere presence would have any effect on Finn. The man didn't care for any opinion but his own. If the brothers had planned this scheme in such detail that they'd taught themselves how to be cowhands, Edward was certain Finn would press ahead with his plan despite opposition, expected or unexpected.

That was what scared him, made him so fearful for Eden. These men had spent years planning their revenge. Maybe the attacks on the ranch had been a warning. Maybe they had enjoyed being able to taunt the Maxwells and get away with it. They had to know they couldn't kill any Maxwell without having the entire family on their trail. No doubt they'd been aiming for one big score, after which they would disappear.

He tried to take some comfort in the fact that no one had proof Finn was trying to hurt Eden, but the conclusion fitted too well with the few facts they did have.

Frustrated with being unable to do anything except watch and wait, Edward worked his way through the throngs, being careful not to cause a disturbance. He didn't want to give Finn any warning of his presence. As he mingled with the crowd, he kept looking for places Finn could use to fire on the riders as they approached the finish line. He could discount the Menger Hotel, but there were several other buildings with windows offering a view of the race. It was impossible to keep all of them under surveillance. Even if he could, he might never see the barrel of the rifle before Finn pulled the trigger.

He wanted to shout to everyone in the plaza that a man calling himself Finn Haswell was about to attempt to commit a murder, that everybody in the plaza had a responsibility as law-abiding citizens to help him stop Finn. But he knew that would only cause a panic. No matter how nearly impossible the task, it was up to him to stop Eden's would-be killer.

"Bring your horses up to the line."

The jockeys broke from their circle and brought their horses toward a line in the dirt that stretched across the road. A couple glanced at Eden, but the others pretended she wasn't there. That suited her fine. She wanted to concentrate on the race, not on what they thought of her or what attempts they might make to keep her from winning.

She moved Crusader toward the line, keeping to the left of the other riders. The start of a race was nearly always the most difficult and dangerous part. Despite the best efforts of the jockeys, not all of the horses would approach the line, nor would they turn in the right direction when the starting signal was given. Pandemonium could reign for a few hundred yards, and she didn't want to get caught up in it.

A shout went up when the starting gun sounded, and fourteen jockeys started driving their horses forward with curses and slashes of their whips. Crusader moved smoothly into a gallop but not before several riders had moved to box him in. They intended to keep her from moving to the lead, but she had planned to keep Crusader at the back of the field for the first mile anyway. Then, using his superior stamina, she would work her way forward and outrun everyone else at the end. Only one thing bothered her. Ulysses had been allowed to take the lead at a moderate pace. If the race was run this slowly, even a sprinter would be hard to catch. Had the jockeys decided to sacrifice their chances of winning to keep Eden from victory?

The sound of the starting gun set a clock ticking in Edward's head. He had less than four minutes before the first riders would reach the plaza. Immediately after the sound of the starting gun, the windows around the plaza had filled with spectators anxious for the best possible view of the race. It was unlikely Finn would be able to force his way to a place at one of those windows, impossible to do so without revealing he was carrying a rifle. As the seconds ticked away, Edward grew more desperate to find Finn.

He returned his attention to the crowd gathered in the plaza and almost at once caught sight of Finn—he was *sure* it was Finn—moving purposefully around a large group of Mexicans in festival dress who were enthusiastically chanting the name of their favorite horse. Setting off at a run that caused him to bump into and anger several people, Edward tried to keep the never fully visible figure in view. By the time he'd worked his way more than a hundred feet down the plaza, the figure had disappeared and twenty more precious seconds had been used up.

Struggling to keep a cool head, Edward stopped and used his superior height to scan the crowd. Finn was here, he was sure of it. He had to find him, and he had less time than ever. He could almost hear the dull thud of dozens of horses' hooves as they pounded into the packed dirt of the road, carrying their riders closer and closer to the city and the end of the race. Their cadence became the cadence of his heartbeat, their efforts to fill their lungs with life-giving oxygen his effort to keep his breath steady, his brain clear and alert. They were all in a race, but his was the one most likely to end in tragedy.

The jockeys' gazes rarely left Eden. Some appeared puzzled by her calm acceptance of being blocked in. Others seemed to believe she'd given up trying to break out of the box formed by a wall of horses in front of her and several on either side, but a couple of the riders apparently couldn't convince themselves she didn't have a strategy for outmaneuvering them.

"Stay closer," one of them kept shouting.

"If we get any closer, we'll stumble over each other," another replied. "I don't intend to be thrown and trampled just to keep some woman from winning the race."

"She's not going to win. She's not even trying."

"Maybe the horse is fast enough to win on his own."

"Then you have to make sure he doesn't."

Their exchanges grew steadily more heated until Eden decided they weren't paying much attention to her. She leaned forward over Crusader's withers, took a stout hold on the reins, and pulled back hard. Crusader slowed so abruptly, the other jockeys didn't have time to slow their mounts. He was in the clear before they knew what was happening.

Angling to the far side of the road, Eden loosened the reins, squeezed her knees, and shouted to Crusader that it was now time to run like he'd never run before. Eden dodged attempts to bump Crusader off stride, to box him in again, to get close enough to push her out of the saddle. She and the horse were repeatedly struck with whips, but that only drove Crusader to run the fastest half mile of his life until he outdistanced all but Ulysses, who had been running a dozen lengths ahead.

The race hadn't been run according to plan. Crusader had been forced to expend an incredible amount of energy to get clear of the field. There wouldn't be any chance to take a breather because, having had an easy lead for most of the race, Ulysses would have plenty of energy for the last half mile. Only an all-out run to the finish line would enable Crusader to catch him. She knew Crusader could run at top speed for half a mile, but he'd never been asked to do more than that. If he couldn't, they wouldn't win the race, Edward wouldn't get his money, and he wouldn't ask Eden to marry him. The race would last about another thirty seconds. That was all the time she had to make her dream come true.

"You've got a choice," she said to the horse. "Win this race and you get to live a life of luxury with all the mares a young stallion could want. Lose, and you could end up gelded and in Arizona running from Indians and chasing cows."

She knew Crusader couldn't understand her words, but he was responding to her urging, cutting into the distance between him and Ulysses with every stride. As fast as he was, she didn't know if he could do it before they reached the finish line.

A feeling of desperation threatened to swamp Edward. He could tell from the cheers of the crowd in the distance that the horses had reached the outskirts of the city. Within a few seconds, they would be racing toward the finish line in the plaza. Somewhere in this crowd lurked a man who was intent upon killing the woman Edward loved. He hoped the reason he couldn't find Finn was that one of the others had already caught him, but he couldn't afford to take that chance. His future hung in the balance, and he had the power to determine its course.

If he could find Finn in time.

He would never have found the gunman if he hadn't heard a child's cry, and looked up to see Finn pushing a young boy from his perch in a tree at the edge of the plaza. No one attempted to stop him, maybe because they were more concerned with making sure the boy wasn't hurt, and also because Finn had a rifle that he raised to his shoulder.

Edward was moving before his mind had finished assimilating what he had seen. He could hear the sound of horses approaching the plaza. They were only seconds away. He didn't have time to wonder whether Crusader was in the lead with Eden exposed to Finn's rifle. Even though it would mean he wouldn't win the race, he hoped she was back in the pack, at least partially protected by the bodies of the other jockeys.

He ran without awareness of the people in his path. He saw nothing but Finn up in the tree, the rifle to his shoulder, the sound of cheering telling him the horses would burst into the plaza at any moment. He had to reach Finn before the first rider came into view.

At the moment he caught a glimpse of the first horses exploding into the plaza, he launched himself at Finn. He grasped the branch at the same moment Finn fired.

Ulysses's jockey didn't waste any words on Eden when he looked over his shoulder and saw Crusader fast approaching. He tore into his exhausted mount with a punishing tattoo of slashing blows that caused the rapidly tiring horse to drift so dramatically, he nearly ran off the course. The jockey jerked him back onto the road so hard, he veered into Crusader, nearly knocking him off stride. Eden held Crusader together and drove him harder to pass Ulysses and his enraged jockey, who was expressing his fury with a string of impressive curses.

Eden ignored the jockey until he leaned out of the saddle and slashed Crusader across the neck with his whip. Crusader veered so abruptly, Eden nearly lost her balance. The jockey swung Ulysses back toward Crusader and raised his whip for another blow. Equally enraged, Eden brought her whip down across the jockey's shoulder so hard he cried out in pain.

"Hit my horse again, and I'll lay it across your face," she shouted at him.

Instead of trying to hit Crusader again, the jockey grabbed Crusader's bridle to slow him down. Eden tried to shove him off, but he was too strong. Crusader couldn't pass Ulysses as long as the jockey held on to his bridle.

They had entered the city by now, and the spectators could see what Ulysses's jockey was doing. Some shouted curses, some shouted encouragement. All knew the finish of the race was in doubt. The two riders burst into the plaza with the finish line looming a hundred yards away. Eden knew Crusader would never win as long as the jockey kept his hold on Crusader's reins. She also knew she wasn't strong enough to break his hold. Unable to think of anything else, she balled her hand into a fist and swung it backward, brought it into contact with the jockey's nose. Once, twice, three times before the beleaguered jockey let go of the reins.

With the finish line practically overhead, Eden urged Crusader forward with all her strength. She felt the response of powerful and well-trained muscles, but the two horses swept under the finish line so close together she couldn't tell who had won.

Chapter Twenty-six

Like a cat, Finn had landed on his feet when he fell out of the tree, his rifle pointed directly at Edward. It was deflected upward by someone in the crowd just as it discharged. Knowing he had only a second before Finn could aim and fire again, Edward lunged forward. He struck Finn in the chest, knocking him backward into the spectators. Being smaller and more nimble, Finn scrambled to his feet, his pale blue eyes searching for his rifle. Someone had kicked it away, where it was picked up by someone else in the crowd. Deprived of his weapon, Finn attempted to run away, but hands in the crowd pushed him toward Edward.

The fight was short and the conclusion foregone. Edward was bigger, stronger, and a natural fighter. Less than a minute later, Finn lay sprawled on the cobblestones.

Drawing a moderately deep breath, Edward turned to the crowd. "Does anyone have a rope?"

No one had a rope, but a rawhide lariat served the purpose just as well. With the help of a swarthy, mustachioed man who knew more about knots than Edward would ever have guessed was possible, Finn was bound to the very tree he'd climbed.

Desperate to find out what had happened to Eden, Edward asked, "Could someone watch him?"

"I watch him," offered a handsome young man with shining black hair and a gaily colored vest. He held Finn's rifle in his hand, pointing the weapon at its owner's chest. "He not get away."

Muttering thanks that he hoped could be understood despite each of their difficulties with the Texas version of the English language, Edward plunged into the crowd once more, headed to the other end of the plaza, where he hoped Eden would be waiting. He didn't care if she'd won the race. He just wanted to know she was okay, that Finn's bullet hadn't hit her.

He arrived to find Eden, Ulysses's jockey, and the finish-line judges engaged in a hot argument. The judges had disqualified Ulysses because of his jockey's interference with Crusader. The jockey, furious at losing the race and second-place money, insisted Eden and Crusader be disqualified because she'd punched him.

"If she is, you won't be the only one receiving a punch on the nose."

Isabelle Maxwell had forced her way through the crowd to face the injured jockey. "After such a disgraceful display of poor sportsmanship, you should be thankful to get off with only a sore nose. Had you been *my* son, you wouldn't be able to sit down for a week."

"*Mother!*" Eden exclaimed.

"And as for you, young woman, I have more to say, but good manners prevent me from speaking before so many ears. I expect your father will have a few words for you as well."

"Don't forget me and Luke," Chet said. "I can't believe you'd do something like that after all the times you yelled at me, saying I was a fool to risk my life going up against gunmen. At least I had a gun."

"I had a whip and the fastest horse," Eden said. "I didn't need anything else."

Edward stepped out of the crowd. "You must have had a guardian angel who twice saved you from a bullet."

Eden spun around to face him; the expression on her face was a mixture of pride, apprehension, obstinance, and a large chunk of love.

In the space of mere seconds, Edward had endured a wide range of emotions. The first was bone-melting relief that Eden was safe. He took his first unconstricted breath in nearly half an hour. That was followed by euphoria that she had won; and amazement she had had to fight with the jockey to do it. Nearly weakened by the force of his relief, he was swept up in a surge of anger that she had been so headstrong that she'd ridden Crusader after he'd told her it was too risky, after her whole family had supported his decision. Didn't she understand the kind of danger she'd been in? Didn't she have any idea how devastated her family would have been if anything had happened to her? How could he possibly want to marry a woman that willful? He might as well hitch his wagon to a loco steer.

Before he had time to decide what he was going to do about it, he was swamped by pride in what she'd accomplished. She'd won a very difficult race against a jockey who had done everything he could to stop her. He was sure others had also tried to keep her from winning. She hadn't hesitated to fight back when the jockey employed unfair tactics. She'd admitted to punching the jockey in the nose, told the judge why, and said she was sorry she'd only bloodied his nose.

Eden fixed her gaze on Edward. "I guess I do have a guardian angel. Without her, I would never have gone to England."

That did it. Any thought of criticizing her left his mind. He could only see she loved him so much she was willing to take the risk to make sure he won the race that would give him a chance at a new life. At the moment, he didn't care that what she'd done was foolish to the point of insanity. All that mattered was she'd done it for him. After a lifetime of being expected to sacrifice himself for others, here was one person who had been willing to sacrifice for him. How could he *not* marry her after that?

Edward closed the space between him and Eden. "I've been

insufficiently grateful to my guardian angel. I've been so focused on what I lost, I didn't appreciate what I've been given in exchange."

Chet walked over, whispered in Edward's ear. "If you're going to ask her to marry you, you oughta wait until we get back to the hotel. After what she's done, people might think you're not sane enough to be trusted with a lot of money."

Edward tried to smother his laughter but gave up and let it roll from him in a long cascade. Jake and Isabelle looked confused, but Eden immediately broke into a smile.

"I don't know what Chet said to you, but don't listen. He used to be much wilder than I ever was."

Chet was honest enough to blush.

Edward smiled down at Eden, took her hands in his. "I wish you hadn't taken such a dangerous risk, but I'm enormously proud of you. You've got courage and intelligence and you don't hesitate to use either of them. You stand behind what you believe even if no one agrees with you, and you don't flinch at facing unpleasant truths. The only misstep you've taken was to fall in love with me." He tightened his hold on her hands. "I'm not going to be a gentleman and step back until you regain your senses. I'm going to take advantage of your momentary lapse in judgment and ask if you could possibly want to marry me."

Luke turned to Chet. "That sounds like something you'd say."

Isabelle pinched him. "It sounds like something only a man who's smart enough to make my daughter fall in love with him would think to say."

Eden's smile was so big it threatened to march right off her face. "Of course I'll marry you. Why else would I risk my neck riding against a bunch of men who should be ashamed to call themselves Texans?"

Edward felt as if his life was being directed by an unseen hand. From the moment he'd almost run into Eden in the upstairs hall in London, nothing in his life had gone as he had expected. He'd been disgraced and disinherited, abandoned, confused and challenged. Yet everything had led directly to this moment, the moment that promised more happiness than he'd ever thought possible.

Isabelle glared at her daughter. "That's not a very gracious acceptance."

Edward didn't take his eyes off Eden. "It sounded wonderful to me."

Jake stepped forward to shake Edward's hand. "She's a lot like her mother. Hasn't given me a moment's peace in twenty-one years, but I wouldn't trade a single minute."

Edward returned Jake's firm handshake. "I expect I'll feel the same in twenty-one years."

Chet shook his head. "If you survive that long."

Isabelle wiped a tear from her cheek and gave Edward a hug. "Welcome to the family. I've been waiting for this moment much too long. But now that it has come, you'll have to wait a while longer. It's going to be a big wedding."

Eden had wanted to have the wedding on the site of Edward's new ranch, but so many people wanted to come, it proved impractical. They ended up arranging to be married on the plaza in front of the Alamo. With the immediate family numbering more than sixty, the guests filled nearly every hotel room in San Antonio. The ceremony would be performed on the steps of the Alamo. A party the likes of which San Antonio had never seen would follow.

The night before the wedding, tables had been set up in the center of the square and the entire Maxwell family, including the six infants in arms, gathered for dinner. Colorful lanterns hung from tree limbs, perched on tall poles, and sat on tables laden with platters, bowls, and pans of food that filled the cooling evening air with a medley of mouthwatering aromas. A mariachi band provided a background of lively music while dozens of young people ran, skipped, and paraded from table to table, catching up with cousins they hadn't seen in at least twenty-four hours. Their parents, relieved for the moment from worries that they'd fall from a rocky cliff they'd been told not to climb, injure themselves with a gun they'd been forbidden to touch, or end up on the wrong side of a longhorn's temper, stretched Eden's goodwill to the limits by regaling Edward with embellished recollections of every piece of mischief his bride-to-be had committed in her twenty-one years.

After one particularly embarrassing story, she took Edward by the arm and led him away. "One more story like that," she told her grinning brother Will, "and the one person in all of San Antonio missing from the wedding will be the groom."

Edward grinned broadly, pulled Eden close to give her a kiss on her forehead. "I wouldn't miss the wedding for the world, but I'm not sure it's safe for us to have children."

"You could always go back to Daphne. I'm sure hers would be extremely well behaved."

Rather than explain that cryptic remark to several interested persons, Edward insisted his future bride begin introducing him to her numerous nieces and nephews. "If you can get them to remain still long enough." He had managed to master the names of her siblings and their wives and husbands because there were only twenty-two of them. Half an hour later he gave up, saying, "We'll probably have a couple of our own before I manage to learn all their names."

Eden surveyed her family with pride and a degree of wonder. Isabelle frequently said she was awed every time she thought of the changes that had taken place in the Maxwell clan. Eden hadn't understood what her mother meant until now. Eden had been born into a large family, took it for granted, took the lives they led, the dangers they had faced, as a normal part of the fabric of her life. Maybe it had been going to England that had brought home to her how unusual her life had been, how fortunate she was to be surrounded by so many extraordinary people.

hat are you thinking?"

Eden jumped, startled to hear her father's voice behind her. "How lucky I am to have such a family."

Jake surveyed his family. "It's right scary when you think of it." He shook his head, as though he couldn't quite believe what he was seeing. "If I'd had any idea this would be the result of your mother showing up on my ranch with her eight orphans from hell, I would have run all the way to New Mexico without my cows."

Eden slipped her arm around her father's waist and pulled him close. She felt incredibly blessed to have her two favorite men on either side of her. "I don't think I'll ever be this happy again."

"Of course you will, dozens of times."

Her mother had come to join them, to link arms with her husband and bask in the glow of love and happiness that filled the plaza. It was so obvious that people passing paused to look, to marvel, and most often walk away smiling. Eden could think of only one thing that would make the celebration better. And then, almost as if by magic, it happened.

Edward was certain he was dreaming. He could think of no other reason why he should see the earl and Patrick walking across the plaza toward him. It was an implausible collision of two worlds, the one that had bred him and the one that had adopted him.

Isabelle moved past her husband to give Edward a kiss on the cheek. "Eden thought you'd like to have some of your family stand up with you. It's not right for you to be surrounded entirely by Maxwells."

Edward was stunned to realize he wasn't imagining anything. They really *were* here. "But how did they know?"

"We sent them a transatlantic cable." Jake chuckled at Edward's look of amazement. "You do know what that is, don't you? It's like a telegraph that works under water."

"Dad!" Eden elbowed her father. "He's not stupid."

Edward shook his head to dislodge the sense of unreality that filled him. When he left England, he'd told himself that life was over, that he had to put all thoughts of seeing his family again out of his head. He'd struggled at first, but concentrating on the race and falling in love with Eden had given him new goals and renewed purpose, which eased the loss of his family. He had missed the earl. The old man was a relic of an earlier time, but he was a decent sort who'd tried to understand Edward. It was Patrick, the only one in his family who truly loved him, that he'd missed most. Though the viscount had tried to keep them apart as much as possible, each had been an important part of the other's childhood—Patrick idolizing the older brother who could do no wrong in his eyes, and Edward feeling free to love Patrick because his brother demanded nothing in return. "I feel stupid, like my brain isn't working. It seems so unreal."

Eden thought Edward's reaction to the appearance of his family was going to cause her stalwart father to tear up. It was a close call, but he managed to remain dry-eyed. Isabelle made up for it. Her eyes swelled with tears that rolled down her cheeks in gleaming rivulets.

Edward hugged Isabelle, but his gaze was focused on Patrick. With halting steps he made his way forward. When Patrick offered his hand, Edward used it to pull him into a fierce embrace.

Patrick hesitated only a moment before throwing his arms around his brother. For Edward it was like a baptism, a re-birth. The presence of the earl and Patrick had given him back his family, and in a sense his name as well. He no longer felt like an outcast. Now he could go wherever he wanted, do whatever he wanted, without feeling that he'd run away.

"I would prefer that you not hug me—I doubt my old bones could survive the welcome you've given Patrick—but surely your brother doesn't hold all your affection. I hope there's at least a little left for me."

The earl's slightly amused voice recalled Edward to his

ion to his great-uncle. "Sorry, sir. I was so overcome by seeing you both here in Texas, I forgot myself."

The earl extended his hand, which Edward clasped in both of his. "I think you did just fine. It does my heart good to see that you continue to hold your brother in deep affection."

"As I do him." Patrick's gaze settled on his brother. "I never thought to see you again. You can't imagine my joy when I read Eden's cable saying you were in Texas and inviting us to the wedding. I gave such a shout, my father feared I'd taken leave of my senses."

Mention of the viscount put a considerable dent in Edward's euphoria. "How is my fa . . . How is the viscount?"

"He's not happy at the moment," the earl said. "When I realized you'd gone, I thought you'd left to avoid marrying Daphne. When Patrick told me the real reason, I nearly disinherited my nephew. Then I realized it was as much my fault as his."

"No, sir, you never—"

He put up his hand to stop Edward's protest.

"I should have stopped him from treating you badly. I was as guilty as anyone of the foolish habit of spending money I didn't have on things I seldom cared about. I didn't realize the cost of what I was doing until you left. Patrick and I had a long talk. The upshot was that we sold the London house to settle most of our debts. Peter Melsome has put us on a strict budget until the remainder have been discharged."

Edward was sure he couldn't have heard correctly. He looked from the earl to Patrick.

His brother chuckled with pleasure. "Don't I always take your advice? Peter has been given management of the estate. He's taken to the job with enthusiasm."

Edward could feel the laugh coming. He followed it as it traveled from his belly to his throat into his mouth and out in a great burst. "If you've let Peter put his ideas about economy into practice, I'm surprised the viscount hasn't tried to kill him."

The earl's amusement nearly matched Edward's. "Cyril's been so unhappy, he has gone to stay with friends. I doubt I'll have the feeding or housing of him for months." He was suddenly serious. "What he did, what I *allowed* him to do, nearly cost us you, Edward. The London house, spending restrictions, what are they compared to the loss of a man I've always held in deep affection and great esteem? You are as much my great-nephew as Patrick—Cyril's sister is your mother. Your illegitimate birth doesn't change that. In any case, I expect to see you in England at least once every two years. I'll come to Texas on the off years. I intend to see what you'll do with this ranch you've bought. I also want to know your sons and daughters. I missed seeing my own child grow up," the earl said, glancing at Isabelle. "I don't want to miss yours."

Edward was so moved, he was unable to speak. Reaching out, he held tightly to his great-uncle's and brother's hands.

"I've learned Englishmen aren't very good at expressing themselves when it comes to their feelings," Eden said, speaking softly into the emotion-laden moment. "I think Edward would like to say your presence, your acceptance and love, mean more to him than either he or I can put into words. He would tell you he's not worth it, but I think he's the best of the Davenports."

Patrick gripped his brother's hand harder. "I've been telling everybody that for years."

Edward had never thought it could happen, but a little more and he'd embarrass himself by crying. He'd be an embarrassment to every cowboy in Texas. It was already bad enough that he talked funny and used a peculiar saddle. He was thankful when Isabelle stepped forward to fill the awkward silence.

"I want to introduce Patrick and Alastair to the family. My grandchildren will ask dozens of silly questions about being an earl, but they don't mean any harm. You're to ignore the rude questions my children will ask. They haven't stopped teasing me about being an earl's daughter."

"Thank you," Edward said, turning to Eden. "Inviting my family was the best wedding present you could have given me." The words fell short of what Edward wanted to say, but talking more wouldn't help her see the joy her thoughtfulness had given him. Nothing could make him as happy as sharing the rest of his life with her, but restoring his family to him had healed a wound that was deeper than even he had suspected. It wasn't simply that she'd done it. It was that she loved him deeply enough to sense the need. She must have known he would never put it into words. Now he didn't have to.

Eden pulled him down to give him a lingering kiss. "Seeing your face when you spotted the earl and Patrick was the best present I could have. Now I can marry a whole man, not one with a chunk of him missing."

He wished the viscount could be here right now, could see that this girl from Texas, a girl whose mother was born on the wrong side of the blanket, was more of an aristocrat than the viscount would ever be. She understood that it wasn't money. It wasn't title, prestige, or social standing that mattered. It was the heart. And when you were loved Texas style, you were loved with the whole heart.

"I love you, Eden Maxwell." He kissed her on her cheek, her nose, her lips. "I don't know what I've done to deserve you, but there's nothing on earth that could change the way I feel about you right now."

Eden's grin was pure devilry. "Hold that thought. You'll probably need it before we get back from the honeymoon."

Davenport Family Genealogy

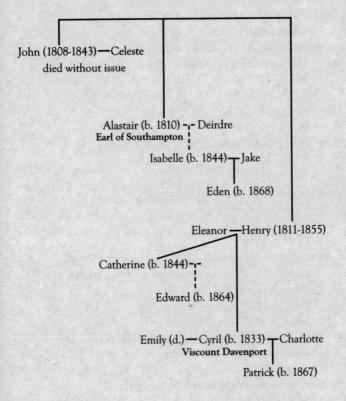

John (1808-1843)——Celeste
died without issue

Alastair (b. 1810) --¦-- Deirdre
Earl of Southampton

Isabelle (b. 1844)——Jake

Eden (b. 1868)

Eleanor——Henry (1811-1855)

Catherine (b. 1844) --¦--

Edward (b. 1864)

Emily (d.)——Cyril (b. 1833)——Charlotte
Viscount Davenport

Patrick (b. 1867)

— denotes marriages and children
-- denotes liaisons and childen

Maxwell Family Genealogy

Jake Maxwell m. Isabelle Davenport 1866
    Eden b. 1868
Ward Dillon m. Marina Scott 1861
    Tanner b. 1862 (married Elise, two daughters)
    Mason b. 1869
    Lee b. 1872
    Conway b. 1874
    Webb b. 1875
Buck Maxwell (Hobson) m. Hannah Grossek 1872
    Wesley b. 1874
    Elsa b. 1877
Drew Townsend m. Cole Benton 1874
    Celeste b. 1879
    Christine b. 1881
    Clair b. 1884
Sean O'Ryan m. Pearl Belladonna (Agnes Satterwaite) 1876
    Elise b. 1866 (Pearl's daughter by a previous marriage)
    Kevin b. 1877
    Flint b. 1878
    Jason b. 1880
Chet Maxwell (Attmore) m. Melody Jordan 1880
    Jake Maxwell II (Max) b. 1882
    Nick b. 1884
Bret Nolan m. Emily Abercrombie 1881
    Sam b. 1882
    Joseph b. 1884
    Elizabeth b. 1885

Matt Haskins m. Ellen Donovan 1883
    Toby b. 1868 (adopted)
    Hank b. 1870 (adopted)
    Orin b. 1872 (adopted)
    Noah b. 1878 (adopted)
    Tess b. 1881 (adopted)
    Matthew b. 1885
    Brodie b. 1886
Pete Jernigan m. Anne Thompson 1886
    Mary Anne b. 1888
    Kane b. 1889
    Kent b. 1889
Will Haskins m. Idalou Ellsworth 1886
    Riley b. 1887
    Isabelle b. 1889
Luke Attmore m. Valeria Badenburg 1887
    Lucas b. 1888
    Valentine b. 1889
Hawk Maxwell m. Suzette Chatingy 1888
    Zoe b. 1889
Zeke Maxwell m. Josie Morgan 1888
    Jessie b. 1889
Eden Maxwell m. Edward Davenport 1889
Junie Mae
    Scott b. 1886

In his darkest hour, Gabriel found Solace. She was full of life, energy and daring. And it was up to Gabe to defend her when all society shunned her for the very individuality Gabe loved. But this time he had the strength and know-how to protect his woman; this time he would have faith that, "Surely goodness and mercy will follow me all the days of my life."

Read ahead for a sneak preview of
Gabriel's Lady by **Charlotte Hubbard**.

"Gabe! Gabe, it's so dang good to see ya! But I'm so—"

When Billy grabbed his hand, the grip stunned Gabe—because it was so strong from his years of working with horses, but also because it swung him into an unexpected hug. A choking sound made Gabe's eyes go wet: for the first time, someone *felt* his pain instead of just giving it lip service. Billy Bristol's arms clamped around his body like steel bands, yet he sensed that his friend—this blood brother of his childhood—would be the one to free him from his misery.

When the redhead stepped back, his blue eyes sparkled with unshed tears. "It's so good to see ya," he repeated, "I don't want to get to that other part. But it tore me up pretty bad to hear about Letitia. I'm real sorry for your loss."

Billy glanced toward the train then, where porters scurried to unload Grace's belongings at the encouragement of her pretty smile. The platform was stacked with an impressive number of trunks and boxes. "Good thing I drove my biggest buckboard," he remarked with a chuckle. "Can't thank you enough for es-cortin' Gracie, since any man with eyes'll try to sweet-talk her. And she so obviously hates that!"

Gabe laughed. "Yes, she could charm the socks off any fellow alive."

"Yeah, well it's what those fellas'll charm off her that scares me."

He stood back then, a rugged man in denim and homespun,

clean but well-worn. *Comfortable* had always been Billy Bristol's way, in clothing and behavior. His hair had turned a darker shade of auburn and he wore it a little longer now. Gabe tried to imagine him as a desperado, like his twin brother had been, yet the direct gaze of those blue eyes bespoke a man of utmost integrity. A man who'd earned his place in the world by the sweat of his brow and the strength of those broad, calloused hands.

"It was a small favor, considering your generous invitation to—"

"Well, how *else* could I get ya here? Been way too long," Billy insisted. "It's a shame it took a situation like yours to get us together again."

He sighed. "Yes, well...situations happen, don't they?"

"And we'll hash all that out after we get you home and outta these fancy city clothes. Gotta say I like that derby, though. Never owned one myself." Billy plucked at the sleeve of his brown plaid suit. "Looks like you've done right well for yourself practicin' the law, Mr. Getty."

"It's what's beneath the suit that's taken the beating," he replied with a sigh. "Appearances can be deceiving, my friend."

"And I want to hear whatever you gotta get off your mind—but meanwhile it appears our new tutor is ready to load up." Billy grinned. "You were the perfect escort, Gabe. Professional, well-heeled air about ya—to discourage anybody else who might be givin' her the eye. And lots of practice at totin' a woman's trunks, I bet!"

"It's amazing how much luggage one tiny female requires. Where would any of them be without men for pack animals?"

For a fleeting moment he wondered how Cranks, the butler, spent his time now that he no longer accompanied Letitia on her shopping excursions. It was a good sign that such a thought didn't depress him today; a better sign that he could laugh at himself for ever depending on domestic help.

It felt good to shoulder those trunks with Billy; they'd worked together as boys, and it was only his bent for book learning that had sent him away from such a salt-of-the-earth existence. As he heaved Gracie's trunks up to the buckboard, his muscles told him he hadn't pulled his weight lately. Maybe this trip to rural Missouri would balance him...show him what he was made of, without stylish clothing and someone else's mansion to live in.

When they pulled into the Bristol driveway, lined with maple trees in their shiny spring leaves, Gabe's heart fluttered. It was still the homeplace he'd envied when he came here for Billy's wedding: the house glowed with fresh white paint and its pillars suggested Southern grandeur of a bygone era. Lilacs scented the breeze, and beyond the large red barn stretched miles of white plank fence. Beautiful grazing horses dotted the lush pastureland.

He couldn't have painted a prettier picture if he'd been Michelangelo.

A dog raced toward them then, white with distinctive markings around his eyes and ears. Some of his fondest childhood memories returned: Billy letting him pick out a border collie puppy born in the Monroes' barn...their four dogs herding Texas longhorns that had cut across their Kansas farms. Those black and white collies were long gone, but Gabe still glowed, thinking about them. Everything about this family took him back to better days, and Gabe felt happier than he had in weeks. Maybe years.

"Rex!" a loud voice called. "Rex, you ornery mutt! We're not finished practicing!"

Billy halted the horses while Grace sat taller on the seat between them. "Don't tell me that's Solace, riding without—"

"Haven't you ever seen your sister practicin' her act?" Billy cut in. "She's trainin' her new dog, and he's a handful."

"Mama would be having a—time and again she's told Solace not to—"

"Which is why Solace loves to come here." Billy leaned his elbows on his knees to include Gabe in his grin. "You and Lily were cut from silk and satin, honey, and Aunt Agatha's academy was the place you needed to be. But while you were away, how do you s'pose Solace entertained herself? She *sure* wasn't perfectin' her needlework."

Gabe chuckled. He gazed at the approaching figure in rapt fascination, for she was standing barefoot on the back of a bay gelding that cantered alongside the driveway. Solace Monroe wore old denim pants and a red plaid shirt, and with her dark brown hair flying behind her—and a daredevil grin!—she seemed like something from a dream. She balanced so confidently on the horse's back that she appeared to be floating. Or flying.

And then, a few feet before she reached the buckboard, Solace dropped down to straddle her mount as though these acrobatics were second nature to her. Such effortless grace bespoke hours of practice, and Gabe wondered how many times she'd tumbled off—how many bones she'd broken—to reach this level of performance perfection.

"Gabe! Gabe Getty, it's been way too long!"

Her hands shot out and he grabbed them. A warm tingle of energy raced through his body when he felt the strength in Solace's sturdy hands. Her face was flushed from riding and her breath came in exuberant bursts as she grinned at him. The little girl he'd danced with at his wedding was anything but a child now.

"I was so happy to hear you'd be—" Her face clouded over then, but her brown-eyed gaze never wavered. "We were all so sad to learn about Letitia, Gabe. How horrible it must've been for you to—but you're here now! Family again, like when we were kids!"

His heart turned a cartwheel. When had anyone ever greeted him with such enthusiasm? Such all-embracing sincerity? He opened his mouth but it took a moment for the words to come out.

"It's good to be back," he murmured. Grace and Billy watched him closely, so he gave them the best smile he could muster. "The past few weeks have been sheer hell. The Bancrofts blame me for Letitia's untimely—"

"How absurd!" Solace had no need for more details. She believed without question in the Gabriel Getty she'd known all her life.

He swallowed hard. Her compassion nearly overwhelmed him. He wasn't sure he deserved such outright confidence in his innocence. Those bold brown eyes unnerved him, too, yet the glow on Solace's face drew him in and warmed his very soul. And she did all this as effortlessly as she'd ridden her horse standing up.

"Don't mind my sister, Gabriel," Gracie murmured. "She wants the best for you—as we all do. But she needs to rein herself in."

Anguish froze Solace's face, and then Gabe watched a play of familiar emotions: despair and betrayal...the sense of being an outcast in her own family. And in that brief moment, he heard the cry of a kindred spirit. How often had he himself felt despised and belittled these past six years?

"Now Gracie," Billy began, "you shouldn't doubt your sister's intentions about—"

"No, Billy, she hasn't a *clue* about what anyone else might think or feel," Solace huffed. "So nice to see you again, Saint Grace. How have we gotten along without you?"

Before Gabe could offer Solace encouragement, she whistled. Her dog leaped onto the horse, in front of her, and Miss Monroe wheeled her mount in a tight circle. Then she charged full-tilt toward the pasture—but the gate wasn't open! He held his breath, wondering if—

As though the horse were a part of her, flying on her will alone, it leaped up and over the white plank fence to land proudly on the other side. The dog was still seated, and so was Solace, who urged the bay into a breakneck gallop. Had he not seen it with his own eyes, he wouldn't have believed it.